BOOK 2  PEACEKE

THE
PEACEKEEPER
INITIATIVE

BOOK 2 ★ PEACEKEEPERS OF SOL

THE
PEACEKEEPER
INITIATIVE

GLYNN STEWART

**FAOLAN'S PEN
PUBLISHING**
faolanspen.com

This edition published in 2020 by:

Faolan's Pen Publishing Inc.

22 King St. S, Suite 300

Waterloo, Ontario

N2J 1N8 Canada

ISBN-13: 978-1-988035-97-0 (print)

A record of this book is available from Library and Archives Canada.

Printed in the United States of America

1 2 3 4 5 6 7 8 9 10

First edition

First printing: June 2020

Illustration © 2020 Jeff Brown Graphics

Faolan's Pen Publishing logo is a trademark of Faolan's Pen Publishing Inc.

Read more books from Glynn Stewart at faolanspen.com

CHAPTER ONE

GUNFIRE WAS GENERALLY CONSIDERED A BAD SIGN AT TRADE negotiations.

Colonel Henry Wong wasn't actively part of the negotiations either, which allowed him to turn to focus on the distant sound. Several of the local security officers standing watch by the conference room's two entrances were doing the same thing, which was not a positive sign.

The tall starship captain was seated on one side of a surprisingly plain table in an almost gaudily decorated room. The table was plain wood, probably local to Tano, the planet they were negotiating with, and barely large enough for the eight people sitting around it. The room itself was painted a deep red color, with gold filigree picking out detailed murals on the wall.

The murals told an ancient story, but the story their *presence* told was the one Henry Wong cared about. The gold mural told a *Kenmiri* story, one belonging to the history of the alien empire that had once ruled Tano and had abandoned the world fourteen months earlier.

Six local officials from Tano's newborn government were seated facing the United Planets Space Force officer and his companion, Sylvia Todorovich, a gaunt and sharp-edged member of the United Planets Alliance's diplomatic corps.

And the woman in charge of the diplomats assigned to the grandiosely named UPA Peacekeeper Initiative.

At this point, the civilians around the table had finally noticed the gunfire, and Henry returned his attention to them with a thin smile.

"Chemical-powered firearms," he told them in Kem. None of the locals spoke English or Mandarin, and he didn't speak any of their native languages—there were three species represented across the table.

But Tano had been a Kenmiri slave world. All of the negotiators spoke Kem, the language of their conquerors and Terra's enemies. That was the language of negotiation and the language Henry questioned them in now.

"That is a lot of shooting," Henry continued in the precision required of speaking a language that wasn't native to anyone in the room. "What is going on?"

The Tano military representative wasn't from a species Henry knew, but the tall woman with the apparently natural purple hair and the almost dainty tusks was of a *type* of species common across the galaxy. General Kansa was Ashall, which basically meant she could pass for human in a dark alley.

"We do not know," she admitted as she rose to her feet. "I am receiving reports from units across the city that we are under attack." She tapped a black piece of plastic in her ear, indicating that she had an active com set.

"I am requesting reinforcements from the other cities, but I am also receiving reports of sabotage at our airports and transport terminals."

Commander Thompson. Local forces appear under attack. Can you and Iyotake sort out what's going on from orbit? Henry had the pure message assembled in his internal network while the local officer was still speaking, firing it off to his GroundDiv commander and his executive officer without even blinking.

The locals didn't appear to have internal networks. Henry understood that the majority of the population was Ashall, which made those implants something the UPA could trade with them.

"Who is attacking you?" Todorovich demanded. "You did not mention any potential threat."

"Because we did not know of one *here*," the senior Tano official named Inbar, an Ashall that really *could* pass for human, snapped. "The Kozun have been threatening us, but they have no soldiers on our world!"

"If it was the Kozun, there would be more energy guns," Kansa snapped. "My apologies, Colonel, Ambassador. I suggest we suspend the negotiations for now. Tano's government is still fragile, and despite our efforts to represent everyone on the Council, there are elements that feel they were robbed."

"Fewer mouths to feed," another Tano official whose name Henry hadn't caught muttered.

"We swore to serve *all* of Tano," Inbar countered.

"Ambassador?" Henry asked, turning to look at Todorovich. She was a practiced ambassador and easily capable of concealing her emotions from almost anyone. Henry, on the other hand, had learned to read microexpressions to be able to follow Ashall emotion.

Unlike most, Todorovich had learned to control those too, but she and Henry had been through worse than this together. He was learning to read her despite everything she could do.

She was *amused*.

"If the government of Tano does not feel they can guarantee our security, it would, of course, be wiser to suspend the meeting for now," she told them.

"None of the attacks so far have threatened the Center," Kansa told them. Tano's Government Center was the former home of the Kenmiri Governor, now the home base for the planet's government. It was *also* the building they were all sitting in.

"We have a number of satellite facilities in the city under attack, and it appears that our ability to bring troops to the city is almost nonexistent until we have completed significant repairs."

"General Kansa is responsible for our security," Inbar said. "We must allow her to do her job if nothing else."

"Of course," Todorovich agreed. "We will return to the suite you assigned us and await an update."

"It's bad, ser." Lieutenant Colonel Tatanka Iyotake's response had taken longer than Henry had hoped, but he presumed his executive officer was using the time productively. Even though he "heard" Iyotake's voice, that was an illusion created by his network.

"Every airport or spaceport on the planet has been bombed. Probably repairable in short order, but out right now. I'd say you've got at least eight active attacks in the city itself, pinning down local forces in their barracks."

"They're removing pieces from the board and heading for checkmate," Commander Alex Thompson added, the GroundDiv officer's message arriving in a slightly different mental tone. "The Kenmiri Governor's House or whatever they call it? They're going to hit it next and they're going to hit it hard.

"I recommend immediate extraction."

"General, is the Center secure?" Henry asked as he processed his subordinates' comments. The dark-skinned and black-haired Chinese-American officer's concern was getting sharper by the second, and from Todorovich's glance back at him, the diplomat was picking up on it.

"What's going on?" she demanded silently via their networks. The sense of sharpness the blonde woman projected was more than merely physical, after all.

"Thompson thinks the attacks are a decoy," Henry replied, his mental voice equally silent.

Kansa looked at the politicians starting to mill around, then gestured for him to follow her as she stepped out into the hall. Like the conference room itself, it was painted deep red and carried a gold mural in the wall.

What little furniture he could see, though, was plain and made of the local wood. That was definitely *not* the style of the Artisan-caste Kenmiri who tended to govern the slave worlds, beings who would never accept something plain if something decorative could do the same job.

The locals had left the Kenmiri walls in place but replaced all of the furniture with their own work. The walls would probably follow, but Tano's leaders had had other priorities so far.

"The Center *should* be secure," Kansa told him once they were clear of her politicians. She looked askance at Todorovich following Henry but didn't argue. "But this is a blatant attempt to decoy forces away from us.

"And I cannot even stop it. Every mobile unit in the streets is rushing to reinforce their home barracks. I have held what troops we have at the Center here, but...the Center is a standardized structure."

"At least in its bones and hardware, yes," Henry confirmed. "The Kozun would know their way through a Kenmiri Governor's House. If there are any here..."

The Kozun had been one of the Vesheron, rebel factions against the Kenmiri Empire allied with humanity. Now they appeared to be the closest example of the warlords the UPA was expecting to rise from the wreckage of the half-abandoned Empire.

"My intelligence was that at least a hundred Kozun special forces were infiltrated onto Tano while they were threatening the Council," Kansa told them. "They will almost certainly be coming here—and they will be better equipped and better trained than my people. My best people served the Kenmiri as slave soldiers. They are not trusted in the capital yet, and they now lack functional airports."

"The rest of your people are, what, rebels turned police?" Todorovich asked.

"Yes," Kansa admitted shortly after a moment of silence. "I have several hundred soldiers in place to guard the Center, but I have less than a dozen energy weapons and limited heavy arms to support them."

"Why are you telling us this?" the diplomat said. "Should you not be briefing the rest of your Council?"

"They have no armies hidden away that can save us," Kansa said bluntly. "I have not seen one of your battlecruisers in action, Colonel Wong, Ambassador Todorovich, but I understand that you *do* carry a ground detachment.

"I hope that the man who ended the Kenmorad can help us."

Henry wanted to grimace. He was mostly past the PTSD nightmares now, but he still didn't like to be reminded that it was his old ship that had wiped out the last of the Kenmorad breeding sects, ending the Kenmiri ability to reproduce and damning them to a slow genocide.

"I am strongly discouraged from interfering in local planetary affairs," he noted. "Ambassador Todorovich?"

They'd walked through the Gathering and the end of the Vesheron rebel alliance together. She *knew* what he was asking for.

Just as he knew she was going to give it to him.

"The evidence does suggest that this is an attack, not a legitimate local uprising," the ambassador said calmly. "An external attack very much falls under the purview of our objectives and your orders, Colonel Wong.

"Speaking for the Diplomatic Corps, I formally request that you assist in protecting the local center of government if at all possible."

Henry smiled, and bowed slightly to Kansa.

"You heard my ambassador," he told her. "Now, *I* have one question."

"Ask, Colonel."

"What is the chance that the Kozun have launched all of this chaos on the surface and do not have a space component to the attack?" he asked.

"We have some defenses, but the Kenmiri took their ships when they left," Kansa told him. "After some...other problems, orbital platforms and a small fighter fleet are all I have. If they can position orbital support..."

"Tano falls," Henry finished for her. "Understood. I need to get to a landing pad, then, General Kansa."

"I'm afraid I do not understand, Colonel."

"My GroundDiv troopers will be coming down on shuttles," Henry explained. "And then *I* will be returning to *Raven* aboard one of those shuttles."

CHAPTER TWO

"I SHOULD NEVER HAVE LEFT *RAVEN*," HENRY MUTTERED TO Todorovich as they reached the landing pad. He was speaking in English, reasonably confident that the locals couldn't understand him. "I could have had Thompson's people on the ground ten minutes ago."

"If you could have had GroundDiv down here ten minutes ago, don't you think Iyotake and Thompson would have at least *asked* if they should drop?" his civilian counterpart said with a chuckle. "You have a good crew, Henry."

"I still should be on my ship, not playing diplomat."

"How many times did you *play diplomat* during the war, Henry?" she asked. "Or watch your captain or task group commander do it? It's part of your job and is only going to be *more* so in this new Initiative.

"*Your* new Initiative," she reminded him.

"You helped get here," he countered. But she was right too. It had taken both of them to get him in front of the United Planets Alliance Security Council, but most people gave him credit for the formation of the Peacekeeper Initiative.

He was just glad no one had tried to promote him to *command* it.

"You have a weight with these people that I don't," Todorovich told him. "Just having you present helps, and we didn't expect an attack. You'll be in space soon enough, my friend."

They could hear the distant rumble of descending shuttles now and Henry shook his head. Sighing, he removed his holstered gun from the weapons belt the Tano guards had given him back, and offered it to Todorovich.

"Take this," he told her. "It's a Kenmiri energy weapon, better than anything the Kozun or the locals have. It was a Consort's sidearm once; my GroundDiv troopers had it regripped for me a long time ago.

"I want it *back*," he stressed, "but it should help keep you alive."

The platinum-inlaid energy pistol was a classic product of Artisan-caste Kenmiri creating something for their Kenmorad parents: both beautiful and *extremely* functional.

Henry found Kenmiri tastes gaudy, but even he had to admit the gun was pretty.

"I'm a terrible shot, even with these," Todorovich told him—but she took the weapon anyway. "I'll bring it back, I promise."

"If it's a choice between you or the gun, remember that I'd rather get you back," Henry said with a flat chuckle.

"Why, Captain, I'm flattered," she replied. "I might almost think you like me."

The shuttles were thundering down now, their conversation carried as much through their internal networks as aloud.

"You're a good friend, Sylvia," he told her. "Stay alive. Thompson understands his priorities; listen to him."

"I will," she promised.

Then an explosion took out the northern perimeter wall and more shooting started.

THE ATTACKERS HAD *PROBABLY* BEEN TRYING to get into the Center before the human soldiers landed. If that had been their plan, they'd underestimated the armament of a United Planets Space Force assault shuttle.

Two of the three shuttles continued their descent, engines flaring to shed their last velocity.

The last shuttle's engines lit up like newborn suns, halting the spacecraft in midair as new control surfaces took shape on its flanks. Hovering in the air, the craft rotated and opened fire.

Explosive shells walked their way along the wrecked wall. Henry couldn't *see* what was going on, but he couldn't imagine the people trying to charge the breach were enjoying the incoming fire.

Two new suns appeared beneath the shuttle, low-yield ground-attack missiles flashing down at the targets beneath the shuttle. A moment later, Henry picked out distant figures, barely more than dots, as the GroundDiv troopers started rappelling down from the hovering shuttle.

The explosion probably hadn't been the only string to the attackers' bow, but that attack was definitely blunted.

As Shuttle One was obliterating the attack, Shuttles Two and Three touched down in front of Henry. He shook his head as he identified the two spacecraft in front of him and watched the GroundDiv companies deploy in rapid order.

"What?" Todorovich asked.

"Take a wild guess, Ambassador, which shuttle Commander Thompson is on," he asked.

She looked at the gray-armored troops spreading out to form a perimeter around the shuttles.

"He just rappelled into the middle of an assault, didn't he?" she replied.

"Bingo." Henry waved the closest of his GroundDiv Lieutenant Commanders over to him. "Lieutenant Commander Rocca, report," he ordered.

Adriana Rocca commanded *Raven*'s second company of

GroundDiv troops, the second-most senior Ground Division officer aboard Henry's battlecruiser.

"Company Two and Company Three are on the ground," she reported crisply. "Scans suggest several concentrations of life signs near the Center walls, but there's a high likelihood that any individual concentration is civilian."

"No preemptive strikes," Henry agreed. It was an order, but it was only confirming what the officer was already telling him.

"Your officers are Kem-fluent, yes?" he asked. He knew the two Lieutenant Commanders would be—there were non-Kem-speaking officers in the UPSF, but few of Rocca's rank or above and even fewer in the Peacekeeper Initiative.

"Ninety-two percent of the battalion's troopers can at least ask for directions," the officer replied brightly. "All the officers are fluent."

"Good." Henry switched to the Kenmiri language and waved a local officer over. "Name and rank?" he asked.

"Captain Install," the Ashall officer replied.

That was one thing Henry had noted. There'd been three species in the Council and he'd seen at least two more around, but every race he'd seen on Tano had been Ashall. Humanoids, some more distinctive than others.

It was a broad grouping. By any standard you cared to apply, *humans* were Ashall, after all.

"Captain Install, this is Lieutenant Commander Rocca, second-in-command of my ground forces," Henry told the local. "Can you link her in with General Kansa and whoever is in command here?

"We have three UPA troopers on the scene, but Commander Thompson is, ah, neutralizing the attack over there." He waved in the direction of the breach and the still-hovering shuttle.

"General Kansa." The officer paused, clearly parsing his Kem slowly. "Left coms with. For you. To coordinate."

From Captain Install's halting Kem, communication might not be as smooth as Henry was hoping, but the local was holding out a box of earpieces that looked like they'd fit humans.

"I'll leave you with General Kansa and Captain Install," he told Rocca. "I need to return to *Raven*."

"Take Shuttle Two," Rocca urged. "Best pilot you're going to find outside a starfighter, ser."

"We haven't seen anti-air yet," Henry replied. "And, Lieutenant Commander?"

"Ser?"

"Make sure you've got at least a fire team with the ambassador at all times. She'll remain down here to negotiate once the situation is resolved."

He'd *like* to haul her back aboard *Raven* with him and lock her in an acceleration tank. His ship's acceleration tanks were probably the safest place in the entire star system right now.

Unfortunately, there was no way in *hell* he was winning that argument, and he wasn't going to try.

"Are you good, Commander?" he asked Rocca.

"I'm linked with Thompson and Kansa," she replied. "North wall is secure. Company One is moving to sweep the outer perimeter while Shuttle One provides overhead. I don't know who's out there, ser, but GroundDiv has the scene.

"These people will be fine."

"Play nice, Commander," he muttered. "Good luck."

With a final nod to Todorovich, he set off for Shuttle Two.

He'd be a thousand times more comfortable on the bridge of a battlecruiser than in the middle of a *ground battle*.

CHAPTER THREE

"WHOEVER THESE PEOPLE WERE, THEY WERE PRETTY confident they'd knocked out the Tano air support," Commander Alex Thompson noted over the com network. "Across three attacks, they had a grand total of four antiaircraft weapons, ser, and they were rockets. Not Kenmiri AA."

"Three attacks, Commander?" Henry asked. "I saw one as I lifted out, but I haven't even made it to *Raven* yet."

Shuttle Two was in the middle of her deceleration burn, the thrust pressing Henry firmly back into his seat.

"We were busy," Thompson said. "First wave, the one you saw with the breaching charges, was the largest. Three hundred troops— but only a single AA rocket and no energy weapons among them.

"The locals make a solid bullet-slinger, potentially better than ours, but it's still just a bullet-slinger. The other two groups were nasty. Maybe three hundred between them, but they were the real push. All of them had real antiballistic body armor, and at least a quarter of each force had energy weapons."

"Any idea on the source for the beamers?" Henry asked.

"We *just* finished repelling the last wave," his subordinate pointed out. "The Center is secure. We're still counting the damage."

"How bad?"

"Need to confirm a couple of troopers where personal telemetry is gone," the Commander said grimly. "Assuming they're alive with damaged gear, forty-six wounded. No dead. Locals weren't as lucky. They had good gear, but today was the first time many of the Center guards had seen the elephant."

That fit with what Kansa had told Henry. The only experienced troops the local government had were ex-enforcers for the Kenmiri. Janissary slave troops, the type the Kenmiri Warrior Caste had used for third-tier security and wasteful frontal assaults.

The Tano didn't trust them yet, which meant they'd been kept out of the capital city. The Kenmiri had used this city as an administrative center, and the Tano had taken over those facilities.

The fact that the city—Arsena was the name, he thought—was an admin center also meant that it didn't have the massive sky-poisoning factories of most of Tano's other population centers. Arsena had been kept "clean," but even there, the air burned the lungs for a non-local to breathe.

Most of Tano's cities required breath masks even for locals. The Kenmiri's factory worlds had been operated with nothing remotely resembling environmental rules. So long as the air was breathable with moderate filtration, the worlds' owners were happy.

And if the air and soil ceased to be able to support food crops, well, that was a *feature*. Not a bug.

"Hold the Center, Commander," Henry told Thompson. "Have a team go through the enemy. See if you can ID any of the gear or any species we're not expecting. Tano has seven major Ashall species making up the population, but if you see anyone *else*, I need to know."

"Like Kozun?" Thompson asked.

"Yes," he agreed flatly. "The locals think the First Voice's people are behind this. I need confirmation, or the Initiative can't do anything."

Not that the Initiative could do much even *with* confirmation. They had a surprisingly broad mandate outside the UPA's borders, but Henry Wong was only too aware of how limited the resources they'd assigned to salvaging the empire they'd destroyed were.

It was better than nothing. But it wasn't going to be enough to save the five thousand stars the Kenmiri had cut loose from themselves, let alone the wannabe warlords like the First Voice of the Kozun.

"We're landing on *Raven* now," he told Thompson. "Keep me and Iyotake informed. I'm expecting a second string to this bow."

The Vesheron would never have kicked off a local revolt without space support, and it was unlikely that there was outside support that hadn't been one of the rebel factions.

Hell, Henry Wong had *worked with* the First Voice in the past. It was only a question of time, and only the lack of the old subspace communicators had forced the attackers to rely on prearranged timing.

"SKIP SIGNATURE," a voice said in Henry's internal network as he strode briskly through the corridors of his ship. *Raven* was three hundred meters long, which made the trip from the hangar to the bridge a job at the best of times.

He wasn't going to *jog* through his ship. Or run, for that matter. Anything above a brisk walk might imply to the crew that the captain wasn't fully in control of the situation.

"What are we looking at, Commander?" he asked. The conversation was silent. He knew from experience that *he* didn't exhibit the visible concentration many people showed when they were talking through their internal network.

"Still resolving," Commander Okafor Ihejirika, his tactical officer, replied. "Looks like a minimum of four signatures, no more than eight. Nothing large enough to ping as a dreadnought, so we're looking at escorts or home-builds."

The UPA had been unusual among the Vesheron in that they'd been outside the Kenmiri Empire. They'd been *El*-Vesheron, outsider rebels, and had brought fleets of their own ships. Most of the Vesheron had been internal rebels of the Empire and had fought with stolen Kenmiri designs.

The Kenmiri only used three ship types: escorts, small laser and missile platforms that they'd built in near-infinite numbers to maintain order across ten thousand stars; gunships, slightly upsized escorts built around a single heavy plasma cannon; and dreadnought, *much* larger ships built around multiple heavy plasma cannon.

Raven's defenses meant she could easily handle four escorts. Eight escorts—or four gunships, for that matter—would be a bit more concerning.

If they were looking at something someone had built in the fourteen months since the Kenmiri Empire had fallen, though, all bets were off.

"Inform me if you resolve them before I reach the bridge," Henry ordered. "Are we ready?"

"All weapons and sensors are green," Ihejirika confirmed calmly. "We are definitely looking at escort- or gunship-sized vessels, no more than six," he continued. "They are now accelerating towards the planet at one kilometer per second squared. Range is ten lightseconds."

In theory, Henry could use his internal network and its ability to generate virtual reality around him to run *Raven* from anywhere aboard the ship. It degraded efficiency—and most importantly right now, he couldn't do it while he was *walking*.

"Moon," he said aloud, connecting his network to his communications officer. "Do you have a link with the Tano defense forces? They've got to have something up here we can work alongside."

"There are definitely ships up here," Lieutenant Commander

Lauren Moon confirmed. "I'm having problems making a connection with whoever's in charge. I'm not sure they know who's in charge."

She paused.

"I think there was some confusion before this even started," she told him, "and while they're not admitting it, I think the most likely person to be in charge was assassinated."

"Of course," Henry accepted with a sigh. "All right. Hack their coms if you must, Commander. I want to be able to talk to everyone in orbit. Confirm with Ihejirika and Iyotake. I want to know how many local supports we can grab."

Most of the factories on Tano's surface had been building starship parts for assembly in orbit. Much of it could have been done in orbit, Henry was sure, but that wasn't the Kenmiri way.

Given time, it would probably become the Tano way—with UPA help, if they wanted it—but what mattered right now was that while those yards had been intended for freighters, they could have easily been converted to build escorts. The locals *should* have warships.

They were the lucky ones, after all. Only one factory world in three had the ability to build skip drives. Tano had clearly found some way to feed their people, too. If they hadn't, well, fourteen months was long enough to run through the food supply of a world that couldn't grow its own.

That was a familiar train of thought, one practice and therapy allowed Henry to pull himself away from as he finally entered the bridge of his battlecruiser.

"Captain on deck!" the GroundDiv guard standing by the door announced.

"As you were," Henry ordered. His *rank* was Colonel, but so long as he was aboard his ship, his *title* was Captain. That rank had never been included in the UPSF's rank structure, reserved for the commander of a vessel regardless of their rank.

His crew had known better than to turn their attention to him with potential hostiles in the battlespace. Their focus was on their consoles and the virtual augmentations their networks would be layering around them.

The consoles had the key data, more than enough to fight the ship if the wireless network that linked the internal networks to the ship's went down. But since they *could* add VR displays, Henry knew his people would be doing just that.

Iyotake rose from the dais in the center of the bridge. Massive screens faced inward from both levels of the bridge, mirroring the displays on their other sides. The bridge had two levels, the "balcony" and the "pit," but both were divided from the central command "bubble" by the two-sided screens.

It separated the captain in a way Henry didn't like, but it put all of the information in the captain's line of sight and accessible to anyone who needed it. Confidential or secure information would be handled in private VR displays, but the battle- and time-tested screens carried every necessary function.

Henry's XO gestured him to the chair with its own set of secondary screens.

"What have we got, XO?" Henry asked as he dropped into the seat, its systems automatically switching from Iyotake's preferred display to his.

The XO's usual battle station was in CIC, but there was a spot for him in the bubble alongside the two observer seats.

The broad-shouldered Native American man shrugged expressively at his boss.

"You've been getting the same updates from Ihejirika I have," he noted. "Four to six escorts or gunships, ten light-seconds and closing at one KPS squared."

"Cautious bastards, aren't they?" Henry observed drily.

If they were Kenmiri escorts, the unknown ships were capable of 1.2 KPS^2. Their compensation wouldn't be perfect, but they'd still only be looking at five subjective pseudogravities to pull that off.

Raven, on the other hand, could only get up to 0.5 KPS^2 before experiencing subjective thrust. Just to match the acceleration his potential enemies were showing would require his entire crew to report to the acceleration tanks to survive the twenty pseudogravities that would leak through.

"Commander Ihejirika?" Henry said more loudly, using the network to send his voice to the tactical officer to make certain he was heard. "Do we have more data?"

"Yes, ser," the Nigerian officer replied. Earth natives like him and his captain were relatively rare in the UPSF, for all that Earth still made up forty percent of mankind.

"We're looking at five ships; all appear to be unmodified Kenmiri escorts," the tactical officer laid out as the data updated on the screen. "I'm guessing they're late. Our updates from the surface suggest that the Tano are getting the upper hand on everything, but these guys are still almost an hour from zero-zero in orbit."

"We'll see if they withdraw," Henry replied. "If they're Vesheron or ex-Vesheron, they know they can't fight *Raven* with five escorts."

"It depends on their orders, ser," Iyotake noted. "Speaking of?"

"Moon, what have we got for the locals?" Henry asked, nodding his understanding to his XO.

"Not much," his com officer said grimly. "I've got links to six orbital forts, but they're standard Kenmiri defensive installations. If our unknowns are remotely competent, they can handle them easily enough. They'll get hurt, but they can take them."

"That's it?" Henry demanded. "These people should be able to *build* escorts, even assuming there was no one local with an ex-Kenmiri one in their hands."

"I've got codes for three squadrons of sublight fighters, looks like twenty-four ships," Moon told him. "I can link you in."

Henry swallowed a sigh and nodded grimly.

"Ihejirika." He turned back to his tactical officer. "What have you got on the local fighter craft?"

"Roughly equivalent to our Dragoons, but no gravity shields," his subordinate reported. "Potentially better compensators, but...they're TIEs, ser."

Henry wasn't sure who had decided to drop *that* particular nickname on Vesheron starfighters. It had been a running joke in the prewar fighter corps, an organization he was probably the only person on his bridge old enough to understand, comparing the terrible unshielded pirate fighters that were the UPSF's bread and butter to the cheap and expendable bad-guy fighters of the old movies.

He'd found the joke a lot funnier when he was twenty, applying it to pirates and scum, than when he was past fifty and seeing it applied to allies. The comparison fit, though. His fighters had gravity shields and could take a lot of hostile fire before they went down.

The local fighters couldn't take a hit at all.

"All right," he finally decided. "Let's get O'Flannagain and her people into space and get us moving out. If the local fighters decide to come with, we'll slot them into the Commander's networks."

He'd barely finished giving the order before his console informed him that Commander Samira O'Flannagain and her pilots had launched. *Raven* carried eight SF-122 Dragoon starfighters, mobile missile platforms capable of augmenting his alpha strike or carrying out independent long-range strikes.

They couldn't fight a battle on their own, but that wasn't their job.

"O'Flannagain, danger close formation," Henry ordered. "For now, at least. You might get some new chicks as we move out."

"I saw the locals," his CAG said dryly. "I could fly one of those if I had to, I suppose, but I'm not sure I'd come back."

"That would be the problem with them, yes," he agreed. "And *Raven* can take five escorts without them, so let's not get our new friends killed unless they volunteer. Stick with *Raven*, Commander."

"I'm aggressive, ser, not *take on five escorts with eight fighters* crazy," she replied. "We'll hide under *Raven*'s skirts till the right time, ser."

She did *not*, Henry noted, promise to stick with *Raven* until ordered to deploy. That was probably as good as he would get.

"Give me timelines, people," he ordered aloud. "Bazzoli, get us moving."

Commander Iida Bazzoli had clearly been waiting for the order. *Raven*'s engines flared to life the moment he was done speaking, setting a direct course for the incoming ships at half a kilometer per second squared.

"Assuming no change to their vector, twenty-four minutes to missile range," Ihejirika reported. "Seven minutes and twenty seconds after that to gravity-driver and laser range."

The United Planets Alliance's major advantage over their former allies and their Kenmiri enemies was a particular mastery of gravity *projection*. The Kenmiri and most of their Vesheron rebels were able to build compensators and similar gravity systems, but they created gravity at the projector itself. Perfect for artificial gravity and good for thrust compensation, but it had its limits.

The UPA's trick had allowed them to build a gravity-based mass driver, a three-hundred-meter-long gun that ran the full length of *Raven*'s hull and fired a projectile at seven percent of the speed of light. Only the heaviest Kenmiri and Vesheron energy shields could take even a single hit from the weapon.

The plasma cannons mounted on gunships and dreadnoughts were just as deadly in their own way, trading far lower projectile mass for a near-cee velocity and higher rates of fire, but if they were only facing escorts, there were none of those in play.

The strangers were in serious trouble if they chose to fight.

Hopefully, that meant they'd talk. Henry's job out there, after all, was to keep the peace.

Not fight Tano's war for them.

CHAPTER FOUR

"Looks like I've got those lost chicks you mentioned, ser," O'Flannagain told Henry. "Do we have com codes for these guys, or do I just need to make sure I keep a couple dozen *idiots* out of my line of fire?"

"Moon?" Henry asked. "Can you link O'Flannagain to the local fighter squadrons?"

"Forwarding the codes to the CAG," the coms officer replied. "We can't guarantee they speak Kem, ser."

Henry snorted.

"Neither do O'Flannagain's pilots," he pointed out. "Hopefully, at least one person over there can translate."

He knew *O'Flannagain* spoke the Kenmiri trade language. She didn't speak it *fluently*, but she should be able to give instructions and coordinate.

He hoped.

"Any sign of our new friends communicating or even getting concerned?" Henry asked.

He was heading out to meet them with a Terran battlecruiser and thirty-two fighters, after all. He doubted there was anyone in the Ra

Sector, what had once been the closest province of the Kenmiri Empire to the UPA, that *didn't* know how dangerous a battlecruiser was.

"They are continuing on course," Ihejirika confirmed. "Range is still well over two million kilometers."

Whoever had set up this attack had shown a surprisingly solid understanding of Tano's star system geography. Generally, you could enter a system just about anywhere along the skip line—the semi-imaginary line drawn in space between two neighboring stars—that you wanted. The downside was that the closer you skipped to your target star, the more likely it was you'd screw up and arrive *in* the star.

But Tano's orbit meant that it was currently as close as it was ever going to be to the skip line. That was still ten light-seconds and an hour's flight away, but it made for a decent "surprise attack."

With the confusion on the surface, it would have been more than enough to get the enemy squadron into orbit...if Henry hadn't been there. But he was there and the unknowns had to have seen him by now.

"Let's start the games up, then," he said aloud. "Commander Moon, get a relay drone out beyond the shield perimeter. Commander Ihejirika...give me my shield."

Moon actually sent out *three* relay drones. They would sit outside a pattern of gaps in the shield, relaying *Raven*'s communications without interference. Henry could talk to the world without them, but they made sure he spoke *clearly*.

Once they were clear, the main shield came up and Henry's power-generation schematics went yellow.

Raven had four fusion plants. Any one of them covered her regular operations—the engines provided their own power. A minimum of two were required to enter skip drive and travel between stars. Her weapons and sensor systems could easily consume the power of the three reactors *not* dedicated to keeping the lights on and the air running.

The gravity shield consumed the full output of a power plant, making combat operations for the battlecruiser a delicate balancing act. Her lasers ran on capacitors that recharged from whatever power wasn't currently being used, which was *usually* enough to keep her running.

Mounting a fifth reactor would have required the cruiser to give up an entire weapon system, rendering the extra power useless, *and* increased the vulnerability of the ship to reactor overloads and failures.

Nine times out of ten, the capacitors recharged fast enough that the power-distribution game was straightforward. The tenth time... the tenth time made heroes of good engineers and corpses of bad ones.

"Shield is stable; we are confirming a fifteen-thousand-gravity shear at all zones around the ship," Ihejirika said calmly. Very little survived going from microgravity to fifteen thousand gravities and back over the space of twenty centimeters. The grav-shield wasn't impenetrable...but it was the next best thing.

It was also *insanely* obvious to anyone watching. If the strangers hadn't known what they were facing before, they did now.

"All right. Commander Moon." Henry smiled as he looked at the five red icons on his screen. "Record for transmission, please."

He faced the camera hidden in front of his chair levelly and with a thin smile.

"Unidentified vessels, I am Captain Henry Wong of the United Planets Space Vessel *Raven*," he introduced himself in Kem. "You might well know me as 'the Destroyer.'"

He hated that the Vesheron had hung that moniker on him, but as wiser heads had told him, he'd *paid* for the reputation. He might as well use it.

"The Tano planetary government is in the process of signing a treaty of trade and defense with the United Planets Alliance," he continued. "That places this world and this star system under the protection of the United Planets Space Force.

"Your approach pattern is highly aggressive and your lack of communication gives the impression of hostility. You will reverse your engines and communicate your intent, or I will have no choice but to assume you are hostile to my allies and defend this system with all necessary force.

"If you wonder why I threaten five ships with one, I suggest you remind yourself *why* you are no longer Kenmiri slaves," he concluded with a light tone he didn't feel. "There will be no further warnings. If you continue your approach, I will open fire to defend this system."

SOMEHOW, Henry hadn't actually been expecting the strangers to reverse course and leave the system. It wasn't a surprise when the five escorts simply broadened their formation and continued toward Tano.

"Incoming transmission, ser," Moon reported. "Vesheron com protocols."

At this point, Henry wasn't sure who in the former Kenmiri Empire *didn't* have access to the protocols the rebel factions had used to communicate with each other.

"Play it," he ordered.

A video image appeared on the screen in front of him. He could see it mirrored on a dozen other screens around the bridge, his officers keeping up with the diplomatic state of affairs.

Henry was familiar with the standard construction and layout of the bridge of a Kenmiri escort. This one had had its lights upgraded—Kenmiri Warriors had *very* capable eyes and needed far less light than most of their enemies—creating an efficient, brightly lit command center.

The camera was focused on a tall figure with pale white hair in the center of the bridge. The man had what would have been called a queue by Henry's Qing ancestors, the front of his head bare with the pale white hair at the back pulled into a long braid.

Of course, Henry's Qing ancestors had shaved the front of their heads. The Kozun officer in the video naturally didn't grow hair there, the space marked by sharply angled natural armor plates coming up from what would have been the eyebrow ridges on a human.

The Kozun had deep purple eyes focused on the camera and wore an unfamiliar uniform of a blood-red toga-like upper body wrap over a full-body shipsuit.

The First Voice had apparently decided to get sartorial over the last year.

"Captain Henry Wong," the man greeted Henry in accented Kem. "I am Star Lance Edritcha of the war fleets of the First Voice of the Kozun."

Star Lance was equivalent to Henry's own rank. A senior Star Lance was probably the commander of the entire five-escort battle group.

"Your presence here is unanticipated and unwelcome," Edritcha continued. "The people of Tano were informed of the First Voice's ultimatum ten days ago. They are now subjects of the Kozun Hierarchy. They should have informed you of this, as they are no longer able to negotiate independent treaties.

"During this sensitive transition phase, foreign vessels are not welcome in the system. I am willing to provide you with updated skip-line charts to allow you to deliver a diplomatic entourage to Kozun itself, but you must speak with the First Voice, not our dependencies.

"As such, I require that you remove all Terrans from the surface of Tano and set your course out-system, so that further discussions can occur without risking conflict over a Kozun internal affair."

The image of Star Lance Edritcha froze as the recording ended and Henry studied it.

"Did the Tano say anything to the ambassador about an ultimatum?" Iyotake asked. "I mean, I don't think it would change much for us, but..."

"They did not," Henry replied. "When the attacks started, they instantly blamed the Kozun and admitted there'd been a delegation from the First Voice recently, but they didn't say anything about an ultimatum requiring their submission to them."

He could argue that the Tano's lack of transparency when negotiating gave him an excuse to leave them to their fate, but...that wasn't the purpose of the Peacekeeper Initiative.

"Commander Moon, prep a skip drone for Admiral Hamilton," he told his coms officer. "Load in everything we know so far, including the Star Lance's message and the response I'm about to record.

"Once you have my response to Star Lance Edritcha, dispatch the drone under Code Marathon."

Until a few months earlier, the Vesheron had had access to an instantaneous FTL communication network using coherent dimensions of subspace. It had turned out that those dimensions had been artificial, created and maintained by the Kenmiri.

Quite reasonably, the Kenmiri had taken their ball and gone home. Henry wasn't sure if there was still a subspace network in the handful of provinces the aliens had kept, but there definitely *wasn't* one outside them.

Fortunately for the UPSF, they'd only learned about the subspace networks during the war. Before they'd met the Kenmiri, they'd used skip-capable robotic ships. One of them was about to carry the same message as the runner who'd named the standard long-distance race: *We are about to engage the enemy.*

He nodded to Iyotake and turned back to the camera, starting a new recording with a mental command to his internal network.

"Star Lance Edritcha, I appreciate your courtesy and your concern," he told the other officer. "However, it is very clear from my conversations with the government of Tano that they have *not* conceded to whatever ultimatum the First Voice has sent. They remain an independent system with a functional local government.

"A local government that has requested the assistance of the

United Planets Space Force in the protection of their sovereign space. This is not a Kozun system. The United Planets Alliance does not recognize your control here.

"Therefore, my orders leave me no choice but to prevent any acts of aggression in this star system by any means necessary. You will withdraw from the Tano System. One vessel may remain to act as host to a diplomatic entourage *if* the Tano agree to it.

"If you continue your advance, I will engage and destroy your fleet. This is your final warning."

He cut off the recording and looked over at Moon.

"Commander?"

"Transmission sent. Marathon drone loaded."

"Get it into space. The Admiral needs to know that we're heading into a shooting incident."

Admiral Sonia Hamilton was the head of the Peacekeeper Initiative, operating out of Base Fallout in the Zion System, the farthest outpost of the United Planets Alliance. She'd backed Henry up when he'd talked the UPA Security Council into the Initiative, and she'd been saddled with the command for her sins.

And even at the best speed the skip drone could manage, she wouldn't get his message for three days. Reinforcements would take at least ten more to get there from the Initiative—and that was assuming Hamilton had anything to spare.

The UPSF had signed off on Henry's grandiose dream of trying to help the people the Kenmiri's fall had left lost, but they hadn't given the Initiative *that* many ships.

The skip drone flashed through a temporary portal in *Raven's* gravity shield, and he wished it godspeed as he turned his focus back to the matter at hand.

"Range, Commander Ihejirika?" he asked.

"Just over two million kilometers and closing," his tactical officer reported. "Assuming they haven't upgraded their missiles, we are five minutes from powered-missile range."

The damnation and the advantage of the situation was that

Henry had fought alongside the Kozun and fought against the Kenmiri. Basically every Vesheron power had used either stolen Kenmiri missiles or a home-built weapon that was extremely similar.

He and Star Lance Edritcha had identical lasers and missiles, but Edritcha only had light energy screens and no heavy weapons. *Raven* had a gravity shield and the gravity driver.

"Any response from the Star Lance?" Henry asked as the range continued to drop.

"Negative," Moon responded.

"We are being pinged with active targeting radar," Iyotake reported from Henry's left. "They're not going to have much luck doing more than detecting the grav-shield, but they are targeting us."

"No surprises there," Henry agreed. "And I guess that's an answer all on its own. Commander Ihejirika, dial them in," he ordered. "Have we IDed the Star Lance's flagship?"

"Negative, ser. They were relaying the transmission to avoid that possibility, ser, and all five of them are identical."

"Understood. Coordinate our missiles with O'Flannagain and the locals," Henry instructed. "O'Flannagain? Are we talking with our friendlies?"

It certainly looked like it. There were twenty-four locally built starfighters flying around his ship, and they'd settled into a decent escort formation that incorporated his CAG's eight SF-122 Dragoons.

"*Talking* is a strong word," the fighter pilot replied. "They have one kid who speaks half-decent Kem, but she's not one of the senior officers." She paused. "Of which, I'll note, we have one where there's supposed be four. The other three are dead. These pilots have no idea what their chain of command currently is, but, well..."

"There's a battle group headed to their planet, so they mounted up and rolled out," Henry finished. "I can respect that. I also think everyone will be better off if they live through this. Once they launch, I want them to break off. They don't have a chance once this gets real, but I'm not turning down a hundred missiles in the alpha strike, either."

"I don't know if they'll *listen*, ser, but I can pass on the instructions. Their homes are behind them. I'd say I wouldn't turn back in those circumstances but, well."

Henry and O'Flannagain had an understanding, but part of that was built on the fact that he had *been* a starfighter pilot once. He still wore a red-and-gold-painted pair of wings on his uniform that indicated that he'd made ace as a pilot—and that he'd been present when the Kenmiri had massacred nearly the entirety of the pre-war UPSF FighterDiv.

He understood rocket-jocks, and O'Flannagain was aggressive even for the type. He wasn't sure what *would* make her turn back—but he was sure she was right in her judgment of the local pilots.

And if the locals didn't speak Kem, there was no way he could change their minds.

"We can't cover them," he warned O'Flannagain quietly. "Our focus has to be on taking down the Kozun."

"I know that. You know that. These guys know that," she replied. "And their homes and families are behind them, ser. They know the game."

"Understood."

What else could he say?

CHAPTER FIVE

HENRY WATCHED THE RANGE INDICATOR DROP GRIMLY. BAZZOLI was adding evasive maneuvers to their base course now, enough to prevent a random long-range shot from getting lucky. None of the weapons in play today were likely to get that shot, but it was always a chance.

"Missile range in sixty seconds," Ihejirika reported. "We have them dialed in and we're feeding the data to the fighters. ROE?"

Rules of engagement. Henry considered thoughtfully for several seconds. Technically, the Peacekeeper Initiative's rules of engagement required him to wait for *clear signs of aggression*, not for the enemy to fire first.

But at missile ranges...they were talking five-minute flight times. With the subspace network down, he didn't need to consider how his actions were going to look to the wider galaxy, but he *did* need to care about how they looked to the general populace of the UPA.

The last thing he and Admiral Hamilton needed was for people to decide the Initiative was out trying to start wars.

"ROE Bravo-Two," Henry finally responded. "Let them fire first.

As soon as you've confirmed they've opened fire, hit your target with every missile we've got."

"Understood." There was a pause. "The CAG and I have assigned the locals their target, and I *think* they've got it, but I don't know if we can trust them to hold fire to match with us."

"We'll live with it," *Raven*'s captain replied, studying the screens and virtual displays around him with dark eyes. "I only have to justify what *I* do to our people."

A calm silence settled over the bridge as Henry's people focused on their tasks. The power-distribution charts on his screen flickered as his engineers adjusted the power supply from the reactors. The capacitors for the lasers were full, allowing them to step two of the reactors down to eighty percent.

That wouldn't last.

"Range," Iyotake whispered behind him.

"Tano fighters are holding fire with us," Ihejirika reported. "I think they think we have a plan."

"We do," Henry replied. "And it depends on the fact that they're carrying full-size missiles."

His fighters didn't. O'Flannagain's birds' main role right now was missile defense. The Tano fighters were bigger and cruder than the Terran ships, but they *did* carry full-sized Kenmiri missiles.

"Launch detected," Ihejirika barked. "One hundred missiles inbound. Acceleration is ten KPS squared. Drive metrics suggest mixed manufacture, but most are Kozun."

The missiles used might be functionally identical, but slight variations allowed the tactical team to identify if they were looking at Kenmiri missiles or locally built copies—and, as Ihejirika's report indicated, often *whose* locally built missiles they were.

In many ways, the missiles only being *mostly* Kozun did more to suggest that this wasn't someone trying to blame the Kozun than a full set of Kozun weapons would have. If Henry was trying to frame the Hierarchy, he'd have made sure he had an all-Kozun-built arsenal.

Whereas the Kozun themselves appeared to have a mix of

weapons stolen from the Kenmiri, bought from the Drifters, loaned by allies, and built by themselves. It was *definitely* them, not that Henry had really expected differently.

"You may return fire at your discretion, Commander," he ordered.

The hundred red icons accelerating toward Henry's battlecruiser and her fighter escorts were definitely concerning, but it definitely felt *better* when *Raven* opened fire in turn. Less than a second later, the Tano fighters followed suit and *over* a hundred missiles flung themselves at the Kozun flotilla.

Of course, thirty seconds later, the Kozun escorts launched another hundred missiles and *Raven* only fired twelve in response.

Henry didn't need to give any orders to O'Flannagain now. The Dragoons were moving up in front of the battlecruiser, positioning themselves to use their lasers against the incoming missiles. Their weaker gravity shields would protect them from stray fire—to a point —and help disorient the enemy missiles.

"Locals are sticking with us," Ihejirika reported. "Looks like the order to break off didn't get through."

"What do they even have left?" Henry asked. He'd expend all twenty-four Tano pilots if he needed to—more people had already died on the surface—but he *didn't* need to. "Are they even useful antimissile platforms?"

"I *think* they've got onboard lasers," Ihejirika reported, "but I don't know if they're trained for antimissile ops. Or if they have the sensors for them."

"Where the hell is the rest of their fleet?" Iyotake asked, the XO sending the question through the network to keep it silent. "The yards only have keels in them. Tano could have built a dozen escorts by now—they had the resources and the industry."

"That's a question to ask tomorrow," Henry replied. "I'd guess these fighters were meant to fly escort on real warships, but you're right. Those ships are missing."

Raven's launchers cycled again and the Chinese-American

captain double-checked his mental stock of the magazines. Without a resupply—a resupply he thought Tano could provide, but he wasn't sure—he only had a hundred missiles per launcher. If they'd arranged resupply agreements *before* he'd got into the fight, he'd have been far more cavalier with his weapons.

"Enemy missiles in laser range in thirty seconds," Ihejirika said aloud. "Lieutenant Ybarra, you have the guns."

Lieutenant Cornelia Ybarra was one of the most junior officers on *Raven*'s bridge, their newest assistant tactical officer. She already had her head down with three Chiefs and the defense team, all of them working together to plan the antimissile tactics.

Henry mirrored her screen to his, dipping into the virtual network the young officer was sharing with the experienced noncoms to make sure there weren't any *major* issues coming up.

He quickly realized that he shouldn't have bothered. Ybarra's second copper bar might be brand-new, but two of the Chiefs were older than Henry's own fifty-one and had served through the entire war, just like he had.

The fire plan was solid and he cleared it from his screens as the lasers started firing. A hundred missiles was a *lot* of firepower, more than *Raven* could bring to bear...but that was a balance the experienced NCOs were all too used to.

The local fighters, however, clearly weren't. At the last moment, they dove forward to use their lasers to cover the battlecruiser. They weren't very *good* at it, Henry noted absently, mostly following the lead of O'Flannagain's fighters.

"They're getting in the way more than they're helping," his XO muttered.

"They'll learn. And our people are good enough not to shoot them by accident," Henry replied.

The end result was probably no better than it would have been if the locals hadn't intervened, but he couldn't begrudge their effort. He could only brace himself as sixteen missiles made it through everything and triggered their conversion warheads a handful of kilometers from his ship's shields.

The escorts couldn't carry a full-size plasma gun, but they could carry a shaped-fusion warhead that duplicated the same effect at close range. Plasma washed over the gravity shear zone of the shield, and Henry's gaze was fixated on his damage reports.

"All warheads deflected; we do not have a blowthrough," Lieutenant Mariann Henriksson reported. Like Ybarra, she was one of the most junior officers on the bridge, an assistant to a more senior department head. Unlike Ybarra, she was the most senior member of her department on the bridge, an Engineering officer whose job was to keep the bridge updated while the rest of Engineering kept working.

"Alpha strike target destroyed," Ihejirika reported. "Multiple hits across the surviving units, but no major damage."

One down.

"Vector change," the tactical officer continued. "Targets are increasing acceleration to one point two KPS squared and breaking into two wings."

The Kozun were trying to go *around Raven*. If they could keep this a missile duel—and their higher acceleration meant they quite possibly *could*—they had the advantage.

Of course, *Raven* had the interior position. She could intercept any of the Kozun ships...but she couldn't intercept both formations.

"Designate Alpha Force and Bravo Force," Henry said calmly. If the Kozun wanted to play games, he could play games. "Commander O'Flannagain, are you getting the force designation and the enemy split?"

"Yes, ser."

"Bravo Force is yours. Take the locals and make them think twice. You don't need to kill them; you just need to do enough damage that they hesitate to engage the orbital forts. Understand?"

"Understood, ser. *Geronimo!*"

Henry had to smile as he shook his head and turned his attention back to the main display. He needed to bring the second force into gravity-driver range. So long as they were headed for the planet, he could *probably* do that, but there were ways to be certain.

"Commander Bazzoli, intercept course on Alpha Force," he ordered. "All hands, report to the acceleration tanks. We will intercept at one KPS squared."

New alert icons flared on his displays as he stood up. A panel in front of his seat slid open simultaneously with dozens of others across the bridge. The mask stand slid up out of the floor and footprints on the metal deck started glowing.

He took a deep breath and closed the mask over his face. His network flashed up an unnecessary warning to close his eyes, and then the ground sank beneath him, lowering him into the acceleration tank directly beneath his seat.

The viscous gel closed in around him, surrounding him as he focused on his internal network.

The fighters were breaking off as ordered, the Dragoons pushing to their full 1.5 KPS^2 of acceleration as they left *Raven* behind. The locals were trailing in O'Flannagain's wake, but the formation closed up as he watched.

A second missile salvo was flashing in as the system started its countdown to full acceleration, matched with a checklist of how many of his crew were in the tanks. A virtual-reality facsimile of his bridge took shape around him in his network, already full of his crew as they continued to perform their roles with only minor interruption.

There was a degradation in performance in almost every sector when they went into the tanks, but the worst was Medical and Engineering. Sickbay had special tanks for the already-injured, but no one could be brought there while they were under maximum thrust.

The tanks would allow humans to survive and function in twenty pseudogravities, but no one was going to be *moving* in them.

"All hands in the tanks, maximum thrust in five. Four. Three. Two. One."

Bazzoli's voice was calm, with no indication that she was counting down to the fist of an angry god. Even with the tanks to render it survivable, that much thrust could never be *pleasant*.

But Henry and his people trained for this. Even as his body was helpfully telling him that he was immersed in liquid and his short-cropped hair was wet—it was *always* his hair that part of him fixated on, for some reason—his mind was focused on the world outside his ship.

The Kozun were trying to go around his forces but they were still trying to get to Tano. His increased velocity meant that even though the enemy were trying to evade him, the closing acceleration had actually increased.

"Fighter-missile range in ninety seconds," Ihejirika reported. "Do you think they realize O'Flannagain didn't fire?"

"They should have," Henry replied. "It's not like our fighters having shorter-ranged missiles is news to the Kozun. They fought alongside us, after all."

It was unlikely that thirty-two missiles were going to finish off two escorts, which meant that O'Flannagain was going to have to close to laser range of the Kozun ships. She was going to lose ships—and Henry was enough of a bastard to hope that those losses were among the Tano fighters.

"We are continuing the missile engagement," his tactical officer continued. "They're focusing fire on us, but the split is wide enough now that they're coming in sufficiently separately to engage each salvo as forty missiles."

There were still missiles getting through, Henry noted. Each conversion warhead had the same small-but-present chance of blowing through his shields. They'd been lucky so far and Henry didn't want to count on that lasting.

"They are focusing their missiles on us and ignoring the fighter strike," Iyotake pointed out. "I'll admit I don't *like* that, but it probably works for us right now."

"Agreed."

"Blowthrough!" Henriksson snapped. "We have a shield blowthrough. Sensors and heat radiators on sector K-ten are gone, but the armor held."

Henry checked his screens. One percent of *Raven*'s heat dispersal lost wasn't the end of the world. Ten percent would be a problem. If he lost that many of the feather-like radiators on the surface of the cruiser, he wouldn't be *able* to sustain all four reactors at full without baking his crew.

"O'Flannagain has launched; thirty-two missiles locked on Bravo-One," Iyotake reported. "She'll be in laser range right after they hit... which is about when our first grav-driver rounds will make contact."

If Henry had been Star Lance Edritcha, he'd have been worried. They'd thrown over a thousand missiles at *Raven* and only scored a single light hit. In exchange, the Kozun had already lost an escort. Splitting their forces would have worked if Henry had *only* had his ship, but the extra fighter strength from the locals meant he could be confident Bravo Force wasn't really going to threaten Tano.

"Ninety seconds to grav-driver range," Ihejirika reported. "Conversion round in the tube. Conversion rounds in the ready magazine. Standing by."

Two more blowthroughs rippled through *Raven*'s shield as she plunged toward her enemy and the odds caught up with her. Neither did more damage than the first hit, the remaining plasma diffuse and off-angle by the time it reached her hull.

The capital ships' lasers would kick in around when the first grav-driver round hit, which meant Henry was hoping to only face one escort at that point.

"Target locked...firing the main gun."

Raven shivered as she created a channel of unimaginably powerful gravity down her core. The projectile went from zero to seven percent of lightspeed along the ship's three-hundred-meter length, the energy release emptying massive capacitors.

"Round in space. Fighter missiles impacting," Ihejirika reported, the two events blurring together. "Bravo-One has lost acceleration and is spinning; she's been hit *hard*."

"Bravo Force is breaking off," Iyotake snapped. "They are rotating their acceleration vector and are burning away from Tano at one point two KPS squared."

"Impact! Alpha-One is hit...Alpha-One is dead in space."

Henry yanked his attention back to the opponents in front of *Raven*. A missile's conversion warhead was designed to create a plasma blast that rivaled a Kenmiri dreadnought's main gun.

A gravity driver round's conversion warhead was designed to cripple or kill a Kenmiri dreadnought, its self-annihilation creating a plasma blast that was unrivaled by any other weapon Henry had ever seen. Ihejirika had lined up his shot perfectly and the blast hit the target escort dead-center.

Energy screens failed against a weapon designed to shatter the defenses of a Kenmiri dreadnought in a single hit. They were still enough that Alpha-One survived.

Theoretically.

"Hold fire," Henry barked. "Order O'Flannagain to hold fire as well. Bravo is already breaking off; let's see what..."

"Alpha-One is abandoning ship," Ihejirika reported. "Alpha-Two has ceased firing and is transmitting. Commander Moon?"

"Star Shield *Konaris* is requesting permission to retrieve *Scimitar's* escape pods as she withdraws from the system," Moon reported. "It's not quite a surrender, but..."

"It's enough for us," Henry admitted. "We are obliged to counter aggression and protect Tano, but we also need to show the Kozun we will not pursue retreating ships.

"We let them go, people." He smiled thinly. "Today, at least."

His conversations with Admiral Hamilton had been quite clear. Regardless of the goals of the Peacekeeper Initiative, there were definitely only so many strikes they were giving anyone.

CHAPTER SIX

"THE KOZUN SHIPS HAVE NOW WITHDRAWN FROM THE SYSTEM," Henry told Todorovich. "What's the situation down there?"

"Ugly, from what I can tell," she replied. "The Council is starting to look a bit less panicked, but it has been almost a day and their control of the situation remains...tenuous."

"How bad?" he asked. The slim officer was pacing his office, bringing up and tossing aside virtual screens around him as new updates came in from his people.

He'd come out of the space battle better than he would have dared hope. All of the Tano fighters had made it back to their bases. All of *his* fighters were back aboard too, and *Raven*'s damages were easily repaired.

The battlecruiser had thousands of individual heat radiators so that she *could* lose them. Drones were already on the hull, installing freshly fabricated replacement units. The estimate on one of the screens he'd closed said the repairs would be done within four hours.

"I don't think Arsena is in question anymore, but some of the regional centers are," Todorovich said. "I think the biggest problem, from the Council's perspective, is that most of the centers are basically under martial law...and the troops are the Kenmiri janissaries."

"Anything we can do to soothe those waters?" Henry asked.

"I don't know yet," the ambassador admitted. "Can you conjure an army out of thin air that they'd trust?"

"I have a six-day communication loop and a minimum-thirteen-day reinforcement timeline," he pointed out. "Assuming that Admiral Hamilton had said army ready to go—and the Peacekeeper Initiative wasn't assigned an army."

"That might yet prove to be a mistake," Todorovich said. "Though I understand the reasoning. Get Thompson on the network, Henry; he's actively working with Kansa."

"Which of us is in charge here again?" he asked with a laugh.

"Both of us. Now get Thompson on the call."

That was the work of a few seconds of concentration, a mental chime announcing that the GroundDiv Commander was linked in.

"Commander, can you update the ambassador and me on the situation?" Henry asked.

"Yes, ser," Thompson replied instantly. He paused to marshal his thoughts before continuing.

"Arsena is secure. I've mostly kept the UPSF out of things and held a careful eye on the Center itself," he told them. "I'm in constant contact with General Kansa, but she understands that my ability to get involved is limited.

"I have deployed GroundDiv to secure critical pieces of the regional infrastructure," he continued. "Working with the General, power and water have been secured across the planet. The Council does not appear to entirely trust the troops General Kansa has used to secure the infrastructure. We're not sure how to handle that."

"She's using the ex-janissaries," Todorovich guessed. "I think that's something the Council will need to get over."

"Honestly, sers? The only real remaining problem is that the Council doesn't trust their soldiers," Thompson told them. "What's left of the Kozun and their local allies are running for the hills. And the hills aren't going to sustain them for long."

Henry grimaced as he brought up the rough ecological data they'd got from the locals. A large portion of Tano's natural fauna was inedible to most Ashall metabolisms to begin with. The flora was better, if you knew what to eat and could check that it wasn't containing toxic levels of heavy metals.

Kenmiri factory worlds were hell—and Tano had only been colonized a century earlier.

"Though that begs the question, I have to admit, of just what the hell the Tano are eating," Henry admitted. "Have we been securing food-supply centers for them yet?"

"Reading between the lines of what Kansa has asked, she is using the troops she is most certain of for that." There was a long pause. "They're sure as hell acting like someone who's expecting to run out of food sooner rather than later."

"Understood. That's useful. Captain Wong, have you sent the follow-up to your Marathon drone yet?" Todorovich asked.

He smiled. He hadn't even told the ambassador he'd *sent* a drone yet.

"I have not, though I remind you that we only have so many skip drones," he said. In theory, the drones he sent to Base Fallout would be replaced by drones sent back to him, creating a continuous sequence of refreshing robotic messengers.

"You still need to advise the Admiral that we don't need a fleet," Todorovich told him.

"Hamilton doesn't have a fleet," Henry admitted. "We all know the Initiative is two battlecruisers and a destroyer squadron. There are a few more ships at Fallout, but they're the base detachment under Admiral Zhao."

"That's our deployed force, yes," the ambassador agreed. "But if we run into a real threat to the UPA out here, they'll find more."

"Probably," he told her. "Probably. You want to add a message to the drone, I take it?"

"We're still a bit from a trade deal, but I can already tell you what they're going to buy," she told Henry and Thompson.

"Food," Thompson concluded instantly. "This is a Kenmiri factory world; they were never intended to support themselves. I don't know how they made it this far, but my guess is that rations are getting tighter. That's at least part of why the Kozun managed this mess."

"I need to get my counterparts back home to organize a relief convoy," Todorovich concluded. "We've sent them before; we know what they need to look like. I think we assumed that Tano had a long-term food solution already, but I'm starting to suspect that whatever it *was* is gone."

"And that's a conversation to have with the Council," Henry agreed. "Do you think you can get them to stop panicking long enough to have it?"

"Almost certainly," she confirmed. "But I can tell you, Captain Wong, that it will be easier with both of us."

"This system was just attacked," he argued. He did *not* want to leave his ship at this point.

"We'll bring you in by holoprojector," she told him in soothing tones. "But I think everyone will be happier if you're at least on the call. I also hope we can get a bit more honesty out of them, because it sounds like they have a lot of problems no one mentioned to us."

⋆
⋆⋆⋆⋆

"ADMIRAL, the situation described in the previous Marathon drone has been resolved for the moment," Henry told the recorder calmly. He and Admiral Sonia Hamilton went back a long way. She now commanded the Peacekeeper Initiative, but prior to that, she'd commanded the UPSF's Fifth Fleet.

Fifth Fleet had been a purely organizational formation, an org chart for a far-flung fleet of scattered battlecruisers and their support ships scattered through the Kenmiri Empire. It had been Fifth Fleet's battlecruisers that had executed Operation Golden Lancelot, the carefully planned and ruthlessly implemented campaign to wipe out the Kenmorad.

Which meant that Sonia Hamilton had dealt with a lot of officers who'd come home to discover their "local strike at the Kenmiri power structure" had been part of a coordinated campaign of genocide. Few of them had handled it well.

Henry suspected he'd handled it worse than most. Therapy helped, but every time he recorded a message for Sonia Hamilton, he had to consciously suppress the memory of the drunken video conversation he'd had with her while his loaded service pistol sat on his desk in front of him.

She'd understood, in a way even many modern fleet commanders wouldn't have. And so, he'd taken command of *Raven* for her and walked into *another* clusterfuck as the Vesheron self-destructed at the Gathering intended to lay out a post-Kenmiri order.

Henry and Hamilton definitely had history. He trusted her, though, and he was reasonably sure the feeling was mutual.

"Full telemetry of the engagement is included on the drone, but it went much as you'd expect a battlecruiser versus five escorts to go," he told his boss. "Unfortunately, it appears that Star Lance Edritcha was killed in action when we hit his flagship with our alpha strike. I doubt the death of the task group commander is going to do us many favors in the halls of Kozun.

"They lost two ships with a third crippled, but we permitted them to collect their escape pods before they withdrew. While I hope that will be seen as a sign of our continuing willingness to negotiate with the First Voice and his people, it may also be taken as a sign of weakness or even condescension."

Henry shook his head.

"I've *met* Mal Dakis and I'm not sure which way he'll read it," he admitted. "Further operations in the region are likely to continue to aggravate him. He clearly regards Tano and, presumably, the other inhabited worlds around here as his property.

"My current orders give me sufficient discretion to disabuse him of that notion. I intend to discuss the local political structure with the Tano Council and establish a plan of action to cut off any tendrils of warlordism the Kozun have sent in this direction."

He paused, considering how best to phrase his next statement.

"In the absence of direction to the contrary, I will continue to act in accordance with my orders and the principles of the Peacekeeper Initiative," he finally said. "I am aware that this does put us on a collision course with the Kozun Hierarchy if the First Voice is intending to set himself up as a warlord here.

"If the Initiative or UPSF command want to avoid major conflict with the Kozun, I need to know that as soon as possible. Right now, it appears that the First Voice is doing exactly the kind of conquest that we intended to stop and I have every intention of stopping him.

"Ambassador Todorovich has requested a relief convoy be assembled for Tano. I recommend that convoy be escorted by a minimum of two destroyers and that those ships remain at Tano to provide us with a secure base for operations in this region.

"If the Kozun want to conquer this region, well, I think it's our job to change their minds. If you *don't* want me to do that, you probably want to tell me sooner rather than later.

"Captain Wong aboard *Raven*, out."

CHAPTER SEVEN

NONE OF THE MEMBERS OF TANO'S RULING COUNCIL LOOKED particularly comfortable to have a hologram in the room with them. Todorovich had set the projector up on the seat and Henry knew, from past experience, that he would look *mostly* right to them.

But only mostly. The lightspeed and encryption delays weren't quite enough to be consciously noticeable from orbit, but they were enough that everything he did would be ever-so-slightly delayed and out-of-sync.

It took practice to get used to, something Henry had lots of from the UPA using subspace-transmitted holograms for major meetings. From his side, he was sitting at his desk, immersed in a virtual reality recreation of the meeting room in Arsena created by his internal network.

The same six locals took up their side of the table and Henry's projection joined Todorovich on the other side.

"The situation has been resolved; I hope?" Todorovich asked in Kem as she took her own seat. "The reports from Commander Thompson were promising."

"The enemy forces have been driven from the cities," Kansa said calmly. The tusked general's species were apparently called the Sana. They were the second-largest population on Tano, though Henry noted she was the only member of her people on the Council.

"Though some question remains as to whether some of the cities are still under our control," Inbar replied. The senior Councilor, first-among-equals by Henry's assessment, could have passed for Ihejiri-ka's cousin. *His* people were the largest population on Tano, the Eerdish. Some of their variations looked highly alien to human eyes, but their features and form were identical and a large portion of their population could pass for humans of African extraction.

A significant portion of the rest were various shades of green.

"You do our soldiers a disservice, Councilor," Kansa insisted. "You mistrust them for their past, but there is no sign that our regional commanders have done anything more or less than their duty. The enemy has been driven from the cities, the civilian governments are in control, and the army maintains patrols because we just fought battles in the cities.

"What do you want of them? To be invisible when you do not need them?"

"That would likely help Councilor Inbar's mood, yes," a third Councilor spoke up. She was another Eerdish, an attractive woman with skin so pale a green as to resemble the finest of jade. "And the General is right, Councilor Inbar. Our soldiers have done exactly what they needed to. You do them a disservice."

"Our time grows short, Councilor Chell," Inbar replied. "When we must rely on warriors who served our conquerors to enforce food rations, I wonder how far we truly are from the imposed governance of the Kenmiri."

"We were chosen, if not perhaps by as broad a crowd as we would desire," Chell said. "And we are trying to find a way forward. I think our Terran friends have proven their good faith. I believe we should make clear the depths of our disaster."

Six heads, each looking human-but-yet-not-quite, bowed almost simultaneously.

"Your disaster?" Henry asked. "I am going to guess that this is related to how you have fed your people since the fall of the Kenmiri and yet are running short now."

"The rebels in the hills will falter and fail," Kansa told him. "But the reason they will fail damns us all. We are only beginning to study the ways in which we can restore the ecology of this world. And as none of us are native to Tano, we must also find sources for crops and food animals that this world cannot provide."

The Kenmiri had populated their specialized slave worlds by drafting vast numbers of people from the occupied homeworlds and moving them across the stars. Zion, the system that hosted Base Fallout, had seen its entire hard-scrabble colony transported to staff Kenmiri factories before the UPA had retaken it.

"We could have built orbital farms," another Councilor told them. "It would have saved us!"

"We all know we could not have built them fast enough, not without crops and herds on Tano to transplant," Inbar said with a sigh. "The deal you have offered us gives us hope, Ambassador Todorovich, Colonel Wong, but for us to rest our food security on so tenuous a supply line..."

He shook his head.

"We can not do it," he told them. "If we sign your deal, we will find ourselves kneeling to the Kozun regardless. In months or years instead of days or weeks, but our fate would be unchanged."

"The UPA can assist you with both orbital hydroponics facilities and planetary remediation and agriculture," Henry's companion told them. "We see this as a relationship with great potential for mutual growth."

Henry had read the terms the UPA wanted. They were *fair*, he supposed, but they were only generous in comparison to the Kozun wanting to take over.

"It will not matter in the end," Kansa admitted. "We are decided, Ambassador. We will sign your deal if you meet our price."

Henry leaned forward. He'd been waiting for this part and he was pretty sure he knew exactly what was coming next.

A map of the region appeared above the table. Its plainness concealed at least one piece of technology, it turned out. The map was zoomed in relatively closely, on an area of what Henry guessed to be about fifteen light years across.

It was a small slice of the Ra Sector, only thirty or so of the Sector's five hundred stars. Two of the stars closer towards the heart of the old Kenmiri Empire glittered red, presumably now under Kozun control.

The Tano System was marked in bright blue but was *not*, Henry noted with interest, the center of the map on display. That was another system, one even his network didn't immediately recognize, marked in orange.

Three more systems were marked in a paler blue, the four blue systems forming a rough square around the orange one.

"Your food supply came from a slave agriworld when you were a Kenmiri slave world," Henry said aloud. "I am guessing the orange marker is that world?"

The paler blue markers would be the other factory worlds. The only real hope any of the factory worlds had had was to build ships and reconnect with the agriworlds that had fed them. Of the five worlds highlighted in the map, only Tano would have been able to build a skip drive without new infrastructure.

The other three factory worlds might have been able to build that infrastructure in the long run, but their main hope for survival would have been co-opting ships present when the Kenmiri left. The agriworld didn't need to worry about starving to death, but their entire technological infrastructure was built on them receiving parts and machinery from the surrounding worlds.

None of the worlds was a complete civilization on their own. The Kenmiri withdrawal had left hundreds of slave world clusters to fall apart. Henry hoped—as the hand that had broken the Kenmiri, he *had* to hope—that most of those clusters had found ways to reconnect.

"La-Tar," Inbar confirmed. "They were lucky. There were a handful of transports in orbit that the Kenmiri did not have the crews to take with them. They managed to take parts they had and rig up an orbital transport and claimed those ships.

"From there, they reached out to us and the other worlds. We were building ships to try and reach them, but we had no idea if we could do it in time."

The Councilor bowed his head.

"They bought us that time. That handful of ships did not *stop* for four months. By the time we had new-build ships to take over, all of the factory worlds were on the edge of running out of food anyway—and we had burned out the skip drives on the ships the La-Tar had found.

"But we built enough ships fast enough, Colonel, Ambassador, and five worlds lived. Over two billion sentient beings lived—and they asked no payment, no fealty, no grand gestures.

"La-Tar gave their food freely, knowing that we would honor our debt to them," Inbar concluded. "And so when we finally built warships, they went to La-Tar, to guard the crops that fed five worlds."

"And they died above La-Tar," Kansa finished softly for the Councilor. "We had built eight ships, functionally Kenmiri escorts, and we tried to protect La-Tar. Instead, our ships were destroyed and La-Tar was invaded.

"The food shipments stopped."

Henry winced. That was classic Kenmiri control tactics, now executed by the First Voice of the Kozun. Many of the warlords they were going to encounter would have learned from their former conquerors.

"We were informed that if we defied the Hierarchy, we would starve," Chell said after a moment, picking up from her fellow Councilors. "If we knelt and acknowledged the First Voice, the food shipments would resume.

"But we would be as we were under the Kenmiri: a builder of

weapons and ships for others. There would be no orbital farms, no remediations. Our world would continue as a factory without a care for the future of our children.

"We would be slaves again."

A long silence filled the room and Henry was glad he wasn't actually there. Even the virtual image around him was bad enough.

"How long do you have food supplies for?" he finally asked.

"We have imposed tighter rationing than I want to even think about," Inbar told him. "With that...thirty-four days. Until you arrived, we had no choice."

"There will be a food convoy on the way from the UPA within the next seven to ten days," Todorovich. "We should have supplies here inside that time frame."

"We have made no—"

"You are worth nothing to us as trade partners if you are dead or slaves," the ambassador snapped. "Consider it an investment that we expect repaid if you must, but a drone requesting the convoy has already been sent.

"Twenty days, maybe twenty-five if it takes far longer to assemble the convoy than I hope," Todorovich concluded. "We will make sure no one on Tano starves."

"We are one world of four," Kansa said grimly. "Ratch, Atto, Skex. They will share our fate if no one acts to save them and I do not believe you can so readily gather supplies to feed two billion people across four stars."

"We owe La-Tar a debt that can never be repaid with money or trade," Inbar concluded. "If you want your treaty, Colonel, Ambassador, you must liberate La-Tar. The Kenmiri bound our worlds together by force, but we are bound together regardless."

"I have a single ship, Councilors," Henry pointed out. "Once my soldiers return aboard, four hundred ground troopers. Retaking a world is not in my capabilities."

"There is...there *must* be a resistance on La-Tar," Chell told him. "We have diplomatic and military codes you can use to get in contact with them. If you can take control of the orbitals away from the Kozun, the La-Tar will fight."

It all sounded very familiar. A strike with an understrength force, hoping to take control of the space above a planet. Relying on an unknown local resistance to finish the job, praying that *enough* of a victory could be achieved to make the conqueror blink when they returned in greater strength.

Henry had served on or commanded a dozen missions like it during the war. At least half had ended in disastrous failure, with the world they were hoping to liberate subject to brutal reprisals from the Kenmiri.

"Colonel Wong and I will need to discuss this in private," Todorovich said swiftly. "Please provide all information you have on La-Tar and the other factory worlds they feed to both myself and *Raven.*

"Understand that we *want* to help," she continued. "But the resources of the United Planets Alliance are stretched thin. *Raven* is all we have available and we must make our plans based on that."

"We understand," Inbar said swiftly, clearly cutting off at least one Councilor who hadn't spoken yet. "But realize that time is only Kozun's ally now. Your victory and your willingness to trade have given Tano a choice. Our friends do not have that. If La-Tar is not freed, those worlds *must* kneel to Kozun or starve."

"I understand," Todorovich conceded. "I can make no promises yet. Send us that information, Councilors, and Colonel Wong and I will see what we can do."

Henry looked back at the holographic map in the middle of the table and nodded his agreement to Todorovich's comments.

The five star systems were inextricably interlinked by the way the Kenmiri had built them. The insectoids had withdrawn from these worlds, but their choices shaped their fates still.

The UPA could potentially feed all four factory worlds in the long run. Enough fortunes would be made in the process that he suspected some of his superiors would want that plan.

But he wasn't sure they could muster enough food fast enough to stave off that thirty-day time limit.

"I appreciate your honesty with us, Councilors," he told Tano's leaders. "We will attempt to repay your honesty in kind once we have some basis for a decision."

CHAPTER EIGHT

THE CHIME ON THE DOOR TO HENRY'S QUARTERS SURPRISED him. He was working in the attached office—just because he wasn't *on duty* didn't mean he wasn't working. He was the captain of a million-plus ton starship with a crew of fourteen hundred human beings, after all.

A check on his internal network told him that Sylvia Todorovich was standing outside his door, which was *another* surprise. He hadn't been expecting the ambassador to return to *Raven* for the discussion they were supposed to have and had been watching his network for a com request from her.

He opened the door with his network as he closed down the files on the desk. The office in his quarters was much smaller than his main office by the bridge, basically just a desk in a closet barely big enough for it.

His quarters were comfortable enough, if nothing anyone could call luxurious. He had a separate bedroom, living room, and office. He had a door into the captain's mess as well, but he didn't really regard that as part of his quarters.

He ate at his desk unless he was having a formal meal, after all.

He entered the living area to find that Todorovich had closed the door behind her and draped herself across his couch, looking up with a surprisingly soft smile as he came in.

Henry wasn't sure what she was smiling at. He'd abandoned most of his uniform in favor of the plain dark blue slacks and turtleneck that served as an underlayer to every UPSF uniform—the ones with the safety features that would allow them to function as an emergency space suit.

His turtleneck had the white collar of a spaceship captain, but he was pretty sure he didn't look much like an officer right now.

"I wasn't expecting you to come back aboard," he told the ambassador. She'd shed a suit jacket over the back of the couch, he noted, leaving her in a pale blue blouse and gray slacks. Her hair, normally done up in a bun or otherwise carefully coiffed and managed, hung down around her face, softening the sharpness of her features.

Just why *was* he focusing on her appearance? That wasn't normal for him.

"If we're heading to La-Tar, it seemed wiser to come back up with the GroundDiv," she told him. "Thompson tells me his people should be clear for action by the time we get there?"

"Two skips, twelve and fourteen hours, with a day's flight between them," Henry said instantly. "Fifty hours. His worst injured were already aboard and being treated. I'd have to check with the medbay, but that timeline seems reasonable."

"That's closer than I expected," she admitted.

"Pretty standard for Kenmiri slave worlds," he told her. "None of the four factory worlds will be much more than forty-eight hours' travel for a Kenmiri transport freighter—none of which accelerate any faster than *Raven* does. They liked to keep the supply lines short."

So far as he could tell, the Kenmiri had agreed with the UPA on the maximum safe length of a skip, too: twenty-four hours. After that, ships started coming out in pieces.

The skip drive wasn't a safe way to travel faster than light. It was just the only way.

Todorovich gestured Henry to his own chair, which he took with a chuckle.

"I don't suppose there's any chance we could *actually* get a fleet out of the UPSF?" she asked from the couch, studying him with oddly intense eyes.

"Give Hamilton time to pull back the rest of the Initiative, we could field two proper battlecruiser groups," he told her. "Of course, *Jaguar* is old and the destroyers are about halfway between her and *Raven* in age."

Raven was still one of the newest *Corvid*-class battlecruisers in service. *Jaguar* was the lead ship of the *Jaguar* class—which meant she was *the* oldest battlecruiser in UPSF service.

He'd still back her against a Kenmiri dreadnought. She'd been designed to kill them, after all.

"That's the entire Initiative," Todorovich countered. "How long to gather that?"

"Depends on what Hamilton's got them doing," Henry replied. "Base Fallout has its own defenders, but we held two destroyers back there anyway. The rest are between three and five days' skip drone flight away. So if we sent a message back and Hamilton recalled the fleet immediately, *Jaguar* wouldn't get the notice for eight days."

His companion snorted as he made it clear he knew *exactly* where every ship in the Initiative was at least supposed to be. The drones they were using for communications now were faster than ships in real space, but they skipped between stars along the same lines and at the same speed.

"And I'm guessing it would take more than twenty-two days for them to all get to us?" she asked.

"*Jaguar*'s the farthest out and it would probably take her twenty-five to get to us after she got the message," Henry agreed. "And that's assuming Colonel Adebayo is in a position to break off whatever she's doing and head straight back.

"She could cut four days off of that by coming directly here, but she'd be pushing her fuel supplies if she couldn't resupply at her mission site. She wouldn't have time to forage fuel on the way."

Geography, so to speak, was as much a factor in skip travel as distance. The larger the star a ship was skipping towards, the farther the ship could travel inside the safe window. Large, uninhabited stars were often used as relay points but there weren't many convenient ones between *Jaguar* and *Raven* right now.

"So we couldn't pull the Initiative together fast enough to take an actual fleet to La-Tar," Todorovich conceded with a sigh. She wasn't concealing her emotions from him, which made sense.

There wasn't anywhere more private than his quarters, after all. If they couldn't have an honest conversation here, there wasn't anywhere they could.

"In theory, there are two carrier groups within five days' skip of Zion," Henry admitted. "If we sent the drone today with a solid enough argument to get Command onboard, one of those could be in Tano in eighteen days. But the entire *point* of the Initiative is not to get the UPA involved in a serious shooting war."

Todorovich studied him for several seconds.

"And one of those is Carrier Group *Scorpius*, isn't it?" she asked.

"The idea of begging my ex-husband to come haul my ass out of the fire has limited appeal, yes," Henry conceded. He and now-Commodore Peter Barrie had been fighter pilots together when the war had started. They'd both even survived the bloody campaigns to stave off the Kenmiri invasion of UPA space.

They'd married during a war and their marriage hadn't survived that war. At fifty-one, Henry could look back and say that had been inevitable.

At thirty-five, two years into what would be a seventeen-year-long war, he'd been enough of a romantic to think their love could overcome those barriers.

"I know you well enough to know the personal angle isn't impacting you much," Todorovich noted. "But...?"

"Either *Scorpius* or *Crichton* could get to Tano in fifteen days from Command signing off on the request," he told her. "But that would require Command to sign off, which adds another six days to the command loop. Hamilton could directly request the Group Commanders to deploy on their own authority, but...I don't know if either would."

"We'd be more likely to get *Scorpius* because Commodore Barrie knows how you think, I imagine," Todorovich said. "Hard to ignore your flag captain's opinion, after all."

"I'd need a lot more than we've got to convince Peter to talk his Admiral into jumping the gun," Henry admitted. "Two billion lives might be enough weight on the scales, but I'm not sure I need a fleet carrier for this yet, either."

"So you have a plan," the ambassador concluded. "Would you care to elaborate, Henry?"

"A plan?" he laughed. "That's a strong word for it."

As he said that, however, he realized he *did*.

"More of a *next steps* than a plan, really," he continued. "We need to know what we're up against. We've already requested reinforcements and humanitarian supplies. They're on their way. I'll note that a *skip drone* can make the trip from La-Tar to Tano or vice versa in thirty-two hours."

The drone didn't have squishy humans aboard. It could cross the gap between the skip lines in six hours instead of twenty-four.

"A drone only has navigation sensors," he reminded Todorovich. "But we can send one *from* La-Tar with whatever we learn.

"Either we need a carrier group or we don't really need reinforcements. *Raven* can handle a lot." He leaned forward thoughtfully, gesturing a map of the region into both of their networks.

"The question, really, is how well defended La-Tar is," he continued. "And, I suppose, whether you and I are willing to stretch the principles and orders of the Initiative far enough to justify an unquestionably aggressive action."

"I think that liberating a world that has been invaded and occupied falls under the principles, at least, of the Initiative," she told him.

"I'll agree that it's pushing your orders, but I think we have to do it, Henry."

"Four worlds. Two billion people," he said aloud, putting the key factors out there. "No one will let their people starve when there's another answer. The Kozun rule will probably be gentler than the Kenmiri rule."

He sighed.

"Or so I would tell myself if I was the leader of one of those worlds," he admitted. "Without intervention, those worlds will surrender to the Kozun inside weeks at most. We might be able to save them."

"You want to go to La-Tar," Todorovich said. "And you want me to back you on that."

"Yes and yes," he confirmed. "If La-Tar is guarded by a handful of escorts, *Raven* can take them out or drive them off. Then you can talk to the locals and see if they can actually secure the planet with limited orbital support."

"How much orbital support can *Raven* provide?" she asked.

"More than the UPA likes to admit," Henry said. "Part of the deal between the member systems that created the UPA was that the UPA would have the only skip-capable warships but those ships wouldn't have ground attack abilities.

"That was a hundred years ago and before we fought the war against the Kenmiri," he concluded swiftly. "*Raven* does not officially carry ground attack munitions. We do, however, have schematics for multiple different systems that can be fired from our missile launchers.

"Fifty hours is enough for my people to fabricate a significant supply of precision bombardment rounds." He shook his head. "I hate using them. *Precision* is a fucking lie when you're talking about weapons of mass destruction."

"Do you need anything to do that?"

"Iyotake is already talking to the locals about replacing our missiles," Henry admitted. "That should be done by morning. Give me eight hours, Ambassador, and *Raven* can move out to wherever we want."

"Enough time to get a good night's rest," she replied, straightening in the couch and stretching. "Gods its good to be back in one gee," she told him. "You don't notice the extra point oh two on a planet like Tano until you *leave*."

"If everything goes right at La-Tar, you'll need to talk a traumatized and mostly shattered government into retaking control and getting food shipments moving *immediately*," he warned her. "Securing the system is the easy part."

"Says the man with one of the most modern warships I know of," she told him. "The job splits the same way it always has, Henry. I'll still need you to play diplomat with me. Even though it *isn't* a game."

"I know," he allowed. "I apologize for that."

"Are you okay?" she asked, leaning forward on the couch to study him more carefully. "You...got out of dodge *fast* when the attack started. You need to be up here, yes, but..."

"Gunfire and I don't get along," Henry admitted. "One of the PTSD responses I'm aware of, but I don't encounter often enough to really deal with."

He shivered.

"I'm not in control in a gunfight," he told her. "Not in a current events sense, not in an emotional sense. Put me on a ship, even in a fighter, I'll handle whatever you throw at me. But I'm a terrible shot and people have died for it.

"So yeah, given the option, I'm going to run for a ship when the shooting starts," he conceded. "It doesn't help that that's usually the right call for me. Hard to fight a habit when it's a good idea."

"It's true enough, but that doesn't help with the underlying problems."

Henry shivered, practice helping him push aside memories.

"Not much can," he admitted. "We both know I'm a patched-up wreck, Sylvia. Find me another senior officer in the fleet who isn't."

"The ones who aren't patched-up wrecks aren't good at their jobs *or* particularly good people," she pointed out. "Are you okay?"

He snorted.

"I'll live, I'll serve, I'll keep my people safe," he promised. "*Okay* is probably too much to ask."

She was studying him with that strangely intense gaze again.

"Aren't you supposed to be allowed to retire when it's bad?" she asked.

"This isn't bad," he told her. "I react badly to being shot at. That's not entirely a PTSD symptom, Ambassador, so much as it's just sensible. Most other responses I've got handled. Our medical people are *very* good."

"I know," she agreed. "I worry about you, Henry. That's perhaps not entirely fair, but this entire Initiative is because of you. We ripped some scabs off getting you in front of the Security Council and we promptly sent you back into space."

"This is where I belong, Sylvia," he said. "Out here, I can save lives. Save *worlds*. Make it all worth it. Which I think is what we're up to right now, isn't it?"

"Depends on what we find at La-Tar, I suppose. Guess we should get that rest?"

Nodding, Henry rose. He walked the few steps to the door with Sylvia, pausing with her as her hand hovered over the door panel.

"I'm here for you, Henry," she told him quietly. "Whatever you need, you know that."

"Likewise," he replied. "You're a damn good friend, Sylvia, as well as a damn good diplomat."

She laughed and hugged him. It took Henry a moment to get over his confusion and hug her back, the two of them leaning against each other and taking solace for a minute.

Then they finally realized she'd forgotten her suit jacket on the couch.

CHAPTER NINE

"CAPTAIN ON THE DECK!"

Henry strode purposefully onto his bridge, nodding to the GroundDiv officer standing next to the door and announcing his presence.

"As you were," he ordered loudly. Ihejirika stood from the main command seat, the big African man saluting as his captain approached.

"Alpha shift is filtering in as we speak," the tactical officer told him. "Shift change isn't for ten minutes."

"And everyone on the ship is expecting us to go somewhere this morning, are they?" Henry asked.

He felt better this morning than he had in weeks. Apparently, he and Sylvia needed to have private chats more often. It helped plan for the work to come and it helped them both feel better about the job they'd taken on themselves.

"Rumor mill is what the rumor mill is, ser," Ihejirika confirmed.

"What's the pool at, Commander?" Henry asked. If the rumor mill was flying, *someone* was taking bets.

"I don't think anyone bothered with a pool," the other man admitted. "Pretty much the whole ship would be betting on La-Tar."

"They would, would they?" the captain said. "Commander Bazzoli. You're not on duty for, what, eight hours?"

The navigator turned in her chair to salute without rising.

"Just being ready for all possibilities, ser," she told him cheerfully. Iida Bazzoli was of mixed Finnish and Italian heritage, a native of the EU's Opiuchi colony. From her Italian side, she ended up with skin nearly as dark as Henry's vague shade of brown, but she had brilliant green eyes and nearly-white pale blonde hair.

"And is one of the possibilities you're preparing for a quick jaunt over to La-Tar to see what the Kozun Hierarchy is up to at the local agriworld?" Henry asked.

"It just might be, ser."

"And what does that course look like, Commander Bazzoli?"

"Two hours, seven minutes of maneuvering here, exactly twelve-hour skip to Ra-Thirty-Five. Twenty-three hours and forty-eight minutes of maneuvering in Thirty-Five, then a fourteen hour and eleven minute skip to La-Tar," she told him instantly.

"Thank you Commander Bazzoli. Commander Ihejirika, the ship is still yours, what is her status?"

"Tano provided us with a full refuel and resupply of missiles, ser," the tactical officer replied. "All repairs were complete six hours ago and we are fully stocked on everything as of an hour ago."

He paused.

"Well, everything except food. I understand that the XO didn't ask and they didn't offer," Ihejirika admitted.

"That was the right call on his part. They could probably feed us without too much difficulty, but why ask them?" Fourteen hundred mouths wasn't much against six hundred million, but it might be enough to change the odds for the most vulnerable.

Henry lowered himself into his command seat, bringing up screens to confirm the key details his people had just given him.

"Give me all hands," he said aloud. He hadn't even realized Lieutenant Commander Moon was on the bridge until she confirmed he was online.

His officers and bridge crew had clearly been expecting *exactly* this.

"All hands, this is Captain Wong speaking," he said clearly. "As I'm sure the rumor mill has made you all aware, Tano is suffering from a food supply crisis. An *artificial* food supply crisis, created by the Kozun Hierarchy invading La-Tar, the agriworld that fed Tano under the Kenmiri.

"Tano and La-Tar had a functioning trade relationship prior to the Kozun intervention that saw Tano provide ships in exchange for food. A full squadron of Tano warships was destroyed in the Kozun invasion of La-Tar, but that is not the problem.

"The problem, people, is that the Kozun now control the food supply for four worlds that La-Tar was feeding and they have stopped the shipments. They will not start the shipments until starvation forces those worlds to bow to the First Voice."

Henry took a moment to clear his throat as he considered his next words.

"This is exactly the type of warlordism the Initiative was created to stop. Therefore, we are proceeding to the La-Tar System. Once there, we will give the Kozun the opportunity to peacefully withdraw.

"If they do not, we will liberate La-Tar and make certain no world starves and no world sells themselves into slavery for food.

"We did not bring down the Kenmiri Empire to install new slave masters. I promise you all that. We are fifty hours from La-Tar. When we arrive, we may well have to fight.

"Be ready. We will not fail."

He cut the channel and turned his focus back to his bridge.

"Commander Bazzoli? Is your course ready?"

"Yes, ser!"

"Then engage."

✦✦✦

EACH SYSTEM the UPA's spaceships had visited in the Kenmiri Empire had a designation based on the same system: the name of the Sector (an ancient Egyptian god, as the Kenmiri designations were unpronounceable and untranslatable concepts from their own ancient myth) and a number, based on how many systems in the sector had been visited by the UPSF before.

Tano was Ra-Forty-Six, visited by a destroyer doing scouting runs shortly before the end of the war. La-Tar *would* technically be Ra-Sixty-One, as no UPSF ship had visited the system before. Where they had local names, though, the UPA preferred to use them with the designation as an organization tool. The Kenmiri tendency to use the same name for both inhabited planets and the star they orbited was something they'd grown used to over time.

Only one of the other three factory worlds La-Tar fed had a UPA designation. Ratch—or Ra-Eleven—had been the scene of an early battle between a UPSF scout fleet and the Kenmiri, while humanity had still been learning about their enemies.

Their first stop, Ra-Thirty-Five, was a red giant with no known inhabitation. Several minor skirmishes had been fought in the system during the war, as larger stars made fantastic relay points for skip jumps, so the Kenmiri had guarded them.

"Skip in five minutes," Bazzoli announced as Henry brought up the data on Ra-Thirty-Five. "All hands stand by for skip."

Henry felt as much as saw or heard Todorovich slip into the observer seat behind him. It was tradition that any passenger watched the first skip on their Force ship. Todorovich had joined him on the bridge for the start of two missions now, and he guessed this excursion warranted the same attention.

"Entrance vector achieved," the navigator continued. "Shutting down main engines and diverting power to icosaspace impulse generators. We will reach entry location one hundred twenty seconds from...now."

The skip drive was more formally the Icosaspace Traversal System. The impulse generators would create a twenty-dimensional kick—in the three spatial dimensions humanity registered and then seventeen they couldn't perceive—and jump the ship slightly out of alignment with regular space.

They could initiate it anywhere, but normally the icosaspatial velocity was lost extremely quickly. A skip anywhere away from a skip line would blip a ship out of reality, but only for a few seconds at most and they wouldn't travel much faster than their existing velocity.

Along a skip line, however, they caught the gravity current between stars and bounced towards their destination. Multiple "kicks" from the impulse generators would be required to keep them going, but the current of the line would pull them along at many times the speed of light.

Larger stars had bigger currents. Skipping between giants was the most effective but skipping from a regular star to or from a giant was still effective. Ra-Thirty-Five, like many other red giants, had been used as a relay point for first Kenmiri, and then Vesheron and Terran, navigation.

"All hands, this is your final skip alert," Bazzoli announced loudly, her voice going through the entire ship. "Entrance in ten seconds. If you aren't strapped in, *get* strapped in."

Henry was already strapped in. The skip drive was neither a safe nor pleasant way to travel faster than light. It was merely the *only* way.

Every time a skip was scheduled, he braced himself. Every time he braced himself, it was not enough.

"Skip...now," Bazzoli said quietly.

The world fell. Sideways. Then forward. Then down. Then up. Each shift threw Henry against the side of his seat and his stomach in the opposite direction.

The impacts weren't heavy. Small objects that hadn't been properly secured would be all over the place, but there shouldn't *be* many such objects aboard a skip ship. People learned. Computers could be taught to handle the rapid gravity shifts.

The human nervous system, even augmented with the hardware of the internal networks, was not so easily trained. Each shift confused the stomach and inner ear, leaving people nauseated and confused.

The compensators that allowed *Raven* to accelerate at dozens of gravities allowed her crew to survive, but they couldn't dampen the rapid random shift of acceleration patterns that lasted for almost half a minute.

Then, thankfully, they stopped.

"All hands, hear this," Bazzoli's voice said over the ship speakers. "Skip insertion is complete. Initial skip complete. Secondary skip will be in two hours, fifty-one minutes. Set your alarms, be prepared."

The secondary skips wouldn't be as bad, but they'd still cause problems if people weren't ready. Worse, gravity was slightly wrong while skipping. *Raven*'s systems kept a solid sense of down, but the continuing eddies of *other* gravity wore on the stomach.

They also wore on the body in subtler ways—and wore on the ship too. There were *reasons* for the twenty-four limit every known species kept on skip jumps.

"That view is still worth it," Todorovich said behind him.

Raven's cameras and sensors were faithfully reporting what they were picking up from the universe outside. Twisted by passage through spatial dimensions the sensors couldn't comprehend any better than humanity could, the colors and lights turned into a kaleidoscopic chaos that couldn't be interpreted into anything useful.

But it was gorgeous, a whirlpool of light and color that threatened to suck a viewer in.

"And I still think you're crazy," Henry replied. The same kinesthetic sense that made him a superb pilot made skipping worse for him than most. His internal network was actively suppressing nausea to let him function.

"I know," she conceded. "How long?"

"Two secondary skips and just over twelve hours," he told her. "Fifty hours all told until La-Tar."

"And then we see how far the First Voice has fallen," she murmured, her gaze focused on the whirlpool in the main displays.

"I've met Mal Dakis," Henry reminded her. "He didn't have very far to fall."

"I need to pick your brain on that," she told him. "It looks like he's going to be more trouble than we originally expected."

"This is about what I expect," Henry admitted. "I'll have a steward prep dinner while we're in Ra-Thirty-Five. Your staff?"

"Felix can join us if you want to include Iyotake," she suggested. Felix Leitz was her chief of staff, a competent if occasionally annoying man sometimes convinced that the entire military just wanted to break things to make themselves feel tough.

"Sounds like a plan," Henry told her. "I'm scheduled to check in on the flight deck while we're in skip. I have simulator hours to put in."

"Sim hours? For what?" Todorovich asked.

He tapped the red-and-gold wings on his checks.

"I'm still a qualified starfighter pilot, Ambassador," he reminded her. "I need simulated and real-space flight hours to keep that up. It's good practice and helps me keep my starfighters' strengths and weaknesses in mind."

He grinned.

"And who knows? It might actually come in handy someday."

"I'm reasonably sure, Captain Wong, that the day you have to strap on a starfighter is a day we're in *serious* trouble," the ambassador replied.

CHAPTER TEN

"I SEE THAT THE GOOD CAPTAIN IS SLUMMING IT DOWN HERE with us," Commander O'Flannagain shouted across the room as Henry stepped into Flight Country. It was a far smaller area on a battlecruiser than on a true carrier, which meant that *Raven*'s flight simulators were in the main pilot ready room.

"Quick, hide the alcohol," someone else replied. "We might lose our wings if we're caught drunk."

Henry paused several steps into the room and surveyed the pilots with a steady eye. If there was any alcohol in the room, it was well-concealed—UPSF regulations limited liquor to the official mess or personal quarters—though there *was* a card game going on with four of the pilots.

O'Flannagain wasn't participating in the card game, the CAG leaning against the wall and keeping an eye on her people while she worked on something on her internal network.

"The card game is clean, I hope," he said with a menacing tone he knew they'd take as a joke. It wasn't *entirely*—there were harsh penalties in the UPSF rules around rigged games or abusing gambling addicts—but he trusted O'Flannagain's eye.

"Connor is *thinking* about cheating," the CAG noted, "but the game is being played for chocolate, so I haven't decided whether to interfere yet."

One of the pilots, Connor Gaunt according to Henry's network, flushed bright red, suggesting that O'Flannagain was reading him far too well.

"I'm here to get simulator hours in before we finish the skip," he told O'Flannagain as he reached the CAG. "I'm running close to the deadline, to be honest."

It had been a busy few months. He wasn't *much* short and he'd got his live flight hours at Base Fallout, but he needed another dozen simulator hours for the year.

"None of the pods are being used; you're welcome to them," the CAG told him. "Hell, I'll fly against you if you want."

Henry shook his head at her.

"I'll be fine," he told her. The suggestion made sense by rocket-jock logic, but as the cruiser's captain, he couldn't allow himself to be shown up as badly as he suspected that would result in. Command was always a careful balance—especially with a hothead like O'Flannagain.

To his surprise, O'Flannagain followed him over to the pod and leaned against the side as he opened the door.

"We have the program loaded for the GMS fighter they're promising us," she told him loudly. "I'll believe in the damn thing when I have eight of them on my flight deck, but the program is in there."

Henry snorted. The Gravitational Maneuvering System had been a holy grail of gravitics research for half a century. In theory, the same system that shielded humanity's warships could be used to create a gravity well they could "fall" into, providing the dream of a reactionless engine.

Unfortunately, managing the tidal forces of that kind of artificial gravity well had proven difficult. A functioning system had been "ten years away" for most of Henry's career. They were supposed to be in production now, but like O'Flannagain, he'd believe it when he saw it.

"It still counts for your sim hours, so you may want to check it out," she told him, now very much inside Henry's personal space in a way she'd never dared before while sober.

He was about to step back and challenge her when she gestured for him to lean toward her.

"Boss, rumor mill spins and rumor mill spins *fast*," she whispered. "I've got a pretty damn good idea how you swing—or don't, from what I can tell—but gossip on the decks is that the ambassador left your quarters late last night all disheveled-like."

He controlled his spike of anger with years of practice. Even if he and the ambassador *were* having a relationship, it wouldn't be his crew's business. His *superiors'* business, yes, given the inherent conflict of interest there.

It *wouldn't* be a violation of regulations, since Todorovich was a civilian. And Henry wasn't exactly leaping into people's beds on a regular basis, regardless. He'd had exactly two long-term lovers in his life: a high school girlfriend and his ex-husband.

"Rumor mill is reading things it shouldn't," he murmured back. "There's nothing going on, Commander."

"Captain, I'll fly for you. I'll die for you. I'll even lie for you," O'Flannagain told him. "But I can't smother rumors; it just doesn't work like that. You either need to watch how things look or accept how the rumors run.

"All I can do is warn you that the decks are speculating, ser."

"I appreciate it, Samira," Henry said softly, intentionally using his subordinate's first name. "I expect the rumor mill to spin as it spins. I don't know if there's much I can do to shut that one down. The ambassador and I have to work closely together."

"Your call, boss." O'Flannagain grinned as she stepped back out of his space. "I could tell you one thing, though, if you wanted. As a woman to a friend."

"Do I dare ask?" Henry replied.

"At least one person in your quarters last night would be happier if the rumors were true!"

V

BY THE TIME the computer opponents had thoroughly wrecked Henry in the simulator four times, he'd worked out that he was distracted by O'Flannagain's final comment. Starting up the program again—the standard one for the SF-122 Dragoon, the starfighters his pilots flew—he spent the seconds of the initial setup confronting his reaction head on.

The problem, fundamentally, was that he wasn't attracted to Todorovich. He liked her well enough, as a friend and a comrade, but he could count on the fingers of one hand the number of people he'd actually been attracted to in his life.

Or the thumbs of both hands, for that matter. He was relatively content being married to the UPSF now that things were over with Peter Barrie.

That thought carried him through the first wave of the scenario, a battle against a collection of the "standard pirate fighters" that FighterDiv used for these exercises. Pirate fighters, in his twenty-year-old experience, had been worse than these and *definitely* more mixed.

The UPSF used their last-generation fighter without grav-shields as their stand-in opponent in these scenarios. Actual pirates were more usually boarding shuttles with a handful of missiles and a laser strapped on.

A wave of virtual wingmen appearing around him announced the beginning of the second phase of the program. A Kenmiri escort appeared ahead of him and Henry gunned the engine.

It didn't really matter, he supposed, if Todorovich was interested in him. Their work relationship meant nothing else could happen even if he was interested, so it wasn't like he would even have to turn her down.

And she knew enough about him at this point to know he wasn't interested in anyone. They'd talked about that once.

A laser blast barely missed his fighter, old reflexes dodging the Dragoon sideways despite his distraction. It was a good thing today that he didn't need to rack up simulator *wins*, just hours.

He dodged his way around the lasers as deftly as he could and triggered his missile launch. As the missiles slashed toward his target, he reflected that it was also a good thing they'd arranged for chaperones at their next dinner meeting.

That hadn't, he assumed, been on either of their minds when the suggestion had come up. It was a good idea to keep *Raven*'s XO and the second-in-command of the diplomatic team up to speed on what was going on, after all.

It also helped keep the rumor mill in check. Not all of his crew would be entirely behind him the way O'Flannagain was. He was the ship's captain. *Someone* on board inevitably hated him.

That thought caught his mind enough that he zigged when he should have zagged, the simulation vanishing in a flash of light. The computer happily informed him that he had destroyed the enemy ship, but not before it had taken him out.

A draw on the second stage. He'd been in the pod for over an hour now, and the timer in his network told him that the secondary skip was fast approaching. The simulator pod was as safe as anywhere, but it wasn't where he wanted to be for getting thrown around like a dog toy.

CHAPTER ELEVEN

"DID I UNDERSTAND AMBASSADOR TODOROVICH'S COMMENTS when she scheduled me for this dinner correctly, Captain Wong?" Felix Leitz asked. "You've *met* the First Voice?"

The diplomatic chief of staff was a heavyset man with short-cropped black hair and a perfectly maintained beard. He'd just finished his soup bowl and was leaning back in his chair, studying the dinner party.

"Mal Dakis," Henry confirmed. "He wasn't the First Voice of the Kozun then. He was 'just' a religious leader and a Vesheron faction leader."

He *watched* Todorovich bite down the automatic correction. The word *Vesheron* meant "rebel faction," so "Vesheron faction" was a redundancy. It was also *clearer* in many contexts, which was why Henry used it.

"We did a lot of operating in the Ra Sector early on as we were learning about our enemy and making contact with the Vesheron," he continued. "We knew the Kozun pretty well, but I met Mal Dakis later on. It would be four years ago now."

He took a sip of water as he considered the story.

"It was my last tour as commander of *Dilophosaurus*," he told them. His second command had been one of the UPSF's most advanced destroyers, a clear sign he'd been earmarked for the battle-cruiser command that followed it. "We spent six months working with several different groups of Vesheron, but the most important was a Kozun religious group.

"The Kenmiri leave conquered homeworlds at least partially intact," he continued. "But organized religion is one of the things they try to dismantle. They don't care what you believe, but you're not worshipping as part of a planet-wide church with the attendant organization and structure.

"Kozun religion recognizes living prophets of the gods. Six gods and six Voices, I believe, but we only got the most fragmented data even then," Henry admitted. "Mal Dakis and his fellows believed that the current Voices, who mostly urged their people to keep their heads down and survive, were false prophets.

"He had not yet, at that point, proclaimed himself a Voice," he noted. "His followers were starting to believe it, though. None of the Vesheron fought overly cleanly, but Mal Dakis's people were among the worst.

"Targeted assassinations are one thing." Henry sighed. "*We* did enough of that, even ignoring Golden Lancelot."

He stared at his plate for a long moment.

"Taking out an entire apartment tower to kill one collaborator and maybe a few Kenmiri Warriors? That's too much by the standards of most Vesheron, even. Mal Dakis would order it, though.

"Make no mistake, neither he nor his people are religious fanatics," he warned. "They use the language and they believe in their faith, but they're not fanatics. They fight sensibly, pragmatically.

"With our help, Kozun ended up being one of the homeworlds the Vesheron did liberate. It was impressive, a big win and a sign that the Kenmiri *could* be beaten."

It had been important. A victorious Vesheron faction completely in control of their system. Of course, part of that had been that the Kenmiri had decided Kozun wasn't worth the effort to retake at that moment.

They hadn't needed new blocs of slaves yet, and that was always the main value of the captured homeworlds for the Kenmiri. If they'd decided to set up a new working cluster in the Ra Sector, Kozun's independence wouldn't have lasted long.

"So, what can we expect from Dakis?" Felix asked.

"He has adopted the patterns and ritual of the role of First Voice in their entirety," Henry said. "But, considering that he sent one of his old assassins to the Gathering as his ambassador, I'm not sure he's changed his ways much."

"What about the other Voices?" Iyotake asked. "Are they the government of Kozun? That would be a theocracy, basically?"

"More complicated than that, but you've read the same briefing I have on that," Henry admitted. "My guess, based on our interactions with them since the liberation of Kozun, and my own assessment of Mal Dakis, is that the other five Voices are completely under his thumb.

"They won't jump without asking him which way. The structure they have is theoretically a theocracy with an elected parliament, but even the Diplomatic Corps thinks it's a one-man dictatorship with good PR."

"The reports suggest Dakis has *very* good PR," Todorovich agreed.

"He liberated their world from the Kenmiri...and he had the previous six Voices publicly tortured to death," Henry told them. "He started with vast amounts of both love and fear, and if nothing else, he is *very* smart."

"And ambitious, clearly," Leitz noted.

"Given the chance, he'll forge himself a new empire," Henry said. "And we're going to stop him. Believe me, people, it's no surprise that the Initiative has collided with Mal Dakis. Not to me. Not to Admiral Hamilton. And not, if anyone was paying attention, to Command or the Security Council."

He shrugged.

"We just hoped it might take a bit longer before the Initiative had to actually *fight* anyone."

✦

THE REST of the meal passed with less-heavy topics. Henry knew the pair of stewards who were assigned to him on a part-time basis looked forward to his dinners with Todorovich and her people as a chance to stretch their culinary legs.

He wasn't one to demand anything complicated for his own meals, especially since he tended to eat while he was working. The two diplomats were perfectly capable of living on the sandwiches and coffee that made up most of Henry's diet, but his stewards took advantage of the excuse.

The jerked chicken was just about perfect, if spicier than Henry's normal fare, and the stir-fried vegetables and rice went well with it. The rice was closer to the Chinese version Henry had grown up with than the Creole version that would have gone with the chicken, but the stewards had mixed the two well.

"So, what happens when we reach La-Tar?" Leitz asked as the plates were cleared away and a bottle of wine was split between the four of them. "I mean, is this a high-speed scouting run? I'm not sure the ambassador and I are needed for that."

"The plan is a high-speed scouting run, yes," Henry confirmed. "It depends on what the Kozun have done. If their dreadnought is at La-Tar with a proper escort, we are getting out of Dodge and calling for a carrier group."

Raven could fight a dreadnought. She even had decent odds against two, or one with a full escort. It was what she was designed to do, after all—but the Kozun had already lost a dreadnought. Their remaining heavy ship was going to be escorted by at least a dozen gunships and escorts.

"I don't expect to see the Kozun's dreadnought here," Henry continued. "We took out their other one at the Gathering—and one of Dakis's favorite assassins commanding her. Intel has confirmed that for us."

Getting information out of their intelligence assets in the former Kenmiri Empire was a nightmare, Henry suspected, but it was at least not *his* nightmare. He knew it was happening and he left it at that.

He hadn't known for sure the ship that had attacked them was Kozun at the time. *Raven* and her crew had defended themselves and the Kozun dreadnought hadn't survived.

"So, you expect to find a force we can potentially fight?" Iyotake asked. "That could be advantageous."

"It would certainly open opportunities," Henry agreed. "If we're looking at a handful of escorts without support, it may well be worth it for us to strike."

"Do you even have authorization for an offensive like that?" Leitz asked sharply. "This was supposed to be a peacekeeping-and-trade mission."

"My orders are to resist and prevent invasion and occupation by any means necessary," Henry replied. "Our job is to keep the peace, yes. Part of that is building trade networks and making sure people are safe.

"Part of that is stopping warlords like Mal Dakis has become."

Todorovich held up a hand before Leitz could say anything.

"I have also signed off on this operation, Felix," she told him. "If we don't stop people conquering worlds in what's functionally our backyard, we can't say we're doing anything to keep the peace and protect people, can we?"

"Do we have a plan?" the chief of staff asked.

"It depends on the situation," Henry admitted. "Most likely, whatever Kozun forces are in the system are in orbit of La-Tar itself. If the forces look too heavy for us to engage without support, we do a scoot around the outer system and fall back to Tano. If nothing else, there are supposed to be two destroyers arriving with the relief convoy.

"The problem, Em Leitz, is that the relief convoy is only enough food for Tano. Three other systems rely on La-Tar for food. Food they won't receive from the Kozun unless they surrender. To protect those systems, as well as the people of La-Tar themselves, we must liberate La-Tar."

Leitz sighed.

"I saw the numbers and data," he admitted. "Six hundred million on Tano. A hundred million on La-Tar itself. Another billion and a half across the other three planets. I agree we have to do something, but we're talking about starting a war, Captain Wong."

"Believe me, Em Leitz, a war is the last thing I want," Henry conceded. "If it appears that we can engage the Kozun force at La-Tar, I will do everything in my power to convince them to withdraw peacefully.

"In a perfect world, we can convince Mal Dakis that he can't conquer worlds while we're watching without having to fire a shot," he told the diplomats.

"And how likely is that, Captain?" Leitz asked drily.

"My most likely scenario sees another several thousand Kozun dead in La-Tar orbit before our visit is over," Henry conceded. "I'm hoping we can coordinate with the local government and resistance to secure the planet in short order once we have the orbitals."

"And if we can't, Captain?" Todorovich asked.

"Then finding an answer may become a political and diplomatic problem," he told them. "And it will be down to the four of us to find an answer."

He raised his glass to them all.

"To a command without instant communication, my friends. To us falls the duty and the glory of deciding for our entire nation."

They raised their glasses in response to his mocking toast.

"It has to be us," Todorovich said after taking a sip. "I don't think anyone in this room is humble enough to think that someone else could do a *better* job."

CHAPTER TWELVE

Exiting the skip was just as unpleasant experience as entering it. In theory, the ship would "fall" back into regular space on its own, but that left the final emergence point to random chance. If the entrance was calculated correctly, the ship would emerge roughly where it was expected to.

Even a slight miscalculation could send the ship careening into the star it was heading toward, so the UPSF and everyone else they'd worked with used the impulse generators to kick the ship back into regular space.

And like every skip along the way, that meant treating the human body to a thousand sensations it didn't quite know how to handle.

"Skip complete," Bazzoli reported, her voice sounding vaguely strained. "We are on target, just over one light-minute from La-Tar."

"Understood," Henry ground out, refusing to let the fact show on his face that his stomach still wasn't sure which of twenty dimensions it lived in. "ETA to La-Tar orbit?"

"Three hours, twenty minutes at standard acceleration," Bazzoli reported. "Your orders?"

"Engage," he told her, his network finally getting a handle on the nausea as he took a deep breath. "Ihejirika, report. What am I looking at?"

The basic geography of the system—F3 star, six planets, two gas giants—was on the screen already. Icons were starting to populate on the tactical displays as Henry watched, the tactical department and their computers going through the sensor take and updating the screen.

"All activity appears concentrated around the second planet, La-Tar itself," Ihejirika told him. "Standard Kenmiri doctrine would have put a fuel station on the inner gas giant, but we're not detecting any artificial signatures out there.

"Most likely, the Kenmiri destroyed it when they withdrew," the tactical officer concluded. "Rebuilding the facility would have required resources that, according to the Tano, they were focusing on getting food to the dependent worlds."

Fuel could be synthesized from water or a captured ice asteroid easily enough. Gas giants just provided a functionally infinite supply of raw materials that no logistics officer was going to turn down.

"So, what are we seeing at La-Tar, then?" Henry asked, zooming in on the planet on the screens on his chair.

"Looks like about half of the orbital infrastructure is just gone," Ihejirika admitted. "Overkill taking down the forts, I would guess, combined with continuing resistance. I make three separate clusters of ships, ser."

Fuzzy orange spheres appeared around the planet.

"Group one, here, is reading as at least twenty contacts. Power levels are low and they're in a stable orbit. It looks like...ships in storage, almost, but the power levels are too *high* for that."

"What about if they're running freighter-scale food-storage systems?" Iyotake suggested. "If the Kozun are planning on delivering food to anyone who surrenders, they want those ships ready to go."

"It looks about right," Ihejirika replied. "If that's the case, we're looking at loaded freighters with minimal or no crew aboard.

"Group two has resolved enough for me to classify them as our main concern, though," he continued, highlighted an orange sphere that now resolved into three crimson icons. "Escort-type vessels. Nothing we'd recognize as an identity code—but given the data from Tano, they're almost certainly Kozun."

"Keep them dialed in," Henry ordered. "Let me know the moment they so much as twitch."

The escorts had *Raven* outnumbered and technically outgunned, but he wasn't overly concerned about their missile launchers and lasers. He could take the brunt of their firepower on his shield and blast them out of the fight at close range.

Four escorts in Tano had left him mildly concerned. Three escorts were barely an annoyance. They weren't entirely harmless—conversion warheads versus the gravity shield was a probability game, after all, and chance played no favorites—but they were outmatched.

And they had to know it.

"What's our third cluster of ships?" he finally asked.

"Looks similar to the first one," Ihejirika told him. "Around twenty ships. Freighters running cold-storage systems. If there's enough between all forty ships to crew one through an actual skip, I'd be surprised."

Henry wasn't surprised to find that there was nothing left of the system's original defenders. Any ships intact enough to be worth salvaging had probably been hauled back to Kozun. The Tano fleet was long gone, one way or another.

A timer in his network softly chimed in his head.

"We should be seeing their reaction to our arrival now," Henry noted. "Are they moving?"

"No response yet," Ihejirika replied. "They might need to wake the CO up."

Presumably, the escorts were at a reasonable state of alert, but they also had several hours before Henry would range on them on his own. For a moment, he considered attempting long-range gravity-driver fire—but at seven percent of light, it would take over fourteen minutes for his projectiles to reach the escorts.

Unless they were ridiculously incompetent, he'd never land a hit.

"All three just went fully active," one of the tactical noncoms reported, the icons lighting up on the display. "Thirty-six seconds after they picked us up. They're not moving yet, though."

"Someone made sure they knew what they were looking at," Henry said with a nod. "And then hit the alert. Maintain our course, Bazzoli. Let's see what they do."

"Do we want to hail them, ser?" Moon asked.

"Not yet," Henry replied. "Let's see how they react before we say hello."

It took almost two minutes before the Kozun ships did more than bring their power cores up to full, and their initial response was a recorded message.

"Incoming transmission," Moon reported.

"Play it," Henry ordered. "Let's see what they have to say for themselves."

A familiar Kozun face appeared on the screen. Henry hadn't seen that particular set of eyebrow plates and crimson eyes for a long time, but he knew the officer on the screen.

"United Planets Space Force vessel, this is Star Lance Kalad of the Kozun Hierarchy," she said in perfect Kem. "While I would normally be delighted to greet old friends, this system is under the protection of the First Voice, and my orders require me to order you to proceed to Kozun.

"By mutual agreement between the Voices of Kozun and the government of La-Tar, we are now responsible for their defense and external policy. This is a sensitive transition time and we prefer to avoid potential confusion or misunderstanding.

"Again, if your mission is diplomatic, I must require you to leave this system and proceed to Kozun with your delegation. If your mission is not diplomatic, you have no grounds to be in Kozun space and I must order you to withdraw."

"Oh, Kalad," Henry muttered. "From liberator to conqueror; what have they done to you?"

"Ser?" Iyotake asked.

"I've *met* Mal Dakis," Henry replied. "Kalad, on the other hand, I've fought alongside and shared drinks with. I'd have said she was damn good people...except right now, she's commanding a squadron in orbit of an occupied world.

"Doesn't leave me with much choice, regardless of my opinion of the Star Lance."

Henry studied the image of his old friend with a feeling akin to grief in his heart. He'd spent over half a year in close company with the woman. They'd been friends, and in hindsight, he could even admit he'd been close to whatever invisible line his brain used to judge someone attractive.

Now she was his enemy.

"Lieutenant Commander Moon, are you ready to transmit?"

"Of course, ser."

It had been a pointless question and they both knew it.

With a mental command, Henry started the recording. He faced the camera directly, straight-backed and cold-faced.

"Star Lance Kalad," he greeted her, the alien syllables flowing a bit more slowly than usual. "My old friend. I wish we met under better terms, but let us not deceive each other.

"The Kozun Hierarchy has conquered the planet La-Tar by force of arms and is holding the food supplies hostage to force the capitulation of the worlds dependent on La-Tar. You stand guard over a strategy that requires the starvation of billions, that will result in the deaths of the most vulnerable on the worlds your master would rule."

He shook his head.

"The Kalad I knew would not have lent her arms to this horror, which means I did not know you as well as I thought I did.

"*My* orders are clear, Star Lance. The United Planets Alliance will not tolerate warlordism and armed conquest. Where our fleets can reach, this kind of invasion will be stopped.

"I *will* proceed to La-Tar orbit and make contact with the local government," he told her. "The only question, I suppose, is whether or not I have to destroy your ships along the way. The choice, Star Lance, is yours."

He cut off the message and sent it with a mental command before he could hesitate.

"Bazzoli, start building evasive maneuvers into our approach," he ordered. "Nothing significant, but enough that we won't get tagged by missiles running cold."

A missile without fuel might not be able to maneuver, but the conversion warhead would be active for another half hour at least. While the warheads were most effective at close range, they could cause real damage at ranges of thousands of kilometers.

And that was one of Kalad's favorite tricks.

"Kozun units have brought up their engines, full acceleration, one point two KPS squared," Ihejirika reported. "Vector...is away from us?"

"On the screen, Ihejirika," Henry snapped. The escorts' course appeared on the displays around him, a thin red line drawn directly away from *Raven*.

"They're headed for the Ra-Fifty skip line," Bazzoli said. "Fastest route back towards Kozun. Still almost ten days' travel."

"We can't catch them," Iyotake said. "They're too far ahead and they have the acceleration edge, even if we go to the tanks."

"We let them go," Henry agreed. "We don't have a choice. Kalad always did have a sense of when to cut her losses."

He studied the display and mentally saluted his old friend. She wasn't running because he'd won some moral argument or because she wasn't supporting her master. She was retreating because three escorts couldn't take down a Terran battlecruiser.

She'd find a heavier force and she'd be back.

"Keep your eyes open for missiles and mines along the way," Henry ordered. "She'll have left something."

"Incoming transmission, ser," Moon reported. "It's the Star Lance."

Kalad's image appeared in front of Henry before he even gave an order.

"Henry," she greeted him, bowing her head to show the close-cropped auburn hair on the back half of her skull. "The gods are cruel, I see. I will not deny your accusations; the truth is carved in stone on the world behind me.

"You may preach morality at me, old friend, but I serve the living prophets of six gods. I cannot fight you with three escorts, so I will withdraw.

"Know that La-Tar remains protected and even her orbits will be denied to you. The will of the First Voice is unbroken. Defy him and you will fail. For the friendship we once shared, I offer this warning: the Hierarchy will not be denied our rightful place.

"I hope that you and yours realize you must negotiate with the Hierarchy as it is, not as you might want it to be. These are our stars."

The transmission ended and Henry closed his eyes. He knew Kalad well enough to understand the layers of her message. She served her world's leaders. What else could she do?

She'd also, however, included a parting gift for him in her words.

"Orders, ser?" Iyotake asked gently.

"Ihejirika, I want scanner probes in orbit of La-Tar ASAP," Henry ordered. "Bazzoli, adjust our course—keep it subtle, at least until the probes are in orbit and Kalad's ships are gone, but we don't want to enter La-Tar orbit.

"Keep a minimum of one light-second's distance from the planet," he continued. "Iyotake, while we're approaching, I want you to dig into our archives. I need every detail we have on Kenmiri surface-to-orbit weapons or anything the Kozun have along those lines."

"Ser?"

"*Even her orbits will be denied to you,*" Henry quoted, translating from Kem to English for his crew. "Kalad is playing a dangerous game, but she's warning us. It doesn't hurt the Kozun for her to tell us that there's defensive installations on the planet, because she knows damn well this ship's ground-bombardment abilities don't have the range to handle them safely.

"She saves my life, for old friendship's sake, and still frustrates our mission."

"And if there are no surface installations?"

"Then she's played a bluff that is only going to buy them a few hours at most," Henry pointed out. "There's no point in her lying to me."

He turned his attention back to the planet at the center of their displays.

"The question, I suppose, is just how heavily *are* they dug in," he murmured. He'd anticipated at least some ground defenses, but Kalad had made it sound like there was no way he was even getting into orbit.

That sounded like a *lot* of guns.

CHAPTER THIRTEEN

"WE HAVE A PROBLEM," IHEJIRIKA SUMMARIZED BLUNTLY AS the senior officers gathered in the conference room. Todorovich and Leitz were together at the opposite end of the table from Henry, studying the screen with concerned expressions.

"I see red icons and I understand that I'm looking at planetary guns, but that's about it," Leitz admitted. "Would someone care to explain?"

"The Kozun knew that La-Tar was going to be their key to holding five systems," Iyotake told the diplomat. "So, their occupation force came loaded for bear. Each of these icons"—the XO pointed at the red triangles on the planet—"is what the Kenmiri called a Guardian platform.

"They're basically tanks the size of a city block. Relatively easily transported if you have the gear and capable of locking down an entire continent against most orbital threats."

"They can't be launching fusion-drive missiles from a surface, though, can they?" the diplomat asked. "And atmosphere would attenuate lasers like crazy, right?"

"Yes and yes," Henry agreed. "The Kenmiri found a solution to the latter problem, though it's incredibly power-intensive. They use a sequence of beams of increasing power to basically burn a channel through the atmosphere for the actual shot.

"It's power-intensive and inherently short-ranged, but it also creates a powerful-enough beam that they have a decent chance of punching through a gravity shield. *Raven* could probably take two or three beams on the shields, but..."

"There are least twenty-four Guardians on the planet," Ihejirika finished for him. "Their positioning isn't perfect for total cover, but it's enough that we couldn't safely enter and stay in orbit."

"And the reason why their positioning isn't perfect is the real problem," Henry concluded. "Look at their locations, Ambassador Todorovich, Em Leitz. You're familiar with our general map icons."

"They're in cities," Todorovich breathed. "All of them."

"La-Tar is only sparsely populated by the standards of home-worlds and Kenmiri factory slave worlds," Henry noted. "A hundred million souls, even with over half the population on farms, leaves multiple cities of a million-plus people.

"The Guardians have been emplaced in parks or central squares or similar structures in those cities. There isn't a single one of them that isn't surrounded by civilian populations.

"Similarly, our scans suggest that the Kozun ground troops have been quartered in the main cities or in facilities built on top of key infrastructure points."

"So, we have to take them out from orbit. I thought that was your precision kinetics were for?" Leitz asked.

Henry swallowed an angry retort, a sharp gesture silencing his people as well.

"Any kinetic-bombardment weapon is inherently a weapon of mass destruction," he reminded the diplomat. "It is almost impossible for us to fabricate weapons of sufficient *precision* to not impact the surrounding region when we drop them on a Guardian platform.

"And even if we managed to build a weapon of sufficiently low power to allow that precision, it would then fail to penetrate the shields and armor of the Guardian. Any weapon we can deploy that can disable a Guardian platform is going to destroy a significant chunk of the surrounding city.

"I am not prepared to accept *millions* of deaths in collateral damage unless there is both a desperate need and absolutely no choice," he continued. "Unfortunately, I can also almost guarantee that the local Kozun commander is well aware of what his living shields are buying him."

"Even the Kenmiri would hesitate to embrace the slaughter of this many potentially useful sentients," Todorovich said in a grim tone. "You will summon the Kozun to surrender?"

"I will," Henry agreed. "But they won't. Both Kalad and whoever is in command on the surface know almost any officer would hesitate to commit this scale of atrocity. They might not realize that we're even *less* likely to than most."

There was a *lot* of blood on humanity's hands. The Kenmiri were on a ticking clock until the last of them died—and their withdrawal to concentrate their remaining resources had left a lot of worlds like Tano to starve.

The victory over the Kenmiri Empire had been humanity's strategy, and it had cost a functionally incalculable number of lives.

Henry wasn't inclined to add to the total if he could avoid it.

"So, what do we do?" Leitz asked.

"We find another solution," Henry told him. "The biggest problem is one of scale. Commander Thompson"—he nodded to the GroundDiv officer—"and his people could take out *a* Guardian platform if we got them in under the line of fire.

"But that would leave twenty-three more and tens of thousands of Kozun troops swarming our single half-battalion of troopers. We can't take La-Tar by force without local help, but the situation on the surface looks extremely under control from the Kozun perspective."

"Not everything is always at it appears," Todorovich noted. "I have contact codes and frequencies for the La-Tar government and for several of their fallback plans. There are continuity-of-government facilities that the Kozun may not have found. Contacting them is a risk, however.

"Mostly for them," she admitted. "We're talking about concealed facilities containing whatever remains of their government. If the Kozun locate those facilities, we could be dooming our only hope here."

"We can use drones to blanket the entire planet with an omnidirectional transmission," Moon suggested. "So long as we have updated encryption protocols that they can decrypt, the transmission will just be garbage data to the Kozun."

"We have to assume that they have their own methods for transmitting safely," Henry agreed. "We can make sure that *our* transmission doesn't reveal them, but they have to be careful on their side. We can't do it for them.

"Once we have localized their receivers, we can use tightbeam communications to make sure we speak securely," Moon noted. "And if we continue to blanket the planet with an omnidirectional transmission that truly only contains garbage data, it will be hard for the Kozun to pick the tightbeams out of the general background noise."

"Is there much point, Ambassador?" Leitz asked. "Surely, if the locals could deal with the situation, they would have."

"*Raven* can't liberate the planet on her own," Henry agreed. "But our presence does open up possibilities if we can coordinate with the locals. So long as the Kozun bases are in cities and on hydroelectric dams, there is little we can do.

"If they deploy into the field, however, *our* options expand dramatically. If nothing else, our presence limits the Kozun's ability to respond to resistance actions."

"But we need to make sure there is a resistance for us to work with," Todorovich noted. "We've all seen this dance before, a dozen times. With the fall of the Kenmiri, I had hoped not to see it again... but we know the steps.

"I will make contact with the locals. Once we have an active channel, I'd like to pull you in, Captain. You are more aware of what we can potentially offer than I am."

"Of course." Henry nodded his agreement. "I will continue to review the data we have. In the meantime, Commander Thompson, Commander O'Flannagain?"

His CAG had been silent throughout the meeting so far but perked up at her name.

"We're no more helpful at taking out those platforms than *Raven* is, ser," she warned. "Less, in some ways."

"I'm not planning on sending you to the planet, Commander," Henry told her. "I want you and Thompson to collect up those food transports. Half of them are in range of the planetary lasers, and we'll need to see if we can at least get aboard them without being seen."

"They're still going to shoot them when the transports start moving," O'Flannagain countered. "And we won't get them far without a real crew."

"I just want them out of laser range," Henry told her. "And the Kozun won't be shooting at them while you're moving them. Once you're ready, we'll take *Raven* in to cover you."

He wouldn't be able to shoot back, but he trusted the Kozun to shoot at the warship over the transports. His ship's shield could take a lot of fire from the platforms, but it would be a risk.

Just not as much of a risk as *not* salvaging the food needed for two billion people.

THE ADVANTAGE of Henry's job, for him, was that he rarely had to send people into danger he didn't share. A captain went with their ship, wherever she went. Occasionally, he had to send GroundDiv or FighterDiv off without him, however, and those moments always grated on him.

Someday, he'd probably get promoted off *Raven*'s bridge. Based off his ex-husband's career arc, he was about a year away from

Commodore and either a carrier or a light battle group. Barrie's rise had been in wartime, but Henry's public profile had been dramatically increased by his involvement in the birth of the Peacekeeper Initiative.

He could send people off to fight without him. He just didn't like it and didn't look forward to when it was going to be most of his job.

Today, though, he sat on his bridge with his hands calmly on his thighs as he watched the shuttles dive toward the cluster of ships in La-Tar orbit. Four of his starfighters went with the shuttles, their gravity shields the only thing that would keep the small craft alive if the surface installations noticed them.

Most of the bridge crew had their own tasks to do, but his two-way screens told him that everyone had at least one eye on the shuttle flight.

"We're ready to start transmitting the ambassador's opening codes," Moon told him. "Should we hold off until the mission is complete?"

"No, I suspect it will make a handy distraction, actually," Henry replied. "Fire it up."

The Guardians were entirely capable of shooting down the drones they'd sent into La-Tar orbit, but so far, the Kozun had chosen to let Henry's eyes remain. The drones weren't easy targets, and the platforms only had one power setting.

He didn't know how much fuel the occupying force had for the big platforms, but it had to be limited. There were refineries on the surface, but he doubted they could stand up to the demands of repeated firing of the Guardians' main guns.

The Kozun would conserve their fire until they had a real target. The freighters would probably qualify when they started moving. *Raven* definitely qualified.

Henry's question was whether the shuttles qualified. Hopefully, transmitting from the drones would raise the robotic spacecraft's profile in the Kozun's eyes—and draw those eyes away from his shuttles.

"Beginning transmission now," Moon reported. "Plan is to continue for one hour or until the first-wave drones are gone."

"Remind me to have O'Flannagain lasso us a small asteroid or two," Henry said. "We'll need to fabricate some replacements."

Raven could, given the raw materials, duplicate almost anything in her stocks. There were a few exceptions, mostly parts for the gravity driver and the skip drives, but her fabrication capabilities were significant and useful.

A nickel-iron asteroid could be easily converted into new probes. Eventually, they'd need more supplies—gold and silicon for the electronics, mostly—but Henry was pretty sure they could build enough drones to keep a constant pattern above La-Tar.

"We definitely have their attention," Ihejirika said after a few seconds of the transmission. "Augmenting the evasive protocols in the drones. They're trying to lock them in with targeting radar."

"I'm happy to trade a few drones for a safe advance for Commander Thompson," Henry said. "Let's give them a few easy targets to draw their attention. Not *too* easy, of course."

The big African man chuckled.

"Understood, ser. We'll see if they take the bait."

HENRY WOULDN'T HAVE WANTED to be in the towns and cities the Kozun had installed their guns in. The lasers themselves were silent, but he knew from close personal experience that *burning a vacuum channel to orbit* was not.

Each time the surface guns fired, the cities around them would be shaking to the mother of all thunder.

The occupiers hadn't been very *successful* at taking Ihejirika's bait, but they were definitely shooting into orbit now. One of the transmitting drones was gone, but the others continued their talkative dance as they tried to reach whatever was left of La-Tar's government.

More importantly, the beams of light flashing into the sky above La-Tar weren't coming anywhere near Henry's subordinates. The shuttles were making contact with the freighters now, off-loading single squads onto their targets before detaching and moving to the next ship.

Thompson had four hundred people to secure twenty ships, and they couldn't be sure the Kozun wouldn't destroy any vessels they left behind.

"Systems are sealed, as expected," Thompson reported.

"Are you supposed to be on one of those ships, Commander?" Henry asked. "Don't you have squad leaders for that?"

"Probably," the GroundDiv officer replied cheerfully. "I'm aboard target six with my command squad. I don't have enough troops to leave anyone behind, ser." He paused. "We've made it to the bridge. There's no one aboard this one, at least."

"Someone was taking care of them," Henry warned.

"I know," Thompson agreed. "My teams were all expecting resistance, but so far, they've been dead. Everything on the bridge here is on standby. Sending you video."

A feed from Thompson's helmet camera opened up on Henry's repeater screens. The freighter bridge was standard enough that it only took him a moment to locate everything he needed to know.

"Can you boot her up?"

"Systems are sealed," Thompson repeated. "We're loading the codes the Tano gave us, but that means we're hoping these are the—"

"We're in," one of the GroundDiv troopers announced.

"From what the Tano told us, they built every ship currently hauling food out of La-Tar," Henry reminded the younger man. "Some might be Kozun, but I suspect these are all the ships that were here when they took over."

"Looks like, ser," Thompson said. "My Marines can't fly these things far, but we can plug in the canned autopilot courses Commander Bazzoli gave us. When do we initiate them?"

"Wait until every ship is secure and then we'll bring *Raven* in to provide cover," Henry said. That was the plan, after all. "We can't afford to lose any of these ships, Commander."

"Status reports show that the hold is full of food, on this one at least," the GroundDiv officer told him. "Grains, dairy, processed food. The works. A few million tons at least."

"Each of those ships should have enough food to cover fifty million people for six months, Commander. Let's hope they're all full."

CHAPTER FOURTEEN

ONCE THE TROOPERS WERE IN PLACE ON EACH OF THE SHIPS IN the danger zone, Henry studied the virtual display for several long seconds, assessing the situation as the last of his crew reported to the acceleration tanks.

The freighters didn't need to move far in the grand scheme of things, barely a hundred thousand kilometers. Their best acceleration was only half a KPS^2, though, which meant that hundred thousand kilometers was going to take them just over ten and a half minutes to traverse.

The transports had no shields, no armor, and limited maneuverability. Straight-line burn was the best they could manage, which meant that if the surface guns decided to destroy them, they were going to be destroyed.

"Is everyone in the tanks?" he asked. The computers said yes, but they had time to validate.

"Yes, ser," Iyotake said. "All hands are reported in."

"All right. Take us in, Em Bazzoli," Henry ordered. "Do you have the course?"

"Yes, ser. We will make a high-speed loop around the planet at fifty thousand kilometers and slingshot back out," she said. "We will be in range of the gun platforms for a minimum of nine minutes, but we'll have just over two minutes of close-range observation of the planet."

"Ihejirika, Iyotake." Henry checked the channel to his tactical and executive officers as Bazzoli brought the engines online. Twenty pseudogravities pressed against his skin, an excruciating sensation even in the acceleration tanks, as his ship headed toward La-Tar at a full KPS^2.

They had a light-second to cross, but they would only be in range for the last hundred and fifty thousand kilometers of that. That final approach, the slingshot, and then their escape...that would give the Kozun nine minutes to try to kill them.

He hoped *Raven* could take it.

"You see the course," Henry told his subordinates.

"Yes, ser," they both replied.

"Does the data from the drones suggest that there is anything on the surface of La-Tar that we can safely engage as we make our pass?" he asked. "The close-range sensor data is worth it, but I'd feel a lot better if we had something to shoot back at."

Ihejirika's virtual avatar shook his head.

"They dug in around targets they knew the Kenmiri or La-Tar's dependent worlds wouldn't attack," he said. "So, major population centers, transport hubs, hydroelectric dams... We can't target any of their guns or major formations without accepting massive collateral damage."

"Twenty-four gun platforms and half a dozen divisions and we can't find a single thing to shoot," Henry said. "I'd be impressed if that wasn't a major impediment to our operations."

"Guardian range in five minutes," Bazzoli reported on the command channel.

"We'll fire up the autopilots the moment you draw fire, ser," Thompson said. "These things are slow and fragile, Captain. Not looking forward to being a flashy target aboard one."

"Best case, nobody even shoots at you, Commander," Henry told him. "Second-best case, O'Flannagain gets lucky." The Dragoons flying escort on the transports had gravity shields, after all. They had a decent chance of surviving a hit from the surface lasers.

A far better one than the transports, which was why O'Flannagain had put her birds *between* the planet and the freighters. They hadn't raised their shields yet—the gravity shear would draw attention the team on the transports didn't need—but they would once the freighters started moving.

Eight Dragoons couldn't form a solid shield, but they cut the odds further in Thompson's favor. That was all Henry could do at this point.

"Shield is live," Ihejirika said, his voice calm as a wave of distortion passed over the sensors. It took a fraction of a second for the computers to adjust to the shield's effect on the scan data.

"Range in one minute," Bazzoli reported.

"We are definitely being targeted with long-range radar," Ihejirika said. "They're having the usual problems dialing us in through the gravity shield, but it won't matter."

Henry tried to nod, only for his head to refuse to move in the tight-packed gel keeping him stable in the acceleration. Starship service wasn't a place for claustrophobes.

At this point, there was almost nothing he could do but project confidence on all of the channels. Unless something unexpected happened, his people were perfectly capable of carrying out the plan —and even if something unexpected happened, *Raven* was committed to her course.

A threat icon flashed on his screen.

"Enemy Guardian platform has fired," Ihejirika reported. "We're still outside their effective range, and they missed regardless. Testing shot."

"Or a warning shot," Henry replied. "Moon, any attempt to communicate from the planet?"

"Negative, ser," she said. "Not a peep since Star Lance Kalad withdrew."

Not even posturing. The Kozun had dug in and shut down local communications. They knew relief was coming and they saw no reason to speak to the UPSF ship that couldn't touch them.

More threat icons flashed across Henry's virtual screens now.

"Multiple shots fired," Ihejirika said unnecessarily. "Two hits on the shield. No contact to the hull."

"Thompson?" Henry asked.

"Activating the autopilots and getting these things moving," the GroundDiv Commander replied. "We'll see you on the other side."

New details flashed up on the icons of the transport cluster, marking vectors and acceleration as the massive ships started moving.

"So long as we get there intact," Henry murmured, making sure his channels were muted.

"Guardians recharging; new platforms are coming into view across the horizon," Ihejirika reported grimly.

"For what we are about to receive, may the Lord make us truly thankful."

More laser threat icons lit up the display in answer to Iyotake's quiet prayer.

THERE WAS something incredibly eerie about charging toward enemy guns, taking their fire, and doing nothing. The good news was that Henry and *Raven* were drawing all of the fire. Only eight of the platforms could currently target the fleeing food transports, and all eight of them were entirely focused on the battlecruiser.

"I have good news and better news," Ihejirika reported as they passed the freighters, diving deeper toward their fifty-thousand-kilometer slingshot.

"That sounds a lot more promising than I expect for getting shot at," Henry said.

"The good news is that we're still here. The *better* news is that two of the platforms that have an angle on us have ceased firing," the tactical officer told him. "Other platforms are still going to get shots in, but the first two to open fire fired six times, then stopped."

Ihejirika paused.

"Others are following the pattern," he concluded. "I'm not sure they're running out of ready fuel or what, but they're definitely ceasing fire after a limited number of shots."

"And they're not targeting the transports," Henry said. "That is good news, Commander. We might just pull this off after all."

"I thought this was a guaranteed plan?" Iyotake asked wryly.

"There are no guarantees until you've already won," Henry replied. "For now, we dance through their orbit like a drunk monkey and we make sure we keep every sensor we can trained on the surface.

"I don't think we're going to find an answer the drones missed, but we may as well take advantage of the close-up."

More of the surface guns were falling silent, leaving it to their siblings coming over the horizon to engage Henry's ship. He couldn't relax just yet, either—the final slingshot half-orbit was almost upon them, and that was when they were going to face the most fire in the shortest period of time at the closest range.

"Angling into orbit now; adjusting thrust to use La-Tar's gravity," Bazzoli said slowly. "Altitude is fifty thousand kilometers and we are commencing our turn."

More lasers were firing now as they circled the planet, opening themselves to the angles of the *other* dozen guns that hadn't seen them yet. Fifty thousand kilometers wasn't quite point-blank range, but it was definitely closer than Henry wanted to be to these guns.

And then *Raven* lurched around them. He barely felt it through the acceleration tanks, but he *knew* his ship now.

"Damage report," he snapped.

"Direct hit to the starboard wing," Lieutenant Colonel Song, his chief engineer, reported. "Armor held, but we lost a lot of surface gear and we may have impact damage throughout. Dispatching drones to investigate."

She paused.

"I don't recommend full thrust until I've been able to review the damage."

"Worst-case scenario, Colonel?" Henry demanded.

"We lose the wing," she snapped. "Four missile launchers, a power plant, and a hundred and fifty crew."

"If we don't maintain full thrust, we could lose the whole ship," Henry said grimly. "We cannot reduce thrust, Colonel. Hold it together."

"It *should* hold," Song told him. "But..."

"I know," he agreed. "We don't have a choice."

Two billion people would starve if Thompson didn't get the food transports clear—and without *Raven* to cover the transports, Henry wasn't sure how far they were going to get.

"Even the drones can't move well under this kind of pseudogravity," she warned. "I can't even confirm there's no structural damage yet."

"Do what you can," Henry ordered. "Hold her together," he repeated.

"Clearing the slingshot," Bazzoli said. "Song, do I have thrust?"

"You have full thrust," the engineer grated out. "Go!"

"First-wave guns are retargeting and firing again," Ihejirika reported. "I guess they found a recharge."

"Or they smell blood in the water," Iyotake said. "Captain?"

"We're clear, Thompson's clear. We *run*," Henry ordered. "Let them shoot our fumes; we need to be somewhere else."

"On it," Bazzoli said.

CHAPTER FIFTEEN

THE DAMAGE WAS LIGHTER THAN SONG HAD FEARED...AND FAR worse than Henry had hoped.

"The structural integrity of the starboard wing is intact," the engineer informed the briefing. "But we lost the feed tubes to the outer four missile launchers. We might have been able to salvage them if we'd slowed, but we might not be here if we slowed," Song concluded. "At this point, it's a quick repair in a shipyard and an almost impossible repair out here."

"Where does that leave us?" Henry asked, glancing around the room. Todorovich and Leitz had once again joined his senior officers, the diplomats doing their best to at least appear to be following the conversation.

"There's a three-round ready magazine attached to each launcher in case of battle damage like this," Ihejirika said. "Unless we get those feed tubes fixed, those three shots are the last full twelve-missile salvos we get."

"Then we hang on to them until we need them," Henry ordered. "What warheads are loaded in them?"

"Standard conversion rounds," the tactical officer said instantly.

"Our shield-penetrator rounds never leave the central magazine without your codes, ser."

The UPSF had made sure they could take out someone *else's* gravity-shield warship when those finally showed up. The shield-penetrator warheads were their answer, a weapon that could completely bypass their own gravity shields.

Conveniently, the same weapons bypassed Kenmiri-style energy shields with equal ease and had allowed more than a few sucker punches over the years. It was always a risk to use them, but the ability to wreck a dreadnought in one hit definitely had its advantages.

"Can we re-equip the missiles with penetrator warheads?" Henry asked. "If we're going to hold onto them anyway, we may as well keep them as our Sunday punch."

"It won't be easy," Song said slowly. "But it is definitely more possible than repairing the feed tubes."

"Do it," Henry ordered. "Where are we at with the food convoys?"

"We have retrieved all forty-three ships," Iyotake told him. "We've settled them into a stable orbit five light-seconds from La-Tar for now. Autopilot will work for that, but they need real crews to fly for any real distance. Or to skip."

"If we strip *Raven* to a skeleton crew, how many can we handle?" Henry asked.

"Three," his XO replied, in a tone that suggested Iyotake had done the math repeatedly. "We could take them back to Tano and pick up crews there, I suppose."

"We cannot rely on La-Tar remaining out of Kozun hands if we leave," Henry said. "Anything we leave behind in this system can be assumed lost to us. Three ships' worth of food won't save four star systems."

"So, where are the crews, then?" Bazzoli asked. "If the Kozun kept them ready to go, surely they had a plan?"

"Some are almost certainly dead, but most have probably been interned somewhere on the planet," Henry guessed. He glanced at Todorovich. "Ambassador, have we made contact with the locals?"

"Not solidly yet," she admitted. "They've responded to our transmission, but setting up a secure communication channel is difficult. All we have so far are coded pulses with minimal information. They're testing us, in a lot of ways."

"We *need* to talk to them," he said. "We don't have any weapons we can use to engage those Guardian platforms without destroying the cities around them. We *need* ground troops. We need a local resistance."

"The difficulty I'm having making contact suggests we might want to start considering alternatives, Captain Wong," Todorovich told him. "If we're having this much trouble linking up for a secure communications channel, they may well not have the resources you're hoping for them to have."

"It's always a chance," Henry conceded. "But we can't take the planet with four hundred GroundDiv troopers and weapons of mass destruction. Not without killing everyone we came here to save."

"Perhaps, ser, we should consider the math," Iyotake said in a faintly sick tone. "There are about forty million people in the cities we'd have to bombard to destroy the Guardian platforms. There are sixty million outside the cities and another two billion on the dependent worlds.

"Can we justify *not* sacrificing those people to save thirty times as many?"

"I will not play games of numbers with lives, Lieutenant Colonel," Henry replied. "We've done that once before. If there is an answer, we will find it."

"And if there is no other answer?"

Iyotake's words hung in the conference room like the Sword of Damocles.

"There is at least one," Henry admitted. "And given the choice between advising the locals to surrender or committing mass murder, we will withdraw. And once we have assembled a real fleet and a real landing force, we will come back and kick the First Voice all the way back to Kozun.

"But we will *not* embrace the murder of millions for expediency. That is not who the UPSF is."

And if it actually *was*, despite Henry's hopes...well, someone else could make that choice this time.

CHAPTER SIXTEEN

"SER, IT'S COMMANDER MOON. ARE YOU AWAKE?"

Henry forced his eyes open and realized he'd fallen asleep leaning forward on his desk. Blinking away fatigue, he made a pointless attempt to sort out his uniform before accepting Moon's call with an avatar.

"What is it, Commander?" he asked. A program in his network started purging fatigue toxins. He'd been *planning* on going to bed, but apparently, he'd been more tired than he thought.

Adrenaline could do that.

"I've been working with the ambassador and we think we have everything in place to establish a link with the locals," Moon told him. "She's requested that you be on the call. We can delay if—"

"No," Henry cut her off. His internal network said he'd been asleep for four hours, which wasn't *great* for having fallen asleep on his desk of all things, but he could function.

"Where is the ambassador?" he asked. "I'll join her in a few minutes and we can see just what we and La-Tar can sort out."

"She's in briefing room six, ser. I'll let her know you're on the way."

Henry cut the channel and looked at himself in the mirror. The slacks and turtleneck undress uniform he'd fallen asleep in was rumpled and probably useless. He'd be better off changing than trying to sort it out.

That would only take him a minute. Thankfully, he knew Todorovich was at least *that* patient.

"CAPTAIN, I apologize for interrupting your rest," Todorovich greeted him as he stepped into the conference room. "I'm afraid I wasn't tracking your schedule and didn't think before asking Moon to get you in."

"This can't wait," Henry told her as he took a seat at the table. "Every hour—every *minute*—we are in the La-Tar System increases the chances that Star Lance Kalad returns with a task force the Kozun believe can take *Raven*.

"And I have every faith that the Kozun can put together a task force that can take *Raven*."

It would probably take a significant chunk of their fleet to do so without getting incredibly lucky, but they could definitely do it. And that was assuming they *hadn't* spent the last year or two working out ways to counter gravity shields.

"Then we should move forward with speed," Todorovich agreed. "I've grown attached to *Raven* and her crew and would prefer she survive, even without my being aboard."

Henry mentally discarded a snarky remark in response to that and simply nodded with a smile.

"Then shall we get started, Ambassador?" he asked.

"Of course. Commander Moon? I believe you have a plan for covering this?" Todorovich asked the empty air.

"Yes, Ambassador," Henry's communications officer replied. A hologram of the woman appeared in the room. He wasn't sure if she'd been listening in before or not. Either way, he was glad he hadn't decided to greet Todorovich more informally.

"We have replaced the drones we were surveying and transmitting at La-Tar with repeatedly as the Kozun have attempted to shoot them down. They now appear to have given up, presuming that we can replace them readily enough that they can't afford the power use to destroy them."

"Can we?" Henry asked.

"We're almost out," Moon admitted. "Colonel Song is fabricating more, but we're down to our last four sensor drones aboard *Raven*. Nonetheless, we currently have twelve drones orbiting La-Tar, and the Kozun appear to be ignoring them.

"To date, we have been using groups of eight to cover the planet in omnidirectional coded transmissions," she continued. "The last two times we did this, the omnidirectional transmissions were pure garbage data, generated to mimic the results of the encryption protocols we sent earlier.

"If they attempt to use the data we've been sending recently to help decrypt the prior messages, it will render their decryption completely worthless," Moon said with a grin. "But the main thing that we have achieved is that they are expecting us to send omnidirectional transmissions across the entire planet at random intervals.

"We are attempting to make it appear as if we have failed to make contact with anyone and are continuing to try to find someone," she noted. "I don't know if we're fooling anybody, but it helps cover our actual communications.

"We will be initiating another eight-drone planetwide garbage transmission. Once that is live, we will be using a ninth drone to establish a direct link with an unmanned relay station in a remote mountain region. We don't know where that station is relaying to and, in all honesty, we have not attempted to find out."

"What we don't know, we can't betray," Henry said with an approving nod. "Are we ready?"

"We are. Wideband transmission begun. You'll have your tight-beam link in thirty seconds. Good luck, sers."

Henry exchanged a long look and a nod with Todorovich and then faced the screen that would show their contact. For a few more seconds, it was blank. Then a wave of distortion passed over it, slowly resolving into one of the more alien faces he'd ever seen.

At first glance, he thought he was staring into a mouth, a gaping maw ringed with long, sharp teeth. After a second, he realized that while that wasn't *wrong*, it also wasn't complete. Two stalks descending from the top of the mouth were turning to face the camera, protective sheaths sliding aside to reveal very human-looking eyes.

That hung from the top of the being's mouth. Henry wasn't sure what the local looked like in person, but he suspected that he wouldn't find them less disconcerting.

"This being is Adamant Will," a clearly computer-generated voice said in Kem. Several different orifices at the back of the mouth seemed to open and close, but whatever sound Adamant Will was making was being replaced by the computer translation.

"I was-am the Third Standard of the Provisional Council of Supply," they continued. "Under emergency protocols and the deaths of First and Second Standard, I am-is the leader of the Emergency Council.

"What is-exists of it."

"I am Ambassador Sylvia Todorovich of the United Planets Alliance," Todorovich introduced herself. "And this is Captain Henry Wong of the battlecruiser *Raven*. We have taken at least temporary control of your star system from the Kozun, but we do not have the resources to deal with the planetary defenses."

"So I presumed," Adamant Will said. "I expected that someone would come. The worlds we feed are-were alone in the dark. We gave them sustenance and they tried to protect us. So many died, ours and theirs."

"The Kozun have demanded their surrender or they will starve them out," Henry told Adamant Will.

The mouth closed, revealing a smooth dark-green skin. A moment later, Adamant Will opened their mouth again and looked at the humans.

"So we feared," they said. "We saw that you retrieved the transports for the worlds we feed. The sustenance was-is loaded aboard them. If you can-will carry those transports, the worlds we feed can-will live and be free for a time."

"That was our plan," Todorovich agreed. "But we do not have the hands to crew forty-three ships. We had hoped to assist your forces in retaking your world and then use the ships' original crews to take the food."

Adamant Will was silent.

"We have-had no forces that can retake our world," they finally said. "Our plans failed. We could-did not move fast enough to retreat to secure bases. Our resistance is-was dead before it began."

That was what Henry had been afraid of. The Kozun had *been* Vesheron. They knew all of the tricks for hiding from a superior occupying power. The First Voice hadn't taken a government into hiding, so they'd missed some of the preparation the La-Tar had done, but they'd made certain there was no real resistance left.

"I am sorry, Adamant Will," Todorovich told the local. "We came here to try and liberate your world, but we need you to be able to fight as well."

Adamant Will closed their mouth again, bowing their head to reveal that smooth expanse of skin again for at least ten seconds.

"The worlds we feed must-can not fall," they finally said, opening their mouth to look at Henry and Todorovich again. "We have no armies, but we do have information. The Kozun guns are-were not perfect. There are-were gaps in their coverage."

"Large enough for a starship to stay in orbit?" Henry asked. That suggested possibilities to him.

"Active you must-will be," Adamant Will told him. "But yes.

Data will-can be provided. The ship crews are-were imprisoned in one camp. Penetrate the gaps in the defenses you must-will. Secure the camp. Free the crews."

"Captain?" Todorovich asked, turning to Henry.

"It may be possible," he said. "We will need to go through Adamant Will's data to be certain, but it may be possible."

The largest problem would be sheer numbers. Forty-plus transports required over two thousand crew. He wasn't sure how many people they could fit onto his shuttles, especially since he'd also need to extract Thompson's troops.

"It must-can and must-will be done," Adamant Will told him fiercely. "But a price for the data and the food must-will be discussed."

"The lives of two billion ride in the balance," Todorovich said. "I do not know what we *can* do for you, though."

"A team can-will be sent to the camp," the local told them. "They must-will meet with your landing. You must-will carry them to the worlds we feed."

"What kind of team?" Henry asked carefully. Adamant Will didn't seem like the type to be causing more trouble for the dependent worlds, but for all his skill in reading Ashall aliens, non-humanoids were still impossible.

"Diplomats they must-will be," the leader of La-Tar's government in exile told them. "They can-will carry the need of La-Tar to the worlds we feed. We must-will stand together or fate-time condemns us to die apart.

"A hundred thousand Kozun are-were occupying my world. If each of the worlds we feed sends forth a mere fifty thousand soldiers, La-Tar can-will be free. We must-will call the debts we have earned. Freely given is-was the food that saved their worlds.

"But if they are-were beings of honor, our call can-will not go unanswered."

"We would be honored to carry your delegation to your allies,"

Todorovich said instantly, before Henry could even consider the merits of the proposal.

Not that he would have rejected it. She was just faster to consider the ramifications and work through them than he was—just as he would be faster to work through a battle situation than she would be.

It cost them almost nothing to lift a delegation from La-Tar and take them to the dependent worlds. If they had the food transports, they'd be visiting each of those worlds in turn anyway. If it made the locals more willing to help them get the transport crews, it was an easy agreement.

And Adamant Will's suggestion for saving their world was probably the only real option they had.

"We will do all in our power to see your world free, Adamant Will," Henry said. "But we must rescue the transport crews and leave. The Kozun will return and their anger will be dangerous."

"We know. But this curse is-was already upon us," the La-Tar replied. "Whether we help you or not, we can-will be punished for your victory. We must-can gain as much from it as we must-can.

"I place the hopes of my world in your hands. The data must-will follow on this channel. I hope we can-will speak again. May fate-time bring us together once more."

"Good luck, Standard," Todorovich told the alien.

A moment later, the channel closed, though Henry's internal network warned him that a data download was coming through.

"Moon, make sure that the data download is stored in a secure offline server until we've had a chance to review it," he ordered aloud, trusting the communications officer to still be listening in. That was her job, after all.

"I am reasonably certain Adamant Will can be trusted, but let's not take any unnecessary risks with strange data files."

"Yes, ser," Moon replied. She paused. "Are we going to do it, ser?"

"If we can, Commander," Henry said. "If we can."

CHAPTER SEVENTEEN

"WE CAN GET IN," THOMPSON SAID CALMLY. "ASSUMING THE data we have is correct, anyway. We can get the shuttles in through the gap in the Guardian firing lines *here* and *here*."

A holographic globe floated in the middle of the room where Henry had once again gathered his senior officers. Pale red hemispheres extended from each of the Guardian platforms now, marking their lines of fire.

The guns didn't have a perfect one-hundred-and-eighty-degree traversal *and* were blocked by buildings and natural features around them. That level of data wasn't something Henry's people had had time to put together yet—but Adamant Will's people had.

There was no way to *get* to La-Tar orbit without taking fire, but there were several blind spots large enough for the battlecruiser once they got there. They could drop shuttles through those blind spots as well, getting them safely to the surface without them coming under firing from the heavy guns.

"*Raven* took a solid hit getting in last time," Iyotake said grimly. "Can we really risk doing a full zero-zero in orbit? The extended flight time could see us torn apart."

"Knowing the firing arcs gives an advantage we didn't have before," Henry replied. "Take a look at this vector here."

A green line appeared on the hologram, connecting the invisible position of *Raven* and the fleet of transports with the planet. It wasn't quite a straight line, coming in at an odd angle and making several distinct changes in acceleration angle along the way.

"Following this vector, we're never in the line of fire for more than three guns at any point," he noted. "We're only in range at all for thirteen minutes, and we spend all of that decelerating towards them. The heat flare from the engines combined with the grav-shield will make accurate targeting almost impossible for them.

"We flicker in and out of the firing lines along the way and spend at least four minutes with only one gun able to range on us before we drop into the gap and are clear from them all."

"Staying in that gap is going to be an exercise too," Bazzoli noted. "They're going to start moving guns pretty quickly once they realize what's going on."

"I know," Henry said. "The Guardians don't move quickly, but they put them in place originally. I figure it will take them an hour at most to move at least one into position to fire on us. That's your time limit, Commander Thompson. Can you do it?"

"Assault a fortified prison camp, neutralize the defenders, liberate the prisoners and organize them onto shuttles, and get them back to *Raven* in an hour?" Thompson asked.

He exhaled a long sigh.

"If it was easy, you wouldn't be calling for Ground Division, ser," he said flatly. "It will take at least two flights to get everyone up once we're in position. Can we even *fit* that many people aboard?"

"This may come as a surprise to some of you who use Kenmiri dreadnoughts for scale, but *Raven* is actually quite large," Iyotake said cheerfully. "Our life support is multiply redundant as well. If we were to try and *keep* an extra several thousand people aboard for an extended period, we'd have a problem, but we can certainly fit them aboard and keep them breathing and fed for a few days while we get everything organized."

"And we won't have them aboard that long," Henry said. "We have lists of the crew of every single ship we've retrieved, and Adamant Will's people have provided us with the Kozun's list of who is in that prison camp.

"Keeping this organized and coordinated is going to be difficult, but the plan is that we lift them up, bring them out here, and then send everyone out to their own ships. They shouldn't be aboard *Raven* for more than eighteen hours.

"We don't even have to find them beds, though our medical team is probably going to be busy. I'll talk to Dr. Axelrod," Henry continued. "We'll want to make sure we have the full files on the Enteni downloaded and reviewed by her staff."

The Enteni were Adamant Will's people, a non-Ashall race that made up about thirty percent of La-Tar's population. The rest of the planet's residents were Ashall, mostly Beren, Tak—and Kozun. There were nine homeworlds in the Ra Sector, and most of the population of the Ra slave worlds would be drawn from those species.

There would be other species present—the Kenmiri were known for hauling people from all over to populate their new colonies—but the people of the five worlds around La-Tar would be drawn from the Enteni and the seven Ashall races of the Ra Sector. The local Kozun population was *probably* more likely to side with their neighbors than with their cousins and wouldn't really add to the complication factor either way.

"Any other concerns?" Henry asked, glancing around the room. "I don't think I need to remind you all that there are two billion lives riding on this. Their freedom, at the very least, depends on us getting the food on those transports *out* of La-Tar, and we can't do that without these crews.

"Let's make it happen."

HENRY WAS ALWAYS the last one out of a meeting like this. Part of that was a security habit, to make sure there were no classified files still on any screens or holoprojectors. Part of it, though, was to make sure that if one of his officers wanted to talk to him, they could.

This time, it was Thompson who was still there after the rest of the senior officers had filtered out to return to their other duties. The GroundDiv officer was still poking at the hologram, shifting the globe aside to bring up the model of the prison camp itself.

"Is there a problem, Alex?" Henry asked gently.

"A few dozen," Thompson conceded. "I'm trying to pick my way around some of them, but this one is probably the biggest."

He highlighted two locations on one of the hills surrounding the camp.

"If Adamant Will's information is correct, there are heavy antiaircraft missile launchers concealed here and here. Worse, they're mobile units, so the Kozun might have moved them.

"My shuttles' onboard weapons can take them down, but they actually have us outranged with the attack geometry." Thompson shook his head. "There's lighter AA gear weapons at the camp itself, but nothing there that can threaten the shuttles.

"Though the rest of the camp defenses are going to be a nightmare. They're designed to stand off lighter armor and weapons than I have, but we're still talking machine guns, barbed wire, and heavy energy weapons."

"And all we have is medium infantry," Henry assessed as he studied the map of the camp Thompson had projected. "Well." He smiled. "Medium infantry and orbital weapons of mass destruction. What's the distance between the camp and those AA positions, Commander?"

Thompson paused thoughtfully.

"About three kilometers, ser," he calculated.

"The angle isn't great, but we should still be able to get sub-kiloton kinetics onto the positions," Henry told his ground commander. "They wouldn't do much against a Guardian platform, but regular mobile anti-shuttle missile launchers? They'll wreck them."

"And the shock zone is less than a kilometer, so the camp prisoners will be fine," Thompson agreed. "That leaves my shuttles' weapons to engage the camp defenses while my people move up on the ground."

"Hopefully, the crews know to keep their heads down once the heavy weapons start shooting," Henry said grimly. "That's not a criticism, Commander. We don't have much choice. Our time limit is harsh."

Thompson nodded and glanced over the globe with its twenty-four red pyramid icons.

"Think they're dumb enough to move a Guardian out of the cities to shoot at you, ser?"

"I can hope," Henry agreed. "But the shock zone on a weapon that can take out a Guardian is closer to ten kilometers than one. They're unlikely to move one far enough out that I can hit it safely."

Ihejirika would be standing by if they did. He wouldn't even wait for Henry's order—if the Kozun made a Guardian platform vulnerable, he'd take it out.

"That's going to be the biggest problem for the landing force if all of this goes to plan," Thompson noted. "Unless someone comes up with a fleet of assault ships in the next few days, we're bringing the troops back in those food transports. They can't take a hit, which means we either need to take out the Guardians or lose ships. Each of them with tens of thousands of soldiers aboard."

"I know," Henry agreed. "I'm hoping to have that conversation with Adamant Will before we leave. They might not be able to launch a full revolt, but if they can disable three guns when we come back…"

"Suddenly, all of this starts looking a lot less like a suicide mission," Thompson agreed. "I'm all the way in, ser. The longer I have to plan, the better, but we'll drop on your order."

"I know you will, Commander. Never doubted you or your people for a second."

CHAPTER EIGHTEEN

As Henry stepped into the acceleration tank for the second time in as many days, he found himself wondering how much progress was actually being made on the long-promised gravitational maneuvering system.

Supposedly, there were fighters in final testing using it. He'd accept better compensators, but the concept of a ship that didn't *need* compensators and could outmaneuver anyone using traditional thrusters definitely had an appeal.

Especially as the viscous gel seeped under and around his ears, a sensation he could never get used to. It was worse, he was sure, for the handful of civilians aboard. Henry knew *exactly* how many times Felix Leitz, for example, had been in an acceleration tank. He'd ordered every one of them himself.

The diplomatic chief of staff would almost certainly stop thinking half those times had been pranks at some point. He might have even done so already; it wasn't like he would tell Henry that.

"All hands are in the tanks," Iyotake reported. "Standing by for turnover."

Their acceleration up to velocity had been at the more sedate half a KPS^2 of *Raven*'s usual cruise thrust. Now that they were beginning the process of decelerating into La-Tar orbit, they'd be burning at full power to minimize the amount of time they were in the firing arcs of the Kozun guns.

They wouldn't be able to use the tanks when leaving, not once they had two thousand-plus civilians aboard. Henry wasn't looking forward to that part.

"Enemy weapons range in thirteen minutes," Bazzoli reported calmly as the ship began to vibrate under the power of her engines. "Orbital entry thirteen minutes after that."

The virtual recreation of the bridge around Henry was far more malleable than the real bridge currently twenty centimeters above his head. He conjured a massive "hologram" of the tactical display in the middle of it, adding in the green line of *Raven*'s course and the red arcs of the Guardian platforms' firing lines.

They'd run the numbers and the scenarios. Everything said they *should* be able to make it to La-Tar orbit without much difficulty. Now if only the enemy cooperated.

"All scans show Guardians in pre-existing positions," Iyotake confirmed as the range continued to drop. "No unexpected maneuvers. They know our weak spots and they're leaning into them as hard as they can."

"And today that's going to work to our advantage," Henry agreed. "Thejirika! Have the drones dialed in the missile-launcher units around the target?"

"They have," the tactical officer confirmed. "Both positions Adamant Will identified have mobile launchers in them. There's also a third launcher that was moved in after we arrived; the drones can even see the tracks.

"All three are dialed in. Munitions will be deployed as soon as we enter orbit."

"Don't miss, Commander," Henry told the junior man. "We need the people in that camp."

"My people don't miss, ser," Ihejirika replied. "Not against targets that aren't even dodging, anyway."

"I have faith, Commander," the captain said. "But consider it a reminder."

He'd taken *Raven* into a contest against another El-Vesheron power's flagship at the Gathering. Their weaker engines had cost them the race—but Ihejirika's gun crews had won the gunnery contest, making it a draw.

He definitely had faith in *Raven*'s gunners—but he'd also never ordered them to fire on planetary targets before. Even the smallest orbital kinetic strike was a weapon of immense potential power.

"Guardian range in three minutes," Bazzoli reported. "Initiating evasive maneuvers around the base course."

Henry swallowed a grunt as the god trying to crush him shifted its angle. The acceleration tanks made twenty gravities survivable. They didn't make it pleasant or ignorable, even when your consciousness was living entirely in virtual reality.

"Three guns have us in their arcs," Ihejirika reported, his voice flatly calm. "They are hitting us with targeting radar. You would think they would learn."

"Shooting at the giant distortion in your scanners isn't all that helpful," Henry said. "Even the garbage they get from the radar pulses can help them try to localize us within the shield. Plus, it helps them get a sense of the angles of the shield and try to line up their lasers to get through the shear zone."

Their odds of success were low, but so were their odds of penetrating the shield in general. The odds were in *Raven*'s favor, but Henry had seen too many UPSF ships rely on their shields only to have a lucky hit doom them.

"Enemy is opening fire."

In theory, they could use the vacuum channels the Guardians' lasers burned through the atmosphere to forecast the path of the beam. In practice, they couldn't detect the precursor beams accurately enough or fast enough for it to matter.

"Two hits on the shield, no blowthrough," Henriksson reported, the engineering officer watching the defensive metrics as *Raven* charged into the teeth of her enemies.

The lasers cycled twice more before they slipped out of the arc of one of the Guardians. Six beams flickered across *Raven*'s shield, and Henry mentally nodded firmly in pride as his ship charged forward.

There was one blowthrough, but the diffuse beam hit in the middle of *Raven*'s engines. Armored nozzles designed to withstand the immense heat of the battlecruiser's fusion rockets ignored the attenuated laser fire like it had never existed.

"Two guns targeting us," Ihejirika said quietly. "Two minutes and we're down to one for three minutes, then we're in range of three for thirty seconds before we're down to two for the final rush."

"We'll make it," Henry assured his crew calmly. "Commander Thompson, what's your people's status?"

"Canned whoopass, ser," the GroundDiv commander replied with a laugh. "Waiting the order to decant and deploy."

The GroundDiv troopers were cargo right now, each fifteen-trooper squad sharing a larger acceleration tank. On Henry's order, they'd decant and load into gear that was already waiting for them in prepared harnesses.

It wouldn't be the first or last time the UPSF's Ground Division had gone into combat with acceleration tank gel in their hair.

"Inform me if there's any problems," Henry told him. "Eight minutes to orbit, Commander."

"Watching every second of it, ser."

"Another blowthrough," Henriksson reported grimly. "This one missed the hull completely."

"They effectively only have one sensor source," Iyotake said. "They can't refine our location from multiple directions. They're struggling to do more than hit the bubble."

"I appreciate their struggle, but I hope they continue to miss," Henry replied. The laser pulses and the acceleration tank were weighing on him more this time than in the previous strike. Old memories were trying to force their way to the surface.

Other landing ops. That was the key, he realized. Pure space battles he could handle, but he was remembering the disastrous operation at Set-Twelve. That was something to flag for his counselors. For now, he ground the memories down.

He'd lost friends at Set, including the original captain of the destroyer he'd been serving on. His first taste of command—but far from his first taste of disaster. The best way to make sure he didn't lose friends *today* was to focus.

And thanks to the work of the UPSF's medical division, Henry Wong knew exactly how to control his memories and emotions.

"WE'RE CLEAR," Ihejirika said, his voice soft as the network carried it to everyone on the bridge. "None of the guns can range on us now."

"Bazzoli?" Henry asked.

"Orbit in twenty seconds," she replied. "We'll be maintaining point two KPS squared throughout. The dead zone isn't big and it is moving."

Metrics hovering on the virtual screens in front of Henry shifted.

"Commander Ihejirika? Are your targets locked?" he asked.

"They are. We are ready to fire."

The prison camp and its covering missile launchers were over the horizon from the closest dead zone. That wasn't going to be enough to save them.

"Commander Thompson?"

"We're ready," the GroundDiv Commander replied.

The metrics shifted again as Bazzoli cut *Raven*'s thrust by over eighty percent. Acceleration tank or not, the reduction from twenty pseudogravities to one was a massive relief.

"Decant and deploy," Henry ordered. "Ihejirika, fire at will."

He waited for the missiles to launch before he activated the exit sequence for his tank, the icons flashing away from his ship as Henry rose out of the thick goo that had protected him from the acceleration.

The same properties that helped keep him safe also meant the gel stuck to itself, most of it flowing back down into the tank as he was lifted out. He was still damp and he still had to shake gel out of his ears, but it could be a lot worse.

Brushing his hair back with one hand, Henry took his seat on the bridge, glancing around as more of his people emerged from their tanks. Most of them came out with the glazed eyes of people focused on their virtual realities, their networks managing a careful transition from the entirely virtual bridge they'd operated in the tanks back to the real-world one.

Being able to see with their actual eyes and control things with their actual hands was more efficient. Theoretically, the opposite should have been true, but human brains were strange and fickle things.

"We have visual on the target zone," Ihejirika reported steadily. "Deployment vehicles in the zone. No counter-fire...impactors deploying."

To an untrained eye, it might have looked like the three missiles they'd fired had just exploded. Even just dropping a multi-ton object from orbit with no additional velocity would have been a more devastating impact than was needed today, however, so the "missiles" were deployment platforms.

Each broke apart into three smaller munitions that activated engines and dove for the surface. Their angles, their thrust...everything about their courses had been carefully calculated for an exact level of force that would do nothing except rattle the windows at the nearby prison camp.

One of those iron "rods from god" would have been enough to take out any of the three missile launchers, but there'd been the risk of losing a deployment platform. Three impactors hammered into each mobile launcher with crushing force.

"Targets destroyed," Ihejirika reported. "The path is clear."

"We are dropping now," Thompson said. "All shuttles away. Make sure there's still a ship for us to come back to, hey?"

"We're planning on it, Commander," Henry told him. "Bring us back some guests."

CHAPTER NINETEEN

HENRY WAS JUST AS GLAD NOT TO BE LANDING WITH GroundDiv. He'd done it often enough to know that he was worse than useless in a surface fight. His job was to command the ship providing orbital support and run the overall operation.

Right now, *Raven*'s job was to keep dancing through the blind spot in the Kozun occupiers' defenses. That was a task he could leave to Bazzoli. Just like he could leave watching the Guardian platforms for unexpected movement to Ihejirika.

He had both of their screens mirrored to his repeater displays, but the main tactical display was an overhead view of the prison camp. Icons marked the positions of the ground troops and fixed defenses identified by the orbital drones, the same information feeding to the incoming shuttles.

Thompson's people didn't have anything heavier than body armor and squad-support weapons. The heavy-weapons emplacements were the biggest threat to Henry's people—but Thompson and his shuttle pilots clearly knew that.

Ground-attack munitions appeared on the display before the

shuttles themselves did, light weapons whose speed paled in comparison to the impactors that had wrecked the exterior positions.

Too slow to take out armor with just their kinetic energy, these missiles carried warheads: fifty kilograms of high-density explosives. Their targets had been chosen carefully. The main gate was left untouched, but every heavy weapons tower on the perimeter was obliterated. An entire hundred-meter-wide section of wall was leveled.

Then the shuttle guns joined the fray, targeting the weapons emplacements closer to the ground—even the lighter ground-attack missiles had been used *very* carefully—in a hail of explosive shells.

The first wave of shuttles slammed to a halt above the camp, doors swinging open and clearing the GroundDiv troopers to rappel down. Door gunners opened fire as the prison guards tried to engage.

Those gunners had some of the few energy weapons in the UPSF Ground Division, heavy plasma pulse guns that ripped through the limited resistance like hot knives through butter.

"First Company is on the ground," Thompson reported over the coms channel. "We are in the camp; resistance appears suppressed. Command detachment moving in with Second Company. Third Company will establish perimeter and watch for incoming."

"Eyes in the sky show you clear, Commander Thompson," Ihejirika told the GroundDiv team. "If they try and move anything significant, we have a few more rods from god waiting for them."

"Good to know. Dropping now."

The shuttle with the command detachment aboard was highlighted gold on the display as it swept over the camp and paused, flaring engines to hover as forty GroundDiv troopers rappelled out the side.

Another three shuttles were around it, dropping their own platoons, while three more settled down outside the camp.

"Send in the support shuttles," Henry ordered. His ten assault shuttles were the armed and armored first wave, the heavy fist of his ground component. Each carried forty GroundDiv troopers and had the ability to hover and fight.

The battlecruiser also had ten support shuttles, multipurpose craft that could carry anything from starfighter fuel to cargo to, as they were equipped today, sixty passengers.

The assault shuttles could also carry fifty people if they weren't carrying their troopers, which meant they *should* be able to lift the two thousand freighter crew in two flights. Assuming they could get the freighter crews sufficiently organized to get them safely and peacefully aboard the shuttles.

That was Thompson's job and Henry didn't envy him it for a moment.

HENRY WAS aware of Todorovich entering the bridge before she reached him, the ambassador's hair pulled back in a severe bun that glistened with the same moisture as everyone else's hair on the bridge.

She made her way across the bridge in silence, making sure she didn't get in anyone's way before taking one of the observer seats.

"How are we doing?" she asked him quietly.

"Better than I hoped up to this point," he admitted. "We didn't take any serious hits getting in, and getting into the camp went smoothly. I'm waiting for the other shoe."

"Is there anything you *don't* have a plan for?" the woman asked, studying the big display. "We have all the shuttles on the ground?"

"Yeah. Thompson is still organizing," Henry confirmed. "He's trying to track down ship captains in the hopes that they can get their crews in line. It's chaos right now, but no one has tried to rush the shuttles yet."

From what he was hearing, Henry was more concerned about the safety of the hundred or so Kozun prisoners Thompson had locked in one of the prison barracks. The now-ex-prisoners were angry at their guards and more focused on that than on any chance of getting off-planet.

Todorovich was silent for a moment, but her next comment suggested she was following a similar thought process as she interpreted the iconography in front of them.

"You'd think the Kozun would have treated the crews they were expecting to have to use better," she said. "Or were they planning on manning the freighters with their own people?"

"I expect they were planning on having a command staff of their own people with the rest of the crew provided by the original hands," Henry murmured. "But the answer to your question, Ambassador, is that by Kozun standards, this *was* treating them gently. Remember that their comparison is the Kenmiri, who never did feel that resources should be wasted on prisoners that weren't working.

"To the Kozun, anything better than forced labor on starvation rations is gentle." He shook his head. He'd pulled enough people out of Kenmiri work camps over the years to remember them vividly. The slave worlds were one thing, bad enough from the perspective of anything resembling freedom, but the work camps were hell.

"That's going to bite them, isn't it?" she asked.

"I hope so. Right now, it's hopefully getting us the crews for our transports. I just hope it does so fast enough." Henry tapped the screen that was mirroring one of the tactical noncoms' stations. "Six of the Guardian platforms are in motion. They're not fast by any means, but every few meters they move reduces the size of the dead zone we're hiding in.

"Thompson only has so much time."

"They haven't been much of a threat so far," Todorovich said. "Why are you worried about the Guardian platforms now?"

"We have *handled* their threat so far," Henry countered. "Right now, we're barely ten thousand kilometers from the surface. That's knife-fighting range for a heavy laser like that. At normal combat range, they have about a one percent chance of blasting through the shield.

"At this range? It's more like twelve percent. And if we're in orbit, they get to *keep* shooting at us."

He shook his head.

"We're more capable of surviving their fire than most of the ships they were built to fight, but the Guardian platforms will kill us if we stay in their arc of fire for long."

The screen froze on one of the massive tank-like vehicles grinding its way along a thoroughfare that had never been designed for it. The only saving grace from the perspective of the people who lived there was that it had crushed the same thoroughfare on its way in.

"So, what do we do?" Todorovich asked.

"We wait," Henry said. "Everything rides on Alex Thompson right now."

He gestured back at the main display.

"The good news is that, unless I'm misreading things, we've finally got people moving aboard the shuttles."

Which meant, of course, that was the moment when new alerts appeared on his screens. A series of red icons popped up above the nearest major Kozun base, carefully situated on a spot where a hydro-electric dam fed a series of canals that provided both irrigation and transportation for a massive array of farms.

The city of half a million people in the flood path if the dam went down was just the cherry on the protective shield.

"Talk to me, Ihejirika," Henry snapped.

"Looks like a dozen ground-attack shuttles, Kenmiri design," the tactical officer reported. "Took them ten minutes to find munitions and troops for them, I'm guessing. Someone was asleep at the wheel."

"Can we take them?" Henry asked.

"They're being careful on their flight plan, but the Kenmiri built that prison camp and it's five hundred klicks from anything. They *have* to move out over unoccupied land to reach the camp."

"Unless they have stand-off munitions with that kind of range," Henry suggested. The UPSF certainly did. "Take the best shot you can, Commander."

He didn't like it, but better a few wrecked farmhouses than four starved planets.

"Understood. Launching."

Eight missiles flashed away from *Raven*, one from each of the launchers that wasn't on the wrong side of a broken feed tube. They dropped into La-Tar's atmosphere like homesick meteors, breaking up much earlier than the munitions aimed at the anti-aircraft tanks.

"Commander Thompson, you have incoming," Henry told his GroundDiv CO. "We're going to try and cut them down to size, but you're almost certainly going to be looking at stand-off missiles."

"Understood," Thompson said crisply. "Five of the assault shuttles are loaded; we'll put them in the air to provide cover."

That wasn't going to be fun for the passengers—Henry knew that from bruising personal experience—but the shuttles' missile-defense systems were designed to have a *chance* against starship missiles. Atmospheric cruise missiles *should* be child's play.

Todorovich was silent behind him, wise enough to know when the situation was outside her skillset. Henry still found himself drawing resolve from her steady presence, like a firm emotional hand on his shoulder that helped him quell the old memories more easily.

"Impactors in the flock," Ihejirika reported. "We got seven of them. Six surface impacts."

These were the same sub-kiloton impactors they'd used to take out the tanks. They had limited blast zones when they hit the surface, but anything inside those blast zones was just as dead as if Henry had ordered a real bombardment.

They probably hadn't taken out more than farmhouse or two, but those were still civilian deaths Henry hadn't been able to avoid.

"Stand-off launch detected at seven hundred kilometers," one of the tactical Chiefs reported. "Estimate twenty hypersonic missiles inbound on the camp. ETA five minutes."

"Commander Ihejirika?"

"Ser?"

"Kill those shuttles," Henry ordered calmly.

"Yes, ser."

A second salvo, smaller this time, of missiles launched. A glance told Henry that they'd now fired almost all of the precision impactors they'd fabricated in preparation for this. They had four of the deployment platforms, twelve sub-kiloton munitions, left.

It was hopefully more than they'd need. The attack shuttles tried to close the distance to use shorter-ranged munitions on the camp, but Ihejirika's second round wiped them out of the air. Only the cruise missiles remained.

As they drew nearer, the rest of the assault shuttles lifted off. Ten armored and armed spacecraft suspended themselves in the air, a frail-seeming shield against missiles traveling at over a dozen times the speed of sound.

The lasers they fired were invisible, but *Raven*'s computers drew them in on the display, white lines that connected the shuttles to the incoming weapons. New icons marked the deployment of decoys while three of the shuttles—presumably ones without passengers aboard—charged forward to draw the fire to themselves.

They succeeded. One of the shuttles took at least three hits and went down, damage icons flickering across the display, but none of the missiles made it through.

"Thompson?" Henry asked, as calmly as he could.

"Shuttle six is damaged and down," the GroundDiv officer reported instantly. "All other shuttles are intact. Six carried no passengers; we have wounded but no fatalities. My command team is already recalculating the trips up."

Not only was that fifty people less in terms of capacity, but it was another forty people that needed to be lifted somewhere else. *Time* was starting to become a problem.

"We're sending the loaded shuttles up," Thompson told him. "That should buy us enough time for those birds to make a third flight."

"It might not be enough, Commander," Henry warned.

"GroundDiv lifts last, ser," the officer said quietly. "Worst-case scenario, I know you'll come back for us."

Henry closed the channel with a smothered curse and turned to Ihejirika.

"Commander, what's the timeline looking like?" he barked.

"If they can fit everybody left on the five shuttles coming aboard now, they'll launch just as the first platform ranges on us," Henry's tactical officer told him. "They have a four-minute flight time *and* they'll spend the last thirty seconds in the Guardian platform's line of fire.

"And that's assuming *we* can take four minutes of sustained fire."

Henry shivered as he ran the mental math. Each platform fired twice a minute. By the end of the four minutes, three platforms would have them under fire. At least a dozen shots. From this range, one would burn through.

Raven still had a good chance of surviving, but even four minutes was pushing how long they could stay.

"Can we save time by dropping deeper into orbit?" he asked.

"Biggest problems are fueling up here and loading the passengers down there," Ihejirika told him. "We can't accelerate the fueling. Bazzoli might be able to buy us a few seconds on the turnaround by dropping another thousand kilometers or so, but not four minutes."

"Let's buy those seconds anyway," Henry replied. "Bazzoli, take us as low as you can."

"This ship is not designed to enter an atmosphere, ser," she pointed out. "I can get us closer, but..."

"Buy me every second you can, Commander," he ordered.

"Understood. Adjusting thrust and dropping towards the surface."

"If nothing else, let's stay as close to the camp as we can," Henry continued. "Seconds are going to count, people."

"Ser, it's Thompson," the GroundDiv officer cut in again. "We have some good news for the ambassador, at least. Our detachment from the La-Tar government arrived. We've got them on one of Third

Company's shuttles; they'll be going up in a moment. Ten people, they're not going to be a problem."

Not compared to losing a shuttle, anyway.

"I'm open to brilliant ideas, Commander Thompson," Henry told the junior man. "Because right now, the only way to get the last lift is by taking the fire of multiple Guardian platforms for several minutes. We can probably do it, but it's going to hurt."

The only upside Henry could see was that even a direct hit was unlikely to take *Raven* out of commission. The problem was that they then had to *escape* the range of the Guardians without being able to use their full acceleration.

That was another thirteen minutes. The Guardian platforms' weapons would get less effective as they ran, but that gauntlet was dangerous enough. A bad hit while they were still in orbit could extend that time and doom them all.

"The last of the shuttles are away," Thompson replied. "We're preparing people to load by section as soon as they return. We might buy you those minutes, ser. We've got their anger focused the right way now."

"Every minute buys us a chance, Commander."

"We'll buy what we can. If we make it out of this, I have someone I need to introduce you to. If we get those four minutes, it's entirely based on how fast she talks!"

CHAPTER TWENTY

"Liftoff. We have liftoff on the final shuttles."

Henry wanted to sigh in relief at the report, but he knew that would be leaping to conclusions. Thompson had got the shuttles turned around faster than anyone had dared hope, but the images across the screens told him any relief was a lie.

"Guardian platform designated Seventeen will be in its new position in forty seconds," Ihejirika said grimly. "We can..."

"It's still in a city, Commander," Henry said. "We take the hits. We reinforce the shield as much as we can."

Part of him wanted to run. They had most of the freighter crews aboard *Raven* now. If he told Thompson to take the shuttles and flee into the mountains to join the La-Tar government, he'd still have crews for thirty-six transports.

But he'd leave behind his entire GroundDiv battalion, four hundred troopers who probably wouldn't make it to safety. Even trying to send them to Adamant Will would risk the entire local resistance.

The only way to avoid the next few minutes was to abandon his people, and Henry didn't have that in him.

"Shuttle ETA?" he asked, his voice calmer than he felt.

"Two minutes, twenty seconds," Bazzoli told him. "As soon as they're aboard, I'm burning for empty space at half a KPS squared."

"Guardian Seventeen is in posi—they have fired!"

Silence held on *Raven*'s bridge for several seconds after Ihejirika's announcement.

"Deflection," Henriksson finally said. "No blowthrough."

Moments ticked away, the battlecruiser's bridge silent as everyone watched the different icons and timers. Guardian Twenty would be in position before the shuttles reached them as well. They'd spend their entire flight out in the line of fire of at least three lasers.

It was going to be a rough flight.

"Deflection," the engineering officer repeated as Seventeen fired again.

"They're adjusting their angles, but they only have so much to play with," Ihejirika reported.

The shuttles were getting closer, Henry urging them on mentally as a third shot hammered into their shields. The grav-shield gave the UPSF's ships a reputation of near-invulnerability, but he was all too aware of their limitations.

"Blowthrough!" Henriksson snapped. "Different angle; we have a light hit on the upper hull. Multiple sectors damaged. Hull is intact, but we just lost a lot of sensors and radiators."

"Guardian Twenty is in position," Ihejirika reported, a bitter edge of helplessness starting to underlie his reports. They were in point-blank range for the Guardian's guns. Nothing else could survive this—but *Raven* was going to get hammered.

Henry checked his reports and concealed a grimace. *A lot* might even be understating the damage. They'd just lost over ten percent of their heat radiators. That was enough that he could no longer bring all four reactors to full power.

It was a good thing he wasn't planning on shooting back! Without sending people out onto the hull to replace the radiators, he'd have to suspend firing the gravity driver to recharge the capacitors for his lasers.

"Guardian Seventeen has fired...*fuck*."

It wasn't a formal report and Ihejirika probably should have known better, but everyone on the bridge was watching. Henry saw the icon of one of the assault shuttles vanish at the same time Ihejirika did.

"Shuttle Four is gone," Ihejirika reported. "I believe Lieutenant Commander Leach was aboard with his first platoon."

The Kozun had realized they could shoot the shuttles even if they couldn't shoot *Raven*—and the shuttles *didn't* have gravity shields.

"Get those shuttles aboard now," Henry snapped. There was nothing they could do to accelerate the process, but he couldn't stop himself giving the order, either.

"First wave is inside the shield and approaching the hangar," Iyotake told him. "We are bringing the rest inside the shield. It's not overly safe, but it's better than letting Guardian platforms take potshots at them."

"Time, XO?" Henry demanded.

"Second set of shuttles is landing now. Twenty seconds," Iyotake replied. "Third set is on appro—"

Raven lurched beneath them. The artificial gravity could absorb a lot, but a solid blow still leaked through.

"Blowthrough, blowthrough," Henriksson reported. "Direct hit on the core hull; breach in sectors D-Twelve and E-Twelve. We are leaking atmosphere and we have multiple crew in the breach zones. DamCon and rescue teams are on their way!"

Coordinating all of that was Lieutenant Colonel Song's job. Henriksson was just the junior officer tasked with communicating it to the captain.

"We've lost the starboard laser, ser," she continued as she received further updates. "Colonel Song thinks it might be repairable, but she isn't sure yet."

"Tell her to focus on getting our people out and getting the breaches sealed," Henry ordered. "I don't need that gun today."

"Iyotake, please tell me those shuttles are aboard," he told his XO.

"Last shuttle landing...now," Iyotake reported.

"Bazzoli! Get us *out* of here!"

There was no perceptible sensation on *Raven*'s bridge as the battlecruiser twisted through a seventy-degree turn and powered up her engines. The relatively slow dance of evasion Bazzoli had been performing to first keep them in the dead zone and then to try to dodge Kozun lasers converted into full thrust in a heartbeat.

The change in vector was enough that the next salvo of lasers missed completely, the massively powerful beams slashing through empty space where *Raven* would have been.

"Just under thirteen minutes until we're out of their range, ser," Bazzoli reported. "Evasion patterns are active; cycling through random sequences every thirty seconds. I can't guarantee anything, though."

"Do what you can, Commander," Henry said. "Just get us out of here."

Raven was like a fish wriggling on the hook, dancing around in random direction but still sticking to the course the enemy could predict. They were evading more beams now that they had more space to play with, but they were still taking hits.

Flashing red icons on his screen warned they'd taken another blowthrough.

"Engine six is down," Henriksson reported grimly. "Heavy hit; the fusion core is auto-ejecting. Commander Bazzoli, we're updating your control protocols; you *should* be okay."

"The day I can't fly at half a KPS squared with only seven engines is the day you can beach me, Lieutenant. I have the update," the navigator replied.

A new icon appeared on the screen, the entirety of a thirty-thousand-ton engine assembly spinning away from Henry's ship. It stayed intact for three seconds...four...five...and then the unstable fusion reaction broke containment.

"Bad news is that the debris field is screwing up my scans of La-Tar," Ihejirika reported. "Good news is it has to be doing the same to them."

Only one of the next salvo of lasers connected with the shield, suggesting the tactical officer was right.

"Well, if I'd known *that* would work, I might have traded an engine for it intentionally," Henry said grimly.

"It bought us thirty seconds, maybe a minute," Bazzoli noted. "I'd rather have an engine for later."

They were halfway through the gauntlet now and Henry still had a ship. She wasn't in great shape, but he still had her.

"Wait." Iyotake's single word hung in the bridge. "Cycle time is thirty seconds, right? Shouldn't they be shooting again?"

Ten more seconds passed. Then thirty.

"They are holding their fire," Ihejirika said. "They did the same last time, watching their reserves. Hell, they might be *out* of reserves now."

"If I had an army right now, that would be useful," Henry replied, then sighed. "Let's not rely on that, people. Stick to the course."

The Kozun probably realized that their likelihood of burning through his shield was dropping with every kilometer he put between *Raven* and the planet. They'd hit his ship and hit her hard, but *Raven* was still there.

Four minutes until they were out of range. *Nobody* was leaving the bridge until then.

CHAPTER TWENTY-ONE

CRAMMING AN EXTRA TWO THOUSAND PEOPLE ABOARD A SHIP meant for fourteen hundred was an exercise in creative crowding. Exhausted and stressed-looking Ashall and Enteni lined the corridors as Henry made his way through his ship to the hangar deck, all of them doing their best to stay out of the way of the crew.

The Enteni didn't look any less strange in person than they did on a video feed. They were tripod-legged creatures with no real head to speak of. Instead, their entire upper torso, with its three evenly spaced arms, swung around with a level of flexibility few humans could match, pointing their massive mouth with its concealed eyes at what they wanted to see.

Henry had dealt with many aliens in his career, but at least two-thirds of them had been varieties of Ashall. *Why*, exactly, half of the galaxy's known sentient races were carved from the same mold was a complete mystery to the UPA.

And every other Ashall race they'd met, for that matter. The Kem word meant *The Seeded Races*, so most of them figured the Kenmiri knew something. The insectoids hadn't told anyone when they were in charge of the region, though, and they seemed unlikely to answer questions now.

When he finally reached Commander Alex Thompson, the GroundDiv officer was surrounded by a collection of people he was giving instructions to. About half the group were Ground Division officers and noncoms, but the other half were aliens, including two Enteni.

"Ah, Captain, thank you for coming," Thompson greeted him. "I need to make some introductions." He waved for two of the people with him to walk with him as he deftly dodged out of the crowd, seamlessly passing the organizational task over to the Lieutenant Commander in charge of his First Company.

Henry knew that the transfer had been accompanied by a silent network conversation and a literal transfer of files, but he saw the confusion in the locals at the smoothness of the handoff.

Several Vesheron allies over the years had told him that Terrans were creepy. Internal networks and similar implants were common enough among the former Kenmiri subjects, but the only people to use them to the same extent as the UPA were the Londu, the *other* major El-Vesheron power who'd fought the Empire from the outside.

If Henry's implants had been made by his greatest enemy, *he'd* probably have mistrusted them too. As it was, he and other UPSF hands were so used to using them, he'd had Vesheron ask if the Terrans had a shared mind.

"You mentioned someone when you were evacuating, that's right," Henry remembered aloud, nodding slightly to the two people Thompson brought over.

One, barely coming up to the tall GroundDiv officer's chest, was an Enteni with pitch-black smooth skin. The resemblance to a mobile eggplant was *not* a thought that Henry needed to share with anyone, especially as he nodded respectfully to the alien.

The other was a Tak woman, a clearly old humanoid with a small forest of gently waving tendrils where a human would have hair. Otherwise, she could easily have passed for an aged Caucasian woman, with much the same wrinkles and liver spots—both extending onto her head tendrils, which matched the rest of her coloring.

"Captain Wong, this is Captain Zast," Thompson told him, switching to Kem as he indicated the Tak. "Captain Zast, this is my commanding officer, Captain Henry Wong.

"Zast is the only reason we got people on the shuttles at all, let alone in time."

"People love to talk," Zast said slowly. "And anger does not help. The Kozun made no friends. But you. You have our ships?"

"We have your ships, yes," Henry confirmed. "They even appeared to be fully loaded. We need you to fly them."

Her lips twitched into a wry smile.

"I flew as a slave for the Kenmiri and a volunteer for the Provisional Council of Supply," she told him. She spoke slowly enough for him to suspect her Kem was rusty, but her use of the language was serviceable. "It was promised I would be compensated in the end, but the concern was to keep people fed.

"I have not changed my mind on that concern," Zast concluded. "I do not think many of the other captains have. We will convince any that hesitate. We owe you."

"And the worlds we feed owe La-Tar," the Enteni interrupted, a computer-generated voice emerging from somewhere around their midsection. "We have freely aided. Debt is-was owed. They must-will save us."

"This is Rising Principle," Thompson said, continuing the introduction. "They are the head of the La-Tar diplomatic delegation."

"I have agreed to carry you to the worlds that depend on La-Tar for food," Henry told Rising Principle. "My own ambassador will work with you to help to conclude the deals you need. You will have all of the assistance that I and my ship can provide, though we should speak in private as to the extent of that assistance."

Most of *Raven*'s damage would be repairable, but he wasn't going to find a new engine assembly out here. Tano could probably fabricate one for him if given the schematics, but their yards had more important uses right now.

"I understand," Rising Principle allowed. "I must-will speak with your ambassador as well."

"I hope you have a plan for getting us back to La-Tar, Rising Principle," Zast told the diplomat. "I can tell you that the only ships in the region capable of carrying an army are ours, so our only hope is to load troops onto our freighters.

"But if we try to fly our ships past the Guardians that Captain Wong engaged, we will be massacred," she said bluntly. "I will take many risks for my home, but I will not accept certain death."

"There is-was a plan," Rising Principle said with a disconcerting spin of their arms. "It could-would not be discussed on radio. Can-will not be trusted, no matter how secure. We must-will..."

The Enteni trailed off, their open mouth rotating to allow them to take in the crowded hangar.

"We must-will speak in private," they finally concluded.

"I know my job in this," Zast told them. "I will work with Commander Thompson. We will get everyone organized and onto their ships; I promise that."

"Thank you, Captain Zast," Henry said. "Envoy Rising Principle? If you will come with me, I will have Ambassador Todorovich meet us in a conference room."

RISING Principle brought one of their assistants, a Tak man named Ilt, with them into the conference room. Since they were the one who wanted to talk in secrecy, Henry figured he'd let them make the call.

Todorovich had brought Leitz, in any case. Henry was the only one in the utilitarian metal room without an assistant. He was a *little* tempted to call one of his officers, but they all had better things to be doing.

"Ambassador Todorovich, this is Rising Principle, the La-Tar envoy, and his aide, Ilt," Henry introduced the La-Tar pair. "Rising Principle, this is Ambassador Sylvia Todorovich of the United Planets Alliance and her chief of staff, Felix Leitz."

"We appreciate the assistance you and Captain Wong's vessel did-have provided, Ambassador," Rising Principle told Todorovich. "While my fellows in the Emergency Council fear Kozun retaliation for your actions here, we recognize that is-was not your fault.

"Without your assistance, there is-was no chance of liberating La-Tar. While we possess more resources than the Kozun likely suspect, we are-were far short of the ability to free our own world. We need ships and soldiers, Captain, Ambassador."

"The only ship I can promise is *Raven*, Envoy," Henry warned. "And what I did not want to speak of among our rescuees is that *Raven* took significant damage extracting you and the freighter crews. While most of it is repairable, we will be operating at reduced efficiency going forward."

He also hadn't heard from Admiral Hamilton yet. Any response to their requests for an escorted convoy would only now be reaching Tano. He was *hoping* to have a destroyer or two for escort when he went back up against the Kozun defenses at La-Tar, but nothing was certain yet.

"I understand, Captain," Rising Principle allowed. "The Guardian platforms are-were a powerful defense, the true iron collar on our world."

"Even if you can convince your dependent worlds to provide armies, which I *hope* should be as straightforward as it seems, we cannot deliver those armies with the Guardian platforms in place," Henry warned. "As Captain Zast warned, it would be a massacre."

"Our calculations suggested this," Ilt said. "We estimate that a minimum of six Guardians must be disabled to permit an initial landing."

"And you have a plan for this?" Todorovich asked. "I hesitate to assist you in negotiating for help if there is no plan to prevent that help dying pointlessly."

Henry studied the two locals. He couldn't read Rising Principle. The Enteni was perched awkwardly on a chair designed for someone with two fewer limbs and a very different symmetry.

Ilt, on the other hand, was Ashall. Tendrils instead of hair or no, Henry had learned to read the microexpressions that were almost universal across the humanoid races. He seemed...confident. That was a good sign.

"We lost a lot of good people when the Kozun landed," Ilt admitted. "The battle was over before we could even attempt to extract a lot of our regular troops. But it was also over before we could even *deploy* many of our elite units. Several strike commando battalions were engaged in an exercise in the polar mountains.

"Unfortunate, in that they might have turned the tide of a critical battle were they in position to oppose the landing," Ilt said. "Fortunate, as they remain available to the Emergency Council. Our emergency plans called for a mass retreat to prepared positions in the mountains, intended to stand off a Kenmiri return."

The Tak diplomat shrugged.

"The Kozun expected something similar and were ready for us," he admitted. "But many of those bunkers and the attached armories remain. The Emergency Council lacks hands but not resources. The officers from those strike battalions have been training the other troops that survived.

"Our remaining soldiers may not be numerous, but they are skilled and well equipped. They cannot retake our world by storm, but we believe we can seize or disable at least eight of the Guardian platforms, clearing the path for a landing by the forces of the worlds we feed."

The *worlds we feed* phrasing, it seemed, wasn't unique to the Enteni.

"All right," Henry conceded. "If you can disable those platforms, that will work. Otherwise, my only option is to clear the way with long-range planetary bombardment of those same platforms. The

Guardians require significant firepower to disable, and firing at sufficient range to avoid their weapons reduces accuracy as well.

"The cities holding the platforms would be annihilated."

Rising Principle's sharp-toothed mouth snapped shut with a loud, unpleasant noise.

"That would-will kill millions," they said.

"And that is why I refuse to do it," Henry told them. "We *need* an alternative option. Your commandos will have to be it."

He shook his head.

"You are going to have to admit to that plan to at least the leaders of the factory worlds," he warned. "That is a risk, since it is certain that at least one of the worlds is already considering conceding to the Kozun. Desperation is a powerful weapon, and the Kozun have wielded it far more capably than I like.

"I understand," Rising Principle said. "Freedom for my world must-will require great sacrifice, but if my world is *not* freed, they must-will all be slaves or die. Surely, fighting for us is-was the better option?"

"I would agree," Henry replied. "But some will have already made up their minds, Rising Principle, and even a decision made in desperation is often difficult to turn aside from."

AS RISING Principle and Ilt left the room, Henry's network mentally chimed to let him know the report he was dreading had arrived. He remained seated, gesturing for Todorovich and Leitz to head out without him, as he opened it virtually in front of him.

Forty Ground Division troopers and four SpaceDiv crew had died when Shuttle Four had been taken out. Another eighteen troopers had been KIA on the ground, their bodies retrieved and brought back for proper burial.

The coffins for Shuttle Four's crew and passengers would be empty. They'd been vaporized with their shuttle.

Most likely, that had been the fate of the eight members of *Raven's* crew currently labeled as MIA as well. Eleven were confirmed dead, but those eight were somewhere in the debris still being cleared. They might get lucky and find one alive.

They probably wouldn't. The damaged zones were still in vacuum. It would be at least an hour yet before Song's teams and drones managed to patch over the hull and restore atmosphere. Their utility uniforms had that much oxygen, but even the slightest tear would have doomed them.

Seventeen more SpaceDiv and fifty-two GroundDiv hands were wounded, a dozen of them critically enough to be under sedation in the infirmary.

The butcher's bill for this stunt was far higher than Henry liked, but his internal network also told him that the utility shuttles were already launching again, carrying crews out to the food transports.

"You did it," Todorovich told him.

He blinked away the virtual display and looked up to realize she hadn't left.

"You got the freighter crews out, enough people to crew forty-plus ships and save four planets," she said in response to his silent question. "It's a start to saving this cluster, anyway."

"I know," he conceded. "And if the La-Tar can clear the guns and you and Principle can convince Tano and the others to provide an army, then all *I* need to worry about is whether the Kozun are going to find a fleet before we get back."

"'All,'" she quoted back at him. "That's quite a bit, Captain Wong. And I'm sure we'll be dragging you into some parts of this mess along the way. It's not going to be an easy vacation cruise around the cluster."

"No." Henry shook his head. "We lost eighty-one people today, Sylvia. I've had worse days, but that hurts."

"My understanding is that it always does for the good officers," she told him. "So people I trust tell me."

"Another day, I'd tell you the same," he agreed. "Today, I just have to wonder what I could have done better." He sighed. "And think about the fact that the Kenmiri had something like five hundred little four-to-six-star clusters like this in the outer provinces they abandoned. How many of them managed to communicate well enough to make sure the factory worlds didn't starve?"

"We don't know," she told him. "We can't know. But I think La-Tar is more representative of those agriworlds than you might fear. They didn't ask for anything, not to start with. They just made sure the food kept moving, knowing that they'd sort out payment and trade treaties later.

"First and foremost, they made sure nobody starved. I think we'll find a lot of cases like that as we reestablish communications across the old Empire."

It had probably helped that they'd *had* communications for the first months after the Empire abandoned its outer systems. The subspace coms had let them find the ships that were in non-Kenmiri hands and bring them to the agriworlds.

He was still grimly certain Operation Golden Lancelot had killed a *lot* of people who'd never been anywhere near its strike forces.

"We do what we can and we save the people who we can reach," he finally said. "But I wouldn't be human, I don't think, if I didn't think about the people I *can't* reach."

CHAPTER TWENTY-TWO

"We now have crews aboard all of the transports," Zast's image told Henry. The Tak woman had returned to her own ship and was settled into the middle of her own bridge like she'd been born there.

"Have you taken any kind of inventory yet?" he asked. He was on *Raven's* bridge himself, watching the displays showing the last of his shuttles returning to the battlecruiser.

"I have managed to pull all of the manifests," she said. "The other captains have elected me to act as our representative to your command structure. They did not want to officially place me in *charge*, but we all know what they have done."

From Henry's limited impression of Zast, most of the other transport captains were going to do what she told them regardless.

"Can you be sure the manifests have been updated?" he asked.

"I can," she confirmed. "I would not be able to tell you what they had replaced containers with if the manifests were not updated, but the automated systems would tell me that containers had been replaced.

"The manifests were mostly recorded prior to the Kozun occupation," she continued. "The fleet was already half-loaded. It appears that they were updating the records properly as well, though we may want to investigate a selection of the storage units to be certain."

"That seems reasonable to me," Henry agreed. "But what do the manifests say you have?"

"A full load," Zast said simply. "Enough food for two billion souls for one hundred fifty days. Mix of processed high-density ration bars, raw crops, frozen meat...averages out to one point three kilograms per person per day."

Henry didn't bother concealing his sigh of relief.

"I had hoped they had been loading the transports all along," he told her. "It made sense, since they needed to feed the factory worlds if they surrendered. But...it was always possible they had not."

"I had not met anyone from the Kozun homeworld before they decided to occupy my home," Zast told him. "My assessment so far is that they are unlikely to assume failure. They planned for success."

"And now we will use that against them," Henry said firmly. "How quickly until the crews are ready to move?"

"My ship is already prepared to go," she said. "Not all the others are. Perhaps three hours. But..."

"Speak, Captain," he ordered. "We are in this together at this point."

"Many of my fellow captains fear that the Kozun will have been moving against the worlds we feed," Zast admitted. "Even if they do not have warships in orbit of the planets, they may well have positioned ships to blockade the logical skip routes.

"Our ships are defenseless, Captain Wong. If we encounter Kozun warships, we will be captured or destroyed—and if we are captured at this point, a swift death is the best any of us can hope for."

Henry nodded, concealing a moment of anger. Too many of the Vesheron had learned how to handle prisoners from the Kenmiri. Though at least the worst the insectoids had tended to do was lock prisoners in isolation to die of thirst and starvation.

Several of the Vesheron factions, including the Kozun, had been far too willing to use torture.

"I understand their concern," Henry allowed. "And what would you suggest, Captain Zast?"

"Most of the worlds we feed should still have twenty to forty days of food left," she noted. "There is enough time for us to visit each of them in sequence instead of splitting the convoy. That would allow your ship to escort us the entire way."

Henry paused thoughtfully. He'd been considering splitting the transports four ways and sending them to the other systems on their own. That would make sure the factory worlds were all fed as quickly as possible, but she was right that they had to have some reserves left.

And he needed to deliver Rising Principle and Todorovich to each world in sequence *anyway*, which brought him back to the original plan.

"As it happens, Captain Zast, my current mission will require me to visit each of them in turn," he told her. "You are aware of the plan to liberate La-Tar."

"You need our ships," she said bluntly. "There is nothing else available that can carry armies. From what I have seen of your ship's small-craft capability, we also have the only heavy-lift shuttles available, too.

"I think, Captain Wong, that every purpose is better served by us traveling under the protection of your warship. My people's fear of the risk is reasonable."

"It is," he conceded. He was running the course on his screens as they spoke. Fifty hours back to Tano. Assume three days in Tano to negotiate matters there and fix up *Raven*. Two skips to Ratch via Ra-Thirty-Nine, but shorter skips so a shorter overall trip. Thirty-six hours. Forty hours from Ratch to Atto and fifty-five from Atto to Skex.

Finally, exactly forty-eight hours from Skex back to La-Tar.

Ten days of just travel, plus the negotiations needed to align armies for the liberation of La-Tar. Three days was the minimum he could see that taking in any system, even in Tano where they'd basically begged Henry and Todorovich to take on the mission.

"We could be looking at over twenty days before we reach Skex," he noted. "That could stretch their food reserves to the breaking point."

"No one eats if the transports are destroyed by Kozun warships," Zast said grimly. "I have friends on Skex, Captain. I have friends on all of the worlds we feed. I do not wish to risk anyone...but I fear we must be cautious or risk losing even more."

"*Raven* will be taking that course regardless," Henry admitted. "If your captains are unwilling to travel alone, then that is the course they will follow us on. All we can do for Skex is hope that they are organized enough to survive until we arrive."

"I know the people of Skex, Captain Wong," she said. "I have faith."

She was better off than Henry in both those regards, then. He didn't know the people he was trying to save...and all he had was worry.

"Inform your captains that we will be getting under way in two hours," he ordered. "Commander Bazzoli will pass along our course to Tano before we leave. Should I anticipate problems?"

"Everyone aboard these ships volunteered for this duty before our world was invaded," Zast told him. "Now they are our people's only hope. They will do all that you ask of them and more. If the food we carry saves the worlds we feed, that is what we volunteered for in the first place.

"If the worlds we feed save our home, then we have served..."

The word she used at the end wasn't Kem, but Henry got the gist of it. *Righteously*, or some close equivalent.

The transports crews had signed on to save lives, to feed people the Kenmiri had abandoned to starve. If they managed to do that *and* liberate their home, well, they were heroes.

CHAPTER TWENTY-THREE

THE EMERGENCE INTO RA-THIRTY-FIVE WAS A WELCOME RELIEF from the pressure of the skip. Henry was on the bridge again, watching for the news his math said had to be waiting for them.

"Ser, we have a skip drone on the screens," Moon reported. "Codes mark it as a response to our Marathon drone. There's an eyes-only code for you from Admiral Hamilton."

"Download the contents and relay the eyes-only to my office," Henry ordered. "I'll take it there."

He rose, glancing around the sparsely-populated bridge.

"You have the con, Lieutenant Commander Moon," he told the communications officer. "Keep me advised if anything comes up."

His office, after all, was less than a dozen steps outside the bridge. He could be back on the command dais in under twenty seconds if he needed to be—and the scans already showed Ra-Thirty-Five completely empty of ships outside their convoy.

Settling down behind his desk, he opened the message from Admiral Hamilton and told it to play with a mental command. A holographic image of the sparsely built and white-haired flag officer appeared above his desk.

"Captain Wong, we received the Marathon Code," she said grimly. "Fortunately, by the time I was recording this message, your follow-up drone had already arrived, which spared me the embarrassment of trying to ride to the rescue with a dramatically tiny fleet."

Somehow, Henry doubted any "ride to the rescue" Hamilton launched would consist of a "tiny fleet." She was senior to Rear Admiral Zhao, the commander of Base Fallout and its defenders, and there was still a battlecruiser in Zion.

Serval might not be authorized to deploy beyond the UPA's borders, but somehow, Henry suspected Zhao and Hamilton wouldn't blink at ignoring that limit if there was a real danger.

"The situation out there sounds like a hell of a mess," Hamilton continued. "I have received Ambassador Todorovich's request for a relief convoy. Hopefully, I'll have an update for you on that in a few days, but I had to bounce it up the chain.

"Base Fallout's food reserves looked a lot more impressive before I compared them to the needs of an entire *planet*." She shook her head. "Food for a quarter-million for a year wouldn't feed a world of two hundred million for a day.

"I'm reasonably sure we're going to get that convoy, but it will take time to assemble. I've requested that an escort for it be provided from one of the other commands, as by the time it gets here, I won't have any actual *ships* in Zion.

"As it is, you lucked out. *Hadrosaur* and *Deinonychus* have returned from their own missions without managing to get into major entanglements."

The destroyers were being sent on scouting missions, investigating old Kenmiri bases and potential threats. Henry had seen their orders—they were supposed to avoid being *seen*, let alone getting "entangled."

"Lieutenant Colonels Spini and Pololáník are following this drone. They're a lot slower, though. They'll reach Tano about eight days after it does and will place themselves under your command.

"Don't let task-group command go to your head, Colonel Wong,"

Hamilton warned. "I'm going to want those destroyers *back*. I'm sure there are more complete briefings already on their way to me that will make me wish I'd done a dozen different things, but that's the reality of our new command-and-control loop.

"I have to trust you and Todorovich to do the job right. Thankfully, I do," she concluded. "Two destroyers are all we can move forward right now, but I'll be watching the drones as you keep us updated.

"No one is particularly surprised to see Mal Dakis causing trouble, not after his right-hand man took a dreadnought at you at the Gathering," Hamilton said. "Which means I need to remind you of one of the unfortunate limitations of our current situation: the Peacekeeper Initiative is not allowed to fight a war.

"Perhaps more accurately, we won't be supported if we start one. There will be no significant reinforcements of the Initiative just because we got in a pissing match with the First Voice. We need to neutralize the Kozun's ambitions around La-Tar without, if at all possible, getting ourselves involved in a longer-term conflict."

The Admiral was silent for a few seconds, then shook her head again.

"It sucks," she said bluntly. "So, deal with it. Whatever it takes, Wong. I'm no more inclined to abandon two billion people than you are, but the limit on how many additional resources we can call on is very clear.

"Good luck."

Henry chuckled in the privacy of his office. Hamilton was always a bit of a breath of fresh air in her willingness to confront the politics of the UPSF head-on.

At least he knew where he stood: on his own. A pair of *Tyrannosaur*-class destroyers was nothing to sneer at, either. They were older ships, but they'd formed the backbone of the UPSF throughout the entire war. The newest of them were only five years old, and all of them had been kept updated.

By the time he made it back to Tano, the destroyers would still be six days away. Knowing they were coming opened up options, though, especially for reassuring Tano that they weren't going to be left to defend themselves alone.

He couldn't afford to leave ships guarding any of the factory worlds right now, but the presence of additional ships should reassure his potential allies.

There was planning to be done.

"Iyotake, please report to my office," he ordered over the ship's network. "Ambassador Todorovich, please join me in my office if you can. We have more information to work with from the skip drones."

WITH HIS EXECUTIVE officer and ambassador in the room, Henry went over the basic summary of the message from Hamilton quickly.

"So, we're getting reinforcements, but nothing heavy," Iyotake summarized. "That could be a problem, ser. We have no idea how significant the Kozun's forces now are."

"It's unlikely that they have more than the one dreadnought," Henry pointed out. "It's really a question of how many escorts and gunships they've stolen or built. They're not going to send the flagship out to secure La-Tar, so I'm reasonably comfortable in our ability to engage a force of lighter vessels with *Raven* and a couple of destroyers."

"I'm more concerned about the timeline on the relief convoy," Todorovich said. "It helps our position here if we can show that we are able to provide some level of assistance even if La-Tar isn't liberated."

"It certainly puts a heavy weight on the concept that they need La-Tar more than us," Henry agreed. "Unfortunately, so far as I can tell, that's simply true. If we'd been out here a few months earlier, maybe we could have positioned ourselves as an alternative supplier —but if we'd been here then, La-Tar would have been actively supplying them.

"The major thing we can provide these people is tech," he reminded her. "The factory worlds desperately need environmental cleanup and safer manufacturing systems. We have the tools for that. Their Kenmiri tech databases don't."

The Kenmiri were perfectly capable of running a clean and safe factory, Henry was sure. The ones they built on the species home-worlds, the planets whose main value was as a source of bodies, had certainly been clean enough.

He doubted that the databases on the factory worlds contained those plans. It would take painstaking effort to turn the factory worlds back into habitable planets, and the temptation to use their massive industrial potential as-is was going to be a problem.

In many ways, the factory worlds were a far greater prize for the Kozun, who would force them to operate as they had before, than they were for the UPA, who would help them rebuild into actual *homes*. On the other hand, that rebuilding process would make at least a few people back in the UPA rich, which was enough for a trade deal.

"We have things we can sell them, it's true," she allowed. "And there's certainly a value for us setting up a stable cluster here. Each system we make secure and safe is a partner not only for trade but in re-stabilizing the Ra Sector."

"Are you sure you can convince the factory worlds to send armies to La-Tar?" Iyotake asked. "I mean, are they even going to *have* armies? These worlds have only been free of the Kenmiri for, what, fourteen months?"

"I suspect we'll be seeing much what Tano has from most of them," Henry said. "The Kenmiri used janissary units for local peacekeeping. They were raised on one world and brought to their current posting, to make sure they had no loyalty to the locals.

"Of course, they also have no loyalty to the Kenmiri. As we saw on Tano, the janissaries immediately threw their support behind the newborn local government. If they *had* officers, they'd probably try and put their officers in charge, but they don't."

"They don't have officers?" Todorovich asked. "That doesn't... make any sense, Henry."

"Their officers were Kenmiri," he explained. "Senior officers were Warriors. Junior officers and senior NCOs were a mix of Warriors gaining experience and Drones." He shrugged. "The Drones wouldn't live long enough to gain enough experience to be senior officers."

Kenmiri Drones grew to adulthood in a single year, versus eight for Kenmiri Artisans or Warriors, but also only lived ten years, versus eighty to a hundred for the other castes.

"All of those officers and NCOs pulled out with the rest of the Kenmiri. I didn't really talk to General Kansa in detail about it, but I imagine they were held together by a mix of long-service troopers everyone respected and the roughly forty percent of their NCOs that were non-Kenmiri.

"It could break down a lot of ways, but I imagine they now have a mix of self-promoted officers and officers provided by the new government. They're desperate to not get massacred by the locals, so they'll sign on with anyone who can protect them."

"That doesn't sound great for stability," Iyotake said. "A group of soldiers willing to fight for whoever can promise them a home?"

"It's worked out so far on Tano. Nothing we've heard so far suggests that the other factory worlds have dissolved into janissary-fueled civil war, either," Henry pointed out. "I don't know if we can find fifty thousand troops on each planet."

"If nothing else, they probably have that many police," Todorovich said. "A hundred million people will have required a lot of police and probably produced a lot of rebels during the Empire. We have to hope that they can provide those troops and leave the task of finding them to the local government."

"If nothing else, they'll have weapons for them," Iyotake said. "I was surprised to see projectile weapons on Tano, even."

"Again, we're back to the janissaries as a component of Kenmiri policy," Henry said. "They intentionally didn't equip the regular slave soldiers with weapons that could penetrate Warrior combat armor. Only select trusted individuals were given energy weapons."

"But they can build them?" Iyotake asked.

"They can and they will. Given time, they'll reequip their entire army," Henry agreed. "We'll probably end up buying energy weapons from Tano or somewhere similar ourselves for a while yet. The Kenmiri guns are just plain better than ours."

"As Captain Wong already noted, though, that ties back into the risks of using their industrial base," Todorovich said sadly. "The only thing, in many ways, that they have to offer any partner is the very thing that will kill their world if they don't restrict its use.

"Tano and the others around La-Tar are lucky because they get to have this problem, but it will take them time to adapt. To update their infrastructure. To move industry into orbit and fuel it with asteroids instead of strip mines."

"I guess if the factory worlds save La-Tar's bacon from Kozun, that will at least help answer the question of what La-Tar gets out of feeding them," Iyotake said. "I'm glad I'm not the one who has to sort out that trading relationship."

Todorovich snorted, bringing a small smile to Henry's face. That she was willing to show that much emotion around him and Iyotake spoke worlds for the ambassador's comfort with his crew.

"I appreciate your vote of confidence, Lieutenant Colonel," she told him. "Because I'm not looking forward to it—and this is what I *do*."

CHAPTER TWENTY-FOUR

"Tano orbital control is requesting our identity codes," Moon reported as *Raven* made her way towards the planet. "They seem both hopeful and rather concerned."

"We left alone and came back with forty-plus friends," Henry replied. "They're hoping we have food and worried we're Kozun. Send the codes we agreed with them and let them know we're escorting a food convoy."

"We have local starfighters heading our way," Ihejirika told him. "I think they've got a pretty good idea of who we are. They only sent four birds and they are not rushing."

"Honor guard," Henry guessed. "Make sure they get our codes too."

Not much appeared to have changed in Tano in the last week. The ships in the yards were a bit further along. The fighters were a bit faster to deploy than they had been. They'd probably sorted out their chain-of-command issues and added a new layer of paranoia to speed things up.

"We need off-loading orbits for ten of the transports and *Raven* herself," Henry continued. "The other ships need holding orbits for now. Once you've got everything sorted out with control, let them know that Ambassador Todorovich and I want to speak to the Council at their earliest convenience."

"Is that their *actual* earliest convenience or 'I have a warship in orbit and want to talk to you' earliest convenience?" Moon asked. "Even in Kem, I can convey a lot with tone."

"Somewhere in between, Commander," Henry said. "We do want to be allies with these people, after all."

Not many people were going to lend a couple of armored divisions to people they *didn't* like.

"Understood, ser. I'll set it up. If they're available, should we set up a holoconference or will the meeting be in person?"

Henry grimaced.

"I'll be phoning in regardless, so check with Todorovich," he told her. "After the last time, I'm not going down to the surface."

He and Todorovich would have to discuss that for the other three factory worlds. Henry had no intention of leaving his ship during this cruise unless he absolutely had to—but he *was* prepared to accept a diplomatic definition of *had to.*

"Understood, ser."

"Fighters are slowing even more," Ihejirika reported. "They are on course to match velocity with us about halfway to Tano, ser."

"Honor guard, like I said. We made friends here," Henry said. "They wanted us to save La-Tar and I don't think they're going to be opposed to helping us do so."

He studied the marred blue-green marble ahead of him and swallowed a sigh.

Unless he was severely mistaken, Tano didn't have the troops to retake La-Tar on their own. They were going to need all four factory worlds on their side to pull this off—and Tano was the only one he'd even been to.

He had no idea how the newborn governments of the other three were going to react to Rising Principle's proposals.

"ALL RIGHT, Song, what do we need from the locals?" Henry asked as he stepped into his chief engineer's office.

Lieutenant Colonel Anna Song looked up from her desk with clear bags under her eyes. Her skin was almost the same darker shade as Henry's, which meant it had to be bad for her to be *that* visibly exhausted.

"A new engine assembly?" she suggested. "Everything else I can fab up, given time and raw materials. We didn't even expend standard missiles, boss."

"What about the laser?" Henry asked.

"If they've got them, I could use a new core optical assembly," she admitted. "We're fabricating replacement parts right now, but it might be faster to just yank the entire assembly and replace it."

"They're probably the Kenmiri version," he told her. "Would that work?"

"It's a set of mirrors and a giant synthetic diamond, boss," Song said with a laugh. "Laws of physics say the component is basically the same for everyone's lasers. I can adjust for any variations without too much difficulty."

"I'll ask," he said. "We're asking for a lot from them over the next few days, but I should be able to get you any parts you need for the repairs."

"So, an engine assembly?" Song asked again.

"I'm not sure I'd trust a Kenmiri-designed engine on my ship, regardless of who built it," Henry admitted. "I'm guessing we can't fabricate ourselves a new one?"

"Give me three months and a mid-sized nickel-iron asteroid cluster nobody cares about, sure," she told him. "Of course, I'm basically building a shipyard at that point, so..."

"Fair," he conceded. "Give me a list of what you need. I'll run it by the locals. They seem to like us so far, so we'll see what we can get. Assume they can't build anything the Kenmiri couldn't, though."

"I'm not asking for engines or gravity projectors, I know," she said. "Most of what I need is just hull plating. Some of the holes in *Raven*'s hull are covered by glorified tarps, still."

That was an exaggeration of the nature of an emergency hull patch...but not as much of one as Henry would like.

"We'll have a couple of days here, but not more than that," he warned. "Can you get us back to fighting shape in that?"

"Forty-eight hours with the engines off and the ship in standby will let me do a lot, but I don't know if I'd call it *fighting shape*, ser," she warned him. "I can't fix the feed tube to the launchers without a proper repair slip, and the engine is best replaced in the same place.

"Take us back to Base Fallout and I can have us in full fighting shape in about three weeks. Two days here? We're going to come up short on any rational standard."

"So I expected," Henry conceded. "What *can* you promise me? We don't have much choice in this."

"If the locals can handle my shopping list, I should have the holes in the armor closed up, the starboard laser online, and the radiators and sensors replaced," she told him. "We'll still be short a tenth of a KPS squared of acceleration, and we'll still be limited to the ready magazines for those four launchers.

"The armor will just be patches, too," she warned. "Reduced thickness, reduced overall integrity. I need more time and more tools to really secure the repairs. Which brings me back to a proper repair slip."

"I can't make any promises on when we'll be back at Fallout," Henry admitted. "Hopefully, I can get the list from General Kansa before we start asking the locals for *big* promises."

"The sooner I have parts, the more work we'll get done before we move on," she said. "The more time I have, the more we can do. I'll focus on getting the gross-level work done first, and then we'll go back and see what we can do to integrate the patches into the hull, for example, once we're there.

"I can give you ninety, maybe ninety-five percent combat readiness."

"It'll do, Colonel," Henry said. "I have faith in your ability to keep my ship running."

"*Your* ship?" the engineer asked. "It's *my* ship that you get to run around with. Stop breaking it!"

"Tell that to the Kozun," he told her. "Somehow, I doubt we're getting through this little affair without getting shot at again."

"At least you're not one of the ones who expects the shield to make you invulnerable," she admitted. "Lost a few too many friends to *those* captains."

"We all did," Henry murmured, faces flashing across his memory before he could stop them. "At least the starfighter pilots who thought that only got *themselves* killed."

"O'Flannagain's done a better job of bringing her ships home intact than you have, ser," Song pointed out. "Not that I'm comparing or anything, but..."

Henry laughed. It was a bitter sound, even to him, but Song managed a grin in response as well.

"So long as we all come home," he told Song, then paused as his internal network chimed.

"The ambassador is asking for my time," he told the engineer. "I'll forward your list to the surface as soon as you send it to me."

She waved a hand in the air and his network chimed again.

"Already sent, Captain. Good luck."

"Thanks," he replied. "Unless I miss my guess, it's time for me to play diplomat."

CHAPTER TWENTY-FIVE

H ENRY ENDED UP MEETING T ODOROVICH IN THE SHUTTLE BAY, where the ambassador was waiting by one of the assault shuttles. GroundDiv troopers were boarding behind her, being directed by Leitz.

"Ready to go?" he asked her.

"Almost," she told him. "Waiting on you."

"I'll conference in," Henry replied, with a look at the shuttle that he realized concealed more nervousness than he hoped even Todorovich picked up. "We've already been attacked once in this system. Everyone is safer if I'm on *Raven*."

Todorovich raised one carefully groomed eyebrow at him, suggesting that she was picking up more than he had wanted to reveal. As usual.

"It's true," he said, perhaps a bit defensively.

"Fair," she allowed. "The delay from orbit shouldn't be too bad." She glanced around the shuttle bay. "The food is being delivered?"

"Captain Zast is taking care of it," he confirmed. "Tano has distribution centers and landing sites already, of course. There's a process and the freighter crews know it. We don't even need to give directions; *Raven* just needs to sit here like an angry sheepdog."

Todorovich gave him a thin smile.

"We're certainly safe enough so long as your ship is here," she said. "Do you need anything, Captain?"

"I have a list of supplies from Song that I'm going to send to General Kansa while you're on your way down," Henry confirmed. "Hopefully, we'll get them to sign off on that before we start asking them for an entire army."

"I'm hoping this will be an easy win," Todorovich said. "They sent us to La-Tar and asked us to free them, after all. I think the Tano will be on board with helping."

"It's the other worlds I'm worried about," he agreed. "I need at least two days here to fix up *Raven* regardless, so you don't *need* to convince them in a single meeting."

She chuckled.

"That's good to know. I hope to not take *months*. These kinds of negotiations are often fraught."

"Even with this food shipment, the factory worlds don't have months," Henry warned her. "And once the Kozun start considering La-Tar under threat, they'll reinforce. Heavily. I can fight a Kozun fleet if I have to, but all it takes is a few lucky hits."

Like the damage *Raven* had already taken.

"And if they reinforce in space, they'll reinforce on the ground," Todorovich agreed. "The timeline is critical. Fortunately, there is nothing like the prospect of hanging to concentrate the mind. They know their risks better than we do."

"I have faith in your abilities, Ambassador Todorovich," Henry told her. "We'll speak again once the conference is underway."

She glanced around.

"I look forward to being back," she said. "*Raven* really is starting to feel like home, you know?"

"I know."

ONE PROMISE from General Kansa to forward the request list to the orbital yard later, Henry took a seat at his desk and checked the status of the Council meeting. Todorovich was still making her way through the Center toward the space, and he leaned back in his chair.

He'd been aboard *Raven* for long enough to begin to decorate the captain's office to his own taste. That was still relatively utilitarian, with the main decoration in the room still being *Raven*'s commissioning seal of a spread-winged bird worked into the wall in gold.

A display shelf beneath the seal now held detailed hand-sculpted models of each ship Henry had flown or commanded, ranging from the old SF-114 Tomcat he'd flown before the war to a model of *Panther*, his command prior to *Raven*.

Three different starfighters, two destroyers and now two battlecruisers. Each of the seven models carried memories and weight for Henry. Each of them had a mental list of names he could never forget, people who'd fought by his side or died under his command.

They were decorations, but they were also memories and reminders. One of his therapists had suggested against continuing that tradition, but he'd pointed out that simply being aboard a UPSF starship was just as much a reminder.

A mental chime told him that Todorovich had reached the meeting room. Refocusing on the task of the moment, Henry linked into the holoprojector waiting for him. It took a moment for the virtual facsimile of the meeting room to take shape around him, but once it did, his office was invisible.

"Councilors, General," Todorovich greeted their hosts in her fluent Kem. "It is a pleasure to meet you again. May I introduce Rising Principle, the envoy from La-Tar?"

"It seems you could not return with better tidings or signs," Councilor Inbar replied. The blond, almost-human-looking Ashall looked pleased with himself. "From the presence of the freighters and the Honorable Rising Principle, I presume that the Kozun have been driven from La-Tar?"

He was to the point, at least. Henry glanced at General Kansa. The Ashall woman's grim expression told him *she* guessed roughly where things actually stood.

"Captain Wong, could you brief the Council on the events of our visit to La-Tar, please?" Todorovich asked, gesturing to Henry.

"Of course," he said with a nod. He turned to look at his audience. It was the same six local officials, the Council and their General, that they'd met with when the Kozun had tried to take the planet by storm.

"The Kozun have heavily invested La-Tar," he told them. "While their mobile forces declined to engage us, they presumably retreated to gather reinforcements. We were left in possession of the star system, but the planetary surface has been fortified against orbital approach.

"A large number of mobile anti-orbital platforms have been installed in La-Tar's cities and critical infrastructure sites. A similar logic has been used to locate their garrisons. Any attempt to neutralize the ground-based defenses or their ground forces would result in massive civilian casualties.

"My *hope* was to coordinate with local forces to achieve an opening, but..." Henry shrugged and gestured to the Enteni envoy awkwardly seated next to Todorovich. "As Rising Principle can brief you, the remnants of the La-Tar government do not have sufficient resources or soldiers to wage a war of liberation across their own world."

The conference fell silent for several seconds.

"But you have food transports, yes?" Inbar finally asked.

"We have enough to provide each of the factory worlds supported by La-Tar approximately six months of food," Henry confirmed. "This was the supply that the Kozun planned to feed you when you surrendered. We stole it."

His bluntness earned him some chuckles from around the table.

"Thanks to the assistance of the La-Tar government, we were able to extract the crews of the freighters from the prison camp they were being kept in," he told them. "The ships were loaded by the Kozun, and we will be delivering them to each of the factory worlds."

"Is...is this enough time for your government to be able to arrange a future food supply?" one of the other Councilors asked.

"It probably is," Todorovich agreed. "Emergency food convoys are already being organized, which should be here in short order to extend your supplies as well. We can negotiate future agreements as needed beyond that, but while that may save your people, it will not save La-Tar."

"May-can I speak?" Rising Principle asked, the awkward translation of their words emerging from a speaker on their torso. "I has-have a proposal. A chance for all of us to win-succeed."

"Speak, Envoy," Inbar instructed. "The words of an envoy of La-Tar are always welcome here."

"We saw-see an answer," the black-skinned Enteni said. "We can-will not liberate our world alone. We lack the strength. But we have-has small elite forces that evaded the Kozun landing. They must-will be able to disable or destroy the Guardian platforms. They can-will clear the way to land an army."

"Our estimate is that the Kozun ground forces number approximately one hundred and twenty thousand," Henry told the Council. "While the UPSF is prepared to cover the transports from any Kozun starships and to provide orbital fire support away from civilian popular centers, we are not able to provide any significant number of ground troops."

"We do not have the soldiers to take on a hundred and twenty thousand energy-weapon-armed Kozun soldiers in fortified positions," General Kansa said flatly. "I would fight for La-Tar, do not misunderstand me, but we do not have the transports to get to La-Tar and we do not have the numbers to win this battle."

"The food transports can-will be converted to carry soldiers,"

Rising Principle told her. "It is-was not a perfect process, but each transport can-will carry at least five thousand."

"Forty-three transports would permit us to transport over two hundred thousand soldiers to La-Tar, with full heavy equipment and armaments," Henry noted. "Only portions of the transports' cargo space can be converted to carry personnel, which leaves you with the ability to bring just about anything you want in terms of hardware.

"Tanks, planes, energy weapons...all of this can and should be brought."

"We can-do not ask Tano to aid us alone," Rising Principle said. "Ten transports must-will remain here, but thirty-three still carry food for the other worlds we feed. We must-will proceed to each world we feed and make the same request."

"The United Planets Alliance is fully on board for this plan," Todorovich said into the silence that follows. "We will put the limited resources we have available behind it."

"And more resources are on the way as we speak," Henry said. "Two UPSF destroyers will arrive in the Tano system in six days. To keep our promises to Rising Principle and his government, *Raven* will have left by then with the convoy. Their captains will make certain of your system's security before proceeding to join us, most likely at the Skex System."

"Councilors. I have thirty-five thousand soldiers who served the Kenmiri," Kansa said slowly. "Despite their best efforts, you still do not trust them. Many, if not all, would gladly volunteer for a mission to prove their value and good faith to Tano.

"While they are our most experienced soldiers, I believe I can muster another twenty-five thousand from our other units that would be worth sending. Only a third of the force would be equipped with energy weapons and we are short on heavy combat hardware, but we could send sixty thousand soldiers to assist in liberating La-Tar."

"And how many cities would be defenseless to the Kozun-funded rogues in our hills?" Inbar asked. "If we strip our world of soldiers, we leave ourselves vulnerable."

"I believe we can field that sixty thousand without exposing our cities, Councilor Inbar," Kansa told him. "Certainly, we can deploy ten brigades without doing so. Seven of the former slave soldiers, three of our own recruits."

"La-Tar must-will take whatever aid can-will be given," Rising Principle allowed. "I am dependent on Captain Wong and Ambassador Todorovich for transport, and I understand we must-will remain in this system for several days."

"*Raven* was badly damaged in the fight for La-Tar," Henry explained. "I have spoken with General Kansa about what parts and materials we could use to accelerate our repairs, but we will require at least two days."

"You have more than earned any assistance we can provide your ship," Inbar said instantly. He glanced around the Council. "The Council must speak in private about La-Tar's proposal. We acknowledge we owe a debt, but we *must* assess whether we can risk our own people to pay it."

"If La-Tar is not freed, La-Tar cannot feed you," Rising Principle said simply. "The decision must-will be yours."

"Come," Todorovich told the Enteni. "The envoy and I will remain in the Center for now," she told the Council. "We await your convenience, at least until *Raven* is able to proceed with the convoy."

"We will not delay you long, I do not believe," Inbar said. "But we must discuss amongst ourselves, Ambassador. You understand."

CHAPTER TWENTY-SIX

HENRY WAS HALF-EXPECTING THE COUNCIL TO MAKE THEIR decisions, one way or another, inside of about five minutes. All he did for the first ten minutes after closing the holoconference was get a fresh cup of coffee.

After ten minutes, he checked in with Iyotake.

"Anything to report, XO?" he asked.

"Not much," the Lakotan man told him. "Just got an update from the locals that they're putting together Song's list of supplies and should have the first wave over to us in a few hours. They asked for pretty specific measurements for the laser optic, so I think we might even have choices."

"Makes sense, I suppose," Henry said. "If they were building lasers here, they'd have been building them for everything from Guardian platforms to dreadnoughts."

"From what I've seen, the entire planet seems to have been set up to supply the shipyards," Iyotake said. "They can build big freighters and have the weapons tech for escorts. Give them a few years to get a handle on their climate and move their heavy industry somewhere sensible, and Tano is going to be a big deal."

"Ten-megaton hulls for freighters aren't dreadnought hulls," the captain pointed out. "They can build big ships, but without plasma guns and heavy armor, they can't build dreadnoughts."

"Do *you* want to fight a dreadnought-sized ship with a hundred escort-grade lasers whose 'heavy armor' is 'just' five layers of the lighter armor they use for escorts, ser?" his XO replied. "Because I can see some nasty ways they can combine what they've got, and I'm willing to assume they have *much* smarter people than me."

"Then it's a good thing we're planning on them being allies, isn't it?" Henry looked at the image of the planet on his wallscreen. "Haven't met anyone yet who didn't deserve better than living on a Kenmiri slave world. I worry for the fate of places like this, but the ones that make it are going to come out a lot better."

"It wasn't us who cut them off to starve, ser," Iyotake reminded him. "We do what we can."

"That we do," Henry confirmed. "I'm waiting on the Tano Council to make a decision. Hopefully, we'll have at least part of the army we need shortly."

"So long as we get the two days you promised Song for repairs, we'll be fine to head out after that. I'd like to be back to top form, but I don't think we have the time to go back to Fallout and sit in a dry dock for a couple of weeks."

"As soon as you build a time machine, XO," Henry told him. A chime on his internal network said Todorovich was pinging him. "The ambassador calls. Hopefully, she has news from the Council.

"Keep me informed if anything changes around *Raven*, Tatanka," he finished. "I have no reason *not* to trust the Tano, but let's not give ourselves enough rope to get hanged, either."

"Understood, ser. Good luck with the diplomacy."

Henry closed the channel, cursed his XO under his breath and then accepted Todorovich's ping. A virtual avatar of the ambassador appeared in his office, giving no clue as to where she'd ended up after leaving the Council chambers.

"Do we have an update yet?" he asked.

"Not yet," she admitted. "I'm hearing more shouting than I was expecting, too. We're far enough that we can't make out details, but I'm starting to suspect that the locals are less of a unified front than they've been trying to show us."

"They had an armed revolt, Sylvia," Henry pointed out. "I wasn't under the impression they were overly united."

"Fair," she conceded. "I think they've been trying to present the Council, at least, as standing on the same ground. Faced with the La-Tar's request, though..." Her virtual avatar shook its head. "They have to make a decision and they know they have to make it quickly."

"They have at least two days," he said. "We're not leaving until then."

"And how long does it take to convert food transports to troop transports and load fifty thousand soldiers in your experience, Captain?" she asked.

He chuckled grimly.

"I haven't been around for doing the former, though Zast gave me the impression it was relatively straightforward for these ships," he told her. "Loading fifty thousand troops? Even with experienced GroundDiv troops and transports that landed on the planet, that would take a day.

"They'll be moving troops and vehicles with heavy-lift shuttles." He sighed. "Three days at least, plus a day minimum for the conversion. You're right. They don't have a lot of time."

"And they know it. Hence the shouting, I imagine. We're asking a lot."

"How's Rising Principle?" he asked.

"I'm not sure," Todorovich admitted. "I can't read them at all. I suspect they're nervous. I think they're a lot younger than they're trying to let us see. Unless I miss my guess, Rising Principle is related to Adamant Will and half the point of sending them as envoy was to get them to safety."

"And they put themselves on my ship," Henry said with a bitter chuckle. "I don't think they know me well."

"They will. I don't think *Principle* wants to be protected. They want to save their people. Hopefully...wait, that's General Kansa. I'll let you know what's going on in a moment."

The channel cut off and Henry sighed. He knew how to negotiate and how to be diplomatic. He'd spent a lot of his time during the war serving aboard or commanding ships embedded into Vesheron formations.

Evidence suggested he was better at it than he gave himself credit for, but he couldn't pretend he *enjoyed* it.

A FEW MINUTES LATER, Henry linked back into the holoprojector as Todorovich and Rising Principle took their seats in the Council chamber.

General Kansa wasn't even bothering to hide her expression. The purple-haired officer was showing her tusks in a broad, probably threatening grin.

That was actually a good sign as far as Henry was concerned. She'd wanted to support La-Tar, which meant they might just have pulled this off.

"Ambassador, Envoy, Captain," Inbar greeted them on behalf of his Council. "As you can imagine, your proposal is concerning to my fellows. We face a difficult era and a difficult task, charged by the people of our world to make certain we all survive the months and years to come.

"Alliance with the UPA is an easy decision. The El-Vesheron helped turned the tide against the Kenmiri. Without the UPA, we would be slaves. Alliance with La-Tar is equally easy. The people of La-Tar aided us when there was no one else.

"But to send the majority of our armies to another world, to fight and die for a victory that is far from certain? This is a difficult task for us to embrace."

Henry waited. Unless he was severely mistaken, Todorovich had just stepped on one of Rising Principle's feet to keep the Enteni quiet as well.

"But." The Kem word hung in the air. "But those alliances that we seek are meaningless if we do not act on them. We can acknowledge debts owed and aid given, but that is *also* meaningless if we do not act on them.

"We owe our freedom to the United Planets Alliance. We owe our lives to La-Tar and the Provisional Council of Supply." Inbar laid his hands down flat on the table and glanced to his left and right, as if waiting for one of his fellow Councilors to object.

"We will honor our debts and commit ourselves to our alliances," he finally said. "We will need to carry out more preparation before we can be certain how many soldiers we can commit to the liberation of La-Tar, but if you leave us twelve transports, we will find something to fill them all.

"It will take us some days to prepare, but you have already told us that there are more UPA warships on the way. We will wait until they have arrived, and then we will proceed to the Skex System with their escort.

"General Kansa and I will both accompany the army into the field, her to command and myself to speak for Tano in the discussions that must follow La-Tar's liberation."

He exhaled a long sigh and faced Rising Principle directly.

"Your people came to the salvation of mine, Rising Principle, in our darkest and most desperate hour," he told the Enteni. "Now you call on us to do the same and I give you the only answer we can give and be who we choose to be: La-Tar calls, and Tano *will* answer."

CHAPTER TWENTY-SEVEN

RAVEN LEFT TANO EXACTLY TWO DAYS AFTER ENTERING ORBIT, thirty-one transports trailing in her wake like ducklings. Henry mentally saluted the twelve ships remaining behind. They were already empty of food, and crews from Tano's shipyards were swarming aboard.

He believed Captain Zast when she told him the ships could be easily converted to carry five thousand soldiers apiece. He did not, however, expect that it was going to be an easy job.

Tano had shipyards, too. He was more concerned than he wanted to admit about the ships to be updated at Ratch, Atto and Skex. The limited information the Tano Council had been able to give him suggested that only Skex had any shipbuilding capabilities.

"Well, Colonel Song?" he asked his chief engineer over a private channel as Bazzoli navigated them toward the Ra-Thirty-Nine skip line. "What *didn't* we get done?"

"You do know how to butter a woman up, don't you?" she asked somewhat acidly. "Our armor integrity is still shot, ser. We *have* armor everywhere, but the patches are just that. If I had more time, I could secure them fully, but as it is..."

"I know," he allowed. "How bad, Chief?"

"They've got maybe fifty percent of the integrity on the joins that I'd want," Song said. "And there's only so much we can do on that front while the ship is under thrust or skip. Nothing's fragile enough to be in danger from even aggressive maneuvers, but the armor is brittle where those patches are connected."

"So, we'll try not to get hit in the same spot again," Henry conceded. He already had the patches highlighted in yellow on his displays.

"They should hold," she admitted. "I'm comparing them to our actual armor everywhere else, after all. They're just not where they should be."

"And I need to know that, Chief," he agreed. "Where are we at otherwise?"

"The optical assembly the Tano gave us was perfect," she told him. "We've got both lasers back; we've got the sensor blisters and the heat radiators replaced... If we could fix it, it's fixed, ser. We even started replenishing our stocks of spare sensors and radiators, though that's going to run down our supply of raw materials."

"Did we restock those from Tano?"

"Of course," she confirmed. "They've been more helpful than I could have asked for. Makes me nervous for an ally to be *quite* that helpful, ser."

"They don't have any skip ships of their own at this point, Chief," Henry reminded her. "You saw their yards. How long until any of those ships are online?"

"Twenty-four weeks, minimum," Song said instantly. "Depends on how many of those keels are gunships versus escorts. They'd got sixteen laid down that could be either at this stage, but gunships will take at least four more weeks."

"They don't have plasma cannon, so they'll all be escorts," he said.

"Then twenty-four to twenty-six weeks," she confirmed. "Six months, give or take. They must have used most of their slips building the freighters we already saw. They've got another ten of those laid down, but those will take a bit less. Four months or so. Simpler ships, in a lot of ways. Lot easier to build a big, empty void than to lay the power lines for a heavy laser."

"Still. Sixteen escorts will make Tano a valuable ally," Henry noted. "Six months, huh?"

In six months, if everything held together, this cluster would probably be able to take care of themselves against most threats. The Peacekeeper Initiative just had to make sure they *made it* six months.

Without ignoring the *rest* of the Ra Sector.

ENTRY INTO SKIP passed with its usual discomfort, and Henry retreated to his quarters at the end of his watch. A new skip drone had arrived shortly before they left, and he wanted to check the updates on the relief convoy.

There hadn't been any direct messages from Admiral Hamilton for him, so he assumed everything was progressing as expected—either there were no updates or those updates were relatively positive. A lack of specific messages meant nothing had changed, for the positive or the negative.

He didn't sit down at his desk just yet, conjuring a virtual screen in front of him with a wave of his hand as he leaned against his office wall. It would be a few more hours until the next adjustment, so he'd take advantage of the chance to not be strapped in.

The drone was full of all of the usual updates and mail. The UPSF was still getting used to not being able to send instantaneous messages, which meant that each drone now carried what would have once been three days' worth of reports, forms, requests, etc.

They'd adjust, but they weren't there yet. Henry was at least able to easily dismiss a third of the messages directed to him as "obsolete by the time a response could get back" with a few minutes' sorting.

There was, thankfully, an update on the convoy. It wasn't *much* of an update, just a note from Admiral Seo-Hyun, commander of Base Skyrim in the Procyon System, that they were assembling a first batch of ships while waiting for further orders from Earth.

The tone of the message suggested that those ships were probably going to end up at Tano regardless of what orders came from Earth. Emergency relief on a planetary scale, though, was going to require more food than was available from Base Skyrim's stockpiles or even the warehouses of Sandoval, Procyon's inhabited planet.

But the UPA could buy the factory worlds more time on top of what the convoy Henry was already escorting was buying. People were going to live because Admiral Seo-Hyun was a grouchy old woman willing to disobey orders if it came down to it.

He closed in eyes in relief, then opened them again as the admittance chime sounded.

Somehow, he wasn't surprised to find Todorovich at his door.

"Come in, Ambassador," he told her. "What do you need?"

"Something to fill the quiet," she admitted, producing a bottle of white wine from inside her suit jacket. "Share a drink with me, Captain? This skip is bothering me more than most, and I could use sitting with a friend."

It was a rare admission of weakness on the ambassador's part, one Henry couldn't reject.

"Come on in," he told her, gesturing her to the couch. "I'll find some glasses."

The door slid closed and he remembered O'Flannagain's warning from the other day. He shook it away as he headed for the sideboard— a fake piece of furniture, actually built into the wall but decorative and functional enough for that—to grab drinks.

The captain was allowed to have friends, after all.

He brought two wine glasses over to the couch, hooking an armchair over closer with his foot as he passed them to Todorovich.

She gave him a sad excuse for a smile as she opened the bottle and poured two glasses.

"Pinot grigio from the vineyards on New Pretoria, in Keid," she told him as she passed one over. "Four years old; it was a good year."

Henry chuckled as he raised the glass in toast.

"You know I can't tell the difference," he reminded her.

"And as I've told you before, I don't keep cheap wine on hand for philistines," she said. "To the United Planets Alliance."

"The UPA," he replied automatically. "The UPA and absent friends."

His tiny living room was silent as they both sipped the wine. It was good, he thought. Sweeter than he expected from wine, but delicate with it.

"I'll teach you something about wine eventually," Todorovich finally said, watching him drink it. "It's a useful skill when dealing with human diplomats."

"You're the only human diplomat I deal with," he told her. "Rising Principle is more my usual discussion partner."

"I know." She shook her head. "They're trying, but I don't think I'm wrong when I think Principle is here to keep them safe as much as anything else. They have the training and a bit of a gift, I think, but no experience."

"If they survive this, they'll have that," Henry said. "Trial by fire with their entire planet on the line. Sounds familiar."

He shivered against old memories. The UPSF's first encounters with the Kenmiri had been bloody on both sides. The insectoid conquerors hadn't been ready for human gravity shields. The humans hadn't been ready to be attacked at all.

The first campaign had ended in Procyon, where the UPSF had finally managed to muster their entire strength in one place. Between six fleet carriers, they'd put almost five hundred starfighters into space—including both Henry and his then-fiancé.

Forty-five of those pilots had come back. They'd enameled the right half of their pilot's wings in red to mark the fact that they were the survivors of that campaign—the survivors of the near-annihilation of the UPSF Fighter Division.

Henry had been far from alone in transferring to a starship track after that. Only eleven of those forty-five were alive now, all starship captains or higher—or retired.

"I'm sorry; I don't mean to bring up bad memories," Todorovich told him.

"We all have them," he countered. "The internal networks watch for them, warn us of them, record them for our counselors, but we all have them."

"Fair," she said. "Part of why I needed company tonight, I guess. Not the first time I've skipped into the dark, desperately hoping to find allies amid worlds at risk."

She stared down into the pale liquid in her glass.

"It didn't always end well," she noted. "For us...or for the people we tried to recruit. I talked a lot of people into going to their deaths, Henry. It was the job."

"I know."

He'd done the same, even if it hadn't been as large a portion of what he'd been doing in Kenmiri space.

"We tried to keep our promises," he told her. "But sometimes, we couldn't. Sometimes, we did and it wasn't enough."

"And sometimes, we lied," Todorovich said bluntly. "I *hope* that the Initiative can avoid that."

"We have to," Henry said. "The only way we can get people to respect us, to look to us as mediators and peacekeepers, is if we keep our promises. We have to be better than the Kenmiri. Better than the Kozun and the other warlords, too.

"We need to be trusted and we need to be worthy of that trust."

"And what happens when we can't be?" she murmured. "When politics back home undercut what we try to do out here?"

"We try not to make promises that can be undercut or will be," he told her. "We make promises that will make people back home money—like trade deals. If an emergency food convoy can open up trade routes for the excess food crops of Ophiuchi or Epsilon Eridani, then certain people are going to make a *lot* of money.

"That helps our case."

"I thought I was supposed to be the cold-blooded diplomat," Todorovich said with a chuckle.

"I learned how to handle the UPA from you," Henry said. "I learned how to handle Vesheron on my own, but money among the Vesheron and the Kenmiri empire was always...odd. Black markets are a funny thing when almost none of your customers ever see currency."

"You just deal in someone else's currency and get your customers used to it," she replied. "Drifter chits, mostly. The Kenmiri even let them on the slave worlds, from what I understand."

"I always wondered just how much money the Drifters were spending to function the way they did," he said. "Tolerated and even semi-welcome as nomadic traders, in an empire of slaves and tributaries. I can only assume they paid enough tribute to not be worth breaking to the Kenmiri yoke."

"I thought they were well protected as well?" she asked.

"Yes, but not enough to really stop the Kenmiri," Henry said. "Most Drifter Convoys had two or three Guardians, the big dreadnought-like ships, and maybe twice that in Kenmiri escorts or equivalent ships.

"The Kenmiri could easily have crushed the Convoys in a few months if they'd ever decided to. But they'd have lost a lot of ships doing it, so I'm guessing it was always a game of making sure they were paying enough tribute and being obedient *enough* to not be worth crushing."

He shook his head.

"As it turns out, perhaps the Kenmiri should have dealt with them. Between the planetary black markets and the Drifters supplying the Vesheron with weapons, they were pretty instrumental in the fall of the Empire."

"I'm not complaining that the Kenmiri didn't deal with them, that's for sure," Todorovich said. "Even if the Drifters don't seem to be *our* friends now."

"Perhaps not, but they enabled our victory." He held up his glass in a toast. "To the Drifters. Our sometimes-friends, sometimes-enemies. Long may they prosper, a long way away from me!"

CHAPTER TWENTY-EIGHT

THERE WAS NOTHING IN THE RATCH SYSTEM TO RECOMMEND IT for much of anything. Eight planets orbited a G-class star very like Sol itself. No dense asteroid belts, nothing particularly unusual about the two gas giants.

The third planet was Ratch itself, a green-and-purple marble highlighted in Henry's main displays. Even from half a light-minute away, it was visibly distorted by continent-sized smog clouds.

Kenmiri factory worlds always looked sad to Henry. He could usually see enough of what the world could be from orbit, but much of it would also be buried under the consequences of the massive factory complexes.

Most likely, Ratch was like Tano in that it was only as clear as it appeared because many of the factories had been slowed or stopped.

"We have contact in orbit of the planet," Ihejirika reported as the convoy traveled toward Ratch. "Looks like a pair of escorts, but their energy signatures are wonky."

"Define *wonky*, Commander," Henry suggested.

"I'm guessing patchwork repair job," the tactical officer replied. "One appears to be running what appears to be a cluster of heavy-vehicle fusion plants instead of a proper starship core, for example. I'm pulling at straws, but I suspect we're looking at ships the Kenmiri abandoned as nonfunctional when they withdrew that the locals have patched up as best they can."

"Potentially not even skip-capable," Bazzoli said. "Wasn't Tano the only system in the cluster that could build skip drives?"

"According to them, yes," Henry confirmed. "Are the guardships responding to our approach yet?"

"They're maneuvering to get in front of us, but they're not coming out to meet us," Ihejirika reported. "There are probably defensive platforms we haven't picked up yet in orbit. Easy enough to rig up a remote-control one-shot missile launcher, after all."

"All right. Any coms?"

"Negative," Moon replied. "I'm picking up the periphery of their chatter, but it's surprisingly well encrypted."

"Then we'll say hello and make it clear we're friendly," Henry decided. "Record for me, Commander."

He waited a second for Moon to set up the transmission, then activated the recorder with a mental command.

"This message is for the government and defenders of the planet Ratch," he said in his soft Kem. "I am Captain Henry Wong of the United Planets Space Vessel *Raven*. I am operating in alliance with the Emergency Governing Council of La-Tar to escort a convoy of food supplies.

"We are not hostile and are prepared to coordinate parking orbits with your government and traffic control. Only a portion of the food convoy can stop here, as we are still moving on to the Atto and Skex Systems, and I am carrying a La-Tar envoy who will need to speak with your government.

"Please advise as soon as possible of orbits and of a meeting time for Envoy Rising Principle and my own ambassador. We need to be moving as quickly as possible to make certain that both your world and others are provided with the food supplies they need.

"I await your reply."

He cut off the recording and nodded to Moon.

"Message sent, ser. How long do we wait for a reply?" the communications officer asked.

"It's a minute just for light-speed turnaround and we're still a few hours out," Henry replied. "We'll give them an hour, and then I'll send another transmission. We're here to help them. I'm sure as hell not fighting them."

"Tano and La-Tar both gave us the same protocols for contacting them, so they should have received the message," Moon told him. "So, we wait?"

"So, we wait," Henry agreed. "Bazzoli, watch our course. Let's make sure we don't commit to getting within range of those escorts until we've heard from the locals.

"Yes, ser."

The one thing Henry hadn't grown used to waiting for in his career was communications. Right up until the Gathering and the Kenmiri remnants' decision to cut off the subspace channels, his entire career had been spent with coms being near-instantaneous.

The rest of his job required enough patience that he was easily able to tolerate the ten-minute wait before the response finally arrived.

"Incoming datapulse," Moon reported. "Looks like a compressed video file, La-Tar coms protocols."

"Secure it and play it," Henry ordered. He didn't need to give the first part of the order, he knew. There were a *lot* of protocols and security measures that automatically kicked in to make sure no one sent a virus over in a video message.

The man who appeared on the screen was Ashall. Henry would *guess* him to be Beren, but that was only because the Beren were among the most human-looking of the Ashall species in the La-Tar cluster. He was a graying older individual who Henry would have assumed *was* human if not for the piercing orange eyes with the cat-like slit pupils.

The man was sitting behind a clearly Kenmiri-made desk that

had probably belonged to Ratch's governor, wearing a toga-like wrap garment in dark blue. The cloth covered most of his skin except his face and neck...but what was visible was enough for Henry to see that he was *very* unhealthy.

The stranger had the saggy skin of someone who had been quite heavy and had lost almost all of that excess weight *very* quickly and *very* recently.

"Captain Wong, I am Father Astemar," he introduced himself in perfect Kem. "I speak for the people of Ratch. You...offer hope. Hope so perfect that I dare not trust it, and yet...I know the name of the United Planets Alliance and, yes, I even know the name Henry Wong."

Father—the Kem word was *otren*—in this case was probably closer in meaning to *don* than the religious title Henry might take it for. The population of a Kenmiri slave world had almost everything dictated to them: where they worked, where they lived and what they ate...for someone to get fat on a slave world, they were probably eating more than the assigned calorie allotment.

That meant he was looking at a black marketeer, one of the locals who'd worked with Drifters and others to provide what luxuries could be found on a world dedicated purely to industrial production.

"Our guardships will allow you to enter Ratch orbit. Their commanders will assign you orbital slots. With La-Tar fallen, there have been no visitors but Kozun warships with their demands."

Astemar bowed his head.

"I was waiting...hoping...for one of them to return," he admitted. "We were out of options. You offer new hope, one I had dared not dream of. I will meet with your envoys, Captain Wong.

"I must ask that the food deliveries begin *immediately* on your arrival in orbit. We are...almost entirely out of food supplies. I beg of you, whatever price you demand, I will meet it, but if you do not start deliveries immediately, people will die."

The transmission ended and Henry nodded slowly to himself.

"Your orders, ser?" Moon asked.

"Forward that to Captain Zast, Ambassador Todorovich, and Envoy Rising Principle," Henry ordered. "Inform Captain Zast that she'll need to prepare for immediate delivery once the first ships are in orbit. I'll leave the details to her.

"I suggest Rising Principle and Todorovich reach out to Father Astemar directly to arrange their meetings," he continued. "This seems fertile ground for the La-Tar's deal, assuming that Astemar *has* the troops to send."

"*Father*," Iyotake muttered. "Why do I get the feeling that's not a religious title?"

"Because he looks like a crook?" Henry asked. "And almost certainly was one. Today, however, he is the leader of a world that needs our help."

"Can we trust him to keep his promises, though?" the XO asked.

"A black marketeer that doesn't keep their deals soon finds themselves with neither customers nor suppliers," Henry replied. "I think we'll be fine."

"I'M sure it's a massive surprise to anyone who saw Astemar's message, but Ratch is in," Todorovich told a gathering of the senior officers later. "He didn't even ask to meet in person. Like Tano, he's mostly committing ex-janissaries, but it sounds like he has a significant force of what used to be black-market security thugs that were being trained up to try and overthrow the Kenmiri, given the opportunity.

"When the Empire left, Astemar was ready to step in. He already had a planet-wide infrastructure, soldiers, everything. He turned from organized crime to governance quite readily, and nothing I'm seeing from here or the Tano files suggests his people mind."

"I'm not always a fan of supporting a dictatorship," Henry noted. "But in this case, he seems to have done well by his people so far."

"They always do at the beginning," Ihejirika said grimly. "That's part of the problem."

"And we'll deal with other potential problems here later," Todorovich told the tactical officer. "Right now, Father Astemar is committing fifty thousand soldiers to the operation on La-Tar. Also, it appears that Ratch was the regional center for manufacturing Kenmiri combat vehicles, so those fifty thousand soldiers represent something like ten armored divisions. Five thousand tanks."

"Kenmiri tanks?" Henry asked.

"From what I can tell, yes," the ambassador confirmed.

He watched several of his officers wince or whistle silently. The Kenmiri had used a variety of ground-combat vehicles, but their actual *tanks* had come in two varieties: a terrifying light tank and a horrifying heavy tank. Even the light version had armor that defied most weapons available to the UPSF and bristled with energy weapons.

"Astemar has committed to providing approximately twenty thousand additional combat vehicles of various types to be transported alongside his troops," Todorovich continued. "They'll be provided to the troops from the other factory worlds once they're on the ground. They won't have them for the initial push, but they'll increase the mobility and firepower of the rest of our allied force once the landings are complete."

Henry was pulling up the information they'd been given on Ratch's troops and ran through it on his network. Most of the soldiers in Ratch's force had the same projectile weapons as the rest of the factory-world troopers would be carrying, but they'd kept the Kenmiri tank plants running at full steam.

That suggested worrying things about Father Astemar's plans, but it also meant that their assault force would have a nearly unstoppable armored fist to carry the battle once they were down. Depending on how brave the Ratch soldiers were feeling, Henry's understanding was that Kenmiri light tanks could be dropped from disturbingly high altitudes, relying on energy shields and inertial compensators to survive their own impact.

"If Astemar is already in, that buys us time we should probably use," he told his staff. "We've been in orbit for less than four hours. We're not short on any supplies the locals can actually provide for us, so I intend to get moving again in another four hours.

"We'll coordinate with Captain Zast and bring the remaining twenty-one transports with us as we set out for Atto. This was smooth and easy, mostly because the locals were desperate."

He shook his head grimly.

"That's not a good sign, in all honesty," he told them. "And even if that is the case at Atto and Skex, we still can't count on things being this smooth. There's too much at stake for us to fail."

CHAPTER TWENTY-NINE

"Welcome to the Atto System," Bazzoli reported.

Henry nodded his acceptance of the report, unwilling to open his mouth just yet. The emergence from skip had managed to punch him in the stomach somewhat more thoroughly than usual, and he wasn't sure he wasn't going to throw up, antinauseants or not.

Blinking and swallowing away the sick feeling, he focused on the screens around him. Like Ratch, there wasn't much to distinguish Atto. Eleven planets and an asteroid belt. Like most factory-world systems, there were plenty of raw materials for the manufacturing centers.

Atto itself was the system's fourth planet, the oldest of the four factory worlds supported by La-Tar. No UPA ships had ever been there before, so they were updating their data as they went, but the planet didn't look like it was going to be salvageable anytime soon.

From space, the planet looked gray. Smog clouds had spread across the entire surface. From experience, Henry knew that the Kenmiri would have set up atmospheric control stations to make sure *enough* light was getting through to support *enough* of an ecosystem that only breath masks would be needed.

But the world was still a grotesque shade of sickly gray from the smoke billowing across its surface.

"Ser, we have a problem," Ihejirika suddenly snapped. "Flagging contacts in orbit, multiple units flying Kozun IFF. Bogey Alpha is a poten—no, sorry.

"Bogey Alpha is a *confirmed* gunship, with two, possibly three escorts in company," the tactical officer continued as the icons lit up in bright red above the planet. "Scans put them directly above the capital city, with the gunship locked on to the main transfer orbital."

"Well, that is a problem, isn't it?" Henry murmured. "Bazzoli, maintain course. Ihejirika, keep the shield down for now...but charge all of our capacitors. This is probably going to get ugly."

"What's a Kozun ship doing here?" Bazzoli asked.

"They've been moving around demanding surrenders from the local governments," Henry reminded his officers. "It looks like we've caught up with that team. The question, I suppose, is whether or not Atto *has* surrendered."

That earned the silence of his entire bridge crew, and Henry smiled mirthlessly.

"For now, we ignore them," he told his staff. "Ihejirika, we'll get ready for a fight, but we'll proceed as we did in Ratch until they actively challenge us. Moon, get ready to record."

He considered his phrasing as the communications officer set up the transmission. There wasn't much point changing things up.

Moon nodded to him and he activated the recorder.

"This message is for the government and defenders of the planet Atto," he greeted his audience, his tone flatter this time. He had more of an audience this time. "I am Captain Henry Wong of the United Planets Space Vessel *Raven*. I am operating in alliance with the Emergency Governing Council of La-Tar to escort a convoy of food supplies.

"We are not hostile and are prepared to coordinate parking orbits with your government and traffic control. Only a portion of the food convoy can stop here, as we are still moving on to the Skex System, but I am carrying a La-Tar envoy who will need to speak with your government.

"Please advise as soon as possible of orbits and of a meeting time for Envoy Rising Principle and my own ambassador. We need to be moving as quickly as possible to make certain that both your world and others are provided with the food supplies they need.

"I await your reply."

He ended the recording and leaned back in his chair.

"Send it, Commander Moon," he ordered. "Both wideband on Vesheron protocols and targeted directly at the capital under the La-Tar protocols. We need the Kozun to know we're here, but we also need to try and put the ambassador in touch with the actual local government."

"If the locals have surrendered, what do we do, ser?" Ihejirika asked.

"That depends on the conversation Ambassador Todorovich has with the locals, assuming we can put her in touch with them," Henry replied. "If nothing else, we fall back on basic principles: the United Planets Alliance does not recognize conquest as a legitimate transfer of government."

That sent another chill around his bridge as his peopled realized he was deathly serious. Unless Atto was as heavily fortified as La-Tar —which Henry didn't expect—he was going to kick the Kozun out of this system.

In pieces, if necessary.

THE KOZUN on the screen wasn't familiar to Henry at all. He was reasonably sure he'd have remembered if he'd met a Kozun officer who'd inlaid gold into the armor plates that rose from their eyebrows.

He couldn't read the characters that the woman had carved into her bone and skin, but he presumed they were religious. It struck him as likely that the Kozun would have a subculture that embraced that kind of self-marking, he just hadn't encountered any of them before!

"I am Star Shield Patrox of the Kozun Hierarchy," the woman told him in harshly accented Kem. "The food transports you claim ownership of belong to the Hierarchy by right of conquest of the planet La-Tar. The only government of La-Tar is that of the First Voice.

"You will surrender those stolen ships and their stolen cargo into the control of my battle group and withdraw from this system. The Atto now acknowledge the rule of the First Voice and the Hierarchy. They will be protected from your lies."

The message ended and Henry shook his head.

"Short and to the point, I see," he said aloud. "Moon, do we have any contact from the actual government yet?"

"No, ser. Should I connect them to you if we get a response?" Moon asked.

"No, send it to the ambassador and the envoy," Henry ordered. "Keep me informed, but I need to focus on our Kozun friend."

He considered the situation.

"Orders for Captain Zast," he said after a moment. "The transports are to begin decelerating immediately. They are not to approach within six million kilometers of Atto until the situation is resolved, and they're to make certain that *Raven* is between them and the Kozun group."

One gunship and two escorts—the final number Ihejirika had confirmed—was stretching the term "battle group" to the breaking point, but he'd give Patrox that much.

"As for us..." He studied the frozen image of the Kozun officer on his screen. "Commander Ihejirika, bring up the shield. All radiators to full extensions, all power plants to full capacity.

"Battle stations."

He didn't give the order with any great urgency. Unless he misread his reports, every member of his crew was *already* at battle stations. Raising the shield and taking the ship to general quarters just made it official.

Henry focused on the camera in front of him and activated it with a mental command.

"Star Shield Patrox," he greeted the Kozun. "The United Planets Alliance does not recognize Kozun sovereignty in the La-Tar System...or the Atto System. I will speak with the proper government of Atto with regards to the disposition of the food supplies from La-Tar and deliver those supplies to the people.

"I have no desire to fire on your ships or to engage in conflict with the Kozun Hierarchy, but I will not permit you to threaten these people with starvation or bombardment," he continued. "I require that you withdraw to a minimum distance of one million kilometers from Atto to permit the delivery of the food supplies and a diplomatic discussion between the La-Tar and Atto governments.

"If you do not withdraw, I must act to guarantee the safety of the food convoy in other ways." He paused, then bared his teeth in what might charitably be considered a smile.

"I will enforce your withdrawal from the system one way or another, Star Shield Patrox. I will not be bullied and I will not permit Atto to starve. Choose your course wisely."

He cut off the recording with a thought and glanced over at Moon.

"Send it," he ordered. "Any word from the locals yet?"

"We just got an encrypted pulse sent via a relay platform," she told him. "I'm passing it on to Ambassador Todorovich, but it looks like they tightbeamed it out and the Kozun may not know it was sent."

"Good. That suggests at least someone on the surface is still pushing back," Henry replied. "What's the message?"

"The encryption isn't any of the codes we were given," Moon reported. "I'm hoping Rising Principle may have a key they didn't tell us about."

"Quite possible," Henry conceded. "Keep in touch with Ambassador Todorovich and fill me in."

He turned his attention back to the main display. Patrox's three ships were moving out to meet him, but their acceleration was low. Barely a third of a KPS^2, which meant the Star Shield was being cautious.

Two escorts *could* threaten *Raven*, but it would take either a lot of bad luck or a surprise for them to manage it. Outside of that, they weren't really a factor in the conflict that was starting to take form.

The gunship, however, was built around a version of the same heavy plasma cannon that formed the main armament of a dreadnought. The UPA preferred the gravity driver for its flexibility, but the plasma cannon definitely had its own virtues.

Most importantly to Henry's current situation, a plasma cannon had a high chance of blowing through his gravity shield. Any individual shot was likely to either miss *Raven* due to the shearing effect or be too diffuse to do too much damage, but the weapon was *far* more dangerous to his battlecruiser than the lasers were.

The gunship was a threat Henry could handle, but it actually presented a threat in the way escorts couldn't without more numbers.

"Update from the ambassador, ser," Moon told him. "Rising Principle had a key for the encryption. It's a secondary code, an emergency backup they didn't expect to ever use.

"The Emergency Governor is trying to validate who we are and why we're here through a back channel," she continued. "Todorovich believes that they *have* surrendered but may be willing to consider a better deal."

"Let her know I plan on running the Kozun out of town unless she gives me a good reason not to," Henry replied. "I'll leave convincing the locals we're the better deal to her. Keep me advised if the situation changes."

"Understood, ser." She paused. "New message from the Star Shield."

"Put it on."

The gold-inlaid Kozun reappeared on Henry's screen, her eyes hard and her lips pressed thin. He didn't even need to pick up her microexpressions to realize she was angry.

"The United Planets Alliance has no authority here and your orders are arrogant and irrelevant," she hissed. "*I* am the proper government of Atto now, until a governor can be appointed by the First Voice. You will surrender those food transports to me or I will take them from you by force."

Henry waved aside the message as it ended, and smiled.

"I don't think that deserves a response," he noted. "Commander Bazzoli, Commander Ihejirika: initiate attack run on the gunship. Maintain point five KPS squared, but feel free to take us to point six if needed. Everyone should be strapped in by now."

"Arming launchers five through twelve," Ihejirika replied. "Range in twenty-six minutes."

"Star Shield Patrox wants to call my bluff," Henry said more loudly, making sure the entire bridge crew could hear him. "Unfortunately for her, I'm quite certain *she's* the one bluffing. And if she isn't, *Raven* will blow her little task group to hell."

He leaned back in his chair and checked the screens. A second datapulse had come in from the local government, and he linked in to Todorovich via his internal network.

"Which way are the locals jumping?" he asked her.

"We've confirmed Rising Principle's credentials and identity and are trading messages with Emergency Governor Setrell via a relay satellite," the Russian woman replied. "She's not jumping just yet, but her position is still pretty clear: she surrendered to the Kozun to feed her people.

"Reading between the lines, there's only a handful of Kozun troops on the surface. If we can feed Atto, Setrell will happily reverse her surrender. But you'll have to make it clear that the Kozun can't stop us."

"Isn't that convenient," he purred.

"That level of smugness doesn't become you, Captain," Todorovich told him. "But it's probably earned in this case. Kick that inlaid spikehead out of this star system and we're well on our way. Sound like something you can manage?"

"With pleasure, Ambassador Todorovich," he agreed.

"She's coming out to meet us still," Ihejirika reported as Henry closed the channel to Todorovich. "But she's not being eager about it. They're still accelerating at point three four KPS squared."

Henry looked at the screen and brought up a virtual overlay on his internal network. He adjusted several lines and then shook his head.

"Bazzoli, double-check my numbers," he ordered. "I make it that if the Kozun vector off for the skip line to La-Tar in about five minutes at max accel, they'll only enter extreme missile range for about ninety seconds."

His navigator was silent for several seconds as she crunched the numbers herself.

"I get the same," she confirmed. "We could increase our acceleration and maybe double that time, but why would they do that? They're not going to do anything to us with a handful of missile salvos."

Most likely, Patrox had about fifty launchers to Henry's current eight. He wasn't going to get missiles through her defenses...and she wasn't going to get any through his, especially not at the kind of extreme range he was looking at.

"'For the honor of the flag,'" he quoted. "In sailing-ship times, a ship that was utterly outmatched would still fire one broadside to make sure they weren't accused of surrendering or running without a fight."

"So, the Star Shield is going to shoot at us...just to show that she did?" Ihejirika asked.

"Otherwise, she'd be burning straight for us at full power," Henry replied. "She's got the same range limitation we do: her gunship's main gun has a range of about a quarter-million kilometers. We're not ending this fight with missiles, so if she *actually* wanted to fight us, she'd be trying to get inside plasma-cannon range."

"If she breaks off on schedule, we'll be in range in twenty minutes," Ihejirika reported, the tactical officer clearly recalculating his numbers on the fly. "Your orders, ser?"

"Let's be generous, I think," he said thoughtfully. "We'll hold course and we'll let her get her salvo in. One return salvo from us, Commander Ihejirika."

"Ser? We aren't going to do anything with eight missiles."

"That's not the point, Commander," Henry told his subordinate. "Star Shield Patrox doesn't actually want a fight today. She knows she can't win it and she wants to protect her people and her ships. But she also has to play the role for her superiors.

"I don't know how dangerous the Hierarchy's navy is at this point, but if she wants to withdraw in a way that makes her look good, I'm willing to play along today." Henry smiled sadly. "That's part of the *being peacekeepers* aspect of this, Commander. We can't press every fight to the knife—letting people go has its risks, but they need to know we will honor surrender and allow retreat.

"Because we're not here to fight a war. We're here to protect people—and I'm willing to make some sacrifices to help Star Shield Patrox protect *her* people as well."

"And if you're wrong, ser?" Iyotake asked, the XO having clearly been listening in all along.

"Then we're going to be in a short-range engagement with a Kozun gunship in a little under half an hour and we are going to blow very large holes in that ship," Henry said calmly. "Playing along costs us nothing but eight missiles I already know Tano is sending replacements for."

"There she goes, ser!" Ihejirika reported. "Vector change on the Kozun fleet; they are up to one point two KPS squared and burning for the La-Tar skip line."

Technically, the skip line went to a blue hypergiant halfway between the two star systems. That star didn't have a name in

Henry's files yet, though, and the only reason *Raven*'s crew cared about it was that it was the route to La-Tar from both Atto and Skex.

It wasn't the fastest route *between* the two star systems, according to the maps Tano and La-Tar had given him, but both systems linked to La-Tar via that giant. Patrox would almost certainly be falling back on La-Tar, but Henry couldn't prevent that.

"Continue pursuit at point six," Henry ordered calmly. "Stand by for long-range fire. Get O'Flannagain's birds out for missile defense."

He looked at the icons of Patrox's ships and wondered if she realized he knew what she was doing. The "I know you know I know" could get pretty deep, but he had to wonder if she realized he was intentionally playing along.

And if so, would that make her trust him next time they met...or hate him more?

THE MISSILE SALVO came exactly on schedule, fifty missiles blazing toward Henry's ship at ten KPS^2. His own single salvo answered, flashing past the eight starfighters hanging between *Raven* and her enemies.

"First contact in one hundred twenty seconds," Ihejirika recited calmly. "All defense lasers online. We're interfaced with O'Flannagain's people. There won't be any accidental hits."

He paused.

"Second launch on screens. We are not returning fire."

"We have as many starfighters as we can launch missiles," Henry replied. "I think they'll realize there's not much point in follow-up salvos." He watched the missiles approach. "I doubt Patrox has done anything to make those missiles less effective, so let's be damned careful here."

"Third salvo on screens, Kozun force is out of range," the tactical officer reported. "Starfighters engaging first salvo."

Missiles started to disappear from the screens and *fast*. O'Flannagain's people were veterans to a one, their skills well-honed in the turmoil of a seventeen-year war.

"First salvo hitting inner defenses, starfighters targeting second salvo."

"And our missiles, Commander?" Henry asked.

"Gone," Ihejirika said bluntly. "*Detonation.* Five missiles got close enough to hit the shield, no blowthrough."

That was the best shot Patrox's people got. Their command-and-control loop degraded as they accelerated away from Henry's ship, each fraction of a second of delay making their missiles a tiny bit more vulnerable.

Two missiles from the second salvo got close enough to detonate. None of the third made it through.

"All right," Henry said aloud. "We can't catch them now." Even if *Raven* still had her full acceleration, she couldn't match the thrust of the fleeing Kozun ships. "Bazzoli, break off and set your course for the planet. Moon, get Captain Zast and the transports heading in to join us."

He chimed Todorovich.

"Ambassador, the Kozun are retreating from the system and the food transports are heading for Atto. I do believe we have created a situation that invalidated the Emergency Governor's surrender, but she should *probably* tell the Kozun that before they leave," he suggested.

"We wouldn't want to risk confusion in the future, would we?"

CHAPTER THIRTY

ANOTHER PLANET, ANOTHER CONFERENCE HENRY WAS attending via holoprojection. A virtual image of the Emergency Governor's meeting room surrounded him.

It wasn't, to his surprise, a space in the former Kenmiri government center. The Emergency Governor had taken over one of the larger residences around the administrative capital that had presumably belonged to a senior Kenmiri Warrior.

The assumption of Warrior versus Artisan came from the lack of decoration. No Artisan would ever build anything without baroque levels of decoration unless forced to. They certainly wouldn't *live* in a space like that if given a choice.

Living in a spacious but undecorated home was something only a Warrior would do. Quite possibly, the house had belonged to the senior Kenmiri commander on Atto.

The Emergency Governor herself was another surprise. She was a Kozun woman with copper-red hair on the back half of her head pulled back into a severe queue-style haircut. *Her* eyebrow ridges, at least, hadn't been inlaid with precious metals.

She was also alone in the room with Rising Principle and Todorovich. There were bodyguards outside the room, Henry understood, but Setrell clearly didn't feel she needed anyone else to approve her decisions.

"Your arrival here was surprising, Ambassador," Setrell told them in slow Kem. "We were expecting a food convoy, of course, as payment for our surrender. The news of La-Tar's liberation had not reached us."

"La-Tar, unfortunately, is-was not yet free," Rising Principle told her. "Captain Wong rescued the transports and their crews, but the Kozun remain on the surface of my world."

Setrell was silent for a moment, blinking in surprise as she considered the situation.

"They have heavily fortified La-Tar's surface," Henry told her. "The La-Tar have commandos they believe can disable the surface guns to allow a landing, but they don't have the numbers or firepower to drive out the occupation force."

"Both Tano and Ratch have committed significant forces and resources to a campaign to liberate La-Tar," Todorovich added. "Between them, they have committed a hundred thousand soldiers and five thousand tanks.

"That is roughly comparable to the forces the Kozun have entrenched on La-Tar, which means we still need more soldiers and more weapons," she continued. "Rising Principle?"

"This food is-was provided freely, as is-was before," the Enteni Envoy said softly. "But we must-will call on the debt incurred, Governor. We need your soldiers. We must-will fight as one or all must-will starve or become slaves."

"I was prepared to accept slavery," Setrell said grimly. "Look through the window behind you, Ambassador, Envoy. My sky is poisoned. My soil is ash. All my world can do now is build the machinery and toys of life for others.

"What does it matter to us if we are slaves of the Kozun or the Kenmiri?"

"The damage done to Atto can be repaired," Todorovich told her.

"It is not an easy course to set your feet upon, but it can be done. You might never breathe the air of your world unfiltered—but your children and grandchildren might.

"That won't happen under the Kozun. As a free world, you can trade what you build for food to feed yourselves—but also for the technology and the knowledge to repair the damage the Kenmiri did to Atto.

"Rising Principle offers your people hope, but only if you fight for their people," Todorovich concluded. "The United Planets Alliance will gladly sign trade treaties with Atto as an independent power. We *have* the knowledge and technology you need, Governor.

"What we do not have is the army to save La-Tar in time. Only you and the other worlds that depend on La-Tar to survive can save her."

Setrell bowed her head.

"You would have me send tens of thousands into the guns of my enemies, to sacrifice their bodies so that the rest of my world can live," she said. "It seems a dark trade to make."

"Would-will you spend your days in a factory, Governor?" Rising Principle asked. "My parent and their parent before them have-has been farmers. Not by choice, but by the will of the Kenmiri.

"Would-will you serve a new master, having experienced a chance to be free? I can-will not. My parent can-will not. My world can-will not. We must-will fight."

The Enteni gestured, palm up, to Setrell.

"We must-will fail if we fight alone," they finished simply.

"As I did," Setrell admitted. "What armies we had are mustered, prepared to defend the cities, but..." Her face was frozen now, but Henry could read her grief. "It was made clear that the Kozun would destroy whatever was necessary to clear the way for their troops.

"Or worse, they would simply wait until our soldiers had starved. I could do *nothing*."

"Now you can do something," Henry told her. "La-Tar is also a choke point on the Kozun approach to the worlds they support. It is not easily bypassed by the skip lines. If La-Tar stands, Atto is free."

The room was silent.

"How long to ready your transports for soldiers, then?" the Emergency Governor told them. "I have thirty thousand soldiers in the field. I can send you no more, but I can send you those."

"Thirty-six hours," Henry told her. "If your soldiers will be ready that quickly, we can wait until they are aboard."

There was an advantage, after all, to arriving in Skex with an actual army. It would be easier to prove to someone that everyone was on board with the plan when *Raven* didn't show up alone, after all.

"My soldiers could march aboard right now," Setrell told them. "We were ready to fight the Kozun until it was clear that there was no purpose to the attempt. Promise me something, Captain Wong."

"Governor?"

"Promise me there *will* be a purpose," she said firmly. "I do not wish to be remembered as the one who brought war to Atto. I only wish to be remembered as the woman who held everything together when the world fell apart around us."

"We are-is better without the Kenmiri," Rising Tide said. "We can-will be better as fate-time passes. The future is promise, not fear."

"So I am trusting," Setrell agreed. "Do not betray that trust. Please."

CHAPTER THIRTY-ONE

MOVING THIRTY THOUSAND PEOPLE FROM A PLANET TO A collection of orbiting transports was a herculean endeavor at the best of times. Moving thirty thousand *soldiers*, with accompanying gear, vehicles, weapons, ammunition and other supplies, multiplied the effort by a couple of orders of magnitude.

Henry had to admit he was impressed by the speed with which Captain Zast had been getting her freighter crews to empty their cargo holds, but this was the first time he'd watched the process in reverse.

First, they'd thrown themselves into reconfiguring the cargo holds. The space to hold ten million tons of food was hardly set up to hold combat vehicles, let alone soldiers. It was more easily used for the equipment and the vehicles, which could simply be strapped onto massive pallets and locked to the floors in the same way as the food had been.

The soldiers required breathable air and gravity, both things that the ships weren't designed to provide for their entire cargo holds. The "converted" space made available for the soldiers still required them to bring their own beds, as Henry understood it, but they were at least flat and had oxygen.

Offloading and switching over had taken a day and a half, and then Zast's shuttles had set back to work. Each of the transports carried twenty of the massive heavy-lift spacecraft, each capable of carrying ten thousand tons of cargo themselves.

Now he watched as a seemingly continuous train of shuttles alternated between the surface and the six ships designated to carry the Atto contingent.

"That will put us at a hundred and thirty to a hundred and forty thousand troops, depending on how many Tano came up with in the end," Iyotake said from behind him. Henry glanced over his shoulder at his XO and gestured the man to the observer seat next to him.

"Think it will be enough?" Henry asked the Native American man.

"Hopefully, we'll fill the rest of the transports at Skex," Iyotake told him. "We *should* be able to bring two hundred thousand soldiers back to La-Tar, at which point the Kozun are screwed."

"Assuming that the La-Tar commandos take down the guns and we can drive off whatever space forces they have," Henry agreed. "We can assume that Patrox and Kalad are both in the system now, which means we're starting to look at a serious force in our way. Six escorts and a gunship is about where I start getting actually concerned, and that's assuming Kalad didn't go get reinforcements."

"Which I'd have done in her place," the XO said.

"I know Kalad of old," Henry reminded Iyotake. "I'm pretty sure she got reinforcements. It's a question of what Kozun has available, and we really have no idea. We know the First Voice only has one dreadnought left, but he could have as many as thirty or forty escorts and gunships."

"Tano had six escorts in La-Tar and the Kozun took them out," his subordinate noted. "What do we do if we're facing a real fleet, ser?"

"Draw them off," Henry said. "They 'know' the planet is secure with the Guardian platforms, so I suspect we can provoke the Kozun fleet into chasing us. We have a few tricks up our sleeve for a running gunfight, and then the La-Tar can clear the way for the landing.

"If the ground troops can seize the Guardians, then the dynamic changes again."

He shrugged.

"The thought of turning those guns on the Kozun warms my heart," he told Iyotake with a smile. "But mostly, I'm counting on the Kozun sending enough ships to handle *Raven* but not enough to handle us *and* two destroyers. Three grav-shielded warships make a hell of a Sunday punch, Lieutenant Colonel."

"And if Mal Dakis is paranoid enough to send a real fleet?" the XO asked again. "One big enough for them to split in half?"

Henry sighed.

"Then things get ugly and we have to hope the La-Tar commandos can take control of some of the platforms they were planning to take out," he admitted. "Because at that point, we might be in real trouble."

"CAPTAIN ZAST, HOW GOES THE LOADING?" Henry asked as the image of his unofficial convoy commander appeared in his office. "I hate to start asking for a timeline already, but I do need one."

"We are progressing roughly as expected," she told him in her slow and precise Kem. "We are mostly loading equipment so far, but approximately six thousand soldiers are aboard. I project we will be complete in nine hours."

"That is it?" he asked. They'd been loading for five already and only moving a fifth of the soldiers aboard.

"Much of the first few hours of a process like this is learning the steps," she explained. "The soldiers now know what to expect when our shuttles land, and we know what to expect from them in turn.

"Everything will move more swiftly now. We will most likely be ready to leave in nine hours. If you can provide eleven, that would be preferable."

"It depends on Skex, I suppose," Henry told her. "Are they likely to be in as bad a situation as Ratch was? After the situation there, I am worried about delays."

"Skex is the newest of the worlds we feed," Zast explained. "My belief is that they will have been able to plant crops or even capture native wildlife. They are the most likely of the four to be able to survive even without La-Tar."

She paused.

"Eventually," she continued. "The transition will be difficult, and without assistance, they will lose many of their people. They, like the other worlds we feed, need us. But not all of Skex's people will starve without us."

"So, they should have time," Henry said. "That is good to know."

It also meant that Skex might be harder to convince to sign on for the joint expedition to liberate La-Tar. If they didn't feel they *needed* La-Tar—they might have a different assessment than Zast, after all— they would be less willing to field soldiers to free another world.

"I understand that we will still be the first to arrive if we wait another eleven hours?" Zast asked.

"It depends on how quickly Ratch got their act together, but we will be at least two days ahead of the troops from Tano and my rein- forcements," Henry agreed. "I am hesitant to return to La-Tar without those warships."

"You are the commander, Captain Wong. We will follow your lead on this, but I do not think..." She paused, trying to find the words in Kem.

"I do not think there is patience for if the first attack fails," she finally said. "If we cannot land when we first return to La-Tar, for any reason, there will be no second chance. The worlds we feed will recall their armies and surrender to Kozun.

"They will have no choice."

"I believe we can keep Tano free if they will work with us, but I expect that, yes," Henry confirmed. "I understand the risks, Captain Zast. I will not order you to take the troops to La-Tar unless I can guarantee a path to do so safely."

"La-Tar is my home, Captain Wong," she noted. "I do not wish to fly to my unquestioned death for my world, but I will take risks for her freedom. We will fight."

"I know," he agreed. "But you should know that if all of this falls apart, you will have sanctuary in the UPA. You have earned that much."

Zast laughed, her hair tendrils rippling.

"I will not hesitate to demand such if it becomes necessary," she told him. "But trust me, Captain. I want to go home."

"And I will do everything in my power to get you there."

CHAPTER THIRTY-TWO

"We're being watched."

Ihejirika's report was calm, given in a regular tone as if nothing important was happening. And nothing important *should* have been happening as *Raven* traversed the empty system around the red giant star.

Henry wasn't even on the bridge. He was in his office, working through the infinite quantity of paperwork involved in running a starship with a crew of fourteen hundred.

"Define *watched*, Commander," he asked. A few mental commands closed his paperwork and brought up a duplicate of the main tactical display in his network. Since it didn't actually exist, it readily expanded to fill his office.

There was a blinking orange unknown contact at the limits of their sensor range, over a light-minute away.

"Unknown contact at twenty million kilometers," the tactical officer told him. "They haven't pinged us with active sensors or anything, but they're keeping pace with the convoy."

"Any details at all?" Henry said.

"She's small, half the size of an escort at most," Ihejirika noted. "Her captain is good, too. I'm reasonably sure she was in the system when we got here and managed to go undetected for six hours before she failed to hide an engine burn."

Henry pulled up a different set of numbers and nodded silently.

"She can skip from here to the same hypergiant we'd leave Atto or Skex for, then skip to La-Tar," he guessed. "Maybe sixty hours at most. Assuming she's Kozun, they're going to have an update."

"Yes, ser," Ihejirika confirmed. "We could send O'Flannagain after them, ser."

He considered. The Dragoons could get up to 1.5 KPS^2, almost certainly more than a home-built corvette could manage, but they were starting from twenty million kilometers away...

"They can't make it before she can skip out," Henry replied. "And it's not like chasing our friend here off is going to change how much intelligence the Kozun get. They know where we're going."

"They're getting quite a bit of data, just sitting there watching us," the tactical officer argued.

"Yes, but if they were watching us for six hours before we detected them, they already know everything they're going to learn," Henry told him. "They know *Raven* is short an engine and they know we have twenty-one transports in the convoy.

"They can probably tell that five of the transports are empty and six are carrying light loads, but they *can't* tell that those six are carrying soldiers. Not unless someone in the convoy is sending them updates.

"So, check with Moon's people," Henry ordered. "If someone has *transmitted* to that ship, we need to know that. But otherwise...she's already learned what she wants to learn and we can't catch her.

"We'll let her think we didn't see her—and we'll send a drone back to the destroyers," he decided aloud. "The Tano convoy will want to take a different route. Let's see if we can keep our reinforcements secret for a bit longer."

It wouldn't be news to the Kozun, after all, that *Raven* was there and was preparing *something*. The two destroyers his latest drones had confirmed were at Tano...*those* he was hoping were going to be a surprise.

V

HENRY WAS STILL WATCHING their unfriendly ghost when Todorovich knocked on his door and entered his office without waiting for a greeting. He looked up at her reprovingly as she took a seat, and she shrugged.

"Is there anything you might be looking at that I'm not cleared for, Henry?" she asked bluntly.

"I might have been in a meeting with someone," he reminded her.

"Which *Raven*'s systems would have told me," Todorovich said. "You didn't have an active call, you didn't have anyone in your office, and I *know* you aren't getting sexual videos from back home."

An almost-laughable attempt by a Vesheron officer to seduce Henry at the Gathering had resulted in a more personal conversation with Sylvia Todorovich on his sexuality than he'd have preferred. Thanks to his extensive encounters with counselors and therapists over his career—the UPSF treated the psychological damage of warfare as careful and thoroughly as it treated the physical injuries— he even knew the label: demisexual. He needed to know someone well before his brain would even begin to consider them attractive.

He'd known his fiancé for almost a year before they'd started dating, both serving in the same fighter wing before the war. He'd known the one girl he'd seriously dated in Montana on Earth for almost two years before they'd dated, though they'd been *much* younger.

"Fair enough," he allowed. He'd transferred the tactical display to the room's holoprojectors, so it now hung in the air around them. He found using the ability of his network to drop things into his vision somewhat *itchy* if he wasn't in full VR.

"Can you even read this?" he asked, gesturing to it.

"Mostly," she said, looking at the display. "There's *Raven* and the convoy. And I don't know what that is, but I'm guessing an unknown contact?"

"Got it," Henry agreed as she pointed at the blinking orange sphere. "We're guessing a Kozun corvette or similar home-built light warship. We picked her up an hour or so ago, but we think she's been shadowing us since we arrived in the star system.

"She's too far out for us to catch with starfighters, so I'm pretending we don't see her while telling my reinforcements to take a different route," he explained. "Hopefully, that will help lull our spiky-headed friends into a false sense of certainty around our firepower."

"Won't they have left by now?" Todorovich asked. "I'm still getting used to the delays."

"They should have left Tano at least a day ago, but the drones update each other with the current locations of their parent ships as they pass each other," Henry explained. "So long as Pololáník and Spini are sending me updates, my updates will reach them.

"Adjusting their course will add a day to their arrival at Skex, but I was already expecting the transports from Ratch to arrive after them. It shouldn't cost us too much time on our schedule for La-Tar."

"That's good," Todorovich said. She studied the icon and shook her head. "Do the Kozun have drones?"

"Not so far as we know, so our friend here will eventually have to skip back to report in," Henry said. "You weren't here to talk about her, though. What's going on, Sylvia?"

"I got an update on the last set of drones that someone screwed up and didn't copy you on," she told him. "Someone even did the math and assumed there'd be multiple factory worlds under threat, and the Security Council opened the coffers wider than I expected."

"How wide are we talking?" Henry asked cautiously.

"When the drone was sent, sixteen days ago, they were expecting to send fifty-two ships out from Sol within forty-eight hours, with a full battlecruiser group as escort," she told him. "They were expecting to pick up more ships at Eridani and Procyon, along with an escort carrier group at Eridani.

"They're not sure on final numbers—and they didn't have our numbers on the factory worlds yet—but they were targeting a year's supply for one and a half billion people, Henry. It's thirty days out, but La-Tar already bought us that much time," she continued. "We... may have both misjudged our government."

His chair wanted to slide out from underneath him. That was *vastly* different from what he had been expecting.

"I'm probably copied on the movement orders for the warships, if nothing else," he admitted, scanning through his own messages. Now that he knew what to look for...

"Yeah, there they are." He pulled them up and exhaled a long sigh. "About what I'd expect. The battlecruiser is *Lioness*, one of the oldest ships still in the fleet. But she's still a battlecruiser and bringing four destroyers with her.

"Plus the escort carrier *Lexington* and two destroyers from Eridani, it looks like."

The delay on the drones meant that the convoy was probably already in Procyon with its escort. Weeks away from Tano still, but on their way.

"That's a hell of a relief," he concluded. "I have to wonder, though...does it change anything for us?"

Todorovich was silent, then slowly shook her head.

"I don't think so," she told him. "Food is...cheap, Henry. Both politically and monetarily. Even on this scale, it's still something that's easy to sell the member governments on and relatively straightforward to pay for.

"Escorting the food? Again, politically cheap. But you have the movement orders for those ships, don't you? They're not being assigned to the Initiative, at a guess. They're just here to make sure the convoy makes it to the factory worlds.

"They're going to have strict orders not to fight anyone except in direct defense of the convoy. I don't know what games you and Admiral Hamilton can play with that, but I doubt you can swing borrowing convoy escorts to support an invasion."

"Admiral Hamilton is a fast talker, but probably not, no," Henry admitted. "For that matter, she's had enough time now to send me orders with regards to the whole invasion plan, and I haven't even received a message admitting she knows about it."

He shrugged.

"Things are far enough along that even Hamilton can't really *stop* us," he concluded. "So, she's choosing to leave things to 'the judgment of the officer on the scene' and pass the reports up the chain.

"If she *could* send me more support than she already has, I'd be frustrated by that. As it is, she's protecting the *Initiative*, so I can't blame her."

"Is there really that much risk?" Todorovich asked.

"The risk is mostly political," he said. "What do you think?"

The ambassador was silent, clearly thinking through the situation.

"If this goes wrong, they'll disavow you," she finally told him. "Both of us, really, though I imagine we'll be dead by then, regardless. They'll have to accept Kozun control of at least La-Tar, though we've probably managed to get the UPA into a position where they have to defend the factory worlds here."

"Probably," Henry echoed. He gestured to the orange contact on the display. "But that that ship exists tells me that the Kozun are doing more than building Kenmiri designs. The Kenmiri didn't have a scout corvette like that.

"If we piss them off badly enough, I'm not sure Mal Dakis will buy that they couldn't rein me in in time to prevent the attack. He's not...an overly understanding man—and if he's building up his own fleet, he may have options available to him that we haven't considered."

Or weapons that could actively threaten gravity-shielded warships.

Todorovich shook her head as she studied the icon herself.

"Then we'd better pull this off, hadn't we?"

CHAPTER THIRTY-THREE

From a distance, Skex didn't have the usual visible wounds of a Kenmiri factory world. There were no massive smog clouds covering entire continents, no leprous seas or poisoned prairies. It was on the small side for an inhabited planet, but it was a dark green ball of life.

"Data from Tano suggests that Skex is denser than it looks," Iyotake told Henry as they scanned the system around them. "High concentrations of heavy metals in the entire system, actually, which certainly makes the whole place valuable.

"And Skex itself has the same minerals as its neighbors. There's already strip mines in place in some areas, but its only been settled for about fifty years. Even to the Kenmiri, it's more efficient to carve off the easy-to-access asteroids first, so more of their industry is in orbit than most factory worlds."

"Which leaves them with some notable benefits," Ihejirika added. "I'm picking up three escorts in orbit. Unlike the ones at Ratch, I think these ones might even be able to skip."

"Are they Kozun?" Henry asked.

"They're not transmitting Kozun ID codes," the tactical officer told him. "It's possible, I suppose. I'm not familiar with the IDs I am seeing."

"Rising Principle says they had some ships," Todorovich advised. "They'd thought all of Skex's skip-capable ships had died in defense of La-Tar, though. Like Tano's fleet."

"So, someone hasn't been entirely aboveboard with their allies," Henry murmured. "A warning sign, if nothing else, though I'd like to talk them into sending those ships with us if we can."

The escorts wouldn't be as survivable as his ships, but he knew how to handle that. It wouldn't be the first time a UPSF contingent had bodily shielded their allies to augment everyone's survivability and firepower.

Gesturing for Moon to get ready to transmit, he considered his spiel.

"This message is for the government and defenders of the planet Skex," he finally said in Kem. "I am Captain Henry Wong of the United Planets Space Vessel *Raven*. I am operating in alliance with the Emergency Governing Council of La-Tar as well as the governments of Tano, Ratch and Atto. I am escorting a convoy of food supplies provided by the La-Tar government as well as a military contingent from Atto that is headed to La-Tar to assist the government in regaining control of their world.

"We are not hostile and are prepared to coordinate parking orbits with your government and traffic control. I am carrying a La-Tar envoy who will need to speak with your government.

"Please advise as soon as possible of orbits and of a meeting time for Envoy Rising Principle and my own ambassador. I must also advise you that we are expecting to rendezvous with other vessels, including both transports and warships, and none of those ships represent a threat to the Skex System.

"I await your reply."

He mentally confirmed Moon's request to send it and leaned back. The situation was as under control as it was going to get—the locals had no reason to shoot at him yet, even if they probably would prefer that he'd asked before he'd used them as a rendezvous point for the invasion army.

He had the food they needed. That would buy him enough of an opening to smooth over any ruffled feathers—he hoped—and get Todorovich and Rising Principle onto the ground.

They'd find out soon enough.

"ESCORTS ARE MOVING to position themselves in our path," Ihejirika reported. "I'm detecting other movement as well. Looks like several flights of fighters and basic repositioning systems on a handful of orbital forts.

"Nothing we can't handle, but they are being more...careful than I might have expected."

"We are an unknown warship accompanied by a flotilla of transports," Henry replied. "Any response yet, Moon?"

"Nothing. It's been at least ten minutes, ser," she admitted.

"All right." He studied the display, considering the situation. "Bazzoli, adjust our course and the convoy course. We'll come to a halt at least five light-seconds from the planet. Well outside weapons range for everybody."

"We don't exactly have parking orbits, so I'd be concerned with trying to drop into orbit anyway," his navigator said lightly. "Passing the course to Captain Zast and the others. We'll be well clear, ser."

"We will *try* not to be aggressive as we let them sort out their own issues," Henry told his bridge crew. "We can only be so friendly if they don't talk to us, but we can be patient."

There wasn't much visible change to their course yet. They'd turn over earlier and hit zero velocity sooner, but that wouldn't be for a while still.

"Ambassador, any suggestions?" he asked Todorovich.

"Give them another twenty minutes, then send another polite

message," she said after a few seconds' thought. "We have ten ships full of food for them. If nothing else, I'd like to deliver that."

"We need their army and I could use those ships," Henry told her. "So far, the food transports have opened any and all doors. I wasn't expecting quite so cold a welcome."

"It could be worse, couldn't it?"

"This is a cold welcome, Ambassador," he said with a quiet chuckle. "A *hot* welcome involves them clearly preparing to shoot at us. This is just them being very cautious and not acknowledging my attempt to talk to them."

"Give them time, then try again," she repeated. "Patience is the only real indicator we can give them."

"Patient is all well and good to a point, but if we're borrowing their troops, we need thirty-six hours to offload and convert the transports," Henry noted. "And the Ratch contingent is going to be here in forty hours. The Tano convoy and our escorts will be about forty-two.

"That's not a lot of time for us to convince the locals of our good intentions and get their commitment."

"They're not even talking to you and you're worrying about their commitment to the invasion?" Todorovich asked. "Perhaps we should focus on the immediate concern, Captain."

"True enough." He checked the time. "So we wait, and then we call again. I can do patience, Ambassador. I just have to watch the timelines."

The silence continued to stretch on and he swallowed his disgruntlement.

"Commander Moon, let's get ready to transmit again. La-Tar and Vesheron co—"

"Incoming message, ser!" she reported. "Took them long enough."

"Our patience is necessary," Henry reminded her. "We did show up unexpectedly with a warship. Is it a live hail or a recorded message?"

"Recording, ser. We're too far away for a live channel."

It was still possible that someone might have tried it, but the question was a leftover from having subspace coms with everyone.

Even Henry wasn't changing his habits as fast as he thought he should.

"Play it, Commander," he ordered.

Something about the man on the screen seemed to project serene calm. He was another Tak like Captain Zast, his skin a pale shade of red no human would ever match that faded through pink to pure white at his extremities. Like his head tentacles, a slowly waving forest of white with a handful of darker spots from his age.

"I am Lord Casto Ran, the Lord Nominated of the Skex System," the stranger introduced himself. "I am pleased to see the food transports from our old friends the La-Tar, but the presence of strange soldiers and strange warships in my system is unwelcome.

"The apparent use of our system as a rendezvous point for a fleet is even less welcome, but I suppose that cannot be undone now. The La-Tar vessels may approach and I will speak with the La-Tar envoy. *Only* the La-Tar envoy. The UPA has no role here."

"Your warship and the transports carrying soldiers are not to approach within five light-seconds of my world, or my fleets will be forced to destroy you. Your presence in my system is accepted on sufferance only."

The recording ended and Henry shrugged.

"Honestly, I'm surprised our welcomes to date have been as warm as they have," he admitted. "He and I apparently have the same assessment of safe distance, too. Ambassador—let Rising Principle know they're heading down to the planet with their own bodyguards. We'll keep all UPSF personnel out of this for now.

"Moon—make sure Zast knows to take the food transports in and begin delivery," he continued. "We may as well pitch for as much goodwill as we can straight away. We'll play nice and we'll let Rising Principle explain their price."

"What do we do if this 'Lord Nominated' isn't willing to pay

Rising Principle's price, ser?" Iyotake asked softly as Henry's words sent people into motion.

"Not much," Henry admitted. "We hope that the heavy vehicles from Ratch make up for the fact that we're dropping almost seventy thousand fewer troops than La-Tar was hoping we'd bring back."

It might be enough. He was reasonably sure the Kozun weren't expecting to see multiple armored divisions hitting their positions on La-Tar.

It also might *not* be, and while Henry was reasonably confident he could get the ground forces down onto La-Tar at this point, he *wasn't* sure what he'd do if it turned into an ugly stalemate on the surface.

Everyone was hoping for a quick victory in the ground war, but he was grimly certain the fight could easily last weeks if it went *well*. If it went poorly, it could last months...and end with La-Tar's allies kicked off the planet.

The more resources they could bring to bear, the more likely it was they'd win quickly or the Kozun would surrender without much of a fight.

La-Tar needed Lord Casto Ran's soldiers. Henry could only hope that Rising Principle was up to negotiating for them.

CHAPTER THIRTY-FOUR

HAVING SPENT WELL OVER A WEEK WATCHING THE CONVOY LIKE they were his own metaphorical children, Henry wasn't really surprised that it made him nervous to send the last ten ships forward without *Raven*.

The single shuttle from *Raven* attached to the convoy didn't help. That shuttle carried ten people from La-Tar, a tiny delegation that right now felt like their only hope.

Despite his paranoia, there wasn't so much as a blip of difficulty, and Rising Principle's shuttle was quickly and efficiently guided down to the surface as the transports began the process of offloading food.

And then the waiting began.

"Dipping into their public communications, they've definitely been doing better than the other factory worlds on food," Moon told him. "There's rationing in place, but they're not reminding everyone of the limits every five minutes."

"Skex has an easier course to becoming a self-sufficient world than the others," Henry agreed. "I doubt they have enough food production to support themselves yet, but with this shipment and the relief convoy coming from home, they can probably stretch it out enough to get there."

"They might not even need La-Tar, then?" his coms officer asked.

The rest of the bridge officers were off duty, Henry trying to get his people rested in case things *did* go to pieces at some point soon. He wasn't expecting it now, but then, he hadn't expected the Gathering to explode into a multi-way melee.

There were enough people on the bridge to handle the ship until everyone made it to battle stations, but the space was still quieter than usual. It was technically ship's "night," except that Henry was still awake.

Technically, it was Moon's watch, but she hadn't even suggested he leave the bridge. She seemed to be drawing comfort from the captain's presence.

"It's possible that they think they can survive without La-Tar, yes," Henry finally confirmed. "They might even be right, but they don't have the strength to remain independent in the face of Kozun aggression alone."

"So, they need La-Tar."

"They need the other factory worlds," he corrected. "They need Tano's shipyards, if nothing else. Skex *would* have had their own in another decade or two, but right now...they can fix ships but they can't build skip drives.

"With Tano's help, they could fix that and provide the cluster with two serious shipyards," Henry said. "On their own, they might manage to combine the skip drives from the ships and whatever science databases they have to build their own sooner or later, but it will take time.

"Time I doubt the First Voice will give them."

"He'll know it's a possibility, won't he?" Moon asked.

Henry nodded.

"Tano, then Skex," he concluded aloud. "Ratch and Atto are valuable, but they can't build starships, so they can be left to concede from hunger in the longer-term. Tano and Skex need to be brought in by force now that we've interrupted the short-term plan to starve them out."

The communications officer looked at the tactical display.

"Do you think the Lord Nominated knows that?" she asked.

"I assume so," Henry said. "Which means Lord Casto Ran needs a way out. I presume he has a plan, but our presence is a new variable for him. We'll see how he judges it."

"Surely, working with us is his best option?" his subordinate suggested.

"That depends on whether you think we'll win," Henry admitted. "In Ran's place...he's got enough security here that betraying us to the Kozun might just buy him enough goodwill to come in with some independence rather than as a slave world."

"Would that be enough for him?"

"In his place? I'd fight," the battlecruiser captain said with a chuckle. "But that's a very human reaction, I think, and even so...I think many people would look at three hundred million people under their protection and make the decision that got them the best you could.

"Even if that 'best' is far from perfect."

HENRY HAD FINALLY RETREATED to his quarters to engage in an unproductive session of staring at walls when Todorovich contacted him. He had been about to use his network to force himself to sleep—the implants were entirely capable of that, though his therapists generally recommended against it—when she called, leaving him grateful for the interruption.

"Ambassador," he greeted her virtual avatar. "There's news?"

"Rising Principle managed to meet with the Lord Nominated more quickly than we expected," she told him. "Unfortunately, they didn't meet with the Lord Nominated alone."

"I'm hoping we're talking a fancy royal court and not what I'm afraid of," Henry said slowly as he processed her words.

"There is a Kozun representative on Skex. The planet hasn't surrendered yet but has apparently been actively negotiating for a better deal."

"If the Kozun envoy was in the same room, that can't have gone well," he said grimly.

"Rising Principle thinks they were provoked and may have screwed up," Todorovich agreed. "On the other hand, from what I've seen of the recordings, I think Rising Principle may be underestimating how well they handled it.

"Casto Ran was clearly intending to set up an argument-and-counterargument session, but the Kozun representative attempted to *arrest* Rising Principle on the spot," she continued. "When Rising Principle, obviously, didn't go along with that, it seems our spike-headed friend *ordered* Ran to intern Principle."

"So, our enemy started digging and kept digging," Henry concluded. "Handy, that."

"They did let Ran talk them down and there *was* a bit of a conversation, but the Kozun very clearly believe that La-Tar is impregnable to anything we can do—and Rising Principle isn't going to tell the Kozun ambassador that his parent has strike battalions ready to knock out the Guardian platforms!"

"Is there any chance of them getting a private meeting with Lord Casto Ran?" he asked.

"I understand the game the Kozun were playing, but I think it was the wrong game to play here," Todorovich told him. "They're trying to present themselves as the legitimate power, with Rising Principle as a rebel. Their arguments for the envoy's arrest came from a position of supposed authority, one that could have supported the sense of legitimacy they're clearly trying to cultivate here."

"And what has it actually got them?"

"An invitation for us to send UPSF troops to reinforce the envoy's bodyguard," Todorovich told him. "*Officially*, that's all."

"And unofficially, Sylvia?" Henry asked.

"Casto Ran is stuck, Henry," she concluded. "I don't know when the Kozun envoy is expecting a courier ship, but its probably before we're planning on deploying. He's been playing for time and the bill is now due: he has to pick a side. He can either go with the Kozun and use one of his ships to warn them about everything we've gathered, or he can side with us and intern their envoy and courier ship.

"And the envoy knows that and almost certainly has contingency plans for it," she continued. "So, he can't openly talk to us. So, you and I need to go to Skex on that shuttle with the extra bodyguards. Officially, it's a minor concession to demonstrate that the Lord Nominated isn't impressed with the Kozun's posturing."

"And unofficially, he wants to meet with you."

"Us, Henry," Todorovich countered. "The name of the Destroyer carries weight here."

"Any one of thirty officers could have ordered the shot that killed the last Kenmorad," Henry said grimly. It had *happened* to be his ship that had destroyed the last breeding sect and condemned the Kenmiri to slow extinction, but it could have been any of the UPSF ships in Operation Golden Lancelot.

"But it *was* you," she said. "And I know you hate it, but it's not a weapon you can lay aside, either, Henry."

He *really* didn't want to leave his ship. It wasn't appropriate. It wasn't safe—technically, Thompson could still overrule him and say he wasn't allowed to leave the ship. His place was on the bridge of his warship.

And how much of *that*, he wondered, was a reaction to everything that had gone wrong at the Gathering and at Tano? That was something to flag for his counselors, he supposed. For today... He inhaled sharply.

"All right," he told her. "I'll talk to Commander Thompson about sorting out the right kind of detail. Remember that he *is* allowed to bar me from leaving the ship."

"This should be safe enough, Henry. I'll talk to him if he decides to be stubborn," she warned. "We need Skex's soldiers and Skex needs us. Even if the Lord Nominated is going to be stubborn about it."

✦✦✦

"MAKES SENSE, SER," Alex Thompson said cheerfully after Henry filled him in. "We'll send down a heavier force than I would send to guard the La-Tar Envoy and we'll use an assault shuttle, though. A full platoon, heavy gear.

"That will help conceal you, too. The Kozun might know what you look like, but they aren't IDing *anything* behind full body armor and an energy weapon."

Henry snorted as he glanced around the GroundDiv officer's office. It was a smaller space and chaotically disorganized. There was presumably an order to the datapads and pieces of gear around the room, but Henry couldn't divine it.

"Aren't you supposed to be the one who *stops* the captain going off on damn-fool missions?" Henry asked.

"Yes," Thompson agreed. "But they hammer that the captain is also a diplomat into us pretty hard. There *are* jobs that require the captain to leave the ship, and the *last* thing I'm supposed to do is stop the captain doing their job.

"What would be irresponsible of me, much as I would like to, is for me to come down with you," he continued. "I'll send Lieutenant Biondo. Peer is my best platoon CO, he's probably due for a bump to Lieutenant Commander and his own company when we get back to Fallout."

"A whole platoon seems a little excessive, doesn't it?" Henry asked.

"Maybe. But the locals didn't specify how large a bodyguard we were allowed to send, only that they wanted us to reinforce Rising Principle's security," the GroundDiv officer told him. "I'd send ten troopers if that's all I was doing, but if we're sending you down as well, I want to send more.

"And it doubles down on the impression that we think the envoy is worth protecting, too."

"Which we do," Henry agreed.

"Exactly. I'm not the diplomat here, ser, but I'm guessing that the more visibly the UPA supports Rising Principle, the better off they are in the negotiations."

"That would be my guess as well, but I'm not a diplomat either," Henry said. He'd done the job before and he'd almost certainly do it again, but he was happy to leave it to Todorovich whenever he could.

"We'll be ready in an hour," Thompson told him. "We should have you on the surface by local dawn in the capital. I can accelerate some of that, but..."

"That sounds fine, Commander," Henry replied. "I could use a nap."

Marine assault shuttles didn't have artificial gravity, only inertial compensators. The faster the trip, the more uncomfortable it was going to be for the passengers. Henry would rather sleep on a shuttle under one pseudogravity than five.

"We'll keep you informed, ser," the other man promised. "It'll be a safe-enough trip, even if the Kozun *do* pull something."

CHAPTER THIRTY-FIVE

THE STANDARD FULL BODYSUIT OF THE UNITED PLANETS SPACE Force that acted as the underlayer to every version of their uniforms was perfectly functional as light body armor. It wouldn't stand up to energy weapons or sustained projectile fire, but it was expected to stop debris and act as a space suit on its own if needed.

Henry had occasionally worn armor over the bodysuit, but that had usually been an ad hoc affair. On one memorable occasion, his Vesheron allies had crammed him into the no-longer-needed armor of a Kenmiri Warrior.

That was probably the closest he'd come to putting on the assemblage the UPSF's Ground Division regarded as "heavy armor." This armor, at least, was designed for someone with the right proportions and number of limbs.

It had taken two of Thompson's armorers almost ten minutes to lock Henry into the multiple interlocking shells and layers that now covered him from head to toe in ballistic- and energy-resistant plating.

The troopers around him moved far more easily in the armor than he would have thought was *possible*. Several of them had helped him get into a position where he could actually sleep on the shuttle, though he suspected he'd pay for that later.

The armor was surprisingly comfortable and supportive to rest in, but it was still armor. *Surprisingly comfortable* didn't mean *actually* comfortable.

His only solace was that Todorovich had been crammed into her own suit of armor, and she was even worse at moving in the equipment than he was.

"Please tell me we can take this off once we're on the surface," she asked him silently over the network as they began their descent to the Lord Nominated's capital. "This is…"

She trailed off into a stream of Russian that Henry didn't understand in the slightest.

"We're following the Lord Nominated's guidance on that," he told her. "We try and look moderately useful alongside the rest of the team while we join Rising Principle's people.

"The envoy will know where to go from there, right?" he asked.

"I hope so," she agreed. "I can negotiate in any situation you drop me into, Captain, but I think I'd *rather* be naked than in this…case."

"The good news is that it will stop an energy-weapon shot," Henry told her cheerfully. "Potentially even two!"

"You're…kidding me, right?"

"We can't build something wearable by a regular trooper that can reliably stop more than one energy bolt," he reminded her. "This armor is rated to stop one shot. Our lighter armors can't even do that."

"Wonderful," she said. "Why did I agree to this?"

"Because the Lord Nominated wants to talk to us in secret and we need him," Henry replied.

"Right," she confirmed. "So, we play along for now. I *hope* that the Skex at least let us change before we meet with him, though. I'm not sure he wants to be talking to faceless statues."

"The helmets *do* come off," Henry said. "We just don't want to do that until we're sure we're in private."

HENRY DOUBTED that he was doing a very good job of dupli-cating the easy motion of the GroundDiv troopers around him. To help, though, it seemed that Biondo had put him in the middle of an entire squad and done the same with Todorovich.

Hopefully, their awkwardness would be disguised by sheer numbers as the platoon of troopers marched off the shuttle. There was a young-looking Ashall officer waiting for them, who seemed more than a little taken aback by the number and weight of the GroundDiv contingent.

"We were...we were not expecting quite so many of you," she finally squeaked out in awkwardly accented Kem.

"The United Planets Alliance values our alliance with the legiti-mate government of La-Tar," Lieutenant Biondo said loudly and clearly in perfect Kem. "We are prepared to respect Skex's sover-eignty, but given the opportunity to protect our ally, we will do so with all necessary strength."

"Of course," the officer said swiftly. "If you will follow me, then. I will have to call ahead and make certain we have enough space."

"We are at Envoy Rising Principle's disposal," Biondo agreed genially.

The UPSF officer couldn't have been doing better, in Henry's opinion. Part of the point of this exercise, after all, was both to make clear to the locals that the UPA backed Rising Principle and their government, *and* that the UPA had the strength to make that a mean-ingful allegiance.

In Henry's opinion, all anyone needed to do for the latter was look at the success rates of UPSF battlecruisers against Kenmiri warships. Send *enough* ships at *Raven* and he'd get nervous—and the Guardian platforms on La-Tar were a giant headache—but there was almost nothing in space he'd worry about facing one-on-one.

The Skex officer led them across a landing pad identical to the ones on any number of ex-Kenmiri worlds to a set of vehicles that were equally standard. She looked at the trucks, then back at the UPSF contingent.

"We did not provide enough transportation," she admitted.

"That is perfectly fine," Biondo replied. "We can march. How far is it to the envoy's quarters?"

"Perhaps three kilometers," the officer said. "If you wish, a portion of your troops can ride with you?"

"I will not ask my soldiers to march while I ride a vehicle," Biondo said firmly. "We march together. Show us the way, ma'am."

Henry agreed entirely with the young Ground Division officer's intentions and principles...but in that moment, realizing he was going to have to walk *three kilometers* in the damned heavy armor suit, he hated the young man.

A lot.

EVEN WITH THE armor's built-in cooling systems, Henry was a sweaty mess by the time they reached their destination and met up with the soldiers Rising Principle had brought from La-Tar.

He doubted the GroundDiv troopers around him were doing *that* much better. They were more practiced at this than he was, but three kilometers in a suit of heavy armor couldn't be easy for anyone.

"Squad Three, reinforce the exterior security," Biondo ordered.

Henry was reasonably sure Squad Three was the one that didn't have a deadweight SpaceDiv officer or a diplomat. Those two squads were quickly ushered in with Biondo and the officer—who'd never given a name or asked Biondo's, he realized.

She paused and bowed slightly to the senior La-Tar trooper.

"The Lord Nominated wishes to speak with the La-Tar Envoy in private in two hours," she told the other woman in the Kem that was everyone's shared language. "Four escorts will be permitted."

"Of course," the La-Tar soldier replied. "I will pass on his request to Envoy Rising Principle."

The Skex woman glanced around, then made a short but sweeping bow that seemed to encompass everyone in the room before silently sweeping out.

"You...fulfilled the Lord Nominated's request?" the La-Tar noncom asked Biondo. "I am Trosh, the head of Rising Principle's security detachment. I am relieved to see you either way."

So far as Henry understood, Trosh only had six people. The other three members of Rising Principle's nine-person support team were civilian staffers. The extra troopers would be the difference between her people being able to sleep and having to somehow manage to stay awake.

"We brought them," Biondo confirmed. "Is this residence secure?"

The building put at Rising Principle's disposal was, like the landing pad and most structures they'd seen on Skex, a standard structure for visiting Kenmiri. It looked like a set of tenements on Earth, a series of narrow three-story houses crammed next to each other.

It looked like the interior had been opened up, with multiple arches linking what had been three units into a single larger apartment intended for a visiting diplomat.

"We are inside the security perimeter of the old Governor's palace, which the Lord Nominated is operating out of," Trosh told them. "We have scanned for electronic recorders, but a second scan would be wise before we treat the building as secure."

"Shallot, Roi," Biondo said loudly, gesturing for his squad chiefs to come to him. "Scan the building," he ordered in English. "The La-Tar scanned for bugs, but we have different tools. We want to be certain before we unwrap the packages."

With the helmet concealing his face, Henry allowed himself to grimace. He was really hoping to be able to *shower* before they had to face the Lord Nominated in person.

He really didn't want to argue the fates of worlds while drenched in old sweat.

CHAPTER THIRTY-SIX

KENMIRI CLEANING FACILITIES WERE ALWAYS AN ADVENTURE, but Henry did at least manage to get himself refreshed before he was helped back into the armor for his role as Rising Principle's "bodyguard" for the meeting with the Lord Nominated.

The officer who guided them across the palace complex didn't seem to know that there were extra dignitaries hidden amongst the Enteni's guards, and Henry wondered just how insecure the Lord Nominated thought his facilities were.

If Casto Ran believed he couldn't hide things from the Kozun in his own palace, he really was trapped. Staying neutral wasn't going to be a good option for Skex regardless, but if the Kozun delegation had been *that* active...

It wasn't a good sign.

Henry was surprised by their destination as well. Their guide took them past the main building, a decorative three-peaked pyramid in a modern Kenmiri architectural style, to a bunker door concealed in the shadow of a natural hill.

"This way, please," the guide ordered.

A Kenmiri governor's palace was a relatively standardized structure. It might be shaped by the standards of the Artisan who designed the final structure, but they all shared certain features, including an underground shielded command center.

The blast door opened to reveal an unadorned security lobby, which they were ushered through without any security checks. Behind the guards was an elevator that dropped rapidly into the ground, and the officer visibly sighed in relief and relaxed.

"Access to the command center is heavily restricted," he told them. "While Envoy Nar Rojan has been here, we swept the facility after he left."

Henry grimaced behind his helmet. He didn't know *Nar* Rojan, but Kozun noble family names worked much the same way as they did in English. Nar Rojan was quite possibly related to Kal Rojan—who Henry had vaporized at the Gathering.

"This is as secure as possible. The Lord Nominated is waiting for you all. Let us hurry."

The elevator came to a halt, and Henry and his companions followed the young Skex officer deeper into the underground complex. Hopefully, all of this rigmarole was a *good* sign.

"YOU CAN TAKE the helmets off, Captain, Ambassador," Casto Ran told them as the door closed behind the last of Henry's bodyguards.

The space they'd been led to was the governor's emergency office. Heavy cloths covered the walls, presumably hiding Kenmiri murals that hadn't yet been removed, but the furniture was still the heavy and functional but baroque stylings of a high-ranked Kenmiri Artisan.

One of the cloths was a tapestry showing what Henry guessed to be a historical scene of a stylized hunt. The animal being hunted was like nothing he'd ever seen and the scene had three moons, so it definitely wasn't from Skex.

Henry checked his network in silence as he removed his helmet and took an indicated seat. The Tak homeworld apparently did have three moons. The scene, at least, was from the pre-Kenmiri history of Casto Ran's people.

The *tapestry* had probably been made on Skex, but the people there had been brought directly from their homeworlds. Even as the Kenmiri had intentionally divided up the ethnicities, cultures and even species they brought to their slave worlds, they couldn't break up people's memories of their homes.

"Welcome to Skex, Captain Wong, Ambassador Todorovich," Lord Ran told them. "I presume Envoy Rising Principle updated you on our previous meeting?"

"The Kozun have an interesting method of negotiating," Todorovich said carefully.

"That they do," Ran confirmed. "Of course, they have all the ships and all the food. Your delivery buys me some time, but I do not see any real new choices present."

"Then why invite us here?" Henry asked.

"To see if you *can* present a new choice," the Skex leader told him. "Are you familiar with the Tak tradition of the Lord Nominated?"

"I have not yet visited Taklan," Todorovich said. "Your people's culture is new to me, beyond the fragments that survive on the slave worlds."

"More survives here on Skex than on other worlds," the old Tak noted. "That would not have lasted forever—I am familiar with the worlds like us—but we clung to it for now.

"The Lord Nominated is an individual granted near-absolute power for a specific term and a specific purpose, nominated by community leaders and approved by as close to a mass vote as possible," he continued. "I have a twenty-seven-month term to stabilize our food situation and set up a long-term government.

"At the end of those twenty-seven months, I will either resign or be assassinated." Ran spread his hands palm down. "It is a very pragmatic tradition."

Earth's history had the Roman dictators, Henry reflected. When the system had worked, it had helped the Republic resolve several key crises. It had also been a contributing factor in why the Roman Republic had become the Roman *Empire*.

"Your food situation is-was a problem," Rising Principle said. "Without La-Tar, you can-will risk starvation."

"But unlike the other factory worlds, we merely *risk* it," Ran replied. "The Kozun control La-Tar. That does not make you a criminal in my mind, Envoy Rising Principle, but it does make them the real power. They control the food supply. They have the fleet to defeat mine. I do not see options to change that."

"They exist," Henry told him. "But you understand that we do not wish those planets to end up in the possession of the Kozun."

"You have one battlecruiser, Captain Wong," the local replied. "Your reputation and the reputation of the UPSF precede you, but you have one ship. The Kozun have many. They were ready for war against the Kenmiri and moved quickly to pick up resources after the Kenmiri withdrew.

"You can't fight a war with one ship. You have soldiers from Atto. I presume Ratch and Tano have put up soldiers as well, but the Kozun assure me that La-Tar is impregnable." He spread his hands palm-down again.

"My first, last and only responsibility is to protect the people of Skex. I swore ancient and sacred oaths and I *will* honor them. The Kozun are not the Kenmiri. They *can* be negotiated with—and Skex is both powerful enough and valuable enough to negotiate my people a better place than as slaves."

"Except you are negotiating with Mal Dakis," Henry said quietly. "I know him of old, Lord Ran. He will keep as few of his promises as he can. If certain individuals must die to make his breaking promises easier, those individuals will die.

"He will not break the letter of his agreements, but he will twist the meaning until the words are useless. You were Vesheron, Lord Ran?"

"I was," Casto Ran confirmed. "The ships in orbit were mine, a tiny squadron of raiders against the might of the Kenmiri—but this was my home."

"And when you returned home, did you murder your leaders and proclaim yourself a prophet as your fastest means to power?" Henry asked.

"No. I placed myself and my ships at the disposal of the leaders here. I did not expect or desire *this*." He gestured at the office. "But my people needed me."

"And now they need you to remember that being a Vesheron meant more than just fighting *against* something," Henry told him. "We were fighting *for* something. All of us. What did you fight for, Lord Ran?"

The Lord Nominated was silent.

"Was it money? Power? Freedom? Freedom for yourself or for your home?" Henry asked. "Would you abandon that now when I swear to you there *is* a chance?"

"My oath is to these people," Ran repeated. "A *chance* isn't enough, Captain Wong, not when failure dooms the people I am sworn to protect to slavery."

"But you'd abandon the La-Tar to slavery? Even after they refused to abandon you to starvation?"

The room was silent again.

"My duty is to *my* people," Ran finally repeated. "I may not like what that calls upon me to do, Captain Wong, but if I must choose my people over the La-Tar, I will. Debts are not forgotten, but I cannot enslave my people for nothing."

"And what happens if we win without you, Lord Ran?" Henry asked. "Do you think the Kozun will feed you then? Or do you think, even as a Kozun vassal, you'll be able to buy food from La-Tar?"

"La-Tar would still sell us food," Ran said calmly. "Wouldn't they, Rising Principle?"

Henry gestured the envoy to silence.

"You know this," he said. "Doesn't that tell you *everything,* Lord Casto Ran? About your people and who will be the better friend to them?"

"I invited you to bring an ambassador and a soldier," Lord Ran said after a few more moments of silence. "I will admit I expected the ambassador to speak more and the soldier to *see* less."

"It seemed that Captain Wong understood your position better than I," Todorovich demurred.

"So he does," the Tak agreed. He rose, turning away from them to study the tapestry behind him. His head-tendrils shivered in some kind of emotion Henry couldn't read at this angle.

"The Kozun have agents scattered throughout this palace, but I do not believe their reach has stretched much beyond this center of government," he said. "I have negotiated with them in honor and I believe that Nar Rojan has negotiated in honor, but I do not know Mal Dakis.

"The terms Nar Rojan has offered are...better than the Kenmiri but hardly full and equal membership in the Hierarchy. You are correct, Captain Wong, that I fought for freedom for my home."

He was silent again.

"For all of the power of the Lord Nominated, this is not a decision I feel I can make alone," he finally told them. He turned to face them—to face Henry in specific, locking gazes with the UPSF captain.

"Swear to me, Captain Wong, on the blood of the Kenmorad, that you *have* a plan. That La-Tar *can* be liberated."

"We have a plan," Henry told him levelly. "The odds without your ships and your soldiers are...even. *With* your support, victory becomes more likely than not, but nothing is guaranteed."

"I would not trust you if you said it was," Lord Casto Ran admitted. "I will speak with others, Captain Wong. I make no promises yet, but you have at least shown me there may be other choices."

CHAPTER THIRTY-SEVEN

IT TOOK LONGER TO GET HENRY OFF OF SKEX THAN IT HAD taken to get him onto the planet. He was reasonably sure it was all worth it, but by the time he was back aboard *Raven*'s bridge, he'd been missing for just under thirty hours.

Long enough that they were expecting the Ratch convoy to show up any minute, resulting in him heading straight to the bridge.

"Ser! Welcome back," Iyotake greeted him, the big man rising from the command chair to yield it to Henry. "I hope the trip was productive."

"I think so, but nothing has been decided yet, so it's hard to be sure," Henry admitted. "My *impression* is that Casto Ran is leaning our way but concerned about Kozun agents in his palace. He could also just be a very good liar."

"I wouldn't side with the Kozun, but I guess that's me," Iyotake replied. "Ratch convoy is expected in the next three hours or so. We weren't getting updates from them, but they seemed to have a solid idea of when they'd be leaving."

Henry nodded. They did know almost exactly when to expect the Tano convoy with its two UPSF destroyers, since there was a steady stream of drones flowing both ways. *Deinonychus* and *Hadrosaur* were due in six hours, along with the Tano forces.

And Councilor Inbar. There was a senior Atto official in the convoy Henry already had, too. If the Ratch sent someone who could speak for Father Astemar, there'd be an...*interesting* cluster of political power in the Skex System as they prepared for war.

So far, the Atto envoy had kept her head down. She might have been helpful in convincing Ran to come onboard, but Henry honestly figured that if Rising Principle couldn't, no one could.

"Skip signature," Lieutenant Ybarra reported. The assistant tactical officer was currently heading up the tactical department for this watch. "Wait...that's on the line from Atris, not the course from Ratch."

Atris was the name of the blue hypergiant that allowed Skex and Atto forty-eight-hour travel to La-Tar. Someone had apparently loaded the La-Tar naming schema into their navigation computers.

"That makes our guest Kozun," Iyotake said. "That's...a problem."

"We knew Nar Rojan was communicating with the Hierarchy," Henry replied. "There was going to be a courier of some kind sooner or later. Right now, Skex is neutral space."

He watched the orange "unknown contact" blob start moving toward the planet.

"We're not actually at war with the Kozun and we're in formally neutral territory," he continued. "We keep *Raven* between the transports and the Kozun, to block their sensors as much as anything else, but we take no aggressive action."

"Do we order them to stay out of missile range?" Iyotake asked.

"If the Skex don't give them an orbit that keeps them at least five light-seconds from us, yes," Henry confirmed. "We'll let Lord Ran's people set the tone for now. We will be completely respectful of neutral space right up to the moment they threaten us or the convoy."

"And then we blow them to hell?" his XO asked.

"Exactly."

"SO, in the absence of a real set of *rules* around this...anybody want to know what Skex is saying to our new friend?" Moon asked. The communications officer wasn't supposed to be on duty for another three hours, but she had appeared shortly after the report of a stranger in the system.

Henry doubted she was the only member of crew hovering around a duty station they weren't technically on. As a department head, though, she had the ability to take over in a way many of his subordinates didn't.

"Should we really be eavesdropping?" he replied. "It seems rude."

"Old Earth international rules would say *no*, but the Gathering blew up before we got anything that looked like a set of 'interstellar waters' laws or anything like that," she said cheerfully. "I've got a drone close enough to pick up the edge of their transmissions, and everyone is sending in the clear right now, anyway."

There was a tiny, futile war between his conscience and his curiosity, and then his curiosity received reinforcements from duty.

"Summarize," he ordered.

"The Skex have ordered them to remain at least five light-seconds from us and are ordering them into a high orbit of the planet, well away from the food transports," she told him. "They're also requiring that the Kozun power down their weapons."

"And how are the Kozun taking all of that?" Henry asked.

"Poorly," Moon confirmed. "They haven't quite proceeded to threats yet, but there's been some *implications* made."

"From here it looks like she's pretty laser-heavy," Ybarra told them. "The Skex *will* be able to tell if her capacitors are charged."

The vessel heading toward Skex was a close cousin if not a sibling of the ship that had been stalking *Raven* before. Today they had a far better view of the ship, an eighty-meter-long needle in space probably built around her lasers.

"She's heading in at point eight KPS squared," Ybarra continued. "Looks like she's got quite a bit of both thrust and compensation in reserve."

"Is she honoring the order to power down her guns?" Henry asked.

"Impossible to tell from here," the tactical officer admitted. "The *Skex* will know once she makes orbit, but we're still five light-seconds out."

"Makes sense," Henry conceded. He glanced at the time. "Their timing could be worse, I suppose," he admitted. "We're still an hour from expecting our first wave of ships."

"There is no way in *hell* that corvette is leaving system before the transports arrive, ser," Iyotake told him.

"I know. But at least we'll be in a better position to *intercept* her once they do," he noted. "I'll honor Skex's neutrality, but that corvette does *not* get back to La-Tar with news of our invasion fleet. We take her in Atris if we have to, but we *take* her."

"Understood," his XO said grimly.

The Kozun ship was no threat to *Raven*. Henry was relatively sure that O'Flannagain's fighters could actually take her down without much difficulty. But if she escaped to carry news back to La-Tar and the rest of the Kozun Hierarchy, the entire invasion plan could be in serious trouble.

"Sounds like the envoy has become involved," Moon reported. "It doesn't sound like Rojan is actually trying to calm things down, though. He *is* conceding the security zone around our ships, but he is refusing to order his ship to power down her guns."

"It sounds like Nar Rojan is much less clever than his brother," Henry said softly. "Threatening the Skex at this point is a *bad* idea."

Moon exhaled slowly.

"It sounds like the Lord Nominated is now involved and has conceded the point," she reported. "The corvette will be allowed to enter orbit with her weapons active."

Henry paused before saying anything, making sure he'd heard Moon correctly.

"That's surprising," he admitted. "I would have expected Ran to back his people up there."

"It didn't sound like the Kozun were going to give way," she said. "If he wants to keep all of his doors open, he had to concede, I think."

He wished Todorovich had come back aboard with him. She was still on the surface with Rising Principle, holding secret meetings with people sent to their quarters by the Lord Nominated. Not only was he lacking her counsel, but he was also suddenly unsure of her safety on the surface.

"I don't like it," he admitted. "The Kozun won't let Skex stay neutral, not at this point."

Which meant he had to start making preparations for if everything went wrong.

"Keep me in the loop," he ordered. "I'm going to talk to O'Flannagain."

It took him a few seconds to open a channel to the CAG.

"Ser, we're awake," she greeted him. "Birds are fueled; missiles are loaded. Give the word and that corvette is *not* getting out of this system."

"It might just come to that, Commander," Henry told her. "You're already loaded?"

"We started prepping the birds the moment we had a skip signature, ser," she said. "Can't be too careful."

"Good call," he agreed. "I don't think I quite need you all strapped into your ships, not yet, anyway." He studied the scans of the ship for a long moment and sighed. "There's a good chance that corvette can match your acceleration, Commander. Her engines are way out of scale for her mass."

"The vector's in our favor for now, plus we *know* when to expect our allies to show up," she pointed out. "That's when everything's going to go to hell, right?"

"Probably," he agreed. "Stay on the command channel for now,

O'Flannagain," he ordered. "Who knows what wrench is going to get thrown in the works next."

"Not me," the fighter pilot agreed cheerfully. "I leave guessing that stuff to you, ser. I just make sure you have eight fighters ready to blow shit up on your command."

Which was an improvement over when she'd barely been conscious of anything outside her own bird, at least.

"Thank you, CAG," he said.

"Corvette is ten minutes from orbit," Ybarra reported. "They're shifting the escorts around to keep them between her and the food transports. I think the Lord Nominated's people don't trust the Kozun *not* to try and blow up the food supply."

"The ships are empty now, aren't they?" Henry asked. "All they'd manage is to piss the Skex off."

"They're practically treating the Skex as a conquered colony already," Iyotake said softly. "They might do it just to make a—"

"Skip signatures," Ybarra interrupted. "Multiple skip signatures along the expected line from Ratch. I'm reading ten ships, exactly as expected."

"We're receiving encoded burst transmissions as well," Moon reported. "A General Olmar sends Father Astemar's rega—"

"*Holy shit!*"

Ybarra's report wasn't formal or useful, but it yanked everyone's attention to the main tactical display in time to watch all four of the escorts in Skex orbit open fire on the Kozun corvette. One moment, the vessel was decelerating into an orbit above the planetary capital, presumably just getting the lightspeed data on the Ratch convoy's arrival.

The next, it was an expanding cloud of debris as sixteen heavy lasers intersected on her hull.

The Lord Nominated, it appeared, had finally chosen a side.

CHAPTER THIRTY-EIGHT

"It appears that our Tak friend was waiting for a sign that we had more going for us than words and promises," Todorovich's hologram told Henry. "He had people ready to move on Nar Rojan the moment he made his decision.

"We've been asked to remain inside the residence we were given, but I've definitely heard gunfire. I doubt the Kozun delegation went quietly."

"If Nar Rojan is anything like his relative, Casto Ran may have underestimated the fight on his hands," Henry said. "I'm holding the convoys at five light-seconds until Ran has confirmed his position and situation.

"There's a General Olmar in charge of the Ratch convoy who I'll invite aboard *Raven* once they join up with us. Current ETA is about two hours."

"I suspect the locals will have everything sorted out by then, but you know better than I how uncertain this kind of situation is," she admitted ten seconds later, their conversation being dragged out by the distance.

"Yes," Henry confirmed. The UPA had mostly sent their diplomats to relatively stable Vesheron bases. While Todorovich certainly hadn't avoided the fighting, she hadn't been on the ground during active insurrections.

Henry had. The memories were part of why he wanted to stay a long way away from anything resembling a ground operation.

"Trust Lieutenant Biondo," he told her. "GroundDiv trains for this and you don't. Listen to your guards, Ambassador."

"I know that much, Captain Wong," Todorovich replied. "We're hunkered down until we hear more from our host. I had to practically sit on Rising Principle to keep them from trying to help."

"That would be a...bad idea," Henry agreed. "We can't afford to lose the La-Tar Envoy at this point."

"They're smart enough to listen," she said. "I'm not even sure I can call Principle inexperienced anymore. They've risen to this pretty well. I've definitely had pupils who were worse at this job."

"Should we be planning on invoicing La-Tar for diplomat training, then?" Henry asked, hoping to bring some levity to a stressful moment.

"Right after we invoice them for rental of a battlecruiser," Todorovich agreed with a chuckle. "I'll update you as soon as I hear from Lord Ran," she continued. "He's made his choice very clear. Now it's just a question of what contingency plans the Kozun had in place."

"We'll be here," he assured her. "We're waiting on my destroyers and the Tano contingent regardless."

He was confident that the Lord Nominated would retain control of the planet, after all...but he also didn't want to underestimate anyone trained by Kal Rojan and handpicked by the First Voice for this kind of situation.

Mal Dakis, after all, seemed to have a habit of sending assassins as ambassadors.

V

THE NEXT TWO hours brought a slew of explosions at key points around the old governor's palace. None were major bombs, but from what Henry could see, they were throwing the Skex response into disarray.

"The good news is that nothing seems to have spilled outside the Palace," Ihejirika told the rest of the bridge crew.

All of Henry's senior officers were on the bridge now. Only Iyotake was supposed to be on watch now; the bridge officers had filtered in as the crisis continued and the Ratch convoy approached.

"There's a perimeter of regular soldiers moved into place to secure the exterior," the tactical officer continued the impromptu briefing. "Most of the fighting seems to be led by a specific unit that was assigned to the defense of the Lord Nominated.

"The fact that the Kozun seem to have co-opted as much as a quarter of that particular unit is probably going to lead to all kinds of witch hunts tomorrow, but the fighting is contained and the situation appears to be under control."

"So far as I can tell, Casto Ran is also only using the surface structures as a decoy," Henry noted. "When we met with him in private, it was in the command center under the palace. Is there any sign those have been penetrated?"

"The main entrance to the bunker appears to be where the fighting is now concentrated," Ihejirika said. "The explosions allowed the insurgents to focus the forces they have, but they're also up against probably the single most fortified point in the complex.

"That Ran hasn't brought additional troops in suggests he either thinks the situation is well in hand or he doesn't trust them," the Nigerian officer concluded. "Either way, there's not much we can do."

"What about the ambassador and the envoy?" Iyotake asked, the XO looking at the overhead image of the palace complex.

"There was an attempt to attack their residence, but it was limited and broke off after they ran into GroundDiv," Ihejirika reported. "It didn't look like they were expecting to succeed, only that they wanted us to know we were remembered."

"Rojan can't have that many resources," Henry said. "He had a delegation of what, fifteen Kozun? Everyone else he recruited on the surface."

He shook his head.

"Money and promises of status in a conquered world apparently go further than any of us expected," he noted. "Any word from Ran or his people yet?"

"I suspect the fact that we have full communication with our people is a good sign, but no," Moon told him. "Not a peep out of the local government directed to us."

Henry looked at the other tactical display, the one showing the Ratch convoy decelerating into company with the transports carrying the Atto troops.

"It appears I will be briefing General Olmar," he said grimly. "The Tano contingent is due shortly as well. Keep an eye on matters on the surface for me, people. The last thing we want to do is intervene, but I'll want a shuttle prepped to pull our delegation out if it looks necessary."

This was already taking longer than he'd hoped.

"CAPTAIN WONG," the Ashall officer in the hologram greeted him. The man had the same tusks at the corners of his mouth as General Kansa, though his short-cropped hair was a shade of black shared by most Ashall races, unlike her natural purple.

"General Olmar," Henry replied. "Your arrival appears to have set off quite the sequence of events on Skex. The Lord Nominated was waiting for us to prove our promises before acting—and your arrival seems to have counted."

"Should I be expecting to need to land on Skex?" the General asked, his Kem perfect. In fact...the Ashall had a *Kenmiri* accent, which meant he was almost certainly one of the janissaries, the slave-soldiers the Empire had used for "peacekeeping" duties across their territories.

"I do not think that will be necessary," Henry said. "Lord Ran appears to have anticipated the problems and have plans in place. The situation is taking longer to resolve than I imagine anyone expected, but it does appear to be resolving."

A chime interrupted Henry's thoughts, and he opened the message in his network.

Skip signature. Lieutenant Colonels Pololáník and Spini send their regards and acknowledge you as Task Force Commander.

That was an unnecessary formality but a useful one. He smiled calmly.

"And another update, it seems," he told General Olmar. "Our friends from Tano have arrived, as have my reinforcements from the United Planets Alliance. Once the situation on Skex resolves, we will be able to discuss our next steps with full awareness of our resources."

"Of course," Olmar agreed. "If possible, we'll want to reallocate the vehicles I'm transporting to the other transports before we leave for La-Tar." He paused. "The training on the heavy tanks is complex enough that I am retaining all of them for my own soldiers. Janissaries from other worlds should have been trained on the light tanks and other combat vehicles.

"I have two thousand four hundred and eighty-two light tanks, eleven thousand five hundred and seventy armored personal carriers, eleven hundred and fifty-six mobile artillery pieces and eight thousand nine hundred and five recon weapon platforms to distribute to our allies," he continued. "They are a *loan* unless payment is established later, but we do not have the personnel to deploy them.

"La-Tar will be better served by us deploying our maximum strength as an alliance than by those vehicles sitting unused in the extra cargo holds of the ships they have loaned us."

"Captain Zast is better able to speak to the transshipment capabilities we have available," Henry admitted. "She is currently in orbit of Skex with the transports that delivered food and are awaiting the Lord Nominated's army.

"We should be able to transfer those vehicles, but you will need to talk to the transport captains."

"Of course," Olmar conceded. "I must also note, Captain Wong, that I have been charged by Father Astemar to act as his deputy in diplomatic matters. He feels that it will serve us well to take advantage of this moment to discuss future relations."

"He is likely correct," Henry agreed. "I know a senior Tano Councilor was expected to accompany their transports. It is not my task to speak to the future of this cluster, General Olmar. My duty here is to counter the Kozun's warlordism.

"I am merely *assisting* in the liberation of La-Tar at the request of its legitimate government."

Olmar laughed.

"I can see that, Captain Wong," he agreed. "I once served the Kenmiri. I am familiar with the games of words played to hide truths from power. We will wait to hear from Lord Ran as to the Skex contribution to our grand endeavor."

He bowed.

"We will speak again soon, Captain, but I believe I must leave you to speak to your newly arrived subordinates. A plan for the future of our expedition must be established, but that is not, I think, a task for any one of us alone."

"It is not, General," Henry confirmed. "I believe we will all be meeting in person aboard *Raven* soon enough."

HENRY WAS INTERRUPTED before he could reach out to the two destroyers by Iyotake stepping into his office without knocking.

"It's over," he reported simply. "Nar Rojan threatened to nuke the palace if Ran didn't surrender—so one of the locals he'd recruited shot him in the back of the head."

"Did he even *have* a bomb?" Henry asked.

"No one sounds certain yet," his XO admitted. "From what I understand of the Kozun, it would be in Mal Dakis's modus operandi for them to have snuck a small-yield nuke in with their diplomatic delegation."

"It would, yes," Henry conceded. "He was always a fan of the nuclear suicide bomber. It's over?"

"The locals who sided with Rojan appear to have decided that backing the people willing to blow them up with nukes if they don't win is a bad idea," Iyotake confirmed. "They've laid down their arms and the loyalists are taking them into custody."

"Thank God," *Raven's* captain murmured. "That was a mess of a complication we did *not* need."

He considered the situation. "I was going to reach out to our destroyers, but I think I need to try to talk to Ran first," he concluded. "We're going to need to host one hell of a planning session, XO. Plan for having at least three people from each planet on board for a meeting."

"On *Raven*, ser?" Iyotake asked.

"We're the neutral ground, the ally from outside that everyone can trust," Henry replied. "We're the guarantor for all of this at the moment—and even if Ran lends us his warships, our three ships are going to do the lion's share of the fighting in space.

"If La-Tar fails to knock out the Guardian platforms, this whole operation is done—but if *we* fail to get the transports past the Kozun fleet, it's just as done."

"No pressure. Right." Iyotake nodded firmly. "Everything will be ready, ser. We can show off if we need to."

"We need to impress our local allies, XO," Henry confirmed. "They're relying on us and we want to show them that we *are* reliable. First things first, let's show we can at least organize a damn dinner party."

CHAPTER THIRTY-NINE

DESPITE HAVING SPOKEN TO HER BY HOLOGRAM AND GETTING continual reports on the status of the surface, Henry still couldn't keep himself from a massive sense of relief at the sight of Sylvia Todorovich stepping off the shuttle.

She was back in her sharp business suit and her full "ambassadorial mask" was in place—but he still saw her look around the hangar bay for him as she returned to *Raven*. He gave her a nod as their gazes met across the deck, which she returned in a momentary crack of her own mask.

"Keep moving, people," O'Flannagain's voice said over the announcer. "There are a *lot* of shuttles coming in, and the sooner you're behind the blast shields, the sooner the next shuttle gets in."

Todorovich turned around to translate the CAG's instructions to the people behind her who didn't speak English. Before Henry could even open a channel to his subordinate, the announcer woke again to the Commander repeating her instructions in Kem.

The ambassador led her party, including Rising Principle, over to where Henry was waiting behind the shields.

"Everyone is present and accounted for," she told him in English.

"I think Rojan was readier than the Lord Nominated expected, but we were able to protect our people."

"Good," he replied before turning and bowing slightly to the Enteni Envoy. "You and your people are all right, Rising Principle?"

"We is-was unharmed," the Enteni replied. "We expected conflict. There must-will be peace, but that fate-time is-was not yet."

"We will have representatives from all of the worlds you feed aboard *Raven* shortly," Henry warned the La-Tar diplomat. "Ambassador Todorovich and I have a role to play in bringing this all together, but it is your people they have been asked to fight for."

"And I must-will speak for La-Tar," Rising Principle confirmed. They seemed confident, though it was always hard to tell when both of you were speaking in a second language—and whatever aspect of the Enteni's massive mouth allowed them to speak clearly couldn't handle Kem.

Computer translators could only ever be so good. It didn't help that the Enteni language didn't appear to have the same rules around tenses as Kem—or English, for that matter.

"*Deinonychus*, arriving," one of the Chiefs announced over the hangar speakers. "Clear the decks." The instruction was repeated in Kem, and Henry smiled slightly at Todorovich.

"I will catch up with you later," he promised her, still speaking in Kem for Rising Principle's benefit. "If you and Rising Principle are ready, I need to meet everyone as they come aboard—especially the destroyer commanders."

"Your ship captains must-are most welcome," Rising Principle told him. "I look forward to meeting them. Later, though. Thank you, Captain Wong, for all that you have-will do for my people."

Henry, all too aware of how badly this could all still fail, gestured for Todorovich to usher the Enteni on. He and the ambassador both had work to do today.

⁘

LIEUTENANT COLONEL ROGER POLOLÁNÍK was a tall, dark-haired man with a hawk-like face and beady eyes that darted from Henry to the next person and back every few moments, continually assessing the situation.

Lieutenant Colonel Parvan Spini, on the other hand, matched his counterpart's Slavic coloring but was much shorter and softer-featured, with a ready smile already on display as he joined the other two captains at the side of the hangar bay.

"Welcome aboard *Raven*, gentlemen," Henry told them. "I apologize for the stern chase we ended up leading you on, but it seemed to work out well for everyone."

"The Tano seem like good people," Pololáník replied. "Nervous types, though. They appreciated having the escort."

"And I appreciate having you here," Henry said. "*Raven* isn't in the best of shape, as I'm sure you noticed. Most of our weapons are online, but we've only got three missiles for four of our launchers before they're empty."

"Good thing we never plan on ending a fight with missiles, then," Spini said with a chuckle.

The two *Tyrannosaur*-class destroyers had the same pair of heavy lasers as *Raven*, combined with eight missile launchers apiece. They lacked the spinal gravity driver of *Raven*'s main gun, but they were capable combatants for that.

They were smaller than a Kenmiri escort, but either of the two ships could have taken all four escorts in Skex orbit without much concern.

"The threat environment we're facing in La-Tar is entirely an unknown at the moment, too," Henry warned, watching as the Atto contingent off-loaded from their shuttle. "The locals don't have that much to back us up with, either."

"The Tano did make an interesting contribution, I'll note," Pololáník said. "They kept two more transports than they needed for their army and stripped all of their shuttles out. Loaded them up with supplies for the entire force but filled their *shuttle bays* with starfighters."

Henry blinked in surprise.

"I didn't even consider that," he admitted. "Their fighters aren't spectacular, but a few extra missile platforms won't go amiss."

"How about thirty?" Pololánik asked. "They've got sixteen birds on one transport and fourteen on the other. From the conversation I had with General Kansa, they've been working on the ships while we were underway and she thinks they could fit twenty-four on each ship.

"It's a tiny flight group when we're talking about a ten-million-ton freighter, but no one is going to be expecting them," the Lieutenant Colonel included. "If we could fill the rest of the bays, an extra forty-eight starfighters is worth bringing along."

"We'll have to talk to Lord Ran," Henry said. "I'm guessing Skex has fighters somewhere, but I've mostly been focused on the fact that he has real warships."

The approach of Atto's representative, an Ashall named Urum who enjoyed the evocative title of the "Emergency Governor's Representative," ended that particular train of conversation. The Beren woman bowed as she reached Henry.

"Captain Wong, I appreciate your hospitality and your willingness to assist us all," she told him. "*Raven*'s efforts on our behalf have made this meeting possible. The Emergency Governor sends her regards."

That *had* to be a formality, since Henry had spoken with Emergency Governor Setrell at least as recently as the Representative had.

"We are here to help, Representative Urum," he replied. "The Peacekeeper Initiative and the United Planets Alliance want to avoid watching the former Empire devolve into chaos and pocket empires.

"Helping you protect yourselves is the best way for us to do that," he assured her.

"Of course, of course," she confirmed. "I assume there is a guide I should be meeting, Captain, so I no longer impose on your time?"

✦✦
✦✦

RAVEN MIGHT HAVE FINALLY BEEN ALLOWED into orbit of Skex, but Lord Nominated Casto Ran was still the last person to board the battlecruiser. The pale-red Tak swept off his shuttle like a conquering king, wearing a black garment that was clearly intended to imitate a Kenmiri warrior's undress uniform.

Of course, a Kenmiri had an extra set of upper body limbs, so the long black tunic looked quite different on Ran.

Henry had a moment of concern from the Lord Nominated's body language and manner—which was promptly alleviated when he realized that Casto Ran had come *alone*. If he had any security, they were remaining on his shuttle as he approached Henry and bowed precisely.

"Captain Wong," he greeted Henry. "It is a pleasure to meet you without the secrecy and games."

"The situation on Skex is under control, I hope, my lord?" Henry asked.

"Nar Rojan had spread his influence more than I had even begun to fear," the Lord Nominated admitted. "My contingency plans were sufficient, but more of my people died than I would have wished."

He shook his head, tendrils twitching.

"Even the ones who took his money were my people, Captain," he said softly. "I mourn every death but Nar Rojan's. I will not underestimate the Kozun again."

"I learned that lesson long ago, when Mal Dakis was at least on my side," Henry told him. "You are the last to arrive, my lord. Are you waiting on anyone?"

"No," Ran confirmed. "I will make enough demands today, Captain, that a gesture of faith is required on my part. I *trust* you, in a way I would never trust the Kozun, so I will place my personal safety in your hands."

"But not necessarily the fate of your world," Henry guessed.

"Exactly, Captain Wong. You understand duty, I think. I do not believe anyone would become the Destroyer of the Kenmorad without understanding those iron chains."

Henry nodded grimly.

"It is not that I oppose your mission or that I can possibly ally with the Kozun now," Ran told him. "But I must serve *my* people first. Do you understand me?"

"I do," Henry said. "I hope we can find a compromise that serves everyone."

"I believe that the stars have aligned and a chance stands before us to shape the fate of worlds," Casto Ran told him. "To best serve my people, I think I shall best serve many others...but those others must agree with me."

"I speak for no one here but the United Planets Space Force," Henry replied. "I am not the ones you must convince."

"Not...yet," the Lord Nominated agreed genially. "But you, like I, have a duty to fulfill and a role to play before this is done."

CHAPTER FORTY

RAVEN HAD BEEN DESIGNED TO OPERATE AS A LONG-DISTANCE raider, providing heavy support for Vesheron rebel groups on the far side of the Kenmiri Empire. It was a role Henry had commanded his previous ship, *Panther*, in several times, and its needs showed in multiple places in her design.

One of those places was that she had the space for a large conference from multiple parties. There were even ways that Henry could set up the amphitheatre-like space to divide groups with energy-weapon-proof barriers.

Today, those barriers would hopefully be unnecessary. He'd taken the precaution of seating UPSF contingents between each of the local delegations, with Pololáník between the Atto and the Ratch; Spini between the Ratch and the Skex; Todorovich between the Skex and Tano; and Iyotake between the Tano and the La-Tar.

Henry himself was at the head of the room, separating the La-Tar and the Atto. All of the groups faced a central dais where a hologram of the current speaker would be projected. The room could be reconfigured into a more traditional conference table, but there were enough people there today to need the more complex setup.

"Welcome aboard *Raven*, everyone," he repeated the greeting he'd given each of them as they came aboard his ship. The entire meeting would have to take place in Kem, the only language they all shared. "I am Captain Henry Wong, commanding officer of *Raven* and the commander of the United Planets Space Force task force now operating in this region.

"Most of you are aware of the UPSF and our role in the war, but our purpose in this region today is more complicated," he continued. "We are operating under a program called the Peacekeeper Initiative, created by our government in the aftermath of the disaster at the Vesheron Gathering.

"The concept is that we are intending to act as neutral arbiters in conflicts between regional powers in the Ra Sector, while enabling peaceful trade and combating warlordism."

He paused, glancing around the room.

"The Kozun's actions in La-Tar qualify as warlordism by the standards I have been given," he told his audience. "The Initiative has therefore deployed three ships to deal with the situation. Unfortunately, what we do *not* have is a significant ground contingent. I have a battlecruiser and two destroyers.

"The La-Tar government, as represented by Rising Principle, has requested the UPA's assistance in liberating their world—and has requested the assistance of each of your governments. Three of the governments in this room have sent soldiers and equipment to participate in that operation.

"Skex has, at least informally, committed to this mission as well, though the Lord Nominated has suggested that he retains some reservations," Henry concluded. "As this meeting is primarily assembled for us to plan our operation against the Kozun forces in La-Tar, I suggest that Lord Nominated Casto Ran take the floor and explain what he needs to commit his people's force to this task."

Henry was willing to accept that Casto Ran had to prioritize his people over everyone else. He was also *entirely* willing to make the

Lord Nominated explain that to the people he and his successors would have to deal with.

The hologram automatically shifted to Ran. He seemed both unsurprised and unperturbed by Henry's curve ball, rising and facing his fellows without hurry.

"Some of you are familiar with the concept of the Lord Nominated," he guessed. "Many of you are not. I am appointed by the community leaders of my world, in an old Tak tradition, to act as a central and absolute authority for a specific term of time.

"It has already been agreed that at the end of that term, I will become the senior officer of the Skex fleet. A fleet, I will note, that currently consists entirely of the remaining four escorts of eight I placed at the disposal of the Skex government."

And in so doing had accidentally bought himself responsibility for an entire world. Henry wasn't sure he'd have done it himself—and he wasn't sure *Ran* would have done it if he'd known what he'd get for it!

"I must make my position clear, I believe. I understand we have the transport capability for some two hundred thousand soldiers and that the other worlds fed by La-Tar have fielded approximately one hundred and thirty thousand such soldiers," he noted.

"Skex was a point of concern for the Kenmiri Empire, partially due to the actions of my own Vesheron forces in the region, and the local peacekeeping forces had been heavily augmented. Those troops have offered their allegiance to the Skex government. Combined with my own Vesheron, we are able to commit the seventy thousand soldiers necessary to fill the transports.

"We are also able to provide three of our four escort warships to assist in the assault on La-Tar," he continued. "We have, through the chances of fate and time, the ability to be the single largest contributor to the liberation of La-Tar except for the UPA."

That was more of a commitment than Henry had expected Skex to be able to make. The newest and least populated of the factory worlds, he hadn't even been expecting to get the fifty thousand soldiers that Rising Principle had aimed to get from each of the planets.

From the quiet murmuring around the room, the rest of the potential alliance were just as surprised...and wondering just what Casto Ran was going to ask for in trade for his armies and ships.

"I am bound by ancient and sacred oaths to serve the people of Skex," Ran told them. "To protect them above all else. Tradition binds a Lord Nominated, and one of those traditions is that the Lord Nominated does not attack. I am called to *defend* my people, not to wage war on others.

"To liberate La-Tar stretches the oaths and traditions of the Lord Nominated and puts my people at great risk," he continued. "It puts *all* of our people at great risk. Merely by being present in this room, we have declared ourselves and our worlds enemies of the Kozun Hierarchy.

"So, before I commit my people to this mission, I must ask you all: what plan do you have for *after* we liberate La-Tar? We face an enemy who was once a friend, and I assure you: the First Voice will *not* tolerate our defiance.

"This will not end once the Kozun are driven from Rising Principle's world," he reminded them all. "Are your people ready for war? Because the First Voice *will* bring one to us."

The old Tak shook his head, his tendrils twitching again.

"My price is simple: if we stand together today, we must stand together tomorrow," he told them all. "I will commit my ships and my armies to a formal alliance, pledged to defend all of our worlds as one. Nothing less."

The hologram of Casto Ran vanished from the dais as the Lord Nominated leaned back in his chair. The murmuring from earlier became arguing now, but no one was hitting the button that would make *them* the central speaker.

Henry met the Lord Nominated's gaze across the room and bowed his head slightly.

A solid alliance of the cluster's worlds was definitely in the UPA's interests, but as outsiders, Henry and Todorovich couldn't push it. All Henry could do was get them lined up and moving towards La-Tar.

Rising Principle *could* have pushed a more formal alliance, but the young Enteni had been focused on saving their people above all else. They didn't *care* what political structure supported the fleets and armies that liberated La-Tar, only that there were fleets and armies.

To Henry's surprise, though, it was the young Enteni diplomat who finally rose and activated the hologram once more.

"Peace," they said loudly. "Calm. This is the fate-time that is-has arrived to us. The Lord Nominated must-does speak truth. Against the Kozun, against others who can-will come after, we must-will stand together.

"La-Tar is-has always seen your worlds as friends. We must-will continue. You fight for our world—and once freed, we must-will fight for yours."

As the Enteni took their seat again, Todorovich rose into the silence.

"It is not the place of the United Planets Alliance to tell you how to shape your affairs," she told them. "We will not insist that you form an alliance. We are here to stand against violence and conquest, not to insist that you do things our way.

"But if you wish to create this alliance, the UPA is willing to support you. I have texts of treaties from our history that may serve as a sufficient basic structure for Skex to join this mission. Any assistance that I and my staff can give, we are more than willing to provide—but I must remind you that we are on a time limit.

"La-Tar is occupied. The Kozun will not be gentle with Rising Principle's people. Every day we let pass is paid for in death and torture of the people who came to your aid when you had nothing. Every day we let pass allows the Kozun to reinforce, to hunt the forces in the hills we are relying on to open the door.

"We cannot negotiate an entire treaty of alliance for five worlds in a matter of hours," she told them. "So, I must ask, Lord Ran, what would you require to immediately commit your forces to this campaign?"

Ran's image took over from Todorovich's and the Lord Nominated looked around, studying his potential allies.

"Each of you has the authority to speak for and bind your worlds," he noted. "Some of you are Councilors, others Generals given that voice, others the chosen representatives of your leaders— but all of you are here because you can speak for your worlds.

"So, I ask you to speak, to bind your people and governments to this pact. The details we can establish later, matters of money and arms and material, but the *principle* must be accepted, that we stand together against the Kozun and any other enemy."

Rising Principle rose to their odd tripod feet and raised his forward arm, not even activating the speaker icon as they spoke loudly enough to be heard regardless.

"La-Tar must-will stand," they said fiercely.

There was a moment of silence, and then General Kansa and Councilor Inbar stood up at the same moment. The two Ashall looked at each other and laughed before the General gestured for her political superior to speak.

"Tano will stand with you all," Inbar told them. "We set this into motion when we asked Captain Wong to investigate La-Tar. We will see it to the end."

Urum rose next, the Emergency Governor's Representative smiling slightly as the hologram focused on her.

"Atto has already made our choice. We stand with this alliance."

General Olmar was already standing, waiting for Urum to finish speaking before he added his own words.

"Ratch was saved by La-Tar once, and by La-Tar and the UPA a second time," he reminded everyone. "We fight for La-Tar. We stand by you all."

Every eye in the room turned to Casto Ran, who looked *spectacularly* smug to Henry's gaze.

"It should go without saying, I think," he told them, "Skex stands with you, side by side. Fate and time have brought us here—but we and we alone decide what we do with the fates before us.

"If we stand together, then I believe La-Tar will be freed and the Kozun driven back—and so Skex will answer the call."

Henry exhaled a breath he hadn't realized he was holding. Ran had got *exactly* what he wanted out of his allies—a commitment to *be* allies after the moment was passed.

And that meant Henry had what he wanted: reinforcements and an army.

There were details to be sorted out, but it looked like it was time to go back to La-Tar.

CHAPTER FORTY-ONE

"Exit skip in thirty seconds," Bazzoli's voice echoed through *Raven*. "Stand by for exit skip."

Henry slowly exhaled, the practice of years to try and minimize the inevitable effects of being punched in about seventeen more dimensions than the human brain was designed to process. He wasn't looking forward to the actual transition, but he was looking forward to being in contact with everyone again.

They'd entered the skip line from Atris in formation and sequence, but there was no way to see or communicate with anyone else while they were in transit. Henry's fleet and the attached convoy had been organized and ready at the blue hypergiant between Skex and La-Tar, but there was no certainty that would have survived transit.

"Exit skip...now."

For a few seemingly eternal moments, Henry felt like he'd been dropped into the middle of a gravitational kaleidoscope. Any time his brain thought it registered a direction for *down*, that direction was suddenly wrong.

It finally faded and Henry blinked away his nausea to focus on the situation.

"Report," he managed to cough out. "Flotilla status?"

"*Deinonychus* and *Hadrosaur* made it through in formation," Ihejirika reported. "*Gardener* and *Carpenter* are off angle by twelve degrees and out of position by about fifty thousand kilometers."

Gardener and *Carpenter* were the two Skex escorts Henry had borrowed for this part of his plan. He was grimly certain that they were the two ships least likely to survive this fight—and their crews knew it.

It didn't seem to be slowing them down, though.

"That's better than I was expecting," Henry admitted. "Hostiles?"

"Nothing on the skip point," the tactical officer replied. "Entry point is secure."

"Moon, get in touch with the Skex ships," Henry ordered. "Get a rendezvous point from Bazzoli; I want us formed up within fifteen minutes. They have twice our acceleration; it should be straightforward enough."

Kenmiri-style compensators, unfortunately, interacted poorly with the gravity shield. The UPA design was less efficient in just about every way, except that it worked just fine with the UPSF's protective fields.

So, the UPSF had slower ships that could take every hit their faster enemies could throw at them.

"We're picking up a new formation of starships above La-Tar, ser," Ihejirika told him. "Resolving details now, but it looks like at least twelve ships."

Henry nodded silently. He'd sent a gunship and five escorts into retreat at various points along the road here, so he'd been expecting at *least* that.

"CIC is flagging an unknown bogey in the middle of the flotilla, ser," the tactical officer continued after a moment. "Estimated mass unknown but significantly larger than the rest of the ships, ser. She's...bigger than we are, if nothing else."

"Dreadnought?" Henry asked.

"I don't think so," Ihejirika said. "We'd recognize a dreadnought."

The icons dropped onto the main tactical display above the sphere of La-Tar.

"Part of what's making both the numbers and ID on the central unit difficult is that there appear to be at least *some* of their corvettes present as well," the Terran officer noted. "We know the primary target is six times the size of some of the units, but we're still establishing if those are escorts or not."

"Understood," Henry said. "Firm up the classes and types, Commander. We want solid data before we play matador."

He had time, at least. The actual landing force wasn't scheduled to arrive for three and a half hours.

Raven and her battle group were three hours and twenty minutes from a zero-velocity entry into La-Tar orbit. That would either require them to destroy the Guardian platforms or get shredded, which meant Henry wasn't planning on taking the battle group in.

Yet.

"Once we're formed up, set us on a course for the Ra-Fifty skip line," he ordered Bazzoli. "Let's see if we can keep our Kozun friends guessing just what we're doing for a few hours yet."

"Yes, ser," she confirmed.

Henry leaned back in his chair, watching the vector lines for his five ships slowly converge while Ihejirika's people worked through the sensor data to firmly ID their targets. At a full light-minute away, it was taking time—and by now, the Kozun had detected *Raven*'s battle group.

They were now at *fifteen* presumed Kozun ships, he noted grimly, and it didn't look like the number was solid yet. The "good" news, Henry supposed, was that there was definitely only one of the big cruisers.

It seemed the First Voice had built himself a counterpart to *Raven*. Today they'd see how good a job he'd done.

"SER, we have an incoming transmission from the Kozun fleet," Moon reported. "Burst recording, standard Vesheron protocols."

"Always helpful to remind each other that we used to be friends, isn't it?" Henry murmured. "Main screen, Lieutenant Commander."

To Henry's surprise, the man who appeared on the screen in front of him wasn't Kozun. The Ashall with dark brown hair and eyes could have passed for human with ease—and could have been a member of any one of a dozen or more other Ashall races.

Despite earlier appearances, it seemed that the First Voice's regime wasn't *entirely* made up of his own race.

"I am Star Commander Tajat Kan," the Hierarchy officer said in flat Kem. Star Commander, according to Henry's files on the new Hierarchy military, was equivalent to a UPSF Rear Admiral.

"There are pretenses I could maintain here, Captain Henry Wong, but I will dispense with them all. You have committed acts of war against the Kozun Hierarchy. You have engaged our fleets in battle; you have assaulted our worlds. You have waged war upon us.

"But my Prophet, the First Voice Mal Dakis, has mandated that your service to him requires mercy. Withdraw, Captain Henry Wong. Turn aside from this war you wage against us. We will not be deterred or intimidated.

"These worlds belong to the Hierarchy. This is not your region of influence. Withdraw or be destroyed."

The message ended and Henry closed the image of Star Commander Kan with a wave of his hand.

"To the point, isn't he?" he asked rhetorically. "Ihejirika, is our friend moving yet?"

"Not yet," the tactical officer replied. "We've got what we think is a solid listing on what the Star Commander has to play with, though."

"Lay it out," Henry ordered.

"Eight corvettes, six escorts, two gunships, and a three-megaton cruiser," Ihejirika listed. "From what we've seen so far, the corvettes aren't worth much alone—but eight of them have the lasers of four escorts.

"CIC and the XO are still making guesses on the cruiser, but she's probably built more like a pocket dreadnought than a scaled-up escort," he continued. "Expect heavy plasma guns and serious shielding."

Henry nodded.

"Eight and a half million tons of warships, give or take," he estimated. "And we've got half of that."

Any Vesheron should know better than to take *those* odds against the UPSF.

"Continue on the plan," he ordered. "Let me know the moment the Kozun move out and if they leave anything behind."

There was a timer on the main display that no one was drawing attention to just yet: the one counting down the hours until the invasion force arrived.

"And Moon?"

"Ser?"

"Get Ambassador Todorovich in contact with the La-Tar government," he ordered. "They need to know the timing on the landing force. We're relying on them to open the door."

HENRY WAS HOPING that his lack of reply to the Star Commander was going to infuriate the man. He doubted anyone that had risen that high in the ranks of Mal Dakis's forces was used to being ignored—and to hold that high a rank as a non-Kozun, he'd almost certainly fought for Dakis before the First Voice had returned to Kozun.

It took almost twenty minutes for the next message to arrive, but when it did, Tajat Kan was clearly trying to appear calm.

Unfortunately for him, Henry was *very* good at reading the variations of body language and microexpressions across the Ashall species. He could tell that the Star Commander was angry.

"So, it seems, Captain Wong, that you have no interest in my First Voice's mercy," Kan stated. "I do not know what you wish to achieve, but I ask you to consider the very people you seem to be trying to 'save.' All you can do is drag out their absorption into the Hierarchy. Already, your actions have brought more pain and more suffering to La-Tar than was needed before your arrival.

"If your course across this system is meant to inform me that you have accepted our terms and are merely on course to Kozun to deliver an embassy, I require that you provide me with the credentials of your ambassador.

"Otherwise, I have no choice but to assume you are attempting to launch some foolish strike deeper into our territory and move to destroy your ships."

Henry checked the maneuver possibility cones in the tactical display. He was a long way—almost twelve hours, all told—from reaching the Ra-Fifty skip point. Everything in Kan's flotilla could achieve a full KPS^2 of acceleration.

The Star Commander had the time to be snarky at Henry. Henry, on the other hand, needed to pull the Kozun fleet out of orbit.

"Should we be responding to the Star Commander, ser?" Moon asked. "We could send him Todorovich's credentials."

"That wouldn't actually serve our purposes," he replied. "Is the ambassador in contact with Adamant Will yet?"

"No, ser," she admitted. "It looks like the relay satellite we used last time was located and destroyed by the Kozun. While I have coordinates for a ground receiver, I don't think I can ping that without the Kozun picking up the beam."

"Can we get a drone into an angle to do that?" Henry asked.

"Already on it, ser," she confirmed. "But it will take time. At least two hours."

They'd already used up most of their first hour of leeway. If they only got in touch with the locals in two hours, then he'd functionally be hoping that they could activate their strike teams and disable the tanks *after* the invasion force arrived in-system and while it was en route to La-Tar.

He'd hoped to give them seven hours' notice and recognized even *that* was asking a lot. Every hour less warning the locals had increased the risk that the Guardians wouldn't be disabled before the invasion force arrived.

The solution to this would have made any Kenmiri Warrior Henry had ever met do the conquering insectoid equivalent of a jump for joy. It was time to *taunt* someone.

"I don't think we're sending the ambassador's credentials over, but I do think I need to get our Kozun friend to actually move," Henry concluded aloud. "Get ready to transmit, Commander."

It took a him a moment to school his features into the exactly right condescending sneer. It had to be an almost-parody to get across the cultural barriers—*and* he had to get himself into the right state of contempt to make sure the rest of his face didn't betray him.

"Star Commander Tajat Kan," he greeted the camera. "Is that the latest title for Mal Dakis's best bootlicker? Or are you so afraid of the UPSF that all you are going to do is sit in orbit and send jokes at me?

"The United Planets Alliance does not recognize Kozun authority in this system. We will never recognize the transfer of authority by conquest. I suggest that *you* withdraw from this system and return control to its legitimate government.

"My ships are in position to escort you safely from this system."

He ended the recording and let his face relax.

"Send it over, Commander," he told Moon cheerfully. "I think that will have the right effect."

His communications officer was staring at him but then nodded and set to work.

"I see the Kenmiri had an apt pupil," Iyotake's voice murmured in his ear. "Do you think it will work?"

"I think he was already furious with me, and hopefully, I just punched a convenient set of buttons," Henry replied. Their channel was private and he was subvocalizing to make sure only his XO heard him.

"We need him out of the way so Todorovich can talk to the La-Tar."

"You did just verbally punch a man with a pocket dreadnought in the nose, ser," Iyotake pointed out. "I *know* what the plan is and I'm not sure I wouldn't be coming out after you."

"Signature change!" Ihejirika snapped. "Multiple Kozun vessels have brought up their engines...looks like some are staying behind, trying to resolve the split."

New data codes flashed across the icons in Henry's displays, and he nodded to himself as they resolved.

"All eight corvettes are remaining in orbit," the tactical officer finally reported. "Six escorts and two gunships are escorting the cruiser out to meet us. Acceleration is one KPS squared."

"Continue on our course for now," Henry told Bazzoli. "Let's get our friend well and truly out of the line of communication for Commander Moon before we turn to play."

"With the corvettes in orbit, they might still pick up our transmissions, ser," Moon warned him.

"I know, Lieutenant Commander," Henry said. "But we don't have a choice. Pick your moments, Moon, but we need to talk to the La-Tar and we need to talk to them *fast*."

"There's half the sensor platforms in play," she conceded. "It'll still be twenty, thirty minutes at least."

"Then we give you thirty," he decided. "Bazzoli? Mark the timer. In thirty minutes, we bring the battle group about to face the enemy."

CHAPTER FORTY-TWO

"WE GOT THROUGH," TODOROVICH TOLD HENRY QUICKLY. "GOT confirmation of receipt back from Adamant Will as well, confirming the timing and that they know about the corvettes in orbit."

"I don't know if the La-Tar can do anything about them, but they need to know," he agreed. "We were expecting the Kozun to keep something in orbit. We have a plan."

"I trust you," she said. "Everyone is trusting you. We're basically asking the La-Tar to commit everything they have left on our word. They'd *better* trust you."

"They'll at least see the invasion fleet before they have to finally pull the trigger," Henry said. "It's all coming down to the wire, Ambassador. We're about to turn to engage the Kozun. Any last political concerns I should be aware of?"

She was silent for a few seconds.

"You have to accept surrenders, which I know I don't need to tell you," she said slowly. "But you also have to let them go if they just run. I know against the Kenmiri, we couldn't let them run—we knew we'd see them again—but like this, right now?

"We have to show that we're only applying the level of force *necessary*. When they break off, you have to let them go."

"That could end up getting used against us," Henry warned. "But I get it." He shook his head. "I wish I could have left you in Skex, Ambassador. There's a few too many critical diplomats flying right into this mess."

"If Inbar or Ran had been remotely inclined to stay in Skex, I might have gone along with that," she said. "But since we have an actual *head of state* in the invasion fleet, leaving our ambassador behind seemed...impolitic."

Lord Ran was aboard his flagship, *Potter*. The escort was the only actual warship with the invasion fleet, which meant that the Lord Nominated was effectively in command of the second wave of the attack.

Most of the invasion-force commanders had been given authority to negotiate on their planet's behalf, which meant that everyone who'd actually agreed to the alliance Ran had insisted on was currently on a ship hurtling toward La-Tar.

Hopefully, their promises would be honored even if some of them ended up dead in the next few days.

"If the La-Tar are updated and on board, then it's time for the next phase of this," Henry told her. "Get your people to the acceleration tanks, Ambassador. I don't plan on pushing past point five KPS squared, but no plan survives contact with the enemy."

"We're on it," she promised. "Good luck, Captain."

"I don't need luck. I have the United Planets Space Force."

"EXECUTE."

Five ships turned in space as one. The course to the skip line had kept them at a constant distance from La-Tar, allowing the Kozun fleet to get up to over eighteen hundred KPS on a straight-line velocity toward them.

Now the allied battle group was accelerating directly toward the

Kozun, the combined acceleration adding a kilometer and a half per second to their velocity every second.

"Just under fifty-seven minutes to missile range," Ihejirika reported. "Two and a half minutes after that to gravity-driver and laser range."

Henry nodded. They'd be up to over one percent of lightspeed relative to each other by the time they reached weapons range. Slowing down was going to be an exercise in patience for both sides, but Tajat Kan was probably relying on La-Tar's defenses to keep the planet secure while he came around for a second pass.

Given that Henry had already demonstrated a healthy respect for the Guardian platforms, it was an entirely reasonable plan. High-speed firing passes were an optimal situation for the gravity driver... but they were also an optimal situation for heavy plasma guns.

"Any solid data on that cruiser's armament?" he asked.

"Power levels are high enough for her to be packing heavy plasma guns, as we guessed," Iyotake told him from CIC. "Assuming a linear projection from a gunship to a dreadnought in terms of mass, she might have as many as five guns."

"*Raven* is supposed to be able to take on a dreadnought alone," Henry observed. "If nothing else, I know Kalad has watched *me* do that with *Panther*, which was an older and smaller ship."

"You think the Star Commander is misestimating the situation?" Iyotake asked.

"Let me loop in the captains," Henry replied. "I'm missing something and I want perspectives."

It was a matter of moments to link in the two UPSF Lieutenant Colonels commanding his destroyers. It took another thirty seconds to bring in the two escort captains, a Tak woman named Ij and a Beren man named Loto.

"My math says the Kozun are completely outclassed," Henry told them all, switching to Kem for the benefit of the two Skex officers. "*Raven* alone is expected to handle a Kenmiri dreadnought, which means that cruiser over there is seriously outmatched. Either of the two UPSF destroyers could handle their entire escort. While our escorts are going to carry the bulk of the missile duel, they cannot really hurt us without getting into close range—where *Raven* will rip their flagship to pieces.

"I may have intentionally aggravated Star Commander Kan, but I doubt he has committed his fleet to a battle he does not believe he has a chance to win. Even if Kan never served alongside UPSF ships, several of his subordinates have. So, what is *he* seeing that I am not?"

He focused on the two Skex officers.

"I am looking for your input, Ij and Loto," he noted specifically. "I know the balance of power between my ships and the Kozun's almost perfectly. You are the outsiders. What do *you* see?"

The six-way channel of his captains and his XO was silent for at least twenty seconds, twenty seconds in which thousands more kilometers of distance vanished.

"I have not seen your warships in action," Ij finally said. "But I was Vesheron and I heard stories. I would likely assume those stories were exaggerations and estimate the strength of my vessels versus yours more highly than you do.

"In his place, *I* would have brought the corvettes and assumed it was an even fight," the Tak woman concluded. "But unless he puts more value on his cruiser than I would, he must see the same variables we do."

"So, he believes he sees a variable we do not," Loto said. "I am but one captain of a small force that had no intentions of waging war on other worlds. I did not see your UPSF as a threat, but even I would have suggested that we seek a countermeasure to your ships once we knew you were operating in our region."

"The Kozun would have been expecting us to challenge them," Pololáník suggested. "Did you not encounter a variety of anti-gravity-shield weapons at the Gathering?"

"We encountered missiles that disrupted our shields in the hands of pirates," Iyotake replied. "We were unsure of the source."

The *other* anti-gravity-shield weapons they'd run into had been

UPSF weapons acquired from lost ships. The penetrator warheads in *Raven*'s magazines would bypass the energy screens of anyone else's ships, but they'd *also* bypass gravity shields.

"If those weapons came from an unknown source, is it possible that source was the Kozun?" *Deinonychus*'s captain asked. "In which case, would Star Commander Kan not only have those weapons but potentially even improved versions of them?"

"Yes," Henry said calmly. That had to be what he was missing. When he'd fought Kal Rojan at the Gathering, he'd intentionally destroyed all of the Kozun weapons to protect his ship. That had, in hindsight, left him lacking a critical piece of intelligence.

"The Star Commander has to believe he can bring down our shields. If he can do that, then the entire balance of the fight changes and his greater firepower could carry the day. He will still get his ships handed to him in pieces, but he has a better chance than I would have given him without realizing that."

He shook his head and studied the tactical display.

"I very much want to know who is providing those warheads," he said quietly, "but that's a problem for another time. That realization won't change our course, unfortunately. We still need to get within three hundred thousand kilometers of their fleet to do the most damage."

"They are going to be sending a lot of missiles our way," Ij warned. "Those six escorts alone..."

"I think I have an answer for that," Henry told his people. "The same one as at the Gathering. In theory, *someone* should have reported on Kal Rojan's fate by now. We'll see if they learned the right lessons."

If nothing else, while they'd confirmed Kal Rojan had been killed, Henry had only crippled the Kozun dreadnought at the Gathering. That the Kozun appeared to believe the ship destroyed told him that the Gathering's hosts had probably kept the ship, but at least *some* of the crew should have made it home.

"This is what we're going to do..."

CHAPTER FORTY-THREE

SECONDS TURNED TO MINUTES TURNED TO ETERNITIES. AT THE velocity the two fleets were approaching each other, Henry calculated that the entire clash would be over in less than four minutes—but it took them almost an hour to even approach weapons range.

"We've got some solid scans on the cruiser now," Ihejirika told him calmly as the range hit a "mere" six light-seconds. "Decent visuals, power lines, the works."

"Does it have any glowing red sections saying 'shoot me here'?" Henry asked.

"No, but I can tell you we overestimated its guns," the tactical officer replied with a chuckle. "She only has four of them, not five. But..."

The "but" hung in the air for several seconds.

"But what?" Henry said, bringing up the visual of the Kozun cruiser. She was a broad flying-wing shape, probably three or four hundred meters across, and at this range, the plasma guns were clearly visible on her profile. There were two weapon mounts on the top of the hull and two below, each of the turrets probably twenty meters across at least.

"They're definitely dreadnought guns, superheavies," Ihejirika told him. "I was hoping for something in between. Even a gunship's plasma gun is a serious weapon, but if they're *building* superheavy turrets..."

"Then building dreadnoughts is simply a matter of time and resources," Henry concluded. None of the systems in the La-Tar cluster could even build a gunship's heavy plasma cannon. If Kozun was building superheavy plasma cannon, they were going to have a real edge over the locals in the medium term.

"Yes, ser."

The United Planets Alliance could, theoretically, build superheavy plasma cannon. They had no practice doing so and didn't have the production facilities. They'd chosen to rely on the gravity drivers instead, a technology they understood.

"Moon, load everything Ihejirika's got onto a skip drone and fire it off under the Marathon codes," Henry ordered. "It's to hold in the system long enough to update the invasion fleet before skipping out. Just in case."

"Yes, ser," the communications officer confirmed. A drone like that was the last distraction he could give her before the fight was joined. In the absence of a flag officer with a staff, coordinating the five-ship battle group fell on Moon as much as it did on Henry.

He exhaled slowly and checked the time. Ninety minutes until the invasion fleet arrived—and Star Commander Kan was almost an entire light-minute away from La-Tar with a velocity of over one percent of lightspeed.

Just slowing down to zero relative to La-Tar at this point would take the Star Commander the same hour and a half it had taken the Kozun to get here. Even if the battle about to occur went sideways, the landing force was going to reach La-Tar.

Henry just had to hope that Lord Nominated Ran could handle the corvettes the Star Commander had left behind. His ability to influence the invasion was limited by the need to deal with the Kozun fleet.

"O'Flannagain, check in," he ordered as the range continued to drop.

"Right where you told us to be, ser," the CAG replied. "Missiles locked and loaded, lasers charged, ready to be your trusty shield."

"What, no request for permission to break and attack?" Henry teased.

"I generally prefer to keep my starfighters from engaging capital ships that *outnumber* us," she replied. "If we had a few more birds, I'd have argued for a high-speed pass to soften them up, but not with eight fighters against nine warships."

"And how many fighters would you have wanted, Commander?" he asked.

"Twelve," she told him, the cheerful tone of her voice suggesting that she was *probably* teasing him back.

Probably. Henry had been a rocket-jock himself and *he* might have been willing to pull a high-speed pass on the Kozun with twelve fighters.

"Missile range in one minute," Ihejirika reported. "Commander Moon, do you have those targeting links for me?"

"All ships are linked in, even the Skex," Moon confirmed.

"You're on the same loop, O'Flannagain?" Henry asked.

"My missiles are toys in this fight, but we're loaded into the firing pattern," she said.

"Then ride fire, Commander," he told her. "Good luck."

He switched to his UPSF captains a moment later.

"Pololáník, Spini," he greeted them. "Forty seconds. We ready?"

The destroyers were the second layer of his formation. The eight SF-122 Dragoons led the way, then came the destroyers, then came *Raven*. The two Skex escorts were at the tail end of a formation five thousand kilometers deep.

Hopefully, that would be enough to keep them protected by the Terran ships' gravity shields.

"It's a bit late for final concerns," Pololáník observed. "*Deinony-*

chus is good to go. We're linked in with Commander Ihejirika and standing by."

"Same for *Hadrosaur*," Spini confirmed. "Time for turning back was an hour ago, ser. We're locked in."

"Good." Henry's attention was pulled inexorably to the tactical display and its countdown to the arrival of the invasion force.

He pulled the Skex officers into the channel and switched to Kem before he continued.

"Just by getting this far, we have already achieved the main objective of our part of the fight," he told them. "We win this by surviving. So *survive*, people. Good luck."

"Range in ten seconds!" Ihejirika barked.

"Engage on the plan," Henry ordered.

THE UPSF HAD STARTED the war with inferior missiles to the Kenmiri, a situation that had lasted until they'd started invading the Empire itself and encountered the Vesheron and the Drifters, people who were more than willing to sell the Kenmiri weapons to the Terrans.

By now, the difference in capability between the UPSF's weapons and the Kenmiri-style ones carried by the Kozun and Skex warships was minimal. All fourteen warships launched their missiles within a fraction of a second of each other.

With the damage to *Raven*'s launchers, the two Skex escorts provided two-thirds of the over sixty missiles that Henry's force launched.

The Kozun launched three times as many missiles in response, a hundred and eighty weapons blazing toward the allied force at ten KPS^2.

"Kozun have flipped and are burning to extend the range," Ihejirika reported. "It won't buy much, but it *will* get the missiles in before we hit laser range."

"Understood," Henry confirmed.

Twenty seconds after the first salvo, the entire process repeated. Then again twenty seconds after that. And then *again*.

Four pairs of matching salvos dotted Henry's display by the time the first salvos intersected and his plan set into motion.

His missiles weren't the conversion warheads intended to duplicate the force of a plasma cannon. They were brute-force killers: hydrogen bombs with five-hundred-megaton warheads that obliterated everything around them, even in space.

The explosions gutted the incoming salvo, wiping over half of the first wave of Kozun missiles from space as both sides launched a fifth salvo.

All of Henry's salvos were programmed the same way. He had enough weapons to have a decent chance of getting hits through, but he was *more* likely to hurt the Kozun in range of his lasers and gravity driver.

They had the advantage at range and he was doing everything he could to neutralize it.

A sixth salvo entered space as O'Flannagain's fighters engaged the first wave. There were still over eighty missiles incoming before they tore into it, and Henry was watching them like an angry hawk.

Raven and the destroyers should have been able to handle eighty missiles on their own. Combined, they would even be able to shoot most of them down—but UPSF doctrine also relied on the fact that any given missile only had a one-in-twenty chance at best of penetrating the gravity shield.

Hits could be taken. Reducing the number was always smart, probability could always turn against you, but their doctrine was around reducing the weapons that hit the shield. Not preventing hits entirely.

Today, he very much wished they could avoid them entirely.

"Clean kills by the fighter wing, fifty-plus missiles still inbound," Iyotake told him from CIC. "Defensive lasers engaging."

"Grav-driver range in fifteen seconds," Ihejirika reported.

Henry took it all in, watching the battle and waiting for the critical moment. It might not come—the entire battle could unfold sufficiently according to plan that the captain merely had to sit in his seat and look confident—but if it did come, he'd need to know everything and act instantly.

"Missiles are targeting *Deinonychus*," Iyotake snapped. "Multiple impacts projected in ten seconds. Pololáník is evading."

The missiles would hit less than five seconds after the short-range weapons reached range.

"Target the cruiser with the gravity driver," Henry said calmly. That was the plan. "Ihejirika, pass me control of launchers one through four."

Those were the ones with only the ready magazines, the missiles he'd ordered reequipped with penetrator warheads. It was an open secret that the UPSF had a weapon that could penetrate energy shields like they weren't even there.

It was the UPSF's heartfelt hope that the Vesheron didn't realize the same weapon could skip their own gravity shield, but someone had tested that theory at the Gathering. Henry didn't know who was setting everyone up, but they'd learned what they needed there.

And they were probably going to learn more today.

"Grav-driver firing."

The report was unnecessary. The gravity driver created a gravity well over a *billion* times as strong as Earth's for an infinitesimal fraction of a second. Constrained and focused as it was, the human body couldn't register what was going on...but it definitely registered that *something was wrong*.

The entire ship lurched with the recoil as it sent the first projectile downrange at seven percent of lightspeed. With the two fleets closing at over two percent of lightspeed, Henry wouldn't want to be on the receiving end of that round.

"Multiple impacts on *Deinonychus*'s shields," Iyotake snapped. "We've confirmed resonance disruption warheads. Her shield is flickering; her shear factor is all over the place."

Very little could survive hitting a region of space where gravity went from nothing to fifteen thousand Gs and back again over the course of a few centimeters. If that gravity level was changing, though, *Deinonychus* couldn't use her own weapons.

And she was more vulnerable.

"Target the cruiser," Henry snapped. "All lasers!"

They were already firing, hammering the heavy Kozun warship with the heavy beams. A second grav-driver projectile flashed out as the computers grimly informed Henry that the first one had missed.

The cruiser's plasma guns were firing now, the entire Kozun fleet focusing their fire on Pololáník's destroyer. Lasers and plasma bolts lashed the gravity shield. The flickering defense somehow held against it all, the destroyer dancing through the fire with enough grace to survive the gauntlet.

And then the shattered remnants of the second missile salvo slammed home on her already-disrupted shield—and for the first time in his entire career, Henry watched a United Planets Space Force Vessel's gravity shield go down.

Deinonychus wasn't unarmored, but she wasn't armored enough to withstand the focused fire of a ship with half the guns of a dreadnought. Multiple plasma bolts struck her amidships...and then she was just gone.

CHAPTER FORTY-FOUR

THERE WAS NO TIME IN THE BLISTERINGLY SHORT HARD-contact portion of a space battle for mourning or grief. There was only awareness, threat assessment, *reaction.*

The next salvo of missiles would miss. Henry knew that in his bones—there was no way Star Commander Kan could have expected the gravity shield to go down in two salvos.

The one after that would be retargeted on *Hadrosaur.* They were only in grav-driver range for another forty-five seconds, and once they passed the Kozun fleet, there was no way missiles could reach each other.

Any missile launched at that point would be trying to come back from a velocity deficit of over two percent of lightspeed, and they didn't have that kind of delta-*v.*

"Grav-driver hit on the cruiser," Ihejirika reported. "Her shields are failing but they're still up! I'm not sure we can get them do—"

Henry hit the command he'd been holding off on in the middle of his tactical officer's report, and Ihejirika fell silent as their four damaged launchers spoke for the first time in weeks.

In theory, the ready magazine could be cycled in just under two

seconds. It took twenty seconds to feed missiles from the main magazines to the outer launchers, and in general, sustained fire was more
effective than a single pulse.

This time, Henry's command sent twelve missiles flashing from
his cruiser's starboard launchers in four seconds. They were almost
unnoticed in the hell of the battlespace, slashing toward their targets
in the mess of other missiles, lasers and grav-driver rounds.

"Missile impacts on *Hadrosaur*'s shields," Iyotake reported.
"She's taken less hits than *Deinonychus* and is maintaining stability,
but we are seeing shear variability and the second salvo is—multiple
impacts, *Hadrosaur*'s shields are critical!"

Twelve missiles *skipped*. Without being on the line between
stars, they didn't leave regular three-dimensional space for long, but
they left for long enough to bypass their targets' shields and deliver
their five-hundred-megaton warheads.

Eight missiles had targeted the cruiser and *six* detonated inside
her hull. Even as *Hadrosaur*'s shields failed, leaving her vulnerable to
the big ship's heavy guns, those guns ceased to exist.

Henry had judged the last four missiles as excessive to the needs
for the cruiser and sent them at the gunships. They had lighter
shields than their bigger sibling and they hadn't been the focus of the
allied flotilla's fire. All four missiles punched through, shattering both
six-hundred-thousand-ton warships like dropped eggs.

Part of him hoped he hadn't just killed Kalad. The Star Lance
had been commanding her forces from an escort before, but it was
quite possible she'd ended up on one of the gunships or the cruiser.
Those were the more prestigious roles, after all.

"O'Flannagain!" he snapped.

"Scale armor, we're on it," she told him. Her starfighters were
flashing backward, pushing as close to each as they dared to form a
defensive layer of their smaller gravity shields. It wasn't perfect, but it
was deflecting *most* of the laser fire still directed at *Hadrosaur*.

Without the cruiser to focus fire on, the Skex warships and *Raven*
now laid into the Kozun escorts as they passed through each other's

formations. A grav-driver conversion warhead smashed one to pieces. Laser fire tore another to shreds.

And then they were through, *Raven* flipping in space to send a final gravity-driver round chasing her opponents. Henry was reasonably sure that was pointless—where they gained two percent of lightspeed closing, they lost that two percent of lightspeed now.

The lasers that continued to be exchanged were more useful for both sides, and he maintained a stony expression as the Kozun now focused on the exposed Skex warships. Four escorts on two wasn't a fair fight, though the two UPSF ships' more powerful lasers definitely contributed.

Red icons flashed across Henry's allies, but no more ships vanished from his screens over the last few seconds of the battle.

"Skex ships are still with us; four Kozun escorts are in retreat," Ihejirika finally reported as the range passed one light-second.

"Begin slowing us down, Commander Bazzoli," Henry ordered. "We'll see what the Kozun do, but I think they might want to rethink their strategy at this point."

Damage reports were coming in from *Carpenter* and *Gardener*. Neither was looking good, though their energy shields had done their job.

"If we slow to zero relative to La-Tar, we'll be at thirteen million kilometers or so when the invasion fleet arrives," Bazzoli reported.

"Watch the Kozun, but that's the plan," Henry confirmed.

"Kozun are decelerating," Ihejirika reported. "They have to. Even if they're going to run for Ra-Fifty, they need to shed the velocity they built towards us."

"And they might well plan to try and catch us between the escorts and the corvettes," Henry said grimly. "We don't know how many of those shield-disruptor warheads they have left."

"Speaking of those, ser," O'Flannagain interrupted. "We tagged a few loose ones that went off course and appear to be intact. Should I play fetch?"

She'd done it for Henry once before, retrieving the wreckage of the stolen penetrator missiles used against *Raven* at the Gathering. *Those* missiles, though, had been UPSF. They'd known their safety features inside and out.

"No," he said firmly. "We don't know what they might have done to secure those weapons, Commander, and the last thing I want is for one of your ships to have a close-up view of a nuclear explosion.

"Am I clear?"

"Yes, ser," she conceded.

"Get your birds aboard to refuel and rearm," he ordered. They'd used up their missiles protecting the flotilla and would need new ones.

Henry's attention returned to the main display, and he looked at the new icon marking *Deinonychus*'s debris cloud.

"And get your shuttle pilot into space for search and rescue, Commander," he told O'Flannagain. "We'll look for Lieutenant Colonel Pololáník's people first, but if we can find any of the Kozun, we'll pick them up, too."

"Yes, ser," O'Flannagain said quietly.

Henry looked across his bridge at Ihejirika, who met his gaze and shook his head sadly.

"*Deinonychus* was the center of a lot of fire, ser," the tactical officer warned. "I'm...not sure we're going to be rescuing anyone."

"We have to try, Commander," Henry replied. "And we have to pick up theirs, too. The war with the Kenmiri might have grown uglier than any of us will like, but *this* fight will be conducted according to convention and military law. Am I clear?"

"Entirely, ser," Ihejirika confirmed. "And agreed with, to be clear as well. I'm just not sure we'll find anyone left from Colonel Pololáník's crew."

"If we can save *one* person, it's worth the fuel."

CHAPTER FORTY-FIVE

"THEY HAVE TO REALIZE IT'S OVER, RIGHT?" TODOROVICH'S voice murmured in Henry's ear. Technically, there was no actual audio involved, with it being transmitted directly to his network...but he *processed* it as her murmuring in his ear.

"They only have to realize they lost that round," he admitted grimly.

Both his flotilla and the Kozun ships were shedding velocity like mad. While he wasn't at risk of accidentally ending up in range of the Guardian platforms, he also didn't want the Kozun commander to realize he was waiting on anyone.

"Along the way, they demonstrated that they could do something no one else has ever done," Henry continued. "They took down *Deinonychus*'s shield. Those disruptor warheads are bad news, especially now that we're facing them in the hands of an opponent who clearly manufactured them in serious quantity.

"They might be out—in which case, it *is* over," he conceded. "If they don't have them stocked on their corvettes, that would explain why Star Commander Kan left them behind in the first place, for example."

"But if they still have them?" Todorovich asked.

"They have twice my acceleration and still have twice my missile launchers," he told her calmly. "If they have a weapon that can reliably bring my shields down from outside the range of my primary weapons, they might still pull this off."

"You don't sound as concerned as I would expect for that," the ambassador said.

"That's because when they zero their velocity relative to La-Tar in fifteen minutes, they will be a full light-minute away from *Raven* and over thirty million kilometers from La-Tar," he told her. "And the invasion fleet arrives in thirty minutes. Three hours for Ran and the transports to reach the planet.

"We'll keep ourselves between the escorts and them until then," he continued. "I'm *hoping* the fighters can handle the corvettes in orbit, though I don't want to know what the price tag is going to be. We'll move in to support as best as we can, though it will take some games to get us on the same vector as the rest of the fleet now."

If nothing else, he could launch missiles at the corvettes from beyond the Guardian platform's range. Once all the cards were on the table, he'd set his course for that. Right now, though, he was still playing head games.

"But the Kozun could still defeat us?" Todorovich asked.

"They'd have to manage decent coordination between the corvettes and the escorts, but they could still set us up to be in range of both forces simultaneously," Henry conceded. "We don't know how many missile launchers those corvettes have. If eight of them can match four escorts for missiles as well as lasers, we're still in serious trouble."

"But?"

Henry grinned.

"Thirty minutes, Sylvia," he told her. "It's chess. Right now, it looks like we've been clearing pieces off the board. In thirty minutes, the piece they weren't paying attention to slides into place...and it's checkmate.

"*If* everything goes according to plan."

"And if things don't go according to plan?" she asked.

Henry sighed and closed his eyes.

"That's the point where it becomes necessary to nuke Guardian platforms from half a million kilometers away and a lot of innocents die," he admitted. "I really, *really* hope it doesn't come to that."

RAVEN and her companion vessels were still moving toward La-Tar when the Kozun force finally reached zero velocity. Now they were accelerating toward Henry and his ship. If they were going to do anything clever, though, it wouldn't show up in their vector for hours.

"What do we do, ser?" Iyotake asked.

"We hold position until the invasion fleet arrives," Henry ordered. "We keep ourselves in the Kozun's path until then. They're supposed to be defending La-Tar, but if we're between them and the planet, how good a job are they doing?"

He turned to Bazzoli.

"Commander, I want you to get *Raven* into a position out of range of the Guardian platforms that will let us get missiles on the corvettes," he ordered.

"Not..." She sighed. "I'm not sure that's reasonably possible, ser," she admitted. "If we're at zero velocity, our missiles basically have the same range as the lasers. With the corvettes' altitude, we can engage them while remaining at extreme range for the Guardians, but we're at extreme range for our own weapon suite."

"Which degrades accuracy and our backstop is a planet," Ihejirika said grimly. "The missiles are probably safe enough in that situation, but I would hesitate to use the driver or the lasers."

"And the corvettes have no such limitations," Henry conceded. "Get us in close, Commander," he told Bazzoli. "We'll send Commander O'Flannagain in with the fighters from the invasion fleet and provide what long-range support we can."

Hopefully, the corvette commanders wouldn't be smart enough to realize that their ships could get as low as five thousand kilometers from the surface, a distance where Henry's ships couldn't engage them without letting the platforms take shots at them.

Of course, if they managed to stick to regions where the Guardians were disabled...but Henry was still waiting for *any* proof of that. He trusted the La-Tar to act, but he wasn't going to risk ships until he was certain they'd succeeded.

"Ser, we're receiving a message from the Kozun escorts," Moon reported. "It appears to be Star Lance Kalad. It's a recording—two-way time delay is almost two full minutes."

The image of Henry's old friend appeared in the main displays again. The bridge of her ship looked completely unshaken, though the scans suggested that all of her ships had taken at least some fire.

"Captain Wong, this is Star Lance Kalad," she greeted him. "I think we can both say that this situation has now escalated beyond expectations. I have detected and appreciate your retrieval of the survivors of our vessels, but the fact remains that we have now fought the opening battle of a war I do not believe either of our nations wants.

"In exchange for turning over those rescued crewmembers, I will permit *Raven* and your escorts to leave this system unhindered. If you remain, I believe we have more than demonstrated that you are no longer as invulnerable as you believe.

"I will regret it, Henry Wong, but I *will* destroy your ship. Even with Hierarchy prisoners aboard. This is my duty."

The image froze and Henry shook his head.

"Bazzoli?"

"Ser?"

"Time until the invasion fleet arrives?" he asked.

"Ten minutes," his navigator reported. "Assuming they entered the skip line on schedule. They were ready to go when we left, so that seems likely."

Henry studied the frozen image of a woman he'd come close to falling in love with once. Life was a funny thing.

"Record for transmission," he ordered.

He faced the camera and switched to Kem.

"Kalad, we both know you can not win this fight," he told her. "My best guess is that you fired off at least three-quarters of your disruptor warheads to take one destroyer. You have lost Star Commander Kan and his flagship.

"You are not going to land the hits you need to take down a grav-shield—and I can assure you that *Raven*'s shield will resist your weapons far better than *Deinonychus*'s did. You can dance around *Raven* for a week, but you cannot hurt me and you cannot stop me.

"You have lost control of this system outside the range of the planetary guns. Again. I suggest you accept this with some grace, old friend. The United Planets Alliance has no interest in a war with the Kozun Hierarchy, but we will also not permit the Hierarchy to conquer worlds without consequence.

"La-Tar will be liberated. These worlds will not merely change their masters from Kenmiri to Kozun. That is the task I have been set, and you know me, Kalad. I will not be deterred from *my* duty."

He considered adding something more, some personal appeal that might change her mind. Instead, he sighed and passed the recording over to Moon to transmit.

"It won't change anything," he admitted. "But we both had to try."

"Yes, ser," Moon said. If there was a sad undertone of understanding to her words, he refused to notice.

"What's the ETA for the Kozun ranging on us?" he asked.

"Assuming we don't maneuver to evade them, over ninety minutes, ser," Ihejirika reported. "Once we start maneuvering for La-Tar, the calculation changes again.

"Of course," Henry agreed. "And our time to range on the corvettes once we start moving?"

"Three hours, ser," she told him. "We can almost certainly time it to arrive at the same time as the invasion fleet."

But Kalad would bring him into missile range before he reached that destination. His own deceleration would make her life easier, though it wasn't like he could keep accelerating *past* La-Tar when he needed to help liberate the world.

If Star Lance Kalad wanted a missile duel, Henry was going to have to give her one—and do it before his invasion fleet even reached La-Tar!

"Ser—we have skip signatures on the Atris line," Ihejirika reported. "*Lots* of skip signatures. The invasion fleet is...exactly on time."

"Between Captain Zast and the Lord Nominated, I had no concerns," Henry said. "Bazzoli, get us underway.

"Let's see what Star Lance Kalad does now that she can see *almost* all of the cards."

CHAPTER FORTY-SIX

"CAPTAIN WONG, IT IS GOOD TO SEE THAT EVERYTHING IS proceeding according to plan," Casto Ran's recorded image told Henry. "We received the update on the corvettes in orbit, and I have passed it on to the squadron commanders on the carriers Tano so cleverly rigged up."

Unmentioned was that half the starfighters on those carriers were from the Lord Nominated's own forces. Skex hadn't wanted to rely entirely on his escorts, so they'd built up a small fleet of the fragile spacecraft as well.

Now most of Skex's starfighters and most of Tano's starfighters were being carried into space on "carriers" that didn't even begin to deserve the name. The carriers might be crap, but the moment they put the sixty ships into space, they'd have proven their worth.

"We are holding off on the fighter launch for a bit longer," Ran told him. "*Potter* can't handle eight corvettes alone, but the longer we keep them guessing, the better."

He paused.

"I have no direct contact with the La-Tar yet," he admitted.

"From your drone, I trust that plans are proceeding on schedule. I do hope that they at least manage to tell us if things *fail*."

Ran pressed his fist to his heart in salute.

"Our next communication should come from La-Tar orbit," he told Henry. "Good luck, Captain."

"The Kozun flotilla has not broken off," Ihejirika reported after it became clear Ran's message was over. "I think they've twitched their vector a fraction of a degree, enough to keep the range open when they actually close with us, but not enough to change the timeline."

"Three hours for the invasion fleet to reach orbit and one hour forty minutes for Kalad to catch up to us," Henry agreed. "The dance continues."

In a perfect world, Kalad would have broken off when she'd seen Henry's reinforcements. Instead, she appeared to be continuing to close, apparently assuming she could take his fleet on her own.

"At what point will we be able to tell if she's going to keep accelerating or head for a zero-zero in La-Tar orbit?" Henry asked as the thought struck him. His course had put him in position where she could do both easily enough.

"About two minutes before our own turnover," Ihejirika said after a few seconds. "Wouldn't even change her engagement time with us by much. A few minutes later."

Henry nodded.

"She'd want to extend her time in missile range anyway," he guessed. "I think we'll see her make turnover for insertion into orbit. If she can blow past us, dodging around laser and grav-driver range, then she can get into position to threaten the transports."

She'd end up fighting him twice. Once she was in orbit of the planet, there was nothing to stop him forcing her into range of his grav-driver, either—except for a desire not to use a planet as a backstop for a projectile traveling at seven percent of cee.

"What do we do if she tries that, ser?" Ihejirika asked.

"We fight a missile duel as she passes us and then we kick her into next week in orbit," Henry told his tactical officer. "She'll have to choose between defending the planet and staying out of grav-driver range. She can't win against *Raven* if we can bring the main gun to bear."

Kalad probably couldn't win regardless, but he had to salute her for *trying*.

Even if it was a pain in the ass for *him*.

"WHEN DO WE LAUNCH?" O'Flannagain asked on a private channel.

"When we get close to missile range with the escorts," Henry told her. "You're still in scale-armor mode. We need to keep those disruptors off *Hadrosaur*."

"Ser, all the locals have are TIEs," she said. "You send fifty of those against eight corvettes, there's going to be a lot of empty bunks in flight country tonight."

"And if I send you to support them, we might lose a destroyer," he countered. "You'll hold back and play missile guard. The locals know what they're doing. Let them do their part of this."

The private channel was silent.

"I don't like it any more than you do," he told her. "And its your job as CAG to make sure I consider that, but that's where we are. Everyone involved has their role to play. Yours is to keep *Hadrosaur* and the Skex escorts alive.

"Theirs is to clear the path for the assault force. Understood?"

"Yes, ser," she ground out, and cut the channel.

Henry trusted O'Flannagain these days, but he *still* was glad she wasn't already in space. He could control when she launched from his seat. He couldn't stop her taking the fighters and buggering off to help the locals if she were deployed.

At least if she did something dumb today, it would be to *help* people. He'd give her that much credit.

"Time," he said aloud.

"Twenty minutes to turnover," Bazzoli told him. "Seventeen and a half to the Kozun turnover if they're headed for zero as well."

"One hundred ten minutes to the transports entering orbit. Should we be seeing some sign of the locals moving?" Ihejirika asked. "I've got probes in position around the planet, but I'm not seeing anything."

"That's probably a good sign," Iyotake noted from CIC. "I don't think the probes are close enough to pick up hand-weapon fire. I didn't get the impression that the locals were planning on rolling out tanks against the Guardian platforms."

"I really hope that Adamant Will isn't trying to do anything *too* clever," Henry admitted. "Those things are fragile on the ground. A satchel charge tossed on the main gun does all we need."

"Which is why they're secured by hundreds of troops," Iyotake countered. "The La-Tar are going to have to assault those positions— unless they've done something clever. And unless they're moving tanks and aircraft around, we might not be able to tell until the guns start blowing up."

"We might not even be able to tell if they're disabling guns," Henry said. He assumed the invasion fleet would launch their fighters as they hit turnover, the starfighters continuing to accelerate while the rest of the fleet slowed down to enter orbit safely.

"We have an agreed signal, right?" Ihejirika asked.

"They're supposed to transmit when they've secured the guns," the captain confirmed. "Any movement on the Kozun's part? We should be able to pick up their transports once they start moving."

"No... Wait." Iyotake stopped himself. "I take that back. Multiple transports just came online across their main bases. I'd say someone just hit a critical alert."

"Anything moving yet?"

"Negative, they have to load troops still. Depending on what the La-Tar had planned, that may not be eno—"

A Guardian platform fired.

No one had been expecting that. None of the attacking forces were close enough to be valid targets, and the thought of the weapon systems being *quietly* taken intact hadn't even occurred to Henry.

The corvette it targeted *definitely* hadn't been expecting that. From the icons, she hadn't even had her shields up. Henry didn't have enough detail at this range to know where it had been hit—only enough to know that the small warship had been cut in half.

The other corvettes started scrambling as a second platform opened fire. The corvette *it* targeted had managed to get her shield up, but she still went staggering off-course, spewing atmosphere—until the original gun fired again and ended her struggle.

A *third* Guardian platform opened fire now as *Raven*'s bridge crew stared in stunned shock.

"Explosions on the sites of two more platforms," Ihejirika said after coughing to clear his throat. "Assuming those five are disabled or in our control, the invasion fleet has a clear path to orbit. It's not a broad path...but it's there."

To finish the metaphor from his conversation from Todorovich, this was checkmate.

"Moon. Lord Ran's people should be able to calculate that, but send Ihejirika's data over anyway," Henry ordered. "What are the corvettes doing?"

"They are *running*," Ihejirika reported with grim satisfaction in his voice. "Fast little fuckers, at that. They've punched clean up to one point five KPS squared and they are heading for the Ra-Fifty skip line."

"They don't know what the hell is happening and they don't trust the ground forces to remain in control," Iyotake said. "Not unreasonable, but...still. Cowards."

The last word wasn't even overly judgmental. Just a statement of fact.

"It might just doom them all. Mal Dakis isn't known for his calm acceptance of defeat," Henry noted. "Can Kalad still break off?"

"For about five more minutes," Bazzoli confirmed. "Maybe six or seven if she's got reserve thrust."

"Most escorts can push one point three if they need to," Henry said. "Record for transmission."

He brought up the recorder linked to his chair and focused on the mental image of his old friend.

"Star Lance Kalad," he greeted her. "You can see, I presume, the fate of your forces in orbit of La-Tar. The planetary defenses are now in the control of the legitimate government of La-Tar."

He shrugged.

"Your forces might be able to regain control of the defenses. I do not project they will be able to do so before the allied forces land. You are in the position of being able to prevent further death by negotiating the surrender of your ground forces before they are defeated."

Or to withdraw or surrender in her own right. Henry couldn't chase down the Kozun fleet, not with the damage to *Raven*'s engines, but he wasn't sure that Kalad knew that.

"Send it," he ordered. "And if we're reasonably lucky, our part in all of this might just be over."

He waited. They weren't light-minutes apart anymore. It should only take thirty or forty seconds for Kalad to respond.

"Vector change on the Kozun flotilla, ser!" Ihejirika snapped. "They're breaking off for the Ra-Fifty skip line. They are withdrawing, ser."

Henry pulled up the data to confirm it with his own eyes. Kalad's flotilla had broken off at their full thrust, pushing past their usual one KPS^2 maximum to make certain they never entered range of his ships or of the Guardian platforms on the surface.

He let some of his iron control slip as he leaned back into his chair, managing to avoid visibly collapsing in relief. He could have taken the Kozun ships, but he didn't *want* to kill more old friends today.

The odds that he'd known at least some of the crew on the ships they'd destroyed were high. The lower the body count, the better.

"Ser, we have a transmission from the Kozun fleet." Moon paused. "I don't recognize the encryption. It's not Vesheron."

He closed his eyes and slowly nodded.

"Forward it to my office," he told Moon as he rose from his chair. "I know what encryption she's using and I'll take this one in private."

"Yes, ser!"

IT WASN'T A COMPLICATED ENCRYPTION. It was an old, pre-UPA-contact, Vesheron protocol, then encrypted using a completely nonstandard key.

There weren't many people in Kozun space who'd have a poem by Yeats memorized, but Kalad had encountered the poet while she'd been learning English from Henry during his sojourn.

But I, being poor, have only my dreams;

I have spread my dreams under your feet;

Tread softly because you tread on my dreams.

The codes of close friends who had only failed to become lovers because of the chains of duty and timing. Henry suspected that Kalad, especially, basically *had* regarded him as a lover at the end, even without any actual consummation of that relationship.

The image of Kalad on the screen was the same as it had been in any of the other videos. She sat in the central throne of a Kenmiri-designed warship bridge, and she looked down at the camera like an angry goddess.

There was a slight distortion to the video that suggested she had a privacy screen up that would prevent her being heard or recorded, but her greatest defense was the language she spoke in.

Henry doubted there were more than half a dozen people working for the First Voice who understood English. There was a *reason* the UPSF had insisted on its officers learning Kem, and keeping their own secrets was part of it.

The Kozun's computers could translate it, but it wouldn't take much distortion to render that almost impossible—but Henry understood her perfectly.

"I have no authority over the ground forces, Henry," she said softly and without preamble. Her English was halting and slow but understandable. "I will not fight you for an already-lost cause. Especially not you."

For a moment, he thought that was all the message and he was reaching to record a response, telling her that *she* didn't have to go back to Mal Dakis, at least.

"I think we both have different opinions of how that battle would end, but I am happier not to fight it. Regardless of the consequences for myself."

She lowered her head, rubbing one of her eyebrow spikes.

"But if I take responsibility for this, others will not suffer," she told him. "I have a mate now. This will not spare him pain, but it will spare him his own death. Star Commander Kan has much to answer for before the Gods.

"I hope the fruits of your victory are worth its cost, my dear Henry," Kalad concluded. "I do not believe we will speak again. Fly true, my human warrior."

Henry didn't need to check the sensors to know that the Kozun flotilla was staying on course. He *could* send Kalad a response, but what was the point? There were ways she could defect, but only by exposing others to the punishment she clearly anticipated.

All he could do was hope that Mal Dakis was more considerate of failure than everyone was expecting him to be. It hadn't been Kalad's failure, not really, but that might not change much.

It certainly didn't change Henry's duty.

CHAPTER FORTY-SEVEN

"The last of the Guardian platforms has been neutralized," General Kansa's image reported. The Tano officer's purple hair was concealed under an armor helmet, but her tusks were visible in the feed in the opened face plate.

"La-Tar orbit is now secure for all ships. All told, we are in control of six of the Guardians thanks to the codes Adamant Will acquired," she continued, her image speaking to the same amphitheatre Henry and Todorovich had used to negotiate the alliance underpinning the attack.

Most of the audience today was also holographic, beaming in from various ships across the invasion fleet.

"That will be a relief," Captain—no, *Admiral* Zast; Adamant Will had made that clear within minutes of establishing solid contact with the allied forces—said. "We have enough ships up here that keeping them in a specific orbit has been burning a lot of fuel."

"We have good news for that, as well," Lord Nominated Ran said. "Captain Ij's report from Atto arrived a few minutes ago. She and Loto have successfully secured control of the refueling facilities above the gas giant.

"There were apparently only a handful of Kozun on the station, and they had no starfighters or other weapons." The holographic image of Ran spread his hands, palms down. "They surrendered without a fight. I was expecting more trouble.

"If we get one of the transports rigged up as a fuel hauler, we should be able to refuel the fleet in short order. Ij's report suggests that there is more than enough fuel present."

"That is-was good news," Adamant Will's hologram said. "The Kozun are attempting to concentrate their forces again. Last reports are-were that they are moving everything left toward our capital."

"They won't make it," General Olmar told them. "The last of our encirclement positions will be in place in less than an hour. Any attempt to reinforce the capital will meet tanks and artillery. Let them come. It will make our lives easier in the end."

"We must-will retake the capital intact," Adamant Will insisted. "I fear for our people."

"We all do," Todorovich told the Enteni. "We are close, Adamant Will. The Kozun forces are in disarray across the planet, and we have both air and space superiority. Hopefully, once they realize they can't reinforce the capital, we'll start to see surrenders across the surface."

Henry was far from qualified to judge the surface campaign, but it *sounded* promising. Over half of the Kozun had already been captured or killed. The remaining units were scattered across the surface, with the largest concentration—maybe twenty thousand—in the La-Tar capital.

"Captain Wong," Lord Ran said, drawing his attention. "We would like to update our home systems on the progress of the campaign and get confirmation of our alliance from the other system governments.

"Would you be able to place some of your FTL communication drones at our disposal for this?"

Henry glanced at Todorovich. She gave him a small thumbs-up, outside the pickup of the recorders creating their holograms on the other ships.

Nodding, he leaned forward into his own pickup.

"Part of our plans for our treaties with your systems will involve a permanent posting of UPA diplomatic personnel. That will require us to set up permanent skip-drone maintenance facilities in orbit of your worlds," he told them. "Since we are planning on arranging for a permanent FTL communication capacity between your worlds as well as with the UPA, I see no reason not to lend you several drones each to maintain a steady communication loop as we move forward."

That would take a large bite out of *Raven*'s drone capacity, but he'd include a request for more drones in his next message back. He was due to record that as soon as this meeting was over.

"We appreciate your assistance as always, Captain Wong," Ran told him. "And the sacrifices your people have made alongside ours. They will be remembered here, as will the UPA's aid in our time of need."

Henry nodded. It was interesting to him that the Lord Nominated had become the clear speaker for the allied forces. He doubted Casto Ran was *intentionally* angling for a new job once his Nomination was up...but if the La-Tar Cluster decided they wanted more than an alliance, he suspected the man was going to find himself with that new post.

"We are here to help keep the peace," he assured them. "The Kozun invasion was a violation of that standard, an act of aggression that the United Planets Alliance couldn't stand for. So long as we are aware of warlords like Mal Dakis is attempting to become, we will act to constrain and resist their actions.

"It is the moral thing to do, the only thing we can do." He shrugged. "We are limited in how far our reach spreads now. In the absence of subspace communications, we cannot send ships to the far side of the old Empire.

"But here, in the Ra Sector, the United Planets can and *will* be a force for stability and peace. That is our promise. That, people, is why the Peacekeeper Initiative was here."

✦

THE UPDATE BRIEFING FINALLY DONE, Henry retreated to his office. He doffed the formal jacket of his undress uniform, put it on the hook meant for it and gestured his computer awake.

"Record for addition to the next skip drone," he ordered aloud. That would be the drone he'd order sent as soon as this was recorded, of course, but that was a *different* set of commands, one the computer didn't necessarily know.

"To Admiral Sonia Hamilton, Peacekeeper Initiative Commanding Officer, Base Fallout, Zion System," he recited. "From Colonel Henry Wong, Captain of UPSF *Raven*. La-Tar System.

"Space and orbital combat in the La-Tar System is complete. Details of the engagement are attached to this message in standard telemetry formats. While our allied forces carried the day, I must report the loss of the United Planets Space Force destroyer *Deinonychus*. Thirty-two crew were recovered from the wreck; the remaining two hundred and seventy-six, including Lieutenant Colonel Roger Pololáník are missing, presumed KIA.

"We are beginning retrieval operations for critical debris and identifiable corpses. *Deinonychus*'s security self-destruct appears to have functioned as designed. Her grav-shield systems and penetrator-missile buses are wrecked beyond retrieval.

"We are forwarding all information acquired in the conflict on the Kozun Hierarchy's new heavy cruisers as well. Their shields are significantly more powerful than anticipated, but our major concern has to be the Hierarchy's possession of an updated version of the gravity-shield disruptor deployed against *Raven* on our journey to the Gathering.

"*Deinonychus* was destroyed after her shields were disrupted and collapsed by these weapons. Our current best estimate is that twenty-five disruptor warheads will bring down our current-generation destroyer shields and that as many as forty to fifty may be required to disable the larger projectors on a battlecruiser.

"We hope to retrieve samples of the warheads from the wreckage and bring them home for analysis."

He paused, considering what to say next.

"Ground combat continues on La-Tar, but the allied forces we assisted have a significant edge in both numbers and equipment. With our assistance, they have secured orbital and aerial supremacy. I expect the situation to be resolved in the alliance's favor within the next twenty-four to forty-eight hours.

"Given that, I am requesting *Raven* be relieved on this post," he concluded. "We took no new damage in the Battle of La-Tar, but our earlier damage is irreparable outside of a UPSF shipyard.

"My recommendation would be that Ambassador Todorovich remain here in La-Tar while *Raven* is replaced by either another battlecruiser or a minimum of two or three destroyers.

"We have made a commitment to support this new alliance against Kozun aggression. We must keep that commitment. But, given *Raven*'s state, I must recommend that commitment be kept by other vessels as soon as possible.

"It was unavoidable that *Raven* carry the fight to this point, from both a logistical and diplomatic point of view," he noted. "But now I think my people need the break, and my ship needs the repairs.

"We will remain on station until relieved or the receipt of new orders. I do not expect a rapid Kozun response. I do expect that Ambassador Todorovich will be successful in converting the promises and intentions that have been committed to by the governments present here into a long-term five-system alliance—and into long-term trade treaties with all five worlds."

He forced something resembling a victorious smile.

"We were sent out here to establish a stable treaty with one world, Admiral Hamilton. I *hope* that you and the Security Council will regard building treaties with *five* worth the additional resources that have been required."

And the sacrifices that had been made. He closed the recording and poured himself a glass of brandy. He stared at the amber liquid for a long time, then raised the glass to the air, to the invisible ghosts of the crew of *Deinonychus* and the now-distant Star Lance Kalad.

"To absent friends," he murmured. "May you find the peace I'm sworn to create."

JOIN THE MAILING LIST

Love Glynn Stewart's books? To know as soon as new books are released, special announcements, and a chance to win free paperbacks, join the mailing list at:

glynnstewart.com/mailing-list/

ABOUT THE AUTHOR

Glynn Stewart is the author of *Starship's Mage*, a bestselling science fiction and fantasy series where faster-than-light travel is possible– but only because of magic. His other works include science fiction series *Duchy of Terra, Castle Federation* and *Vigilante,* as well as the urban fantasy series *ONSET* and *Changeling Blood.*

Writing managed to liberate Glynn from a bleak future as an accountant. With his personality and hope for a high-tech future intact, he lives in Kitchener, Ontario with his wife, their cats, and an unstoppable writing habit.

VISIT GLYNNSTEWART.COM FOR NEW
RELEASE UPDATES

 facebook.com/glynnstewartauthor

OTHER BOOKS
BY GLYNN STEWART

For release announcements join the
mailing list or visit **GlynnStewart.com**

STARSHIP'S MAGE
Starship's Mage
Hand of Mars
Voice of Mars
Alien Arcana
Judgment of Mars
UnArcana Stars
Sword of Mars
Mountain of Mars
The Service of Mars
A Darker Magic (upcoming)

Starship's Mage: Red Falcon
Interstellar Mage
Mage-Provocateur
Agents of Mars

Pulsar Race: A Starship's Mage Universe Novella

DUCHY OF TERRA
The Terran Privateer
Duchess of Terra
Terra and Imperium
Darkness Beyond
Shield of Terra
Imperium Defiant
Relics of Eternity
Shadows of the Fall
Eyes of Tomorrow (upcoming)

SCATTERED STARS

Scattered Stars: Conviction

Conviction

Deception

Equilibrium (upcoming)

PEACEKEEPERS OF SOL

Raven's Peace

The Peacekeeper Initiative

Raven's Course (upcoming)

EXILE

Exile

Refuge

Crusade

Ashen Stars: An Exile Novella

CASTLE FEDERATION

Space Carrier Avalon

Stellar Fox

Battle Group Avalon

Q-Ship Chameleon

Rimward Stars

Operation Medusa

A Question of Faith: A Castle Federation Novella

VIGILANTE
(WITH TERRY MIXON)
Heart of Vengeance
Oath of Vengeance

**Bound By Stars: A Vigilante Series
(With Terry Mixon)**
Bound By Law
Bound by Honor
Bound by Blood

TEER AND KARD
Wardtown
Blood Ward (upcoming)

CHANGELING BLOOD
Changeling's Fealty
Hunter's Oath
Noble's Honor
Fae, Flames & Fedoras: A Changeling Blood Novella

ONSET
ONSET: To Serve and Protect
ONSET: My Enemy's Enemy
ONSET: Blood of the Innocent
ONSET: Stay of Execution
Murder by Magic: An ONSET Novella

FANTASY STAND ALONE NOVELS
Children of Prophecy
City in the Sky

Lightning Source UK Ltd.
Milton Keynes UK
UKHW011827230321
380868UK00001B/27